HIGHLAND TREASURE:
The Enchantress

May McGoldrick

AN ONYX BOOK

ONYX
Published by New American Library, a division of
Penguin Putnam Inc., 375 Hudson Street, New York, New York 10014, U.S.A.
Penguin Books Ltd, 27 Wrights Lane,
London W8 5TZ, England
Penguin Books Australia Ltd, Ringwood,
Victoria, Australia
Penguin Books Canada Ltd, 10 Alcorn Avenue,
Toronto, Ontario, Canada M4V 3B2
Penguin Books (N.Z.) Ltd, 182–190 Wairau Road,
Auckland 10, New Zealand

Penguin Books Ltd, Registered Offices:
Harmondsworth, Middlesex, England

First Published by Onyx, an imprint of New American Library,
a division of Penguin Putnam Inc.

ISBN: 0-7394-1184-5

To Hilary, our favorite Ross

Chapter 1

Fearnoch, the Northern Highlands
December, 1535

The gold coin tumbled slowly across the knuckles of the silent Highlander standing against the sandstone wall. When the group across the open square stopped at a stall containing bundled wool, the coin paused as well, its Tudor rose gleaming even in the shadows.

"The one with a face like a pig's arse called her Laura, master." The toothless farmer talking to him spat into the half-frozen mud and glared across the market square. "The lass might be dressed only in the rags they've given her, but she's of quality, there's no doubtin'."

Across the cold, windswept square, the two watched the Sinclair men herding the women along. The gold coin resumed its journey along the deft knuckles of the tall Highlander.

"Though she's a young thing, from the way she talks, there's no doubt she's English. If 'tweren't for that, I'd wager more 'n one of yer crofters would have stolen her already from these swine." He spat again. "Aye, 'tis a fearful shame, master. Why, if I were twenty years younger, I'd . . ."

William Ross of Blackfearn left the farmer without a word and, tucking the gold sovereign into his wide leather belt, stepped out of the shadows of Fearnoch Cathedral and into the midday sun. As he strode through the scattered crowds of townsfolk and farmers to a cart by the ancient stone cross at the center of the square, he was immediately joined by two of his men.

" 'Tis *her*, master! 'Tis the same one you've been looking for!"

William absently dug the fingers of one hand into the coarse wool bundled in the wagon.

"And all of them don't go together. The two other women are nuns from that tumble-down convent near Little Ferry."

Watching the group stop by another stall, William stared at the hooded Englishwoman's back. Encircled by the Sinclair brutes, she appeared to be a wee, fragile thing. At this point, though, he didn't want to even think about the hardship she must have gone through over these past three months, living as a captive among those blackguards. He reminded himself that there couldn't be any bloodshed. Not while he was trying to rescue her, at any rate. He'd promised his brother that much.

"Should we take her now?" his man continued, glancing at the scar-faced farmer standing with them. The other man's hand moved to the hilt of a dirk half hidden beneath the red and black plaid of the Ross tartan. His face showed his eagerness for a fight. "They've been plenty rough with her. The ugly one shoved her—without so much as a 'by yer leave'— right out of the wool seller's tent up by the north road."

"There was talk of the dungeons at Rumster Castle."

"They've been locking her up for months, master."

"The lass had her hood pulled low over her face to hide the tears."

"Aye, and her shame, the poor woman."

"There's only a half dozen Sinclair men with her. We can take them, master!" the first man growled. " 'Twould be a good deed to help the wee lass and set the bastards back a—"

"Wait here." William turned his back, leaving the two looking helplessly after him as he strode unhurriedly around the stone cross toward the wool merchant's stall.

As William approached, the Sinclair men visibly stiffened. They knew who he was. He ignored them.

The two nuns, gathered right outside the wool merchant's stall, were whispering in French, and William heard snatches of their conversation. They, too, seemed to know him, though he couldn't for the life of him imagine why. He'd never had any dealings with the little group of French nuns living at the convent on Loch Fleet.

Brushing past the Sinclair men, William sauntered into the stall, casually picking up a piece of fleece and setting it down. The Englishwoman, reaching over, immediately picked up the fleece and set it in another pile. Though she was speaking quietly and continuously to the merchant, she appeared resolute about bringing some organization to the jumbled piles of wool the man had carted to market.

Suddenly, William found himself listening intently. There was something captivating about the soft lilt in her voice. Although her timid attempt at mimicking the Highland tongue was charming, her English accent—as Ren, the old farmer, had said—gave her away immediately. Peering covertly at her, he could just see a lock of black hair that had fallen free of her worn hood. Looking back down at her small hands, chafed by hard work and cold weather, he realized that she was sorting the fleece by color and quality.

An amused smile tugged at his mouth.

Out of the corner of his eye he could see that the leader of the Sinclairs was watching him carefully. William picked up another fleece, one that still retained marks of black tar in the thick wool. He intentionally dropped the fleece on the ground and moved over a step.

The Englishwoman immediately picked it up, but as she did, raised voices could be heard from the square. Glancing around, the Highlander realized that a shouting match between a haughty townswoman and a crofter driving a dozen red shaggy-haired steers through the market square had drawn the Sinclairs' attention momentarily.

William looked at the Englishwoman. She was standing with the fleece in her hand, ignoring the commotion in the square. She was clearly undecided about which pile the fleece belonged in. Without a word, he took it out of her hands and placed it on the pile of fleece that she'd deemed of the poorest quality.

She turned in shock at his forwardness, a scowl darkening her face. But then, for William Ross of Blackfearn, something stopped, and the world stopped with it. Perhaps it was her eyes that halted him in his tracks. Their deep, violet-blue color was not like any he'd ever seen. Except perhaps for Molly, the wench he visited occasionally at the Three Cups on the Inverness road. Nay, these eyes were even deeper, more violet than Molly's.

An eon may have passed—William couldn't be sure—and still he found himself staring. It occurred to him that perhaps it was the surprise in her pale face that made his heart pause for that lingering moment. It was a face of an enchantress, English or no.

William thought she was about to speak, but the woman hesitated as one of her captors eyed her menacingly. She said nothing and looked away.

When he glanced back at the Sinclair men, he saw the nuns had separated themselves from the party, each moving toward a different part of the marketplace. Turning away, William ambled as casually as he could out of the stall, stopping a young lad who was walking about and hawking apples. The uproar had died down, and the cattle were disappearing down the dirt street.

"Hurry on, lass!"

Shooting a quick look back at them, William could see that the Englishwoman was still standing in the stall. The Sinclair men had no patience with her, and the leader tugged at her elbow.

"If you're not back by vespers," the leader growled, "it'll mean a dozen lashes . . . if you understand my meaning."

With a hasty nod she left the fleece behind, and immediately the group moved through the crowd toward a group of tented stalls belonging to traveling merchants in from Inverness.

At the next stall the woman paused again, but this time only for a moment as she straightened out a display of women's shoes. The disgusted curses of one of the Sinclair warriors rose above the sounds of the market throng.

Flipping his uneaten apple to a street urchin running by, William crossed the way and slipped into the alley between the merchants' tents and a low wall behind them. Beyond the wall was a ditch, and a stand of trees was visible beyond that.

Working his way past serving lads sitting idly on half-empty carts of merchandise, he moved silently into the alleyway between the third and fourth tents. A merchant selling brightly colored Flemish cloth was calling out to the guarded woman. The cloaked and hooded Englishwoman drew near the tented stall, and William stepped back into the shadows.

As he did, a gypsy band came to life across the way, their tambourines and bells and flashing-eyed women immediately drawing the gazes of the Sinclair warriors.

The Highlander seized his chance. With a silencing look at the merchant, William reached out, grabbed the startled woman by the wrist, and dragged her in one quick motion into the alleyway.

"I am a friend!" he whispered against her ear.

Covering her mouth with his hand nonetheless, William took her around the waist with his other and speedily backed along the alley. As they reached the low wall at the end, the Ross turned and released the squirming woman, setting her back on her feet and turning her to face him. Her hood was pulled forward, and a lock of thick black hair had tumbled out across her eyes.

"We've only a moment before they discover you're missing. But I've horses waiting beyond that stand of trees. You're safe now." The Englishwoman was clearly stunned. The corner of his mouth turned up in a half smile. "You've nothing to fear. You've been rescued."

The woman's eyes swept questioningly over him, focusing on the coin that he suddenly pulled from his leather belt. The Tudor rose flashed in the sunlight.

"I've no time now to explain. If we're to get you out of Fearnoch, we'll have to—"

William Ross's words died on his tongue as the woman's full-throated scream—loud enough to be heard in Edinburgh—cut like a sword through the crisp winter air.

Chapter 2

Gilbert Ross leaned into the fireplace and tried to peer up the chimney. Seeing nothing, the young priest got up from his knees and straightened the iron pokers leaning neatly against the wall. The smoke continued to back up in the fireplace, drifting into the room and hanging like a pall just above his blond, tonsured head.

The sound of the door opening behind him drew his gaze. Two clerics hesitantly peered inside the chamber.

He gestured to them. "Father John, 'tis time we sent for the mason."

The younger of the two men nodded vigorously and withdrew, immediately disappearing down the corridor.

"And Father Francis, if you find this chamber too suffocating for our work . . ."

"I am used to this, Provost." The older priest stepped into the room and closed the door. "For as long as I can remember, this chimney has smoked. Father Jerome gave up on it long ago, I think." He shook his head. "'Tis a nuisance during the winter months."

Giving up on things had been his late predecessor's guiding rule, Gilbert Ross had quickly realized after taking over the position as provost of the Church of St. Duthac. Gilbert stepped over Willie, his barrel-chested dog, who continued to snore unconcernedly while his master pulled open a shuttered window. Gilbert filled his lungs with the cold winter air that swept in beneath the escaping smoke.

"One of the fishermen from the village has just returned from the market at Fearnoch, Provost. She is there."

Gilbert turned and found the priest already positioned at his customary position at the trestle table—his gnarled hands untying the black ribbon around an oversized account book.

"And my brother?"

"He is there as well. In the company of Ross farmers already at market, but with *none* of his warriors."

The hint of criticism was obvious in the old priest's tone, and Gilbert stiffened a bit defensively. He and his older brother William had been pupils to Father Francis from the time they were lads, packed off by their mother—over their father and their eldest brother Thomas's objections—to the ancient church school. Even though William was now laird of the Ross clan— and Gilbert himself was now the provost of St. Duthac's— he knew that Father Francis would always view them as lads to be scolded.

Aye, he knew what was coming.

"Gilbert . . . er, Provost . . . for a man of William's position to act—"

"Father Francis, I thought William showed great wisdom when he assured me—and you were sitting right where you are now—when he assured me that he would take care of this problem without bloodshed." Gilbert moved as well to the table and took his place across from his old mentor. "Considering the fact that, since Thomas's death two years ago, Ross and Sinclair men have not clashed seriously, don't you think it a responsible step for William to avoid starting up the fighting again?"

Francis grumbled under his breath, his fingers traveling across the pages.

The old priest was still scowling darkly as he carried on with the pretense of looking for the last ledger entry. Gilbert braced himself. He knew Father Francis was not finished. Provost or not, he would hear the frequently repeated reprimand once again.

"There was something else, Father?" Gilbert said gently.

The old man exploded. "Aye, there's something else, as you well know! William can no longer hold to the reckless, ne'er-do-well days of his youth. By Duthac's Shirt, William is laird now! The leader of the Clann Gille Aindrias, the ruler of all this land from Fearnoch Firth to The Minch. He carries in his veins the blood of his namesake, the great William, earl of Ross, who led our own kinsmen under the Bruce at Bannockburn. 'Twas his hand that put the Ross seal on the Declaration of Arbroath!"

"I know, Father Francis," Gilbert interrupted softly, stopping the older priest's ardent sermon. "I am William's brother. I, better than anyone, know of our name, our blood . . . and William's responsibilities."

The priest nodded sternly. "Aye. You are a fine man, Gilbert, and I am as proud of you as if you were my own son, but 'tis time you used your power as provost of St. Duthac's to benefit not only those who make the pilgrimage here, but the people of Ross as well."

"Father Francis, I've been provost of this church and its lands for a wee bit more than a month now, and if you are saying that my desire to bring some semblance of order to this place, that my plans to stop the deteriorating condition of St. Duthac's is somehow compromising my responsibilities to the people—"

"I am saying no such thing." The old priest placed both elbows on the table and stared evenly into Gilbert's eyes. "What I am saying is that for the first time in your life you can wield some authority over your older brother. You can influence William, direct him in the affairs of—"

"William is the laird of Ross, Father. I am a priest."

"Aye. You have spiritual authority." Father Francis pointed

a long, bony finger at Gilbert. "I have seen how he treats you—now that you are provost. He does not deal with you as he did when you two were growing up—when you were just the younger brother to banter with and to battle constantly. There is a new respect that he is giving you now."

Only in the presence of others, Gilbert thought. "So what is it exactly that you recommend I do with this new power over my brother?"

The semblance of a smile increased the deep wrinkles of the old priest's face.

"You must order him to change."

"To change?" Gilbert repeated, not comprehending. "William?"

"Aye! 'Tis time William Ross of Blackfearn grew up. 'Tis time that he began putting more value in his own life. By the saint, Gilbert, he thinks more of the lowliest shepherd lass's well-being than he does his own! You know as well as I that he'd sleep in his stable if he thought some old beggar woman would be more comfortable in the laird's chamber." The old priest leaned over and lowered his voice. "'Tis time that he learned to act the part of laird. 'Tis what I *tried* to prepare him for. He should pick up where Thomas left off by reno-vating that holding of his—bringing back some of the grandeur of Blackfearn Castle. Blackfearn is the largest castle this side of Inverness. He must stop ignoring his position in life. Stop acting like a common crofter—eating and sleeping in the fields and in the stables. He must take his place as the leader of his warriors and his people."

Gilbert opened his mouth to speak, but the priest rolled on.

"'Tis true that the title of earl was stripped from your great-grandsire all those years ago. But in the eyes of these people and every nobleman in the Highlands, William is now the true earl of Ross. He is their chieftain. He is the laird." Father Francis laid a gnarled hand on Gilbert's wrist. "And as such, he is responsible for marrying properly and begetting a bairn to keep your great lineage alive."

Gilbert again began to speak, but Father Francis raised a hand to him and gestured toward the mantel above the fireplace and the simple sketch there on a wooden board. A sketch of a little girl's face.

"And I'm not even mentioning William's failure to bring Thomas's wee daughter, Miriam, back to her own clan folk."

Gilbert sat back in his chair and nodded thoughtfully at the elderly priest. There was no purpose in arguing. Half of what the chaplain said was true. More than half. Still, though, there was no way that Gilbert could see his brother marrying.

Much to Gilbert's chagrin, William openly preferred the company of the fallen women at the Three Cups Tavern to any lass who had been properly brought up. In fact, this past fall when he'd finally allowed Gilbert to drag him along to visit with the earl of Caithness's daughter—under the pretense of a hunting party—William had said as much to the poor lass herself. Gilbert cringed at the memory of the young woman running, horrified, across the heather-covered meadow back to the arms of an indignant mother.

Gilbert and William were only two years apart in age while Thomas had been more than twelve years their senior. As the result of this age difference, the younger brothers had been inseparable as lads. And later on, when Gilbert had pursued a life in the church and William had been sent away to St. Andrew's—and later to the household of Lord Herries—the two still had managed to remain close. They were not just brothers but friends as well. And it was as a friend and not as kin that Gilbert Ross had determined that his older brother was perfectly content with whom he'd become—despite the fact that he had been called upon to be laird. Changing him at this stage in his life would be as difficult as chiseling in stone with a willow branch.

"'Tis up to you, Gilbert! You have the power and the in-

fluence to do a great deal more good than repairing an ancient chimney. St. Duthac's will survive. You, however, have
the ability to preserve the Ross name and, in so doing, save
that undisciplined rogue you call brother at the same time."
Father Francis lowered his eyes to the open page of the ledger.
"You have the insight to force him to settle into a calmer and
more respectable life. To find the right lass. That's what he
needs, Gilbert. Just the right lass to calm his wild ways."

Perhaps, Gilbert thought with a resigned smile. But pity
the woman.

William Ross cursed out loud as the squirming, kicking
banshee landed a solid punch to the small of his back. Who
would have thought that fighting off an entire company of
Sinclairs would be easier than controlling the woman he'd
thrown over his shoulder?

The woman's scream had brought all hell down around
their ears. The moment he'd tried to drag her over the low
wall, she'd dug in her heels, caterwauling as William had
never heard before. For a wee thing she was . . . vigorous.

The riot that immediately ensued upturned carts and tore
down tents. The Sinclairs were quick to pour into the alleyway, but the Ross farmers were equally quick to head them
off once they knew the laird was involved.

Grimacing at the pain shooting through his lower back,
William swung his sword at the advancing leader of the Sinclairs, and the sound of clashing steel rang out above the
sounds of the shouting crowd.

Shoving the Sinclair warrior back into the tumultuous battle behind him, William once again tried to back over the low
wall. As the Sinclair leader lunged at him again, the toothless
old farmer from the market square tackled him with a vital-
ity that William would have never thought he had in him,
thumping the man's head resoundingly on the frozen earth.
The Sinclair sword clattered against the wall at William's feet.

As the farmer sat up on the man's chest and winked, the woman dangling over the laird's shoulder dug her claws into William's buttocks. He shifted her weight farther up over his shoulder and heard her gasp at the threat of dashing her head against the wall.

"We're going out the south lane to a boat at the firth," he shouted to the old farmer. "Keep these blackguards busy for me."

"Aye," the crofter shouted back before two brawlers came tumbling over him.

She was again using her fists on his buttocks and legs.

"Quit your squirming," William growled, vaulting the wall and starting across the ditch. "Or I'll ding you so hard, lass, you'll think you're back in England."

"Let me go, you filthy brute, or I swear I'll dig your ugly eyes out of their sockets with my own fingers."

He started up the far embankment toward a stand of trees and the horses. "Is that not a wee bit violent for a mild and gentle English damsel? Nay, let me think on this again. You'll take my eyes out so you can put them back in my face, and more to your liking. How do you sort eyes, m'lady? By color or—?"

"I'd stuff one into that gaping maw of yours if there were a chance you'd choke on it!"

"Now, there's an arrangement I would never have thought of." Reaching the two waiting horses, William hesitated and sheathed his sword. He could hear the brawl still going full-tilt in the market square. There was no way that the woman clawing his back was going to ride alone. Yanking free one of the tethers, he swatted the horse on the rump, sending it trotting off a ways.

Her gasp of shock at being thrown like a sack over the withers of the other horse brought a devilish smile to his lips, and he leaped onto the animal himself. As William spurred the steed into action, he took a firm hold on the cloak at the

nape of her neck, keeping her draped precariously over the
horse.

"I'll kill you," she screamed, eliciting a gruff laugh from
him. "I swear I will!"

The jump over a low stone wall and down across an icy
brook turned her threats into another gasping cry. Her hands
clutched his boot in desperation as he looked over his shoulder. Three of the Sinclair men had broken away from the
chaos and were running across the market square after them.

In a moment William and his prize had entered the scrubby
pines to the south of Fearnoch, and he abruptly wheeled his
charger to the west, galloping over stony, uneven ground—
and away from the boat landing on the firth.

"Let me up, you blackguard," she cried out, squirming
again. "The little I had in my belly is ready to . . . is ready
to . . ."

"Feel free, lass. 'Twould be far better to get rid of it down
there than in my lap."

In a few minutes of hard riding, they broke out of a patch
of trees and onto a well-traveled road that led from the town
along the line of hills to the west.

The woman was now groaning at every dip and turn in the
road, but William was not ready to slow their flight. When
the road turned southward again toward Fearnoch Firth, the
Ross laird reined his horse sharply to the right, leaving the
main road and continuing west through thick groves of pine.

Looking back over his shoulder again, William could see
no sign of the Sinclair men. They were on foot and heading
south toward the firth. It would be far too late once they realized their mistake. The pursuers would never catch them
now.

Swerving just in time to dodge a low-hanging branch, he
shoved the woman's head hard against the flank of his horse
to avoid her face being whipped by the lower branches.

After a few more jumps over fallen trees, they splashed

through a half-frozen stream. Slowing on the far bank, he peered down at her. She was no longer squirming or even groaning.

William eased the pressure on the back of her neck and raised her face a bit. It was a rather odd shade of green, he thought. Well, she hadn't been exaggerating about being ill. His horse's shoulder and forearm showed signs of the woman's breakfast.

At the foot of a stone ledge beside the stream, the Highlander reined his horse to a stop and climbed off. The sight of her, draped like a rag across the withers of the horse, brought a frown to his face. He reached across the animal and dragged the Englishwoman toward him. His frown deepened as she drooped over his arm in a dead faint. He crouched on the gravel of the bank and cradled her in his arms.

Pushing the hood of her heavy cloak over her head, William stared at the woman. Something tightened in his chest at the sight of her pale and disheveled condition. Her black hair had for the most part escaped its braid and now was lying in a tantalizing array around a perfectly formed face. Her eyes were half closed and her full lips were parted, her breaths unsteady. Even in her tousled condition—nay, perhaps because of it—William knew that she was the most beautiful creature he'd ever seen.

Shaking off such thoughts with a snort, he pulled at the tie that bound the cloak at her throat. With little help the outer garment dropped away, revealing the careful embroidery work in the soft gray wool of her dress. A pulse fluttered at the base of her ivory throat, and William's gaze swept downward over womanly curves not even her demure dress could hide. He looked away at the gurgling stream, feeling a sudden ache in his loins at the sight of a woman so beautiful . . . and so vulnerable.

"Easy does it, Will," he murmured to himself. "This is not the lass for you."

When he looked back at her a trice later, her eyes were just beginning to focus. The violet-blue orbs gazed up into his face without recognition for a long moment, and then suddenly narrowed. A wry smile tugged at the corner of his mouth, but he quickly subdued it and looked away from her face. Wrapping his arm around her shoulder, he stood her up, gently leading her to the edge of the stream.

"I can see you're not much for riding."

"I hate you!" Her voice was a mere whisper.

"Nay, you do not." Seating her on the ground by the running water, William dipped his hand in the icy water and wiped her chin, the silky softness of her cheeks and brow. "You are grateful to me. For saving your life. For rescuing you from those rascals."

Her eyes were fixed on his face, and when he glanced at them, he could see the anger blazing in their depths. She slapped his hand away from her face, and he sent a silent prayer of relief heavenward. He didn't need to be touching that face right now.

Rising to his feet, the Highlander took a step back. Try as he might, though, he couldn't tear his eyes away from her slender back as she leaned over the water, washing her face and drinking from the icy brook.

A long moment passed. The woman was kneeling beside the water, tidying her hair with her back to him. Suddenly William realized she must be cold. Striding across the loose gravel, he was reaching down to pick up her cloak when another thought struck him. Despite being a captive for months and despite what he'd gone through to save her life, she was still no more than a pampered court lady. And an English one, even worse!

"Are you a madman?"

She was standing up and facing him, her hands on her hips and eyes flashing. He threw the cloak at her, and she caught it. Yanking it around her shoulders, she quickly fastened the ties at her throat. She looked like a warrior donning armor for battle.

"Mad? Nay, I am a Ross."

The anger in her gaze flickered with uncertainty, a frown replacing the glare for just an instant before a very tantalizing half smile broke out on the corner of her lips. Shaking her head slightly, she turned away, using the corner of her cloak to dry her face. It took great willpower on his part not to close the distance between them and take over the task himself. If she was not who she was, he would easily give up a night's sleep kissing away those droplets, drying each glistening bead with the soft touch of his mouth.

"I don't know enough of the clans and the ways of you Highlanders. Am I to understand that being a madman and being a Ross are the same thing?"

"Mind your tongue."

She carefully tucked a loose strand of hair into her braid and glanced at him, catching him staring. He scowled at her and looked over at his horse.

"Why did you take me from the village?"

"I—I did not *take* you. I rescued you." He shook his head and cast a quick look at her, grumbling, "Most likely saved your life."

She rolled her eyes in disbelief and pulled the heavy hood over her hair.

"Och," William uttered under his breath. He was a fool to think she'd actually appreciate what he had done. "'Twas not my choosing to come after you. And if you give me trouble, woman—"

"Do you intend to do me harm?"

The Highlander grunted an obscenity and, turning around, whistled for his horse. "So like the rest of them!"

"The rest of whom?"

"The rest of your type! Selfish! That's the whole lot of you. 'Tis bred into you and nurtured at every turn. And ungrateful, too. You'll bite the hand that feeds you! Of that I've no doubt."

"Ungrateful?"

He led his horse back to the brook. He could hear her approaching behind him. Ignoring her, he crouched down beside his horse and started rinsing off the steed's shoulder and leg.

"I'm supposed to be grateful because you turned a peaceful market square into a battleground in a matter of moments? Because you took me, against my will, from the people who—?"

"I am finished talking to you, woman. The sooner I'm rid of you, the better." He stood up beside the horse. "If you give your word to behave, I'll let you ride behind me this time. Gilbert is no doubt thinking I—"

The blow to his head was sharp and heavy, and William stumbled forward against his horse. The flashes of a thousand suns exploded in front of his eyes, but the Highlander half-turned in an attempt to see the woman behind him.

"Wh . . . yer . . . message . . ."

He tried to take a step toward her as she swung the rock again. He watched, unable to lift his arm and ward off the blow.

"Sis . . . ter."

And then, suddenly, he was falling. The woman disappeared from his sight. The flashing suns disappeared. Even the gravel of the streambed disappeared, and an abyss opened beneath him, as black and silent as a grave.

Chapter 3

"She may be the gentlest creature I've ever known." The old nun pursed her wrinkled lips. "She is certainly the smartest and the most agreeable woman her age I've ever met. *Oui*, I tell you, Laura Percy was an angel sent from God above to help us in a time of greatest need."

The wiry, squint-eyed monk motioned to the three burly Lowlanders to remain in the corridor as he followed the aging nun into the cold work room. Peering critically about the sparsely furnished room, the clergyman's gaze came to rest on the tiny fire burning in the hearth.

The nun gestured toward a pair of low three-legged stools set by the hearth, and the monk wordlessly removed a small basket filled with spools of fine colored thread from one. The old woman sat on the other and picked up a stretcher of half-embroidered linen, waiting for the monk to continue.

"So then, it must be at least three months that she's been here."

She nodded. "She arrived here at a most critical time. I had been bedridden with the flux for days. My own nuns were distraught at the thought of me dying and leaving them to fend for themselves. What with our little bit of planted ground ready for harvest, and the linens we'd completed needing to be taken to harvest markets—'twas all too much for them, I'm afraid. And then . . . well, suffice it to say that we were in great, great need."

The monk idly picked up a rough-cut block of peat from the floor beside the hearth and examined it. "I assume she arrived by boat?"

"Oui," she said in response, her hands deftly working the intricate design with her needle. "I was far too ill to notice, but from what my nuns have told me, the same storm that flattened our flax field beside the storage shed brought her to us. 'Twas a fierce storm, they tell me, and the ship bringing Laura north was forced to take shelter here at Loch Fleet rather than try to make the journey back into Fearnoch Firth. Of course, I did not learn of the details until I began to recover weeks later. By the grace of God, Laura simply took over, calming my nuns and managing to bring about order again. Why, the child even took charge of my care."

The mother superior's hands paused in their rapid movements, and her dark eyes focused on the monk.

"Some of my nuns believe that 'twas their prayers that directed the storm's winds—and that ship bearing Laura—to our little bit of coast."

The monk stared at the woman a moment, and then threw the block of peat into the fire.

"Aye, no doubt," he growled. "And you say you are expecting her back anytime now?"

"Oui." The woman's busy hands returned to their work. "Before dark, to be sure. But first, I must tell you as much as I can about all the good deeds that Laura Percy has done around here. Since you have the privilege of escorting her back to her mother, I want you to have all the details. You must compliment Lady . . . Lady . . . what was her name again?"

"Percy!" the monk grunted, tossing another block of peat on the fire.

"But wasn't she a Scottish lass? From what Laura has said—"

"Aye, Nichola *Erskine* Percy. She is Scottish."

"*Oui!* Lady Erskine!" The nun nodded agreeably, ignoring the growing note of irritation evident in the monk's tone. "She has done a very fine job of raising her daughter."

The monk came restlessly to his feet and walked to the small window that looked out over the road from Fearnoch. "I'll tell Lady Nichola."

"Laura has a gift, I believe, for managing things. All it takes her is one look at things and then—"

"How many went to Fearnoch with her this day?"

The nun paused, surprised at the monk's question. "Ah! Well, you are correct in assuming that we don't send her there all alone. With our little Convent of St. Agnes on the road from Rumster Castle, I could see no sense in risking her life. I simply asked a favor of Sir Walter, our benefactor, and he happily agreed to it."

"What kind of favor?" The monk half turned toward the nun, rubbing his hand over his grizzled chin.

"The favor of an escort on market days, of course. Since Laura is half English . . . and a pretty thing, at that . . ." The nun's hands paused again mid-stitch. "I thought it best for everyone involved. From what I hear, Sir Walter's men have become quite protective of her over these months. With so many rogues traveling along these coasts, 'tis quite important to protect a thing as precious as our Laura."

The monk nodded and, frowning, turned his attention back to the window and the road beyond. The shadows were lengthening rapidly.

"The only complaints that I hear, every now and then, is that our Laura likes to take her time when she goes to Fearnoch. Did I tell you that she is really good at—"

"You did," the monk interrupted bluntly and turned again toward the nun. "Did she arrive here with many possessions?"

"Possessions? Nay, not our Laura."

"How much? A trunk?"

The nun paused suspiciously for a long moment before finally nodding with understanding. "Of course. In taking her back, you need to know of—"

"How much, woman?"

"So little," the nun blurted, appalled. "Nothing that would require a trunk. She had only a small traveling bag."

"And that contained what?"

"Personal items. Necessities. Nothing more." The nun stopped abruptly and then glared in annoyance at the monk. "I don't believe the contents of Mistress Laura's traveling bag are anyone's—"

"Since she has been here, has she received anything from her mother?"

"Her mother?" she asked, surprised, before shaking her head. "Nay. I believe that she does get lonely every now and th—"

"So she hasn't heard anything from the mother."

The monk's sharp tone again caused the nun to pause in mid-stitch. "That is correct. She has not. You are the first to bring any news of her from the Borders."

"Or from her sisters? Has she received anything from them?" He stepped into the middle of the room. "A message? Or perhaps . . . a package?"

"A package?" The nun's eyes narrowed in concern. In an abrupt motion, she rose to her feet, dropping her work into the basket on the floor. "I don't believe I care for these questions. In fact, I think I've already revealed more than I should. I certainly have no wish to confide anything Laura would want to tell you herself."

"Was there a package?"

"Laura will be here soon enough herself. If she wishes, she can answer any other questions that you have. For now, you may remain here where 'tis comfortable and warm. I, however, must go to see to it that there is enough to feed you all."

The monk stepped between the aging nun and the door-way, blocking her exit.

"*Was* there a package?" The cleric's face was dark and threatening. "If you will not answer, I am certain I could call in one of your other nuns and get the answers I seek."

The woman set her jaw obstinately. "I am in charge of this convent. Now, I don't know what kind of behavior is acceptable in the Borders—or wherever 'tis you come from—but here you have no right to speak this way."

"Remember that I have been sent by—"

The nun held up her hand sharply, silencing the surprised monk as her eyes continued to blaze.

"For someone put in a position of trust by this young woman's kin, you certainly disappoint me. Now, sit back down by that fire . . . and compose yourself. I'll send Laura to you as soon as she returns from Fearnoch."

With a curt nod of dismissal, the mother superior of the Convent St. Agnes stepped nimbly around the monk and swept out of the room.

"What about my sister?" Dropping the rock into the sand and gravel, Laura knelt beside the sprawling body of the unconscious Highlander and poked his shoulder with one finger. Getting no response, she shook him. "What were you trying to say about my sister? Which sister?"

There was no answer. Perhaps she hit him too hard, she thought. Moving quickly around to the other side, she peered carefully at the face speckled with sand and pebbles. Laura carefully brushed away some sand that was clinging to the man's long eyelashes. Cautiously, she pressed her hand against the side of the warrior's throat. She could feel the blood pulsing beneath the taut skin, but his face had taken on an ashen hue. He looked none too healthy.

Feeling through the thick waves of dark chestnut-colored hair for a lump—or two—she drew back involuntarily when her fingers encountered the warm wetness of blood on his scalp. Parting the hair, Laura bit her lip at the size of the gash that she'd given him.

Drawing from her sleeve the finely embroidered kerchief that the mother superior had given her as a token of gratitude, Laura dabbed the gash gently. In a moment the snow white linen was crimson with his blood.

Looking about her at the surrounding groves of pine as she rinsed out the kerchief in the icy stream, Laura considered her next move.

She'd delivered the blow, certain that the man must be in the service of vile Sir Arthur Courtney . . . or another of the English king's deputy lieutenants. Certainly, the Tudor coin he had been tossing around when he first dragged her out of the market square had hinted as much.

But now, looking at the insensible creature lying beside her—vulnerable and injured—Laura began to have misgivings about her earlier assumptions.

What had he said? she thought. He had somehow been under the impression that she needed to be rescued. But rescued from whom, she wondered? And then, his final words before . . . well, before passing out. Laura was sure he'd said the words "message" and "sister"!

It *was* conceivable that Catherine or even Adrianne had indeed hired this man to bring her a message. It was also conceivable that, seeing her in the company of those Sinclair warriors, the man thought that she needed help. Suddenly, Laura began to feel a bit queasy.

He'd said he was a Ross. Looking at the red and black weave of his tartan, she'd learned enough about the Sinclairs' rival clan to recognize it. The Ross clan controlled huge tracts of land to the south and west of Fearnoch. And from what she'd gathered from the Sinclairs, the two clans had been feuding over the lands to the north of Fearnoch Firth since the dark days of the Viking marauders. Quickly, she untied the scabbard of his sword from his belt and laid it aside with the man's dirk.

Suddenly, everything made sense. As far as her two sisters knew, she had gone not to the Convent of St. Agnes, but to a little convent connected with the Shrine of St. Duthac, just to the south in the village of Tain.

South of Fearnoch Firth.

South . . . in Ross lands.

The revelation made her feel no better.

Laura quickly bent down and soaked the kerchief again in the cold, clear water. As she gently cleaned the wound, she chided herself for her error. It was only natural that her sisters would contact someone from the Ross clan. And it was also natural, given the animosity between the Ross clan and the Sinclairs, that this man would think she was being held against her will.

"Why couldn't you explain this to me before?" She knelt over the unconscious warrior. "'Twould serve you right if I just left you here to freeze . . . treating me as you did!"

But Laura knew she couldn't do that. In all probability, no one would be passing through this thickly wooded glen until spring. And though the blood had stopped flowing from one of the two wounds and the man's color was improving, she had no way of knowing how long he'd be unconscious. If the cold didn't kill him, some wild animal would certainly drag him off.

Glancing over her shoulder, Laura saw his horse standing quietly and watching her curiously. "You won't let me leave him here, will you?"

The handsome steed snorted and pawed the ground.

"Very well! Then come and help me." Stretching one hand out toward the animal, she quietly waited until, after a moment of hesitation, the horse moved across the gravel and came right to her—rubbing his muzzle in her open hand. Taking hold of his reins, Laura got to her feet and, for assurance, tied the animal to a tree branch hanging down from the steep embankment above the rocky ledge. Two large leather bags hung across the steed's flank, and she turned her attention to the bags' contents.

"We can't take him back to your own people," she said, pulling a plain gray blanket from one of the bags. The horse tossed his head and snorted in response.

Laura frowned. "No matter what you say, we cannot do that. I have no knowledge of the roads leading to the south. I have no idea how far 'tis to Tain. And besides, even if I left it to you to take us there—and we made the trip successfully—my life will be forfeit for certain for dealing such a blow to one of their kin."

The animal flicked his ears at the woman and looked away.

"I am *not* going south," she said adamantly, opening the blanket and putting it to the side. Next, she leaned down and again checked the man's head. The bleeding had stopped.

"At the same time, it would probably not do to be found by the Sinclairs. Heaven knows what they'd do to your master after all he did to them back in Fearnoch. Then I'd never find out what he knows of my sisters."

The horse's next snort had an agreeable tone to it.

"Aye. The Convent of St. Agnes 'tis, then. But I'll need your help, my friend, to get him on your back." She leaned over the Highlander again and rolled him onto his back. He groaned as his wound touched the stony streambed, and she paused to look at him.

By the Virgin, he *is* a handsome man, she thought self-consciously, kneeling down beside him. But then, she'd known that from the moment she'd first gazed into his deep blue eyes in the market square. Tall and lean with shoulder-length hair framing sunburned and strong features, he had a reckless air about him. Involuntarily, she touched the thin scar that ran along the left side of his jawline. Not just reckless. He'd looked dangerous. Very dangerous.

He groaned again, and she snatched her hand away and stood up.

"Leave it to my sisters to pick a man with looks this fine to come after me!" Moving between his legs, she reached down and took hold of both his hands. Pulling with all her might, she managed to get him to a sitting position. But the horse was still too far away, and she realized now that, at any rate, she simply could not lift the man's dead weight onto the horse's back. She was trapped. She let go of the man's hands and winced at the sound of his head thumping on the frozen ground.

Deciding on an alternative method, Laura rummaged through the Highlander's travel bag again and took out a coil of rawhide, leaving the man's tam and an old, oft-mended shirt in the bag. Tying his hands and ankles was easy, but dragging him up onto the narrow rock ledge beside the stream bed was extremely difficult. It took far longer than she would have thought.

Totally out of breath, Laura hung the man's legs down over the ledge and sat him up.

"Stay." She propped the Ross warrior up carefully. Quickly, she climbed down and maneuvered the horse into a position where she could pull the man across the animal's back. Standing in one stirrup, Laura pulled the man's wrists, and—as she fell backward onto the stony streambed—he dropped heavily across the steed's withers. She eyed the result with satisfaction and scrambled to her feet, wiping the sweat from her brow. The horse snorted and flicked his ears.

"It serves him right to ride in the same fashion as he forced me to ride. And no matter how sick he gets, we are not stopping until we get back to the convent."

Using the remainder of the leather cord, Laura tied the sword to the saddle behind her. She picked up the warrior's dirk and looked at the weapon thoughtfully. Then, cutting a small slit in the lining of her cloak, she slid the dagger into the opening. Next, she picked up the blanket off the ground and covered the Highlander's large frame with it. Finally, she climbed up behind the man and, with one hand looped in the belt of her captive, clucked encouragingly to the horse.

With a quick look at the descending sun, Laura turned the horse's head northward along the path next to the stream.

Even if he had lied when he'd shouted to his cronies, even if he'd headed west instead of south, Laura was confident she could find her way back to the convent. Loch Fleet, where the convent was located, stretched a few miles inland from the sea. She knew that she could not fail to find her way home.

But as she rode northward, the afternoon sun continued to fight its way through an encroaching patch of dark clouds and sink toward the western mountains, and the chill wind of the Highland winter began to bite into her skin. Her passenger had not stirred once since they began, and only the warmth of his body against her legs kept her anxiety at bay. Then, just as dusk began to descend in the forest, they broke out of a grove of trees, and Laura spotted the shimmering waters of the loch. The setting sun reflected warmly on the buildings of the small convent across the silvery body of water.

Luck was with her, she thought with a smile, for the Highlander had indeed taken them to the west of Fearnoch. Riding around the loch, past the ruins of the old castle on the western shore, would take no time at all.

It was nearly dark when they drew close to the convent, and Laura eyed the chimney above the chapter house with curiosity. The mother superior was extremely frugal with her fires, and yet the clouds of smoke billowing from the top of the chimney showed that she was still burning a fire there.

Knowing how little these nuns spent in terms of their comfort, she found that sign of extravagance somewhat alarming. But that was not the only thing that made her pause as she approached the convent's low stone walls. As she peered through the small orchard past the outbuildings and the chapter house beyond, she could just make out the shadows of a number of horses tied by the convent gates.

Laura reined the steed to the left, off the path along the loch, spurring the animal along the wall toward the back gate, which led into the orchard and to a small stone hut just inside the walls.

The Convent of St. Agnes was not like so many other religious houses that entertained a steady stream of travelers. Though the nuns there were not cloistered, the meagerness of their existence was generally known, and better food and lodgings could be readily found nearby. As a result, with the exception of a weekly visit of a few Sinclair warriors coming to escort Laura and the other nuns to market, no one ever stopped here.

Climbing down from the horse to open the gate, Laura had a vague sense that these visitors were not the neighboring Sinclairs coming to report the news of her abduction at Fearnoch.

As she led her mount through the gate, Laura was delighted to see Guff, the convent's laborer, come out of the hut and shuffle hastily toward her.

"We have visitors?"

"Aye, mistress. And a miserable lot, if ye ask me!" the farmhand grouched irritably.

As he took the reins from the young woman, he eyed the horse and the blanket-covered body suspiciously.

"There's not a man among 'em, mistress, with as fine a steed as this 'un. Did you commit murder to get 'im?" he asked, hitching a grizzled chin at the unmoving body.

She smiled at the question and pulled the blanket off the Highlander.

"Haven't the Sinclairs returned from Fearnoch?" Laura moved around to the other side of the horse to look at the wound on the Highlander's head, and Guff followed her.

"Nay, not a soul has returned as yet! I was thinking you got 'em tied up in one of your ideas. 'Tis hardly a . . ."

Glancing at the farmhand, she frowned to see him standing beside her, his mouth hanging open in shock.

"He is not dead, Guff. I just laid a small rock against the side of his thick skull . . . for his own good."

"The laird!"

Laura looked from the farmer's shocked face to the Highlander and back. "What did you say?"

"The laird, mistress! The Ross himself! William . . . William Ross of Blackfearn. His brother's the new head priest at St. Duthac's. They are a mighty family to the south—a good one so long as ye're not a Sinclair. But I do not think murdering their laird will set well with 'em, mistress!"

Laura winced at the sudden knotting in her stomach, accompanied by the certain knowledge that something had indeed gone terribly wrong. Glancing back at the Highlander, she hesitantly pushed back the loose strands of hair from the man's brow and looked into his face. Even in a dead faint, he suddenly looked murderous.

"Whist, Guff! He isn't dead. Help me bring him into the chapter house."

"Nay, mistress. Ye cannot take him there. I do not know who these Lowlanders be, but the rascals have been hanging about here for most of the day, and I do not like 'em a bit."

"Lowlanders?" Laura glanced at the direction of the chapter house. "Do you know what they want?"

"Aye. You!"

Laura tried to keep down the bile moving up in her throat. She could feel the fear burning in her face, and she tried desperately to fight off the panic. But then, the memory of her family being torn apart . . . of her father being taken from them by the English king's soldiers . . . of learning later of his death in the Tower . . . nay, the memories were all too vivid. All too recent.

"The mother superior came out of there just once this afternoon. But the crabbed old monk with 'em sent for her right off." Guff pulled the laird from the horse, hoisting him onto his shoulder. "I'll take him inside my hut. Ye'd best tie his horse behind those trees and out of sight, mistress. From the looks of things, I do not think it wise to have him found by these blackguards. I'll tend to the horse later."

She nodded quietly, and as soon as Guff disappeared through the low doorway, she led the charger to the grove of trees that the laborer had indicated.

Lowlanders! And a monk leading them! This could mean many things, none of which gave Laura any comfort. The visitors' arrival could mean news from her mother, but somehow she didn't think so.

After her father died in the Tower of London, for defying the king and refusing to sign the Oath of Succession, Laura's entire family had been forced to flee England for the land of her mother's birth. Lady Nichola had arranged for each daughter to go into hiding in three remote corners of the Scottish Highlands while she herself would remain in hiding in the Borders.

From the first day of their initial flight, one thing had been clear. They were not to trust *anyone*. The danger threatening the Percy family originated not only from the English king and his hatred for the family. Laura, her sisters, and their mother were also being pursued by enemies far more ancient—and far more powerful—than any single king.

Tying the horse, Laura picked up a half-eaten apple from the ground, and after feeding the fruit to the mount, she started back for the hut.

Of the three daughters, Laura had always been the closest one, in every way, to their mother. While Catherine, the eldest, had always been the dreamer of the three, and Adrianne, the youngest, the most reckless and courageous, Laura had somehow ended up as the voice of reason among them.

And it was because of her likeness to her mother that a warning bell sounded in Laura's head. If she was to be contacted, sending a group of men—who could easily be followed—would not have been Nichola's way.

A chill running up her spine, Laura ran the last few steps and ducked inside the stiff leather door covering. Once inside, her eyes quickly adjusted to the darkness of the single room, and she made out the form of Guff leaning over the Highlander in the farthest corner.

"He is coming around a wee bit, mistress. But I have to say, he is mighty—"

The head and broad shoulders of the Lowland warrior pushing into the hut behind Laura silenced the farmhand's complaint. She whirled in surprise as the man, long sword in hand, stepped to the side, making room for a wiry little monk who entered behind him.

"Mistress Laura!" the monk growled menacingly in English. "Somewhat ungracious of you to keep us waiting so long."

Clutching her cloak tightly about her, Laura jumped back a step as the cleric lurched across the hut toward her.

Chapter 4

The bitter wind raced across the loch, whipping up the black waters into a boiling, heaving mass. Across the moor, over rock-studded braes, shrieking it came, slamming finally against the gray stone walls of Hoddom Castle, seeking entry.

In the recess of the stone wall, a guttering candle, flickering wildly, wept its dying wax tear. Shadows loomed over the bed, climbing the walls, clutching at her. Quivering like a leaf, Miriam Ross tugged the heavy bedclothes, hiding herself beneath them. The wind outside, howling and wailing, hammered a fastened shutter. With a deafening crash the wooden latch gave way, and the winter gale exploded into the chamber.

Throwing the bedclothes aside, the little girl leaped from the bed and scurried across the floor. Tugging open the ponderous oak door, she ran barefoot down the corridor to the winding blackness of the stone staircase. At the sound of a cry somewhere behind her, she lost her footing, tumbling down the last few steps to the stone landing.

Never pausing to nurse the scrape on her knee, Miriam raced through the narrow passages into the amber light of the castle's kitchens.

Scurrying between the sleeping bodies of the kitchen workers, she gradually made her way to the hearth and nestled into an empty space.

Pulling a bit of coarse sacking around her, she glanced about at the soft shadows. Breathing in the kitchen smells, she listened for a few moments to the familiar sounds of snoring and then closed her eyes for what remained of the night.

The leather skin covering the doorway jerked to the side again, drawing Laura's gaze over the monk's shoulder. She could see the dark shapes of his Lowland escort peering in from outside, but the men parted as an aging nun, grumbling loudly, pushed her way through them. In an instant she was in the hut.

"There is no reason to create trouble, Mistress Percy." The monk stopped in the middle of the hut, his eyes glittering even in the darkness. "The horses are ready, and we'll be taking you—"

"Makyn!" the mother superior cried out, brushing past the monk and rushing toward the slowly retreating Laura. "Guff has been ill with worry that you wouldn't arrive by nightfall. With the cold settling in, we were all worried about you catching your death in the darkness."

Laura lost only an instant before realizing what her mentor was doing, and quickly fell in with the ruse. Dropping to her knees, she took the nun's gnarled hand and kissed her ring. From the corner of her eye she saw the monk hesitate, looking on with suspicion.

"Oh, my dear, you are shaking!" The nun turned and cast an angry glare at the monk. "You've scared the poor child witless. And who could blame her? The young thing is mute, and here you are frightening her!"

Mute? Laura threw a quick look at the monk. A shadow of confusion flickered across his features.

"Eh? You say this one's not Laura Percy?" He took a step closer. His squinting eyes never leaving the faces of the two women. "But I say, let the torches be brought in. I want to see for myself."

At that moment, from the corner of the hut, William Ross of Blackfearn groaned loudly, silencing the clergyman. The ancient nun whirled, hiding her look of surprise as she turned her gaze on Guff, and on the Highlander trying to sit up beside him.

Laura, coming quickly to her feet, turned her back on the two and rushed to the side of the Ross laird.

"Makyn, here. Well, ye can see she brought . . ." Guff began haltingly, quickly stepping around Laura and shielding her from the rest. "She brought . . . her husband, Mum. And he's godawful sick, from the looks of 'im."

"Sick?" the nun asked with genuine alarm.

Laura's mind was racing. Now it wasn't only her own life in danger but the Highlander's as well. Using all her might, she pushed the laird down on his back and then started to tuck the blanket around his body. But in his half-conscious state, he pushed the covering away and let out an obscene oath as he tried again to sit up.

Lord have mercy on her soul, she thought, she could still handle him. Using the heel of her hand as a weapon, Laura directed a solid hit to the lump on his head.

The Ross laird responded better than she'd anticipated. Jerking his hands to his head, he fell backward on the straw and groaned in pain.

"Ye do not want to be close to him. My—my daughter's husband is out of his head with the fever." Guff shuffled closer to the group, lowering his voice to a confidential tone. "If ye ask me, mum, I think 'tis the same fever that killed off the crofter and his little 'uns up on the Skibo Brae at Michaelmas."

The Lowland warrior edged toward the door, but the monk held his ground. "I don't care a whit about the man. But bring the lass around." He shouted over his shoulder at the men gathered outside. "Bring a torch in!" He then turned again to the nun. "I want to see her face for myself."

With her hands planted on the Highlander's chest to hold him down, Laura was fairly certain that she had never seen this monk before. Still, though, her mother's face had been well-known in both the Scottish and English courts before Edmund Percy's beheading. And considering the fact that she resembled her mother so much, Laura knew she was in grave danger of being identified.

The fate that awaited her if she was to be abducted by these people would be worse than death. It was riches that they were after, and she knew they would stop at nothing until they found it. Her only chance lay in devising some plan. Behind her, the mother superior and the monk were continuing to argue. Putting her hand quickly into the lining of her cloak, Laura searched frantically for the Highlander's dagger. She would do what her younger sister, Adrianne, would do in this situation. She would fight her way out.

But what were her own chances of surviving past the door? Not very good, she decided, considering she couldn't find the weapon. The dagger must have slipped through the slit she'd made. . . .

"A torch," the little monk shouted, shoving the warrior towering over him. "I want light."

The crumbling walls of the hut lit up as the torch was finally handed through the door. Beads of cold sweat began to run down Laura's back. But then, suddenly, she found herself staring into the blue eyes of William Ross of Blackfearn. Her heart leaped in her chest. He was fully conscious, though his face was still pale and strained.

"Bring her to me."

One of Laura's hands was still on his chest, and she felt the Highlander's muscles tense beneath her fingers. In the space of a heartbeat she realized he was about to put up a fight on her behalf. But she couldn't allow another innocent life be lost over her family's ordeal. Considering their sheer numbers, Laura was certain they would kill him, and she had seen enough of that in the past.

Pushing his chest, she tried to stand. But William Ross's

solid grip on her wrist took her by surprise, and she fell forward against him. His breath caressed her cheek, and she fought back the shocking thrill of her body pressing against his.

"Are you deaf?" the monk shouted. "I said, bring her to me."

Guff continued to block them from the monk's view. Laura glanced over her shoulder, only to see the mother superior taking up a position beside Guff. Not that it would make any difference if the hulking Lowlander behind the monk decided to act.

"Can't you see?" the old nun responded harshly. "The husband is dying. In the name of Heaven, you should be able to respect a moment of peace between them . . . before he goes to meet his Maker. 'Tis certain that your order cannot . . ."

The older woman carried on loudly, but Laura's full attention turned to the Highlander's dark expression. Their faces were so close, and she was so aware of the warmth of his body, of his earthy, masculine scent. At the further tightening of his grip on her wrist, her eyes dropped to his lips. They were so tantalizing.

She watched him mouth the words, *my sword*.

Laura placed a hand shakily on his forehead. Leaning closer, with the pretense of placing a kiss on his cheek, she whispered her answer in his ear.

Thankfully, his gruff curse was muffled by the rising pitch of the nun's continuing harangue. 'Twasn't her fault, Laura thought, that she'd left the Highlander's sword strapped to the back of the horse.

She leaned down again and brushed her face against his. The tremor that coursed through her at the feel of his unshaven face against her skin was unexpected, startling her. "I—I slid your dirk into the lining of my cloak . . . but I can't find it."

Laura felt her face flush hot as he held her with one hand

while the other delved into her cloak, touching her intimately as he searched for the weapon. She held her breath, trying not to be affected by the feel of his strong fingers moving across her back and her buttocks. Confusion was quickly added to the tumult of sensations, though, when she raised her face and met his gaze. The Highlander's blue eyes were glinting mischievously.

She pressed an elbow into his rib to curtail the roaming of his hand over the front of her dress, and continued looking for the weapon herself. She found it pressed between their bodies. Raising her weight off him slightly, she reached into the slit in the cloak, feeling for the dagger. But the rounding of the rogue's eyes, followed by the suggestive gleam from the dark depths, caused her to hesitate, burning with discomfiture.

"Get these two out of here and bring the lass to me."

At the sound of the monk's sharp command, Laura quickly withdrew the Highlander's dirk. The laird closed his huge hand over hers, taking the weapon from her.

"But the fever—" the Lowland warrior complained.

"By 'sblood, it hasn't killed the girl. 'Twill surely not kill you."

William Ross pressed Laura's head tightly into the crook of his neck. She had no idea what he was planning to do, but whatever it was, she couldn't imagine they had much chance of surviving. Still, though, she went along with it, finding assurance in his protective grip.

"Stay away, you great baboon." The mother superior's voice rose to a screech. "I tell you Makyn is this man's daughter. Take your hands off me!"

Laura froze at the sound of the old nun being manhandled and then pushed the man's chest, but William Ross's firm hand held her in place.

"Let me go."

"Wait!"

"They are hurting her. Let me—"

A woman's shout cut through the din, silencing everyone inside. "They've returned!"

No one moved in the hut, and the tension hung in the air, sharp and palpable. Laura was afraid to breathe.

There was a slight commotion outside, and the Highlander eased his grip on her. Laura's head turned in time to see Sister Beatrice appear in the doorway.

"They are here, Mother."

Every eye in the room was fixed on the tiny nun.

"Sir Walter's men are back," the arriving nun said breathlessly. "And they are waiting to see you at the chapter house."

"What of Laura Percy?" the monk rasped, turning sharply on the diminutive woman. "Is she with them?"

Beatrice's eyes fleetingly searched the hut and barely paused on Laura before returning to the monk's face. She frowned darkly.

"Come and see for yourself," she snapped, and then turned to her leader. "The Sinclair men are impatient, though, to speak with you, Mother Superior. With the darkness and with snow in the air, they are anxious to go on to Rumster Castle."

This appeared to be all the encouragement the mother superior needed. Immediately taking charge, she shook off the grip of the Lowland warrior and began to fire instructions at everyone.

"You, monk, come with me, so you can at last meet our precious Laura. But I am warning you now, I won't allow you to be dragging that child out into a cold and stormy night."

"Now, just a moment—"

"Nay, not another word on it. The morning will come soon enough for you to take her from us. Out with you!"

Laura didn't hear the monk's mumbled answer as he stepped out into the night.

"And Guff," she said loudly, turning back at the door. "You

see after your daughter and her husband. I'll have Sister Beatrice bring back some broth for his fever."

But her look did not match her gruff words, and Laura did not miss either the affectionate nod or the subsequent wave of the old woman's hand, telling her to get out while she had a chance. Both women knew that this was their moment of good-byes. Their moment of parting. The mother superior turned and stepped out into the darkness.

No sooner had the thin leather door dropped back into place than Guff was there, peering out. The Highlander was on his feet, too, and checking the crumbling walls of the hut for an alternate way of getting out.

"They'll be right back, laird," Guff mumbled with an anxious look at Laura. "They've left a man standing by the apple shed. He's watching the hut."

William Ross began to kick some straw near the spot where he'd been lying. "I could feel the wind pushing through this wall."

"There's a goodly hole here." Guff nodded, shuffling over to the corner. "And we'd best hurry. That monk'll be back as soon as he sees Mistress Laura isn't with the rest of 'em."

The laborer was on his hands and knees, pulling a loose block of stone from the base of the wall and adding to an already good-sized hole.

Laura picked up the blanket that had been thrown aside by the Highlander and rolled it under one arm. She turned uneasily to William Ross of Blackfearn.

"So you will help me, then? You'll help me escape these men?"

Even in the semidarkness she could see anger blaze in his eyes.

"By Duthac's Shirt, lass! If it weren't for your interfering . . ." He let his words trail off with a disgusted shake of his head.

Heat rose to Laura's face. "How was I to know that you

weren't one of *them*? I mean, the way you acted . . . abducting me . . . stealing me from the market square in broad daylight!"

She jumped when he started toward her, but he simply brushed past, going to the doorway. She felt the cold wind push around the leather covering as he peered out.

Guff stood up, brushing the dirt from his hands. "Mistress Laura tied yer horse out by the trees beyond the walls. Ye'll not miss it if ye go out this way and straight over the wall. Ye'd best go now."

Laura moved quickly to the door when the laird crossed to Guff. She could see the single man the farmhand had pointed out earlier. But there could be even more that she could not see.

She strode back to Guff, knowing her best chance of escape lay in taking charge. She hurriedly removed the jeweled cross that she always wore around her neck—a present from her mother—and pushed it into the laborer's hand.

"Bless you for everything. Now you must get away yourself. And later, when they've gone, tell the mother superior that I'll send word as soon as I can."

That said, Laura threw a hopeful look at the tall Highlander, tucked the blanket under one arm, and crawled out into the wet and stinging cold of the Scottish night.

Behind the dais in the ancient hall, a huge, jewel-studded cross hung from the wall, a blue veil fringed with gold draped around it. In the very center of the chamber, the flames of the freshly lit bonfire licked at the pyre of oak logs.

Suddenly, as the blaze leaped upward, the jewels of the cross seemed to come alive, casting their glittering brilliance on every wall, on every face, silencing the jangling din of the gathered throng. Agitated knights who had been arguing for hours suddenly paused, awed by the spectacle of color and light. The complaints and the grumbling ceased in an instant.

The voices all hushed. But for the crackling of the fire, the hall was suddenly silent.

A tall, gray-haired knight standing by the dais stepped forward, addressing the group.

"I know that we are restless. We all feel the urge to act." His piercing gray eyes swept over the nodding warriors. "It has been five months now. And five months is a long time to wait."

Murmurs of agreement echoed through the hall.

Another aging knight stepped forward. "But time means nothing to a Knight of the Veil. Whether it be five months, five years, or five hundred years, we would never be so unsettled if we were sure the treasure was in safe hands."

"Aye, but as far as we know, the treasure *is* safe," a warrior called out.

"But for how long? And how can we be certain? We've been warned of the danger."

"And the maps. What of the maps?" another knight barked. "We were promised the maps."

The leader raised his hand and silenced the group. "We were promised only that the Treasure of Tiberius would be returned to its rightful place. Should we ride in and take it by force from the family of our brother?"

"Aye! Perhaps we should!" another knight asserted hotly. "We know nothing of our brother's promise passing on to his wife and daughters. What happens if these women decide on a different path? What if someone fools them? Or wrests the treasure from them? Even worse, what if they are so blinded with the power of Tiberius that they decide to keep the treasure for themselves?"

"I tell you this," the leader stated sharply, quieting the growing uneasiness in the chamber. "Nichola Erskine is a most honorable woman. The delay has only to do with the fears she harbors for her daughters' safety. Would you deny her that? And you know that as long as rumors continue to circulate of the existence of a map—or of three maps—no one would foolishly kill these daughters."

A tonsured knight-priest spoke for the first time. "But we've heard reports of so many in pursuit of them."

"Aye, men like the English king! But Henry Tudor knows nothing of the treasure. He only wants their Percy heads."

"The three are safely tucked away in Scotland."

"What about Sir Arthur Courtney?"

"He was killed by his own men."

"And the monk?"

"The monk!" The leader's voice dropped down low. "We have reasons to question his loyalty."

"If he has fallen, then we cannot afford to wait."

"We cannot wait!" several men shouted.

"Brothers!" A knight clothed in black pushed himself away from the wall at the far end of the hall and strode toward the dais. As he passed the fire, his tall build cast a shadow on the other warriors, and more than one of them eyed the gold brooch holding a tartan at his shoulder. In exquisite workmanship using tiny colored gemstones, a red hand clutched a blue cross. "I have something to say."

"The Blade of Barra!" Nodding with satisfaction, the leader of the knights turned his gray eyes on the approaching man. " 'Tis time you took up the quest."

Chapter 5

Damn the woman! Of all the troublesome, ungrateful...! William peered through the darkness as the wind whipped his hair across his face. His head was pounding between the goose egg and the open gash she'd given him, and it felt as though he'd been beaten with a stick across his ribs. He wondered if she'd dragged him all the way to the convent behind his own damned horse.

And now where was she? She'd only gone out a moment ahead of him. After first finding out how large an escort the monk had with him—and making sure the old farmhand had a plan for saving his own neck from the wrath of the monk and his Lowlanders—William had quickly crawled out after her. The Sinclair men would have to look after the nuns.

Still, in that instant the thickheaded Englishwoman had disappeared like some wood nymph. Their only chance lay in the hope that she had gone directly to the horse.

As he broke into a trot, a wave of nausea swept over him. Fighting it off, he moved in the direction Guff had said to go. There was a definite smell of snow in the wind.

The grove of trees loomed before him in the darkness, and he stopped. Still tied to a branch, his horse Dread stood pawing the earth beside a shivering Laura Percy. Upon seeing him, the giant horse tossed his head in greeting and then sniffed the ear of the young woman.

"I was beginning to think you were lost," she whispered,

patting the head of the horse. "They must know by now that I did not come back with the Sinclairs. We must hurry."

She was taking it for granted that he'd take her with him. William could feel the devil urging him to mount Dread and ride off, leaving her. He would thoroughly enjoy paying her back for all she'd done to him. But on the other hand, the thought of listening to Gilbert whining if he was to return empty-handed was too much. He frowned and stepped toward the animal.

Her voice was quavering. "If we go around Loch Fleet and then move south the way we came . . ."

She jumped as he yanked his sword sharply from the back of the giant steed. He loosened the weapon in its sheath before strapping it onto his own back.

Her breath spilled into the cold air. "As I was saying, I can lead us back as far as . . ."

He mounted his horse and, wheeling the animal in a circle, nudged him toward the path. It occurred to William that he wanted her to call after him. To ask him again to take her. He wanted her to be terrified at the thought of being left alone, but, glancing in her direction, he found her standing expectantly, a wee shivering bundle of eyes and cloak and blanket.

"Damn!" He moved Dread to her side and stretched a hand out for her to take. She put an icy palm in his hand and placed her foot on top of one boot. He pulled her up behind him, and she immediately wrapped her hands around his waist. Even with the cloak and the blanket wrapped around her, he could feel her shivering violently with the cold.

Shouts came from the direction of the convent, and the laird kicked the warhorse into a gallop, following the path westward along the loch for a short time before changing direction and veering to the north across a stony meadow. Their pursuers would overtake them for sure if he tried to make a run straight for Ross lands.

The night was black, and the wind was picking up. William

slowed his horse as they reached the far side of the meadow. As the two rode on, he could feel the tightness of her grip around him, and he tried to ignore the pleasant chill that ran up his spine as the woman's face rubbed against the wool tartan on his back.

Reaching a wide creek, William followed the path along the bank through thickly wooded glens and open ground that he knew led to rolling moors and eventually to Rumster Castle. But all was now simply a black, empty void. At one point the creek branched off, and the Ross chief splashed across the icy water, still keeping to the right branch of the stream. He knew where he was going. At the convent Guff had told him how many men the monk had with him, and that had given him the answer he was after. There was no way he could have fought the blackguards successfully. Especially not with Sinclair men arriving. They would assuredly have sided with the Lowlanders against him.

In a few more miles, the stream bent sharply to the east, and they continued to follow it as an icy rain began to fall.

Throughout his years growing up in this region, he and Gilbert and the other young lads their age had many times traveled onto Walter Sinclair's land. Always being told by Thomas that they were too young to accompany the Ross warriors in their raids, they had often taken it on themselves to raise cain in their neighbor's lands, "conveying" back to Blackfearn Castle livestock and anything else of Sir Walter's they could lay their hands on. That was many years ago, he thought with a pang of nostalgia. But as the woman behind him tried to snuggle closer against his back, it occurred to him that the Sinclair chief was not yet free of Ross incursions.

A stinging shower of sleet whipped in on a driving wind, and in a few moments the frozen rain turned into a heavy, wet snow, covering the ground quickly with a shroud of pale white.

Damn, William thought, glancing back at the tracks they

were making. He pushed Dread into the shallow water of the creek's edge.

"Do you think that any harm will come to Mother Superior and the nuns?"

William felt a pang of relief that her voice was still strong. But he knew that he needed to reach shelter before long, or the shivering heap behind him would be frozen solid.

"You should have thought of that before bringing those villains to their door."

"I did not bring them! Somehow, they found me on their own."

"And would it not have been safer for all if that scrawny excuse for a monk had found you where you should have been—in the abbey convent of St. Duthac?"

"I see no difference," she grumbled, rubbing her forehead again on his back.

Though he didn't think she was even aware of the action, he took a deep breath. How was it that he could be so annoyed and so excited by such a simple act? And by a wee, bullheaded court chit at that.

"No difference at all," she repeated quietly. "I would have been forced to flee that place as well."

"Who is the monk?"

She paused a moment. "I've never seen him before."

"Someone must have paid him to come after you. And those Lowlanders. Gilbert never said a thing about them."

"Gilbert? You mentioned that name before."

She tightened her hold as William nudged his steed up an embankment. Through the whirling snow he could see a dip between two rocky braes. "Who is this Gilbert?"

"The provost of the Shrine of St. Duthac." He spurred the horse into a canter. "Your mentor and protector. The one who was so worried about your whereabouts. The one who came begging to me for help."

He thought he heard a snort of derision, and considered dumping her right there in the meadow.

"Guff told me that you are William Ross of Blackfearn."

He spurred Dread into a canter over the hard ground. The snow on the meadow brightened the vista considerably.

"It would have been much simpler if you had explained that much to me in the market square."

"And when are you thinking I was supposed to do that? While you were caterwauling and bringing every Sinclair in the Highlands down upon us? Or should I have waited and told you after you tried to kill me?"

William reined in the mount as they reached what appeared to be a path winding between the snow-covered hills.

"You deserved what you got." She tried to take her hands from his waist, but he reached down and trapped them with one of his own.

"You keep those where they are, lass. You've done more damage to me in one day than I've had in ten years of fighting."

"Then you've led a soft life."

This time he was the one to sputter derisively. To think, this from her, the very picture of the spoiled brat!

"I thought we would be going around the loch and to the south."

"You thought wrong."

The wind swung around, stinging their faces with a mix of sleet and snow. He felt her adjust herself and nestle closer against him.

"What is your plan?"

"I have none."

He felt her stiffen. It took only a moment, but he could feel it coming.

"Then perhaps if you'd listen to what I have to—"

"Hold tight."

William nudged Dread down the steep, rocky path, and

Laura again had to tighten her hold so she wouldn't fall off the horse. In a few moments he pushed the horse around a boulder, and they were suddenly out onto a stony strand, the roaring sea before them. Pushing the giant animal to the very edge of the foaming water, William again turned them northward.

The riders were now taking the full brunt of nature's forces, but the Highlander kept his horse at a canter along the sea's edge. He knew this was the best way to hide their tracks. With the howling wind in their faces and the froth of the waves soaking them as high as their waists, they pushed onward.

The uncertainty in her voice belied her words as she called out against the wind. "We must be close to Rumster Castle!"

William didn't bother to answer her, for his eyes were riveted to the first of the abandoned fishermen's huts he'd been looking for. Even in the dark he could see that the thinly thatched roof had collapsed in on the splintered pile of sticks swaying in the wind.

"I thought we were running from the Sinclairs as well. Why have you brought us into Sir Walter's lands?"

Ignoring her, he spurred Dread on. Rather than moving inland and into the hills, William had decided instead to take shelter in one of the fishing shacks he knew existed along this stretch of coast. Used only during the warmer seasons, these places might offer no more than some loose timber to break the wind. But the fact that they lay in the shadow of Walter Sinclair's castle made the huts an unlikely place for anyone to search for them.

"Other than soaking us to the bone, would you be kind enough to tell me your plan?"

"I told you before. I have none."

Her frustration was all too obvious in the way she banged her head against his back. The thought of her organizing the piles of wool in the marketplace flickered through his mind, bringing a devious smile to the Highlander's lips. What a perfect punishment for someone like her—to be left alone with *him*!

A dark line of bluffs had risen up just beyond the strand, and when they reached a notch in the low cliffs, William pushed Dread up the stony incline of the beach. Three tiny huts lay huddled against one another in the protection of the rocky ledge.

Even before plague had struck Inverness and Fearnoch and the surrounding areas a few years ago, wiping out whole villages and cutting down the numbers of people who lived here, these huts had always been empty at this time of year. When the harsh winters ravaged the coast, keeping even the hardiest fishermen from venturing out of the lochs and the more protected firths, those who lived here in the summers were tucked away snugly at Fearnoch or in the village beneath Rumster Castle, a few miles up the beach.

Unwilling to throw caution completely to the wind, though, William ordered her curtly to stay where she was. Then, drawing his sword as he dismounted from Dread, he approached each of the cottages in turn.

They were indeed uninhabited, and after inspecting them closely, the Highlander nodded toward one of them as he returned to his steed.

"This one is the only hut sturdy enough to house us all. I dare say 'tis no English palace, but at least it has a bit of leather across the door to keep out some of the weather."

His charge appeared to bristle, but then she checked her tongue. When he held out his hand to help her, she waved him off, swinging her leg over Dread's back. She dropped to the snow-covered ground with a thud, slipping and landing on her hands and knees. Again ignoring his outstretched hand, she pushed herself upright and trudged wearily toward the hut. He followed her in.

For the next few minutes she was silent. But then, as soon as he started making a place in a corner for Dread and set-

tling the animal for what was left of the night, she began with
her questions again.

"How long do you plan to keep me here before we leave?"

He peered about in the darkness and then squatted before
a small circle of ashes. Rubbing some between his thumb and
forefinger, he smelled it. It was old.

"Who said I plan ever to leave?"

He glanced at her over one shoulder. Even in the darkness
of the hut he could tell that she was watching him with weary
eyes. She started toward him. He turned to face her fully.

"First show me you've nothing in your hands."

She didn't even pause as she advanced on him. "Have no
fear. If I had a weapon, I'd give you a bruise worthy enough
to match the others on your thick head."

"Aye, I've no doubt of that. But you don't have to stay
here. You are free to sleep outside."

She moved past him to the pile of wood. "True. But what
chance would I have then of knocking you out in your sleep
and taking your fine horse?"

"We hang horse thieves in the Highlands."

"Well, I might just take the chance, considering the fact
that you yourself have not been hung yet."

He'd have liked nothing more than tossing her delicate butt
out onto the beach right now, but the memory of Gilbert's patient expression and his sincere plea to bring this woman safely
back to St. Duthac's halted him again. He watched her start
carrying back pieces of the driftwood and stacking them for
a fire beneath the smoke hole.

"And what do you think you're doing?"

"I'm going to make a fire."

"And invite Sir Walter for dinner, I suppose." He shook
his head. "There will be no fire."

"But—"

"No fire."

She sank to her knees on the dirt floor, her hands making a weak attempt to rub warmth into her arms.

"You picked a fine place to bring us. Now we can just freeze."

The Highlander turned his back on her and went to where she'd dropped the gray blanket on the dirt floor. Shaking it out, he tossed it to her.

He wasn't going to let her get on his nerves. He wasn't going to feel sorry for her. And most important, he wasn't going to be charmed by her pretty face and violet-blue eyes. All he had to do was ignore her. Pretend she wasn't there. And try to protect his head.

Chapter 6

"I believe 'tis time you began to worry."

The provost responded to Father Francis with a vague nod as the two made their way back to the provost's work room after their morning meal. Gilbert's huge hound Willie trotted on ahead.

"Even the farmers made it back from Fearnoch before dark. And you know how recklessly William pushes a horse. By the saint, Gilbert, they should have been here by vespers last night at the latest. But still we've not heard a word."

Gilbert paused to look out of the small slit of a window in the long corridor. He *was* becoming concerned about the whereabouts of his brother—and Laura Percy. Heavy snow had been falling through most of the night—a mix of snow and sleet continued to fall—and the bitter north wind was surely adding to the dangerous conditions for wet travelers.

And what if William had been injured in taking the woman? What if his horse had come up lame? Perhaps, he thought, it would be best to summon some of William's men, perhaps just a couple of them to go out in search of their master.

But in the back of Gilbert's head a nagging voice kept telling him to wait. Indeed, the busy little voice was saying, If the two had stopped somewhere along the way, this might be the best chance he'd ever have of getting his brother alone with an eligible and marriageable noblewoman—even if this one *was* half English. Hiding a grin, he sent a prayer heavenward to forgive him for his deviousness.

"You are not listening, Gilbert. Shall I send Father John to Blackfearn Castle?"

The young provost stepped over Willie, who had stretched himself comfortably in front of the door, and walked into the work room. "You said the farmers saw them leave Fearnoch during the fighting?"

"They did."

"And we've had no word from the Sinclairs?"

"Nay, Provost. Nothing yet."

Gilbert shrugged and turned to the older priest. "Well, Father Francis, 'tis just possible that—out of consideration for the Englishwoman—William is taking his time. I say we give them another day."

Before Laura was even awake, she was conscious of the wind whistling into the hut, and she pulled the blanket higher on her face. Gradually, her eyes focused on the small opening of a smoke hole in the thatched roof, and she watched snowflakes dancing in the dim light of dawn and falling to the dirt floor of the hut.

She shivered as a blast of wind shook the cold walls of the hovel.

Though it had been long dark by the time they reached the deserted hut, the coldness inside and the storm raging outside should have made for a sleepless night. But the last thing she remembered was moving to the farthest corner of the hut from the Highlander, who had simply pulled his tartan around him and sat against his saddle, long sword in hand.

Aside from his pigheadedness, William Ross had been a stunning vision of power and gallantry. And Laura had forced herself to close her eyes—and her mind—to the mixed images she had of him.

Not admitting it openly, she would always remember him

as the fearless warrior taking on at least ten Sinclair men while holding her squirming body on one shoulder. She would also never forget the calmness he'd instilled in her when she'd just pressed her body against his chest in Guff's hut. At that moment she had no idea what fate lay ahead.

She snuggled deeper into her blanket and smelled his scent. How strange that a day later, the memory lingered of the nearness they'd shared. She could still feel the strange warmth that spread through her whenever she looked at him—talked to him—even argued with him as if he were the veriest villain north of the Yorkshire.

But in many ways he was a rogue, and she would simply never be a woman to hold her tongue.

He was obstinate, and she could already tell that he scorned her for her sensible logic. Well, that was her nature. How could she ever change?

This meandering stream of thought carried some of the laird's less than admirable qualities to Laura's mind. Despite his pleasing looks and undeniable courage, the man was a scoundrel. A reckless, unmanageable rogue with no sense of planning at all. He hadn't answered any of the questions she'd asked of him. Nothing about the length of their stay, or even about how he would get them to St. Duthac's.

Perhaps after all, Laura thought, she *might* have been better off fleeing with his horse when she'd knocked him on the head outside Fearnoch. If she had, she could right now be planning and proceeding without any interference from William Ross of Blackfearn.

Nay, that would never have done. She hadn't the slightest idea about where she could find safety in this wild country. Her two sisters were far away to the south and to the west. This had been the result of their mother's planning to send her children to three separate corners of Scotland. If danger was to find one of them, the other two had at least a chance of escaping it.

Still, Laura thought, if she set her mind to it, she could find her way to another convent. From what she'd learned from the sisters at the Convent of St. Agnes, there were a number of religious communities huddled along this coast.

A gust of wind swirled through the hut, and Laura shifted her position a little, letting her eyes drift toward the ill-fitting flap of leather that served as the door. It was doing nothing to keep out the weather. With a frown she turned her gaze to where the Highlander had spent the night.

He was gone.

Jolted into full consciousness, she hurled herself to a sitting position and looked nervously about her in the semi-darkness. The shelter was empty of both man and horse.

He was gone.

She shuddered as all the images of his chivalry crumbled before her eyes and a sickening feeling of loss swept over her. *He* was the one who had up and decided to leave *her* behind. Throwing off the blanket, Laura came quickly to her feet.

A quick search told her that everything was gone. Horrified to think that he'd just waited until she was asleep and then left without a word, she clutched her cloak fiercely around her.

"The knave!" Laura pressed the heel of her hand against the sudden knot in her belly, a painful sensation that seemed to be gripping her midsection more and more at moments like this. "Of all the churlish, ill-bred . . ."

She glanced again in the direction of the partially open door. Snow was swirling in on the strengthening wind and coating the dirt floor of the hut. She had to do something. She was not about to sit here and freeze to death. But what?

Last night she had been too blinded with weariness and the weather to judge how close they were to Sir Walter's castle. Though she'd never been there herself—she had yet to meet the aging warlord—she knew Rumster Castle lay to the north, along this rugged stretch of coastline. It couldn't be far.

What other choice did she have? Laura quickly decided. She could stay here and freeze, or she could try to reach the Sinclair keep on foot. Not a difficult choice.

Having decided, Laura shed her cloak and quickly pulled the blanket over her shoulders. Donning the cloak again and pulling her hood forward over her face, she stepped out into the storm.

The blast of the wind nearly pushed her back into the wall of the hut as she turned toward the stony beach. The mix of icy snow and the whipped-up sea stung the exposed skin of her face with the sharpness of a fistful of needles. Drawing a sharp breath, she clutched the hood tightly to protect her face as well as she could, and squinted up the beach through the storm. She could hardly see fifty paces in front of her. No matter, she told herself, leaning into the wind. This was the time to travel—while she still had strength in her bones.

This weather was far too foul for traveling, he decided, peering out of the protective grove of stunted pines by the creek. He'd wait out the storm and then take the woman to St. Duthac's.

"Come now, Dread, you've had your water, and there's not enough grass there to fill your belly, anyhow."

William Ross tugged the horse's head away from the tufts of yellowed grass and led the animal through the trees and away from the road. He mounted the steed and started along the edge of the creek again.

With the stormy weather and the night working against them, it was possible that the monk and his men might not have gotten too far from the convent.

William considered this for a moment. If he was foolish enough to head right now for St. Duthac's, he would quite likely cross paths with the blackguards. Nay, it would be best to wait a few hours.

One thing he was certain of, though. His enemies had separated. In a wind-sheltered spot not far from where William had watered his horse, the Highlander had found the tracks of a band of warriors heading north. There were no horses, and he knew the group was headed toward Rumster Castle. It had to be the Sinclairs.

Suddenly, William found his thoughts lingering on the Englishwoman waiting for him, and he frowned. Though the storm was now roaring like an angry beast, it occurred to him that he might just prefer staying out in the weather to spending any more time than he needed to with Laura Percy.

She was a sea of contradictions. In her waking hours, annoying and arrogant. But in her sleep, as he'd watched her last night, she'd rested less comfortably than anyone he'd ever met in his life. Fretting, moving around, and then sobbing quietly in her sleep with such heart-wrenching sadness that he'd not been able to hold back. Moving to her, he'd stretched out beside her, smoothing her hair, brushing away her tears, whispering comforting nonsense in her ear. She'd slept through it all.

But for him the night had grown more torturous with every passing minute.

Though common sense told him he was a fool, the woman aroused him. When he looked at her, when he felt the softness of her skin, his loins stirred with desire. Even the memory of her hands about him as they rode, and last night, the scent of lavender in her hair as she lay sleeping, was enough to set his blood on fire.

By God, he thought, even her sharp tongue, with those unceasing demands for a plan to do this and a plan to do that, served to stir life within him.

The stinging wind hammered him as he rode down onto the beach. The sea and sky—what he could see of either—

were a fierce gray-green color, and he shook his head, feeling himself growing angry at the direction his thoughts were going.

William had left in the morning to avoid this. He'd left her sound asleep, a heap of cloak and blanket, because he knew he needed to get away. Distance—that's what was called for—before she awakened and he fell further under her spell. She was a damned enchantress.

Aye, distance was the answer. His own past—a past that still gnawed at him—had taught him that this was the only way to deal with the likes of her. True, she was not Mildred, but the woman came from the same privileged life and upbringing.

Reaching up, he felt the lumps and the clotted blood beneath his tam. Then again, for a wee thing she could swing a rock as well as any Scottish lass.

"By Duthac's Shirt," he swore out loud. He'd been away from women too long! That was it. That was the whole problem. "Dread, we're going to pay a visit to Molly at the Three Cups once we're free of this arrogant court chit."

Aye, he nodded, turning the steed toward the hut. That was all he needed to forget Laura Percy.

Leaping from the horse, William quickly brushed the worst of the snow off Dread and shook himself. Looking up, he realized the snow was falling even heavier than before.

The Highlander pushed open the door flap and began to lead the horse in. But Dread was only halfway inside the hut when William realized that Laura Percy was not there.

He called out to her, but the sharp whistle of the wind was his only answer. Pushing the horse back out the door, he called again. Nothing.

Searching the ground, the Highlander could see now the soft impressions in the snow. A single track of footprints showed that she had indeed left the hut on her own.

Following the tracks back down onto the beach, the Ross

laird looked about in frustration. The waves were crashing high on the beach, and the spray filled the air. He could see nothing. As soon as he was beyond the protection of the bluffs, the footprints disappeared, obliterated by the snow and wind. She had not passed him on the beach, and the bluffs would not have offered an easy climb in the best of conditions. Her only route led to the north.

"Damn the woman!" William swore, running back to the hut and leaping onto his waiting steed.

Chapter 7

Laura stood in stunned disbelief beside the broad gray-green river and stared at the churning, wind-whipped froth of white on its surface.

No longer even aware of the shudders that were wracking her body, she lifted her gaze gloomily to the towers of Rumster Castle rising in the distance beyond the impassable stretch of water.

Seeing the river jolted her for only a moment out of the numbing weariness that had crept into her body. She vaguely recalled being cold, but now she could not even feel that. As her disappointment dissipated, she realized she simply wanted to lie down on the soft white ground and sleep.

Nay, a nagging voice called out. Follow the river until you find a place to cross. There must be a place to cross. There must be a place.

But Laura's body was growing too numb to respond immediately to the commands from her brain. She stood, her body slumped and shaking, her eyes hardly even able to focus on the great stone edifice across the water.

After leaving the hut, she had stubbornly pushed on through the storm, always keeping her destination in mind, always certain that the castle would suddenly appear. But as she trudged on with increasing fatigue, the wetness of the snow and ice had gradually seeped into her clothes, chilling her until her thoughts began to grow fuzzy, until the world around her began to take on a vague, distorted, dreamlike quality. Until it slowly registered in her brain that she no longer could feel the body encasing her soul.

And then she had found the river, nearly stumbling into it before drawing herself back.

Laura turned her back to the river and stared blankly at the stretch of beach she'd just covered. She did not recognize it. Everything appeared strangely tilted, unnatural. She tried to focus her eyes on the track of dark footprints snaking away from her in a long meandering trail, but she could not even do that.

Then, suddenly, she was looking across a moor in York-shire. The snow that covered the ground would soon disappear in the lightly falling rain. Her sisters' tracks led just over that hill. Laura could hear the sounds of their voices calling her.

Her mother had begged her to leave the house, to escape with her sisters. But as the three had run across the courtyard, Laura's hand had pulled out of Catherine's. She'd stopped. She couldn't help herself. She could hear the screams of the serving folk as the king's men cut them down. They were tak-ing her parents away. They were killing any who raised a hand.

They were killing them, but there was nothing she could do to fight the evil.

Nay, Laura realized vaguely, that was past. She knew she was not in Yorkshire. There was no moor. The smell of salt from the sea penetrated the vision, and she turned her head slightly to look at the wind-whipped froth. She shivered and her gaze turned downward. Her feet were planted in the snow, but they seemed to belong to someone else. She could not move them.

Her mind wandered again. She could see the crenelated towers of their home above the crest of the moor. Was it spring already? Laura could smell the lilacs on the soft breeze.

She would stay here until her sisters came for her. Only vaguely could she feel the warmth of tears on her face.

"Laura!" Her sister's frantic call reached her ears, but she remained still.

Oh, Virgin Mother, she prayed. Protect them. All of them.

"Laura!"

She slowly brought her hands to her ears to block out the distant sound of her name. They were dying in the household. The monsters were cutting them down!

"Laura!"

She shook her head. She couldn't go. She couldn't leave them behind. If it was her parents' fate to die, then she would die, as well.

"Laura!"

She opened her eyes and saw him.

Out of the mist he came. So huge on his charger. His long, dark hair streaming in the wind.

"Nay!" she tried to scream. "Leave me to die."

But she knew the sound was only in her head. The cold had robbed her of her voice.

William Ross leaned down on the side of his horse and hauled the soaked body of the woman onto his lap. Like a frozen branch floating on an endless sea, there was no fight in her when he tucked her closely against his chest. Her bare hands were colder than ice—her exposed face red with the weather. He saw her lips move, but the words never broke through.

He didn't pause more than an instant before yanking his horse around and charging down the beach. This was the last thing he needed right now—her dying of the cold.

With the wind at his back, it was not long before they reached the hut. Laura Percy's life, though, seemed to have slipped from her body as he carried her inside. He knew there was still a very real danger of them being found if he was to start a fire inside the hut. The wind would carry the smell of smoke a long way. But laying her unmoving form on the packed dirt, he suddenly didn't care.

After leading Dread in and closing the door against the invading wind, William quickly built a small fire from the driftwood. Once the blue flames were crackling in the center of the hut, he moved to Laura and went down on one knee beside her.

"Och, only a madwoman would have done what you did this morn."

William continued talking to keep his mind off the chore he knew he must do. The cloak and blanket still half wrapped around her were stiff with ice. Carefully, he peeled both of them from her still body, hanging them over the rawhide cord he quickly strung up beneath the thatched roof. He placed her stockings and shoes beside the fire.

Her eyes were shut. Her chest barely moved as she breathed. At least, she was alive.

"As I said before, your kind think only of yourselves."

William used the inside of his tartan to squeeze some of the water out of her streaming black hair. It had come completely free of the braid. The long shining waves gleamed like the wing of a raven. Looking away, he remembered the old shirt he carried in his saddlebag and got up to fetch it. He then pulled her into his lap. Her body draped over his arm, as limp as the wet woolen dress that clothed her.

"I'm telling you now, lass . . . I hate doing this." He pulled her close to his chest and reached for the laces on the back of her dress. Her face rolled on his shoulder slightly as he swept the long ebony locks out of the way. The laces gave way slowly. As the soaked wool parted, his fingers came in contact with a linen shift. It, too, was soaked through. With a low curse, William started pulling the wool dress forward, off her shoulders.

"I do not like you," he lied through clenched teeth. "And

I do not like any of your kind. In fact, I'll take a fistful of needles in my eyes and a dirk in my back before ever conceding that this gave me one whit of pleasure."

He averted his eyes from the dark circles of her nipples showing through the transparent undergarment. Putting his old wool shirt quickly over her head, he relied on his sense of touch to push the wet shift down her arms. Holding her by one arm, he pulled the gray dress and the shift off her legs, and worked her arms into the sleeve of the dry shirt.

The woman made an incoherent sound deep in her throat. As he watched, her hands fisted, suddenly clutching his tartan and shirt. He pulled her more tightly to him, laying her head against his chest. As he held her, he gently rubbed one hand over her arms and back, warming her skin. Slowly, he felt her begin to relax.

By St. Andrew, he thought, he'd asked for distance and here she was, naked as a bairn beneath his shirt. He tried to not think of how soft her skin felt beneath his fingers or how full and round her breasts had looked. He tried not to remember the gentle curve of her hip and backside where he'd touched her just a moment ago. He felt the heat again stirring in his loins and took a deep breath. Her hair smelled of lavender, just as it had last night.

"By Duthac's Shirt, woman! Have I told you how much I hate you?" He pulled her knees up and covered the exposed skin with the soft wool shirt. "As soon as this damnable weather lets up, I am taking you straight to the church and dropping you at the gates of the place. Gilbert can do whatever he wants with you. I'll have no part of it!"

He felt her hand again clutch his tartan tightly, and she stiffened momentarily. As she did, her cheek accidentally brushed against his neck, and he felt the wetness on her face. He pulled back slightly and saw the tears. The silent tears that were streaming down her cheeks. Just as they had the night before.

"Laura!" he called gently, wiping away the wetness. "You're safe, lass."

Tears continued to fall as her features shifted, the muscles moving beneath the skin, a display of anguish and hurt that showed clearly even in the flickering firelight. The point of some invisible blade slipped between his ribs, and he breathed in sharply as the point touched something deep within him.

William edged closer to the fire and stretched, placing another piece of driftwood on the flames. She continued to cling to him. In a strange way, he realized that he was beginning to take comfort in that. It was true that she represented everything that he didn't want in a woman. And yet, thrown together as a result of the storm and the danger around them, he would be a foul, unfeeling fiend not to give the simple aid that she needed.

A few hours later Laura came fully awake.

As the clouds began to part, she tried to focus on her surroundings. A thatched hut. A small fire crackling a few feet in front of her. Certain she was still dreaming, she gazed for a moment at the strong hand wrapped protectively around her shoulder. A woollen cloth of red and black plaid appeared to be draped around her. In one ear she could hear the comforting sound of a heart beating strong and steady.

It took her a few moments to comprehend fully where she was and in whose lap she lay curled up. She lifted her head slowly and looked into his face. His eyes came open, and he stared into her face.

They were so close. So intimate. She felt the warmth against her fingers and realized her hand was tucked inside his shirt, resting against the warmth of his bare skin. She held her breath, unable to move, her own heart beginning to pound out a wild rhythm.

His eyes were as dark as a moonless night. And yet, reflected in their depths, a private battle was brewing. Perhaps because she was still floating somewhere in the space between dreams and reality, she couldn't focus on the great danger that lurked so close at hand. The danger of lying half dressed in the arms of this reckless Highlander. The danger of finding herself attracted to something very real—to something forbidden.

Her eyes roamed his face for a long moment. She studied the dark slant of his brows—the eyelashes that were longer and more beautiful than any she'd ever seen on a man. Her eyes lingered on the scar by his chin, and then her gaze came to rest on the firm set of his lips. She felt a knot form in her throat just as a tingling heat began to surge through her belly.

Perhaps it was the tightening of his chest muscles beneath the tips of her fingers, or perhaps the hardness she felt pressing against her hip. Whatever it was, Laura found herself scurrying off his lap in a wink of an eye.

Springing to her feet, it took her another long moment before she realized he was regarding her with an almost amused expression. Looking down, Laura was horrified to discover she was wearing nothing more than a man's shirt—a thing that came only to her mid-thigh, a thing riddled with more holes than a tinker's promise.

She turned her back on him, trying to pull the shirt down over her legs, only to have it slip over her shoulders. She gave up struggling and half turned, scowling at him as he continued watching her every move.

"Could you do something other than stare at me?"

He stretched his long legs out before him and then rose to his feet. Laura felt the hut shrink by half when he stood up.

"I can certainly try." He casually lifted a gray wool dress off a few pieces of wood by the fire. Without glancing back at her, he hung the garment on a leather cord stretched above the fire. He then picked up a very wet bundle that proved to be her shift. He shook it out, and then let his eyes travel from the wet and transparent material to her half-dressed body and then back to the undergarment. She was sure she heard a low chuckle as he hung the shift beside her dress.

"There must be something you could be doing outside." She saw his horse watching them with a bored expression. "Like watering him or . . ."

Laura stopped. William Ross was frowning at her.

"Aye, you were saying?"

She felt her face turn crimson. "You needed to . . . to take him out . . . this morn . . . for watering."

He simply nodded as he turned and stepped to Dread's side. The horse still carried its saddle, and the man moved around the animal, tending to it.

Embarrassed that she had thought the worst of him—that she had not even considered a practical reason for his absence this morning—she turned her back to him as she moved toward the fire, crouching beside it and hugging her knees to her chest.

"I suppose I should . . . well, I am sorry," she mumbled.

"So you assumed that I had abandoned you here, is that it?" He dropped the saddle somewhere behind her.

"I . . . I did." She never lifted her gaze from the blue-tinged flames.

"Actually, I wanted to. But Dread had doubts as to whether you'd survive without us."

"I would have managed." Her weakness. She couldn't hold her tongue. "I was taught long ago how to fend for myself."

"Och! As you did this morning, I suppose."

She had no answer to that. When the animal was settled, she heard the Highlander rummaging through his travel bags. She didn't look at him as he lowered himself beside her at the fire, though her gaze flickered toward the leather flask in his hand and the pieces of dried meat and an oatcake that he placed on the ground between them. She gnawed her lip and forced herself to look away, but the growling of her stomach made her face burn with embarrassment.

"Aye, you were taught to fend for yourself, but I say your teacher should be hung."

He extended the flask toward her, but she shook her head.

"Come, lass. 'Twill do you good."

He pushed it at her again, and she reluctantly took it. The liquid burned her mouth and throat, but a heavenly warmth quickly spread through her belly. When she lowered the flask from her mouth, she found his eyes lingering where she could still feel the liquid on her lips. Stunned by the look and the jolt that coursed through her, she quickly ran the back of her hand over her mouth and handed the flask back to him.

"What is that?"

"'Tis the 'water of life.' Usquabae, they call it. Straight from the kitchens of the Shrine of St. Duthac."

She pulled her hands tighter around her knees and tried to shake off the light-headedness she suddenly felt. Whether it was the liquid or his nearness, she simply could not tell. Looking at him, however, did not help, and she focused her gaze on the fire. "I believe we've been hostile to one another for no reason. Perhaps we started off on . . ."

"I had reason enough."

"And so did I," she retorted, her temper flaring.

They sat in silence for a few moments, but then he shook his head before offering her a piece of the dried meat.

"You seem to have only enough for you. I'm very well."

He pushed the piece into her hand. "I did not bring you back frozen and half dead just to watch you starve before my eyes."

His chivalry had reared up once again, and she accepted a bit of the meat with a grateful smile. A moment later, he broke the oat cake and handed her half as well.

As she ate, her eyes traveled from the wet clothing hanging by the fire down to the large shirt that was covering her. A warm flush began to creep again into her neck and cheeks. With difficulty she swallowed the mouthful of food.

"Did—did you—undress me?"

"It was either Dread or me. We drew straws and I lost."

Laura leaned her forehead against her knees and tried to ward off the embarrassment. She'd reached the age of twenty without ever allowing a man to seriously pursue her, never mind kiss her. And here, in a single day William Ross of Blackfearn had already carried her off, seen her naked to the skin, and awakened with her curled contentedly in his arms. By the Virgin, she thought with rising panic, and none of that was even in response to the lustful thoughts she had of the man.

"I would eat that if I were you." He nodded toward the food in her hand. "You're far too thin already. By his Shirt, as lean as the wenches are at the Three Cups, I still think every one of them has more meat on her bones than—"

She shoved him hard enough to send him rolling onto his side. Pretending as if nothing had happened, she quietly tucked the shirt around her legs.

He pushed himself back up into a sitting position. "I take it from your actions that you do not care to be compared with . . ."

"Don't say it."

". . . Wenches."

This time the attack was less than successful. Before she could lift the closest weapon at hand—in this case, the leather flask—he had trapped both of her hands in one of his own and pinned them to the ground. Her face was only inches away from his. This time, though, she was taken aback at the sight of the soft wrinkles at the corners of his eyes. He was a breathtakingly handsome man, she found herself thinking. Especially when he was amused by her actions. Her gaze drifted uncontrollably to his lips.

"You have a temper, lass."

"I am the calmest of all my sisters," she said, struggling to free her hands.

Holding her until her efforts subsided, he finally let go of her hands, and she quickly pulled them a safe distance away. He reached over, though, and pulled up the neckline of the shirt onto her shoulder. Laura again felt a feverish warmth creeping into her face. She gnawed her lip and gazed at his booted legs as they stretched before him.

"And how many are there?"

She stared at him a moment until it registered in her brain what he was asking her. "Oh, two. My sisters are . . ." She stopped. "You have news of them! You started saying something . . . something at the stream about a message from my sisters?"

"If I knew how the mere mention of them would affect you, I would never have done so, I'll tell you that."

"But I struck you before you mentioned them."

"And why was that? A strange thing . . . to reward kindness with violence."

"I told you before. I thought you were one of them."

"One of who? You tell me you've never seen that monk before, and yet you knew they were coming after you. Why?"

Laura didn't look away. "You are William Ross of Blackfearn. The laird of clan Ross. 'Tis very little I know about you."

"Are you saying that you don't trust me?"

"Aye." She nodded with conviction. "You mentioned a provost's name. Gilbert."

"Gilbert Ross. My brother."

She narrowed her eyes and gave him a look of suspicion. "When I was being sent into the Highlands last fall, the name given to me was not Gilbert Ross, but—"

"Father Jerome," William cut in. "He passed away about the same time that you were expected. Gilbert was chosen as his replacement."

"And how do I know what you say is the truth?"

"You can believe what you will." His scowl darkened. "I'm a fool to . . . och! Think what you will!"

She tucked the tips of her toes under the shirt. The Highlander was staring into the fire, the muscles in his jaw clenched hard.

"I—I believe I was wrong in not believing you." There was no response. She softened her tone. "Does this mean you'll not tell me what you know of my sisters?"

William continued to stare into the fire for a long moment before finally cursing under his breath. He turned his blue gaze on her. "First, you tell me why you did not arrive at St. Duthac's three months ago . . . when you were expected."

"A storm blew us off course." She shrugged. "The ship I was sent on was pushed north and forced to anchor at Loch Fleet. We very nearly ran aground at the entrance to the loch itself."

"That is only a day's ride from Tain."

She didn't like his accusing tone. But knowing the man was obstinate enough to withhold any information until she'd answered all his questions, Laura bit her tongue and forced down her temper. In measured tones, she gave him an account of the disastrous conditions she'd found upon arriving at St. Agnes's Convent. She had been needed there, so she had stayed. As she spoke, she thought he should be at least a little impressed by the account of all she'd been able to accomplish there. But the Highlander's hard look never softened.

"And you could not send a message to St. Duthac?" he said accusingly.

"I did. I sent word with the same sailors who had brought me here."

"The same sailors?"

She nodded.

"And let me guess, were they Lowlanders?"

"The ones assigned to take me here were."

He looked at her as if she were a simpleton. "And you

thought, 'tis so easy to maneuver a ship . . . 'twas a ship, was it not?"

"Get on with what you have to say."

He nodded. "You thought, 'tis surely no trouble for a ship to move out to sea and back again into Fearnoch Firth, just a wee distance down the coast, to deliver a message . . . for a spoiled English chit."

She tore her eyes away and, resting her chin on her knees, stared into the fire. The taste of the food in her belly had turned sour. Well, what was she supposed to think? It was their duty to go to Tain. At the time it had seemed reasonable to expect them to proceed as planned.

"I assume no message arrived at St. Duthac."

His snort of disdain was her answer.

"Coddled!" he muttered. "What else is to be expected!"

She pushed away a lock of hair that fell across her face as she snapped her head in his direction. "I'm not coddled. I never have been. I don't know what you mean."

"The noble! The rich! Your kind think they can do as they wish and have everything their own way." He shook his head. "And the English are the worst."

"I won't let you insult me." She threw her head back. "I am sitting here in a ragged shirt with all my worldly possessions hanging above that fire. I think the people you are talking about are *your* kind . . . not mine! The only people I have are a mother, whom I haven't seen in months, and two sisters—and *you* refuse to tell me what you know of them. So if you'd be courteous enough to turn your head, I'll be putting my clothing back on and leave this place so you won't have to suffer any more because of *my* kind."

She waited for him to turn his head, but he stubbornly refused to look away.

Laura was too upset not to go through with her threat. "Damn you, you've seen what there is to see." She scrambled to her feet and, stepping behind him, tried to reach for her dress, but his strong grip around her ankle stopped her.

"Sit down."

"I will not! I am leaving!"

"You'll stay here and wait out this storm with me . . . if I have to hang you by your hands right there beside your wet clothing."

She shivered as his eyes turned on her face. There was no mistaking that he meant everything that he said. Still, she waited as long as she dared. She would not let him bully her.

"I'll stay . . . for now." He let go of her ankle, and Laura retraced her steps, crouching again by the fire. This time, however, she made certain to sit farther back, where she could watch him.

They both sat in silence. Laura listened to the sound of the wind buffeting the hovel walls. Steam was rising from her clothing. They would be dry soon, thank heavens. A fine mist was swirling above them, mingling with the wood smoke. Smoke and mist. The Highlander's horse shook his head and shifted in the corner, and she turned her gaze to where he stood. A magnificent animal, she thought.

She stole a secretive glance at William Ross of Blackfearn. He too was magnificent. And very much a man. Muscular thighs well defined beneath his red and black kilt, and—as he sat back—strong arms supported a broad, powerful body. Tucking her knees closer to her chest and pulling the long sleeves over her cold hands, Laura tried to bury her face in her knees. Please, Virgin Mother, she prayed, let my clothes dry soon.

"I have news from only one of your sisters."

Startled by his words, she focused her eyes on him. He had once again taken out the Tudor coin that she'd seen that first time. He was studying it in the dim light of the fire.

"Which sister?" she asked unsteadily. A sudden burning tightness gripped her belly. What if something was wrong with one of her sisters? What could she do? Her eyes involuntarily followed the movement of the coin in William Ross's hand.

"The message Gilbert received brought word of Catherine Percy Stewart."

She tore her eyes away from his hands and looked with confusion at the Highlander's profile. His attention was still focused on the coin. "What did you say?"

He gave her a side glance over one shoulder. "If you have no sister by the name of Catherine, then I've been searching for the wrong—"

"I do!" she quickly interrupted, shaking her head. "But you called her Catherine Percy . . . Stewart."

He nodded. "Aye. Catherine Percy Stewart, countess of Athol. Mistress of Balvenie Castle."

"She is married? She . . ." Laura couldn't continue. As his words registered, her eyes clouded with a jumble of emotions. Joy and happiness, curiosity, disbelief, even a pang of loss. She quickly dashed away an escaping tear, forcing herself to think on this as good news. As the best of news.

Looking away from his watchful eyes, she dropped her chin on her knees and looked ahead into the dimness beyond the fire. This news changed everything, though. Nothing would ever be the same. Married! A husband to protect her. To love her . . . Catherine Percy Stewart.

For the first time since fleeing England—for the first time since separating from everyone she held dear—Laura felt truly alone.

"John Stewart is a good man." William's voice was gentle as he stood up and shook out the drying clothing. "He has title and wealth. Good land. He is blood kin to the king himself. And he's a generous man. She'll have all the comforts money can buy."

Laura bristled. "All three of us could have had whatever we wanted in England, but together we chose integrity over selling ourselves."

"And what makes you think she's sold herself? What self-respecting Highlander would buy such a wife?"

She hadn't meant for her self-pity to sound so accusing. "I didn't . . . I'm sorry. That's not what I meant."

He stared at her for a long moment before talking. "I know nothing of your life. Or your family. But it has not been easy spending time with you." A grim half smile tugged at one corner of his mouth. "Nor safe, either. I can only imagine what a sister of yours would be like."

"Catherine is a fine woman!"

"Aye, I've no doubt she is. Athol wouldn't have her otherwise." He paused. "His letter to Gilbert said more."

She held her breath, waiting. But the rogue said nothing, letting the sound of the wind fill the dim light around them as he absentmindedly rolled the gold coin a few more times across his knuckles.

"Please tell me what the letter said."

She could actually see a mischievous glint flicker in the depths of his blue eyes.

"I do not know all of it." He furrowed his forehead as if digging deeply into his memory. "Aye, one thing. Gilbert remarked that Athol sounded almost foolish at times in the letter, considering how serious a man he is. The earl kept referring to the . . . to the blissfulness of married life."

"Really?" Laura asked happily. "He said 'blissfulness'?"

"Aye. Hard as that is for me to believe." Laura's eyes narrowed, and William fought back a grin. "Ah, and he said something of opening his wife's school. And a curious mention about some half brother that he never knew he had."

His voice trailed off as he appeared to be considering the last bit of news.

"Anything else?"

"Aye, there was something else." He held the coin up before his eyes, studying it carefully. "Something about the springtime. Aye. He had some important news of the spring."

"What of the spring?"

"What was it . . . ?" He eyed her.

"Please?"

"Ah, that's it. A bairn. They've a bairn coming in the spring."

"A bairn!" she whispered in shock. "My sister . . . with child?"

"Aye."

One by one the tears welled over, rolling down her cheeks. She looked about her hurriedly in search of something to wipe her tears with, but there was nothing but her sleeve. She covered her eyes with her arm, but she could not quell the sobbing.

"If you act like this when you are happy, I do not have any great wish to see you when you're sad."

Laura jumped a little at hearing him next to her. When he put an arm around her, she gnawed her lip and dabbed her eyes with her sleeve. But then gradually she relaxed against him.

"But these are tears of happiness, lass. Are they not?"

It took great courage to lift her head and look into his eyes this close. The wrinkles at the corners of his eyes deepened a little, and she looked down at his full lips, curled into a warm smile.

She nodded, then shook her head, then nodded again—before surrendering to the jumbled mix of feelings racing through her. She laid her head against his chest and cried.

Chapter 8

There is an intense satisfaction in watching snow falling, Gilbert thought, as long as you are looking out at it. As the world disappears beneath the blanket of white, one sees the power, the plan, and the accomplishment of the Maker's work. The dead world of autumn is covered, if only for a short time, and the whiteness of the snow produces in the mind a feeling of hope where disappointment had lingered.

Death, rest, and rebirth in the spring. A good plan.

Unwilling to tear his eyes away from the scene outside, Gilbert only heard the door of the work room close behind the last of the departing priests.

He was undeserving to ask a favor in prayer for himself. But it had been a long time that he'd known the truth. The confession he had heard from Mildred had been meant for the Lord, but yet had fallen to him to hear it. It was he who had carried the torment of it for so long.

Gilbert Ross had prayed. He'd sought guidance. He'd begged for direction. And here, after all this time, after he'd all but given up hope, the Maker was giving him his answer.

"Not only an answer, Willie," he said quietly, petting his dog as the giant head nosed its way into Gilbert's hand. "The Maker is taking charge. Rebirth lies just beyond that drift of snow."

Gilbert turned and smiled at the simple drawing of the young girl smiling at him from above the fireplace.

"All will be well, Miriam!" he announced with certainty. "The Maker is indeed taking charge."

Snow floated in on a cold gust of the wind, swirled around them, and settled wetly on his neck as he tightened his hold around her shoulders.

William Ross's reason kept telling him to push her away and put as much distance as possible between them. But his body was obstinately ignoring any message that smacked of reason. Looking down, he watched his hand gently combing through the thick silk of her long black hair. Her head rested lightly against his chest. His eyes followed the line of the shirt, lingering on the ivory skin peeking through unpatched holes, taking in the curves of her body and the shapely calf extending beneath the ragged hem of the garment.

He'd always liked that shirt . . . but never as much as right now.

For the hundredth time since returning with her, William felt heat stirring in his loins. He took a deep breath. By St. Andrew, he thought, she wasn't helping matters any. As he stared at the dying fire, she turned her face and rubbed it against his chest. Her one hand was tucked around his waist in back and the other was placed, palm flat against his chest. Obviously, she was determined to torture him to death.

William took another slow breath and tried to regain some grip on his sanity.

"Do you know . . . ?" Her soft voice scattered his thoughts in an instant. "Do you know how their marriage came about so quickly?"

His fingers brushed back the hair from her face. She was so beautiful . . . so trusting. Her body fit against his so perfectly.

"I have—"

She shifted slightly and her hand slipped downward onto his stomach. William had to clear his voice and tear his eyes from her face. Staring into the fire, he tried to think of the snow, of sharpening his sword, of any one of Gilbert's tedious reprimands. He tried to think of anything but Laura Percy writhing in ecstasy beneath him on this dirt floor.

"You were saying? About my sister and John Stewart?"

Say something innocuous, he thought, searching around in his scrambled brain. He lowered his head and found her violet eyes looking up at him. They were like jewels in a field of ivory.

"I would say if your sister looks anything like you, Athol was a lost man before he even knew it."

The prettiest of smiles broke across her lips as his face flushed with heat.

"That was the nicest thing you've said to me since we met."

"Aye, well, it just slipped out. Lack of sleep, probably."

"Will I see you at all? That is, if we make it safely back to St. Duthac's?" A deep crimson began to creep up her neck and into her cheeks. "I mean, since you are brother of the provost . . . I hope . . . I don't mean to sound forward. I just meant since you . . ."

Her broken words were a perfect match to his inner turmoil. He raised a hand to her cheek. His fingers were large, brown, and rough against her skin. Her eyes, large and bright, watched him questioningly.

" 'Tis a dangerous thing we're starting, lass." He brushed his thumb across her lips and felt the sharp intake of breath. "I'm telling you now, use whatever weapon you have in your possession. What I'm thinking of this moment . . . well, another blow to the head may be in order."

She didn't pull away or smile. Instead, he felt her press closer in his arms. Her eyes focused on his mouth.

"By his Shirt, Laura, you do not know what's good for you."

"Don't I?"

The words were scarcely breathed when he drew her up and kissed her waiting lips. It was a chaste kiss, a brush of lips, a tasting of her nectar and a testing of her experience. He drew his face away slightly. He told himself he was a fool for doing it. But she was indeed sweeter and more tender than the most exotic of delicacies—and he wanted more.

William watched her as she brought shaky fingers to her lips and touched the surface where his mouth had been an instant earlier.

"I have never been kissed."

"And you still have not," he stated, letting his eyes hungrily roam her face and body. "Not properly, anyway."

He bent his head again and plundered her willing mouth. There was no longer any gentleness, only desire. No restraints, only passion pure and unreasoned. He felt her open her mouth beneath his, but he was too far beyond care to notice if her groan was uttered in complaint or passion. His tongue swept in, and he knew that she was his.

Flashes of rational thought, instants of sanity, occasionally flickered through his heated brain, but he ignored them as he held her body tightly to his own. He pulled her onto his lap, and Laura, too caught up with the power of their kiss, came willingly.

She wrapped her hands around his neck, and he felt her responding to him. She was pressing herself to him. As his mouth continued its onslaught, his hands roamed her back, brushing the soft fabric of the wool against her softer skin. She pulled back a bit to catch her breath, but he was relentless, following her and recapturing her mouth. All he could think of now was the sight of her naked skin—the feel of her firm flesh where he'd touched her as he'd undressed her earlier. He ran one hand to the side of her breast, groaning at the feel of the hard nipple erect beneath the shirt.

She tore her mouth away from his abruptly and placed a hand against his lips. His heart was pounding, his body throbbing with need, and he looked down into her flushed face. The intimacy of her fingers on his lips was almost more than he could stand. As his heart pounded in his chest, he gazed at her, vulnerable and his alone.

Her lips were full and tender, her cheeks the color of the wild roses. She was by far the bonniest lass he'd ever held in his arms. Nay, she was the most beautiful woman he'd ever seen. But just then her gaze lifted, and the sight of tears again pooling in her bright eyes carved a frown across his face.

"I'm sorry," she whispered, pushing his chest. Moving awkwardly, she fell off his lap and onto the floor. She struggled ineptly for a moment, crawling backward and pulling the shirt over her legs. "I am not . . . I should not have . . . I've never been so reckless in my life. I can't."

William didn't need to hear any more. Rising abruptly to his feet, he ran a restless hand through his hair. He wanted her. And deep down, she wanted him, no matter what she said.

But damn him, he decided bitterly, if she was a mistake he would indulge in again.

Snatching up his sword, he stomped to the door, yanked the leather flap aside, and marched out into the storm. The bitter wind, laced with icy snow, cut his face, but he never even noticed it as he stormed down the beach.

Almost in a daze, Laura watched the flap of the door fall back into place. Unexpected tears welled up and ran down her cheeks, their wetness startling her into alertness. She dashed them away, but the sharp knot of regret that she felt rise in her throat made her stare once again at the doorway.

The madness, the burning desire to melt against him, into him, to become one with this man—these were sensations totally unknown to her. And yet she'd acted as boldly and as brazenly as some—as some tavern wench. But then, how she could not feel what she did when he had his arms about her?

He was simply far too irresistible for someone of her sheltered background. It was no wonder, Laura realized, her sister Catherine had decided so soon to wed. If the earl of Athol was anything like William Ross, she now understood very clearly why her sister would have given up the fight so quickly.

Using the Highlander's retreat to her advantage, Laura rose quickly to her feet and started pulling down her garments from the leather cord. Damp but dry enough, she thought. She needed to be fully dressed, and she wanted to have a logical explanation for her lapse of sanity ready before his return. And he would return, Laura assured herself, glancing at the watchful horse in the corner.

"You must think humans to be daft creatures."

The horse's snort brought a smile to Laura's lips.

She turned her attention back to the clothing in her hand, but her mind was engulfed with images of herself in William Ross's arms. The feel of his mouth, the intimacy of his tongue as it had caressed her own. She brought a shaky hand to her swollen lips and tried not to think of the pleasure she'd felt at having him touch her breast.

She'd become corrupt. She was so willing. So *very* willing. Nay, she had to stop. She could not continue this way. What of her soul! What of his!

As she dressed, she decided to leave the laird's shirt on beneath her dress and pulled her clothes on quickly.

The small fire in the middle of the hut had burned down to embers and a mere wisp of smoke, but Laura didn't dare put another piece of wood on top of it. William had put them both in danger by lighting the fire so close to Rumster Castle. She knew it was done solely to save her life, but she was far from the point of perishing now.

Laura had just finished pulling her damp boots over her warm wool stockings when she heard the sound of voices. Standing stock still, she strained to hear the voices again over the wind. Running to the thin wall of the hut, she peered through a crack. The wind pushing through was frigid, but she immediately spotted three men huddled against the battered wall of the hovel across the small opening. Ice and snow covered their tartans and beard, and they were casting suspicious looks in the direction of the hut where she was hiding. Laura looked over her shoulder in panic at the thin smoke rising through the small hole of the hut's roof.

Worry of the whereabouts of William brought Laura's head around with a snap. She couldn't tell if these were Sinclair men or not, but seeing their drawn weapons sent a cold shaft of fear straight through her. What if they had already injured or even killed him? He might be out there even now, his blood staining the snow as his life ebbed away.

Her mind whirled, and anger boiled in her veins. The thought of these men hurting the unsuspecting laird was made even more terrible by the guilt of knowing that he'd rushed from the hut because of her.

She had no time to think beyond the present. She would escape and save him—or she would avenge his death. One way or the other, she would have to fight her way past these men.

As the group started toward the hut, Laura quickly ran her eye around, searching for a weapon. She had few options. Picking up one of the larger pieces of driftwood, she clutched it tightly and moved into the shadows. The leather door of the hut lifted, and with a gust of cold air, one of the men stepped in.

"His horse is here," he shouted over his shoulder. "Just as I thought, he didna go south."

Laura watched as the man's two companions followed him in. Stepping in behind them, she smashed the heavy stick over the last entering man's head. The man fell forward a step into the Highlander before him, knocking him down. Swinging the rude cudgel again, she struck the surprised leader in the ear and then scrambled to pick up a sword that had fallen to the ground.

"This will teach you," she shrieked, struggling to swing the heavy blade, "to kill unsuspecting and innocent men."

Before she could deliver the blow, however, strong hands grabbed her from behind, yanking the sword from her hands and lifting her by the waist off the ground. As she thrashed, the wide-eyed group of men struggled to their feet. Kicking out with one foot at the closest one, she sent him sprawling and drove her—and her captor—crashing into the doorjamb.

"By the devil . . ." he cursed, stopping her cold.

"You!" she gasped, twisting around to look at him.

William Ross put her down abruptly and then grasped the shoulder that had hit the doorway. He was glaring at her with a murderous look in his eye.

"They did not kill you," she cried.

"Nay, but *you* almost did."

She turned abruptly toward the three men crowding the hut. One of them was still sitting on the ground, holding his head in his hands. The leader was standing and nursing an ear that was already beginning to look like a mutton chop. The third, a wiry older man, was grinning toothlessly at her and at the laird behind her.

Laura turned again to William. "Where were you?"

"On the beach trying to cool off, so I wouldn't have to murder you."

"So you just let them walk right in here?" She cast a look meaningfully at her dress. "Knowing how you had left me, you just let them march right in unannounced?"

"I did not see them until they were stepping through the door."

"Then I am correct to assume *now* that these are your people?"

The chuckle from behind turned to a cough when William shifted his angry glare from her face to the men. When he shifted his attention back to her, the violence of his anger was like a blast of Highland wind.

"For someone who pretends to require a logical plan for every step she takes in life, your actions are more impulsive and more foolhardy than any bairn's."

"Foolhardy?" she snapped. "You thankless villain! And to think that I had every intention of spilling their blood simply because they'd taken your good-for-nothing life."

"Is that so? And how were you *planning* to do that? By hitting them over the head with a worm-eaten stick of wood? Jocky's head is a wee bit thicker than that. Get up, Jocky, you fool! Damn, woman, do you think any of these dunderheads will die of a splinter or two in their hair?"

Laura threw a defiant glance at Jocky, still sitting and rubbing his head. "I'd say I gave him a wee bit more than a splinter."

He angrily waved at the other two men watching the exchange curiously. "And what were you going to do with those two, if they had come to cut you into—?"

"I had a plan," she lied. "I'm quite capable of thinking on my feet. I *had* a plan!"

"Plan, my arse!" William gave a loud snort as he took a threatening step toward her. It took all of her courage not to back up. He pointed a finger accusingly. "If you had any sense in that stubborn head of yours, as soon as these three started toward the hut, you would have climbed on Dread and run the three of them down as they reached the doorway. Why, you'd have trampled two of them, at least, and been away down the beach before they knew what hit them. Plan, humph!"

Pushing roughly past her, William moved to the remains of the fire and kicked a pile of stony, sandy dirt over it.

The one named Jocky pushed himself to his feet and grinned sheepishly at Laura. "Mistress, I'm glad ye decided to follow yer own plan. I'll take a ding in my skull anytime over being stepped on by that beast."

"Hold your flapping tongue, Jocky. You do not want to be encouraging her in such pastimes."

"I hope I didn't—"

"You gather your things," William snapped at her, stepping between them as she started toward the injured man. His eyes were like daggers. "I'm taking you back to St. Duthac today if 'tis the death of me."

Laura felt an ache claw into her chest as the Highlander summarily dismissed her, turning his broad back on her. Clearly, he couldn't wait to be rid of her. Ignoring her completely, he began to question the men regarding how they'd found their hiding place.

As Laura listened to what they had to say, she picked up her cloak and tied it around her neck. From the sound of things, these men were apparently quite familiar with their laird's impulsiveness. After learning that he'd never arrived at the waiting boat by the firth, the three men had begun trekking northward in search of him. After the storm forced them to spend the night in the ruined castle by Loch Fleet, they pushed northward again to the huts that Jocky knew William had occasionally used in his youthful raiding. The guess had been confirmed by the sight of smoke issuing from the hut.

Laura's spirited defense of the hut, however, had completely surprised them. She forced down a self-satisfied smile as William snorted scornfully.

It was amazing to her that as laird of the Ross clan, he didn't travel with an entourage of warriors. In fact, listening to the men's talk, she realized that the three who had followed them were chiefly employed as farm help on the clan lands. It also was very clear that the three men were happy-go-lucky mischief makers who had shared—with William—a number of violent clashes with the Sinclairs in the past. But if there was one thing that Laura had no doubt about—listening to them—these men would lay down their lives for their master.

Shaking her head, Laura moved quietly to the giant horse

and ran one hand over his neck and chest. His skin was warm, and the animal's smell suddenly made her homesick, triggering thoughts of her family's stables in Yorkshire. As Dread nuzzled her with his great head, Laura forced herself to think of the present.

The past was gone.

With Catherine already married, the sisters' plans needed to change as well. And it was up to Laura to design a new one.

Chapter 9

The two monks, silent and grim, stood back as a pushing, laughing swarm of young children tumbled out of the small chapel's door, pursued by a number of scolding women. In a moment the laird and his wife followed, smiling as their little ones pelted one another with snowballs as they ran ahead through the snow. Their childish voices rang out happily beneath the arched passageway leading to the courtyard of Ironcross Castle.

When the small group of servants had passed by as well, the taller of the monks—a man with a battered face and a slight limp—cursed under his breath as a heavyset priest, spotting them by the doorway, waddled toward them. The two clerics stepped into the chapel.

"Jacob!" the priest called jovially, addressing the smaller monk. "'Tis a delightful surprise, seeing you back so quickly. The weather didn't hinder you on your travels?"

The wiry, squint-eyed monk gave a quick nod, growling, "No hindrance."

"I'm certainly glad about that. And were you successful in your charitable work to the north?"

The old monk's eyes darted questioningly toward the scarred face of the taller cleric, who spoke up immediately.

"I told our friend about your desire to go and look after our ailing brother at Inverness." The tall monk looked meaningfully into the face of the wiry monk and then back at the fat priest. "Jacob's journey was indeed futile. You see, our brother in Inverness had already died."

The priest shook his head with a look of sympathy. "Sad news, indeed. A loss to your order . . . and to Holy Mother Church, I'm sure. But there is something to be learned by this, my friends. You English monks need to put some meat on your bones if you hope to last through a Highland winter. If you go and see Gibby in the kitchen, I have no doubt that the good woman will help you do just that. Why, when I arrived here, I was only a twig of a man, and now—"

"Father." The tall monk held up his hand, silencing the priest. "I'm afraid we're going to need your assistance there. The cook has taken an unfounded dislike to us for some reason. She refuses to allow either of us into her kitchen. She instructs the serving folk to give us the smallest portions. Whether it is because we are Englishmen who have come here to escape persecution in our own country, I know not. But if . . . if you would kindly intercede for us? We believe a good word from you, Father, would make all the difference."

The priest rubbed his jowly chin doubtfully for a moment and then nodded in agreement. "I can do that, my friends. I will just see to my—"

"No need," the tall monk cut in. "The good Jacob and I would be happy to put up your vestments. You be on your way and—through your kindness, Father—secure us a decent meal, would you?"

The portly priest nodded and, talking softly to himself, left the chapel and hurried toward the great hall of Ironcross Castle and the kitchens beyond.

The two men watched until the priest, puffs of breath hanging in the cold air behind him, finally disappeared from view.

The wiry monk cringed involuntarily as the taller man slammed the door of the chapel shut and whirled on him.

"'Twas so simple," the man hissed, his battered face livid

with anger. "Everything had been arranged for you. All you had to do was escort her back here."

"Aye, but I tell you she wasn't there when we arrived. Then that cursed mother superior deliberately misled us, pretending that Laura was some crofter's lass. We were distracted long enough for her to escape with—"

"Fool!" The scarred monk raised himself to his full height, silencing the other. "You know very well the punishment for failure."

"But I did not fail. I just—"

"You lost her!"

"I didn't lose her. I didn't!" the wiry man stammered. "In fact, I know exactly where she is hiding now."

"You should have gone after her, then. You had the men to help you. You had information. Instead, you scurry back here with your tail between your legs."

"But we couldn't foresee the Ross laird kidnapping her at the same moment we were waiting at the convent!"

"Kidnapping her? You just said she escaped."

"Aye, with the help of the Ross himself! I think she may have even arranged for him to kidnap her. Aye, that's it. Why, the man took her from the market square and then helped her escape the convent. Then they disappeared in the storm." Jacob peered at his superior and quickly continued. "But the rogue took her to St. Duthac's at Tain, I'm certain."

"Damn these Highlanders." The tall monk turned sharply and limped to the altar, the other at his heels. "The fools at St. Duthac's didn't even know she was missing."

"They must have just realized their mistake." The wiry monk took a hesitant step forward. "I chased after them until we were well into Ross lands. I didn't think you would want us fighting the entire Ross clan for her."

"So close!" The man banged his fist on the altar. The candles flickered madly. "But you say she is at St. Duthac's?"

"Aye! The shrine at Tain. The Ross laird's brother is provost there. They *had* to be going there."

"And that was where she was originally destined to go." The lame monk turned again sharply. "Were the Sinclairs any help?"

"Nay." The monk shook his head. "Because of that nun. The woman in charge of the little convent. She convinced the Sinclair warriors that Laura went willingly with the laird. She is a shrewd woman, that nun. It gave them an excuse for losing her. And if I wanted to go after Laura, she said, all I had to do was go and ask the Ross laird." The monk wrung his hands together angrily. "I tried to catch them. I did."

The taller man glanced down at his misshapen hands. The knuckles were swollen and white, pushing out the skin as if they had been badly broken at one time. He stared at them for a long time before speaking.

"We missed our best chance of capturing her on our own," he said, his voice low and assured. "But Fate still smiles on us. The Knights of the Veil, fools that they are, have chosen the Blade to assist me!"

Gratefully accepting the dry clothing from the hands of the novitiate, Laura closed the door of the small chamber. She had agreed to meet with the provost in his work room as soon as she had changed out of her wet clothing. Though it was late, she was anxious to meet Gilbert Ross.

Her three-month delay in arriving at St. Duthac's and the failure of her message to reach the new provost combined to make her feel quite uncomfortable. She wanted to apologize as soon as she could and try to establish an appropriate relationship with the man—one marked by a little less hostility than the relationship she had succeeded in forging with his older brother.

"Well, this younger brother is definitely more thoughtful,"

she murmured, eyeing the pile of clothes. They had been sent over from the convent at the provost's request.

Laura shed her clothing but stopped when only William's shirt remained. She stared at the rolled cuffs of the baggy sleeves and the gaping holes in the body of the shirt, and a sudden thrill ran through her body as she thought of the intimacy she'd shared with the Ross laird. Taking a deep breath, she quickly peeled that off as well and cast it aside.

As she cleaned up at the washbasin and pulled a comb through her tangled hair, she couldn't help but think back over all she'd been through in so short a time. She cringed at the memory of her blunders.

"Well, that journey is over," she muttered. "Count your blessings. No more of his arrogance, silence, or—or his nearness!"

Laura pulled the shift over her head as her thoughts returned to the ride from the fishermen's hut. Leaving his three men to follow on foot, William had driven his horse south as if the devil himself were on their trail. The Highlander had not once spoken a word to her that might indicate that his mood was improving. Laura stepped into the oversized dress and pulled the laces tight in the front.

But what had she done, she thought, to bring on such anger?

Laura doubted somehow that it was her failure to use Dread in escaping from the cottage that left him silent and sulking. But if it was because she'd put a stop to their passionate encounter in the hut, then he should be . . . well, thankful.

But whatever his reason—if he had any reason—he was still angry enough that he'd practically dumped her in the yard at St. Duthac's Shrine. Why, he'd never even looked at her again. After storming into the chapter house, he'd simply climbed back on his weary horse and ridden away.

Not that she had been watching for him out the small window, but how could she miss his loud cursing when they opened the gates too slowly for him?

A rather gruff old priest by the name of Father Francis had welcomed her, bringing her to this room in a building connected to the chapter house, and the dry clothing had arrived almost immediately. Hastily, she neatened the thick braid of hair that fell like a rope down her back, and headed for the door.

Her urgency in seeing the provost actually had two reasons. True, she wanted to express her regret for any inconvenience and get into the good graces of Gilbert Ross if possible. But she also knew that the provost held a letter for her from her sister. Laura ached to read the news of Catherine and learn whatever she could after these months of separation.

The serving man was still waiting in the corridor in anticipation of taking her to the provost's work room. Passing through the quiet passages of the place, following in the footsteps of the silent young man, Laura studied every aspect of the place. The long, empty halls, the serene orderliness, the warmth and cleanliness of what she'd seen already of the place, all spoke volumes of Gilbert Ross and his administrative abilities.

Her guide's knock on the provost's door was answered from within, and the young novitiate opened the door for her. As she strode in purposefully, her entrance was thwarted when she stumbled over some huge sack stretched the entire width of the door. Sprawling flat on her face, she immediately felt the provost's strong grip on her arm, helping her to her feet and apologizing profusely.

"I am so sorry, mistress! Willie has a knack for always being in the way. I hope you're not hurt."

The giant dog never even lifted his head as he looked at her with raised eyebrows. Stretching a paw at her direction, though, he yawned, displaying the largest set of teeth Laura had ever seen on a dog.

"Willie," Laura repeated incredulously, red in the face with

embarrassment. "Willie is a big dog, Provost. But I hope I
didn't hurt *him*."

"I don't believe you did, or the beast would be yelping like
a bairn right now. An oversize and oafish cur he might be,
Mistress Laura, but he is really very dainty when it comes to
being stepped on."

Recognizing the amused tone of the priest's voice, Laura
turned to Gilbert Ross and smiled in surprise. Other than his
great height, the provost of the Shrine of St. Duthac didn't
look at all like his brother. He had a lighter complexion and
more refined features, but the major difference lay in the
provost's bright and open smile. Laura was quite certain
William Ross's face would crack if he ever dared to smile
this broadly.

"I am grateful to you for granting me an audience at this
late hour."

" 'Tis a pleasure for me to meet you finally. I hope your
chamber is comfortable."

"Aye. Thank you for everything, Provost." She paused before continuing. "But before I say anything else, I sincerely
hope you will accept my heartfelt apologies for not arriving
here when I was expected and for failing to secure a better
messenger to carry my letter to—"

"There is no need to apologize, mistress, since I am the
guilty one here."

"Pardon me?"

"Aye, you see, until I received the letter from the good earl
of Athol, I was not even aware that you should have been
under our protection." The provost gestured toward the bench
at the long table, and Laura gratefully took a seat. "With the
unexpected passing of the previous provost, the correspondence that had been exchanged between your mother and St.
Duthac's was unfortunately lost—along with other important
papers."

"Lost?" Laura eyed the far end of the table, where stacks

of papers and a number of books were arranged in an orderly fashion, with a pot of ink and quills nearby.

"Well, misplaced would perhaps be more accurate. However, we have since located your mother's letters, and I understand better now the reason for the secrecy behind your arrival. No doubt to protect you, my predecessor decided not to announce your coming, not even to the nuns at the adjoining convent, until you were safely within our walls."

Laura was uncertain how much her mother had revealed in the letters. "If you have no objection, I would very much like to read the letters my mother sent."

"Of course. I will share them with you tomorrow, if that suits you."

"Thank you."

"After receiving the letter from your sister's new husband," the young priest continued, "my earlier negligence became quickly apparent. That was when I sought my brother's assistance in seeking you out."

Laura cringed inwardly, thinking of her response to William Ross's "rescue" of her.

"Fortunately, my brother was born with the ability to cultivate many friends in . . . well, in every class of society. So it was a matter of just a few days before he learned of your frequent visits to the market square in Fearnoch." The provost moved to the far end of the table and then hesitated, looking up at her with a spark of genuine interest in his blue eyes. "I forgot to ask if you had a pleasant and uneventful journey from Fearnoch."

Uneventful? She repeated the word in her mind and fought down the color she felt creeping into her cheeks. William had spoken with his brother, and Laura wondered just how much the priest already knew.

"Everything was just . . . fine. Except that I've—I've never traveled in weather as severe as we encountered during this journey. Except, of course, for the storm at sea that blew our ship far to the north of Fearnoch Firth."

"Och, weather!" The priest nodded thoughtfully and moved to a cabinet in the corner. As he opened a door, Laura could see rows of shelves neatly filled with bound books, papers secured with ribbon, bulging leather packets, and scrolls. She lifted her gaze and found the man studying her seriously. Suddenly, the foul possibility of how William Ross might have described their journey sprang into her mind, tormenting her.

"Did Wi—the laird . . . your brother . . . have the same complaint?"

A sparkle suddenly lit Gilbert's eyes, dispelling the look of seriousness. "If you are asking whether 'twas *weather* that William complained of—the answer is nay, mistress."

Trust the rogue not to keep silent about her errors in judgment.

"Very well, then. There was more than just the weather that went awry," Laura blurted out wearily. "I did not know your brother when he approached me in the market square at Fearnoch. And aye, I created a bit of a ruckus. In fact, a great ruckus, and that was just the start of it. . . ."

Letting out a frustrated breath, she told the attentive priest everything that had happened in the past two days. With the exception, of course, of those moments of lunacy when she had found herself kissing William Ross.

"So I know he loathes me. He must be quite angry with me for turning his simple mission into a painful journey. But despite what he has surely told you about my rude disposition and my selfishness, I am very grateful to him for his rescue . . . as I am thankful to you for the shelter you are offering me now."

A lengthy silence descended upon the room. When Laura looked up nervously, the provost—who had seated himself across from her as she told the tale—was studying her with interest.

"Was there anything else, Provost, that your brother told you that I failed to mention?"

"The saddle?" the young priest suggested, his face brightening with a smile. "William marched in here, announced your presence, and then proceeded to complain for a rather extended period about the saddle that I had made for him when he became laird. I couldn't get a word in at all. He said the thing was too narrow, then too broad, then too ornate, then too plain. The stitching was shoddy and the leather too stiff. But to be honest, mistress, he complained about nothing else. In fact, I had no idea your journey was so, er, eventful."

"And was the saddle a recent gift?" Laura asked, not knowing what to say.

The provost gazed at her a moment speculatively and then shook his head as a smile continued to tug at his lips. "Nay, 'tis more than two years old. And prior to your journey, I had heard nothing but praise for the thing."

Laura felt her face beginning to burn with embarrassment. An unspoken suggestion hung in the air. Looking around the room in an effort to compose herself, she noticed above the mantel the simple sketch of a young girl. The large, bright eyes smiling down at her immediately looked familiar.

"'Tis a sketch of my niece, Miriam. Just a wee lass, she is."

Laura took in the dimpled cheeks of the child. "Does she live nearby?"

"She should, considering both her parents are dead, and the man who should be caring for her lives here. But to answer your question—nay, she does not."

"Why is she not here, then? Who is responsible for her?"

"Aye, fair questions, mistress." Father Gilbert gave an approving nod before getting up and taking a letter out of the open cabinet. "That is a long story, though, which I'll be more than happy to share with you once you are rested and settled into your new quarters. But for now, I believe you must be anxious to read this letter from your sister. It accompanied the earl's letter, which is here as well."

Laura's heart rose into her throat as she took the packet from him.

"And I believe that since you are now safe and sound here at St. Duthac's, I'll answer the earl of Athol's letter." The young priest came around the table. "'Tis so much more pleasant to correspond with a powerful nobleman when you don't have to tell him you've lost his new sister."

"Provost, I am deeply sorry for any trouble I might have brought you."

Gilbert Ross shook his head good-naturedly as he escorted her to the door. "Please, don't give it another thought. Tonight, you read your letter and then have a good rest. Tomorrow, I'll escort you to our convent and introduce you to the prioress and some of our fine people there. I have to warn you, though, life at the convent of St. Duthac shall not be nearly as exciting as the life you've been living."

"I assure you, Provost," Laura said, nodding gratefully. "Excitement is *not* what I need right now."

A dog rose, stretched lazily, and moved closer to the hearth. A serving woman carrying a stack of wooden bowls walked past the little girl toward the kitchen. The sound of men arguing behind the closed doors of the laird's chamber drifted into the Great Hall. Miriam lifted her face from her work and stared timidly at the closed door.

"Is my grandsire still angry with me, Nanna Jean?"

"I shouldn't blame Lord Herries if he was." The heavyset woman shifted her weight on the bench and peered more closely at the pattern of needlework spread before them. "You are seven, Miriam. Seven! And do you know what most lassies your age are already capable of?"

The young girl bobbed her head of dark curls as she kept one eye on her grandfather's door. "They stitch and they weave. They sing and entertain. They take care of their younger siblings, if they have any, and are polite to their older ones, if they are still living."

The woman's eyebrows arched. "And . . . ?"

The young girl's shoulders slumped. The soft voice dropped to a whisper. The blue eyes reflected a sadness far too deep for one so young. "And they are not afraid of the dark."

"Afraid of the dark," the woman repeated with ridicule. "Escaping one's own comfortable bed and sneaking into the kitchens at night like some petty thief. Spoiled! That's what you are, Miriam Ross, since I know of no other orphaned seven-year-old who has been as coddled as you."

Miriam tried to focus on the work, but her needle slipped past the white linen and stabbed her finger. She stared at the crimson drop of blood forming on the pale skin at the end of her finger.

"Now look what you have done!" The heavyset woman pulled the linen off the little girl's lap. "Away with you and don't get that blood on your clean apron! Come back when you've stopped your bleeding."

The child rose slowly to her feet and stared anxiously at the closed door at the end of the Great Hall. "Could I go and show grandsire my finger?"

The woman shook her head adamantly. "Lord Herries told you before that he does not want to see you. He is a very busy man, Miriam, and has no time for you. Now, be on your way."

Chapter 10

Everything in the laird's chambers seemed to stab at him. All an ugly reminder of the past. All a reminder of Mildred. Her presence was everywhere in the room.

In William's mind, this remained Thomas's quarters. This was his *brother's* bedchamber. Next door, *Thomas's* work room, where he had attended to the business of the Ross clan. Out of respect for his memory, William had left the chambers virtually untouched. But whenever he was forced to step inside those walls, his inability to breathe, to be able to clear his mind of the memories and the guilt, made him want to lash out in anger. Everything—from the exquisite tapestries covering the walls to Thomas's ornate desk with its matching cabinets, brought at Mildred's direction from Paris—bespoke the shallow elegance that she had demanded.

It all filled him with disgust. For her. For himself. For everything.

"I told the messenger from Hoddom, m'lord, that we did not know how long you were planning to be away. But the man has been very content to stay and sit by the fire in the Great Hall since Lord Herries ordered him to await your answer."

William turned his back on Edward, the seasoned leader of the Ross clan warriors, and walked hastily to the closest window. Throwing open the wooden shutter to a bitter rush of morning air, he filled his lungs and looked out at the snow-covered courtyard and the countryside beyond. It was all so clean, he thought, out there.

But beneath the cloudless sky, a piercing wind raced out of the mountains to the northwest, scoured the crystalline landscape in search of victims.

Edward's tap on the worktable got William's attention. "I left Lord Herries's letter here, m'lord, with the other correspondence you might care to look at."

William didn't have to turn to know where the folded parchment lay. He didn't have to break the seal to know what the old man wanted.

"When you are finished with your work in here, Will, I was hoping you might meet with a few of us." There was a slight pause in Edward's voice which made the laird glance over his shoulder at him. The warrior, obviously uncomfortable, avoided meeting the Highlander's direct gaze.

"Is there a problem?"

Edward shook his head. "Nothing too important. But . . . odds'blood, Will! When the men learned of your going to Fearnoch and not taking any of them—us—well, a few were a wee bit disappointed. Some were thinking you do not think us worthy to face a few miserable Sinclairs."

"Edward, tell your men that I consider all of them—all of you—a match for any clan."

"They need to hear that from you, m'lord." The warrior met William's gaze with the quiet strength of a seasoned fighter. "They miss you training with them in the yard."

William turned fully and faced his man. "I grew up with most of you. In fact, you, Edward, were the man who first put a sword in my hand. Thomas said that the Ross fighters have always been—and still are—the best group of men a laird could have behind him. My brother—"

"Nay, m'lord. Speak not of Thomas." His gray eyes were hard and direct. "*You* are our laird. Will, *you* are our master now. The Ross clan needs you, m'lord, to lead us."

"By the devil," William exploded. "Is there no . . . ?"

The Highlander stopped, his fists clenching and unclenching at his sides as he forcibly regained his composure.

Edward's words were said simply and without malice, and William knew that. These were plain facts that he could not change. No matter how hard he cared to fight it, he was still laird—by blood and by the choice of his clan. It appeared to matter naught how unworthy he was of the position. They wanted a laird, and would take the empty shell of one if that was all they could get.

Well, William thought, I can give them that, at least.

"Aye. Tell the men to prepare to take a beating from their laird tomorrow morning."

Edward gave a satisfied nod and started for the door, but then hesitated.

"There is more?"

"I know, m'lord, you've been back here only a day. But there are two crofters from out by the fork of the Strathrory who've been awaiting your return. They're ready to kill each other over a cow and a bucket of oats. And old Raulf from Kinloch sent word that the Munros have been raiding his family's lands again."

"Aye, Duncan Munro hasn't much to do once the winter sets in. Very well, send a half dozen men to Kinloch. I'll see the crofters today."

"And then there's the question of repairs to the east wing. And the matter of choosing a new steward. I never knew how good a man Robert was until the old bastard died. I'm not the man to run things, Will, and Blackfearn Castle is just not a fit place without a steward. If anyone of quality should come, there's no one to serve them. And then, the kitchens—"

"The kitchens?" William asked crossly.

"The new cook ran off a fortnight ago with one of the scullery lads." Edward shrugged. "Not that she could bake worth a damn, anyway."

"Why is it that Thomas has been dead for two years, but everything falls apart at just this moment?"

The warrior shook his head. "It has been coming for some time, m'lord. Even while Sir Thomas was laird. When he and Lady Mildred started spending less and less time at Black-fearn . . ."

Edward continued, but William already could taste the bitter recollection of those times in his mouth. Mildred never intended to be happy in what she called "the wilds" of the Highlands. She needed her comforts, her friends, the excitement and the extravagance and the recklessness of court life. It was because of her unreasonable nature that Thomas agreed to take her south in the middle of winter. They drowned because of her arrogance and her selfishness. It was only a miracle that the bairn . . .

William's gaze fixed on the waiting letter on his desk. He stared at the seal of Mildred's father, Lord Herries.

"And one thing more." Edward's voice cut into William's thoughts. "There is the message from the provost."

"You can send a word back that I'm through with rescuing damsels in distress."

Edward's face broke into a grin. "No wonder you did not want your men crowding about you. Was there a good reward that went along with the lass?"

"Reward?" William snorted dismissively, turning away. "Only if you consider a cracked skull a reward."

Damn, he didn't want to think about her now. It had been hard enough to have his sleep plagued with dreams of Laura Percy—her soft white skin beneath his fingers, her warm flesh pressed tightly to his own, her mouth so tender, willing . . .

Nay, the woman was poison. Strong-willed. Meddling. Far too orderly. Trouble, pure and simple. That should be simple enough to remember.

"What was it my brother wanted?"

"Just to speak with you. But he sent word that you should

not worry yourself about making the trip to Tain. He is coming to Blackfearn himself once the weather eases up." The tall warrior put a hand on the door, ready to depart. "His man mentioned 'tis advice the Provost seeks."

"My advice?"

The warrior nodded. "Aye. That was the message."

There was no challenge in her life. No excitement. Nothing to urge along the cold winter days—or the seemingly endless nights.

For nearly a fortnight bitter winds had ripped through the walled-in clusters of buildings that formed the Shrine of St. Duthac and its adjacent convent. Snow had fallen several nights, and an icy rain had now coated everything.

Stepping through the gated wall separating the convent from the shrine, Laura pulled the wool cloak tightly about her and winced at the sight of the cleared and tamped-down pathways leading to and from the chapter house.

Once again, everything was taken care of.

The orderly community at the convent at St. Duthac was an unexpected vexation to Laura. The methodical order of things at the shrine had quickly proved to be another torment.

What was she to do when *everything* was being done?

Relentless in her pursuit of usefulness—in finding some value for her existence in the peaceful and well-managed community—Laura had been reduced to begging for chores. The response, though, from the very first moment, had been the same.

Laura was a guest, and she was not to fret over mundane details.

The truth of it was, Laura thought, that Gilbert Ross was too much of a man in control, too much of an organizer with clear views of order, too much of a person like herself.

And the situation was about to make her daft.

Intentionally avoiding the path and digging her boots

through the icy crust into the knee-deep snow, Laura buried her face deeper under the cloak and made her way toward the chapter house. There, at least, she knew she should be able to charm old Father Francis into giving her *some* task to do. Word had come to the convent that the provost had ridden out and would be absent for the day, so this was Laura's chance to find something to alleviate the boredom of her enforced idleness.

With nothing to focus on, her thoughts had all too often drifted to William Ross. She'd even fallen so low as to ask some casual questions of one of the younger nuns about the Ross laird. It appeared that he rarely visited St. Duthac's, though Laura already knew that. Days had come and gone, and there had been no sign of any visitors from Blackfearn Castle.

Foolish, idle thoughts, she chided herself as she neared the chapter house. Kicking snow and ice with her foot, she pushed onto the cleared pathway.

The old priest was waiting for her on the steps before the door and watching her. Spying the curmudgeonly expression on his wrinkled face, Laura smiled innocently and stamped the snow off her feet onto the path. As he stepped aside, she quickly moved past him into the vestibule and stopped to unfasten her cloak.

He eyed the ice clinging to the hem of her dress and cloak. "You'll need to go back, mistress."

Laura glanced down at the snow that had fallen to the floor and shook her head.

"Oh my," she exclaimed, feigning horror. "Well, before I go, Father Francis, I'll just go to the kitchens and get a broom. I would be a very ungrateful wretch not to sweep these floors before going back to the convent. And then, while I'm at it, perhaps I'll just ready the fires in the refectory for the afternoon meal, and see if Brother Hugo needs any help in the kitchen. I believe he is beginning to value my expertise with a paring knife. And I know that the candles in the chapel need tending, for I noticed yesterday as I watched the workmen—"

"And this will be the last time you see me here."

"Pardon, Father?"

"If I simply allow you to wander about and accomplish all of the tasks that our young men should be doing, the provost will be sending me off to tend sheep in the glen beneath Carn Chunneag when he returns." The priest pulled on an ear and shook his head resignedly. "But an educated lass like you must be doing something, I suppose. Come along, then."

With another shake of his hoary head, he turned down the corridor, and Laura fell in happily beside him.

"Of course," he grumbled. "He might still send me there if he learns that I gave you work to do, yesterday as well as today."

"Meaning no disrespect, Father, but I don't consider copying text from a manuscript hard work." Upon seeing the priest's sharp scowl, Laura smiled sweetly. "But I'm thankful to you for allowing me to do it, all the same."

"Hmmph."

She followed along as Father Francis made his way through the chapter house. And she held her tongue, practicing restraint, as she observed workmen and their helpers laboring away at changes the new provost had in progress. Carpenters were at work in the chapel, repairing a great carved screen of oak. Stonemasons were replacing ancient bosses in the ceiling arches. She listened quietly as Father Francis paused to discuss future plans with one master mason for chimneys and modest fireplaces that were to be built in a variety of different chambers when the weather improved.

Reaching Gilbert Ross's work room, Laura sat down at Father Francis's gesture, positioning herself at one end of the large trestle table. Soon she was busy copying ledger lines and columns onto the blank pages for the coming year's figures. The task of copying was simple and tedious, but the thought of complaining never entered her head. She was grateful for the opportunity to work.

Finishing in much less time than Father Francis had anticipated, Laura found the old priest engrossed in his ledgers, so she quietly rearranged the books in an orderly manner and resharpened her quill. Letting her eyes survey the work room, she again fixed her gaze on the portrait of the young child sitting above the mantel. The large bright eyes, the innocent smile, lifted Laura's spirits.

"From what I hear, she is not such a wee thing anymore. The lass is three years older than she was when that sketch was drawn."

Laura glanced over her shoulder and studied Father Francis's thoughtful expression.

"Her name is Miriam. Miriam Ross."

"The provost told me that her parents are dead." Laura rose to her feet and moved closer to the fireplace to get a better look. Even though she had never seen the mother, Laura was certain that the little girl took after the Ross side of the family. The resemblance to William was exceptional.

"Thomas and Mildred died fording a river by Ben Wyvis, not a half day's ride from here. Mildred's horse stumbled, throwing her. Thomas went after her, but the icy river just washed the two of them away. Over two years now the lass has been orphaned."

"She is all alone." Laura wrapped her arms around her middle as a cold draft suddenly chilled her. She glanced over at the priest. "Who is looking after her?"

"Her grandsire, Lord Herries. That started as a temporary arrangement, and 'twill soon come to an end."

"And why is that?"

"Lord Herries is an old man, and ill, and he wishes to send Miriam away while he can."

"Where is he sending her?"

"I would imagine to some priory, to be raised by some ill-tempered, though godly nuns who'll have hardly any appetite for the antics of a young and spirited lass like Miriam." The old priest dropped his gaze to the ledger. "Of course, this will only happen if her rightful guardian fails to stand up and accept his responsibility."

Laura returned to the table and sat across from the priest. "And I assume William Ross is that guardian."

Father Francis pushed aside the ledger book. "You're very observant, mistress. Other than her grandsire, Miriam's only kin are her two uncles, Gilbert and William. I suppose Gilbert could keep the lassie here, but 'twas her father's expressed wishes that if anything should happen to him and his wife, Miriam was to be raised at Blackfearn Castle, under William's protection."

"Then why is the laird not honoring the wishes of his brother?" Laura's voice quavered. "What does he have against the child?"

"You might ask, what does he have against any semblance of order? Or discipline? Or responsibility? Why, after two years, is he still unwilling to take control of what is his by right?" The priest laid both his hands flat on the table and stared at them for a long moment. "'Tis a mystery, lass, why William is so pigheaded. But he has his virtues—"

"He is quite brave . . . but he seems to be quite set in his own ways. But then, I thought 'twas only I who brought out the worst in him." She stopped, letting the thought hang in the air. The old cleric was eyeing her carefully.

"Nay, Mistress Laura. You might as well know that there is not a more undisciplined, obstinate ne'er-do-well than William Ross in the entire Highlands."

Laura stared at the man for a moment and then shook her head. "But from what I've seen, the people truly respect him as their laird."

"Aye, that is true enough. Every Ross man and woman

looks fondly on him. And that's because the rogue is a born leader with a heart of pure gold. William is a fierce fighter but kind-hearted to those in trouble. The lad is forceful but humble. He has a dangerous temper and yet has compassion as well. And he has greatness in him, make no mistake."

"Well, I've seen samples of his courage . . . and his temper." She wasn't going to add to the list of his qualities, even though thoughts of William Ross's passionate nature had been keeping her awake for the past two weeks. "I'm certain there is greatness in him . . . if one were to search."

The hint of a smile softened the man's furrowed brow. "I won't argue against you, mistress, since I believe that for all his faults William Ross is a fine man. But I also believe that he needs the right person to rein him in. Only then will he become a great one."

Chapter 11

The stable was warmer than the courtyard, and the smell of horses and cattle mingled with the smell of sweating men. Gilbert Ross lifted the hem of his cloak and stepped over a pile of fresh manure and followed his brother into the semidarkness.

Two stable men went by, nodding cheerfully at their laird and the cleric, while a young boy rushed forward with William's shirt in hand.

"Sorry, master. Didn't know you'd be finishing in the yard so soon."

The Highlander gave the boy's scrawny shoulder a gentle pat and took the shirt. "We were interrupted by the provost."

The young boy took a step back and eyed Gilbert Ross's black robe cautiously. Gilbert raised a hand to bless him, but the lad quickly crossed himself and took off as if the devil were on his tail.

"What's the matter with the lad?"

William snorted and turned away.

"Wait a moment, brother. What have you been saying about me?"

"Only that you are forever on the lookout for likely lads to steal away to St. Duthac's dungeons."

"Dungeons? We don't have . . . Now, listen to me, Willie."

The laird scowled and gestured toward the huge dog lazily

scratching an ear by the stable door. "Willie is that foul beast over there, in case you've forgotten. I'm William."

Gilbert followed as his brother started off again through the stables. "I do not believe poisoning a wee one's mind, *Willie*, is in the best interest of anyone. Especially when you're filling the lad with wrong-headed notions of the church and its servants."

By an open stall the Ross laird abruptly turned, and Gilbert nearly barreled into him. The two eyed each other pugnaciously.

"Is that the reason for your trip out here, Provost? To lecture me on the church's concerns?"

"Nay, but that is as good a place to start as anywhere."

Though they were nearly the same height, the difference in appearance between them was telling. Gilbert, blond and tonsured, was lean and well appointed in his fine robes and cloak. In contrast, William, his thick chestnut hair tied back, was shirtless, muscled, unshaven, and glistening with sweat from the recent exercise in the yard with the men.

He gave his brother a murderous glare before picking up an empty bucket from the floor of the stall and shoving it into Gilbert's chest. "Right behind you. Get me some water. I'll wash in this stall."

With a curt nod Gilbert turned toward the cistern, only to have his boot sink deep in another pile of manure. William's throaty laugh was far louder than the cleric's grunt of displeasure.

Ducking as the bucket sailed past his head, William found himself lifted off his feet as Gilbert shot across the enclosure, sending them both sprawling in the straw and muck. Recovering quickly, William launched his brother across the stall and pounced on him, putting a knee in Gilbert's back and shoving his face into the foul dirt.

"By the saint, William, get off me, or I swear I'll have you excommunicated."

With a grunt the older brother retreated to the other side of the stall, and plunked himself down on the fallen bucket. Gilbert turned over and sat up, picking dirt and straw out of his mouth.

Two matching sets of blue eyes glared for a moment. The black dog lumbered into the stall and stretched out between the two brothers.

"Good dog." William chuckled. "A real protector."

As the two men laughed, a half dozen men watched wide-eyed from the stall entrance.

"Robbie!" William called out, standing and stretching a hand out toward his brother. Gilbert accepted it and rose to his feet as the lad peeked cautiously through the crowd. "Run to the laird's chamber and fetch a clean tartan for the provost."

"Aye, m'lord."

As the boy disappeared from the stable, the workers, realizing there would be no more entertainment, drifted off to their various tasks. William picked up the bucket and scooped water from the cistern.

"I'm sorry to be the one to tell you, Your Holiness, but you look and smell far worse than your position dictates."

"I believe you're correct . . . *Willie*."

As the Highlander undressed and washed, Gilbert shed his own soiled cloak and sat himself down on a pile of straw.

"I should get to the reason for my visit, brother, before you manage to distract me again."

William's snort was loud and clear.

"I've received a letter from Lord Herries of Hoddom. Regarding Miriam's keep."

"Why should he write to you?" The Highlander poured icy water from the bucket over his head. "I've already answered the man."

"Not to his liking." Gilbert shook his head. "And I must say, not to my liking, either. The child is too young to be sent away to some convent in France."

"'Tis a school as well as a convent," William asserted, pushing the wet hair off his face and scooping another bucket of water from the cistern. "She can learn something there. Who knows, she might turn out better than . . ."

"Than whom?"

"Than—than those other wee court brats."

"She is a Ross, William."

"Aye, and Mildred's daughter, too," William asserted harshly. "'Tis in her best interest that we give the lass a better upbringing than her mother got."

The stable boy ran into the stall and cautiously handed the folded tartan to the provost.

"Thank you, lad." Gilbert walked to the bucket as William dried himself. "Well, she doesn't want to go."

"She's only a bairn. She has no choice in the matter."

"Thomas's wishes were for his daughter to be raised here, at Blackfearn Castle—not in France or some convent far from the only kin she has left in this world." Gilbert fixed his gaze on his brother's face. "Thomas wanted *you* to raise her."

Scowling, the laird angrily yanked his shirt over his head and wrapped his kilt about him.

"Will, give the lassie a chance. Bring her here, even if 'tis only for a wee time."

The Highlander's glare was hard and cold. "Blackfearn is no place to raise a bairn."

"This castle is strong, and you could make it better. But you must take control of it. You're laird now, William. Like it or not!"

William pulled his sword belt tight, avoiding Gilbert's accusing gaze.

"I do not know what 'tis you fear, brother, but I've decided I can no longer wait for you to act. I've taken the steps I should have taken two years ago."

"What the hell have you done, Gilbert?"

"I wrote to Lord Herries and told him to send Miriam here."

William took an angry step forward. "What right have you to do such a thing? I tell you this is no place to raise a child like that."

The provost matched his brother's angry stare. "You and I were raised here. There's nothing wrong with the place, William."

"Those were different times. There were servants who knew what needed to be done. Hell, we had parents, Gilbert."

"Aye! Who, for most part, had no idea what you and I were up to. But still, all in all, I'd say the two of us grew up fairly well."

"Och, she's a lass. What do I know of—of womanly things? By St. Andrew, Gilbert!"

"You can learn, William. And if I were you, I would learn quickly, since the lass should be here no later than a fortnight."

"Nay, I'll not do it. You can keep her."

Gilbert stood for a moment. "I'll tell you what. You keep her for a month, and I'll send you help to see that she's cared for."

"Och, by his Shirt! Now I've got bairns *and* pudding-faced nuns running about the place. What next?"

Gilbert backed away and turned toward the door before William could find a reason to thwart the plan. "If you care to see me before I return to St. Duthac, I'll be in the chapel, fulfilling the spiritual needs of some of your crofters."

"Where you ought to be, you meddlesome priest."

"And concerned brother. And uncle. Remember, William, the two of you are my last remaining family." He threw a departing look at his brother. "Don't let the past ruin the future blessings the Lord has in store for you. Go along with me for a change, Will. I know best."

Silent but hardly convinced, William stared sullenly at the retreating back of the provost.

*   *   *

"The place is a shambles. Certainly, he's got the folk and the gold to put things right, but the amount of work that needs to be done is nearly unfathomable. The organization . . ." Gilbert shook his head. "Though he does have the best of intentions, if you understand my meaning, Father Francis."

The older priest nodded solemnly. "I do. Indeed I do, Provost."

As if having just remembered her presence, Gilbert Ross turned abruptly to the young woman who was sitting on the bench at the trestle table and listening quietly to their conversation. "Please forgive me, Mistress Laura, for boring you with our local concerns. I will refrain from any further talk of my visit to Blackfearn Castle, and—"

"Nay, please don't," she blurted all too enthusiastically, quickly containing herself and running a calming hand down the front of her dress. "By all means, please continue, Provost. 'Tis most interesting to hear the account of your visit."

Gilbert paused for a long moment, while Laura looked down and held her breath. When she glanced up again, he was looking at the old cleric.

"A talent for organization has never been William's strong point."

"He's always been willing to let others do their job," the provost stated in defense of his brother. "But with the arrival of the wee Miriam so imminent—"

"Will she arrive before Christmastide?"

"Aye." Gilbert nodded. "One would assume so. Though there are so few days left. I wonder if he'll be ready to receive the lassie properly."

Laura hung on every word that was said. The provost had returned from Blackfearn Castle only the night before, and she was delighted to be included in these discussions.

So William Ross *was* taking charge of his niece. The child would need so many things, though. A safe place for her and someone to watch over her. A tutor to keep her mind active.

"He will not be ready and you know it, Gilbert. Perhaps 'twould be better for her to come in the spring."

The provost adamantly shook his head. "Nay. If Lord Herries passes away this winter, there'll be no one to look after the lass. Do we want her in the hands of strangers?"

"Couldn't she be brought here?" Laura blurted out the question. "I mean, until such time as your brother is ready to receive her."

Gilbert and Father Francis looked at each other for a moment. Then they both firmly shook their heads, and the provost spoke. "Nay, that will not do."

"And why not?" she asked, realizing as she spoke that it wasn't her place to speak. "I apologize for my interference. But I just thought . . . that might be the best of solutions for . . . for all involved."

Gilbert walked to the hearth and stood there with his back to the other two. The older priest rubbed his chin before turning to Laura. "You see, mistress, as intelligent a solution as your recommendation might seem, the provost and I believe 'twill be a grave mistake to give William a way out."

"A way out?"

Gilbert turned and nodded. "It has taken two years for my brother to come to the point of even accepting the lass at Blackfearn Castle. If he gets any notion that there are other places—especially one as convenient as St. Duthac's convent—to shelter her . . . Nay, we can't allow it."

In an instant, it all became clear to her. William Ross wasn't taking his niece willingly. They were forcing him to face up to his responsibilities, and using the poor health of Lord Herries to do it.

But this was a child they were talking about. Men!

Well, it was time for someone to speak in the child's defense. Staying at the convent with her was the best course of action. With Laura to take over the girl's instruction, the situation would be good for Miriam, and she herself would feel useful.

"Provost, considering the fact that I'm not much use as things stand . . . you haven't much work for me at St. Duthac's . . . perhaps you would allow me to . . ."

"My dear, that's extremely generous of you."

Laura, with the words still hanging on her tongue, turned to look at Father Francis, who looked almost gleeful. "I consider it my duty to be of service, Father."

"Are you positive about this, mistress?"

Laura met the provost's brilliant blue eyes, and suddenly she wasn't certain what she had said and what she hadn't. Before she could say anything, though, Gilbert continued cheerfully.

"From what I understand, you're an excellent organizer."

"I believe I have some ability in planning," Laura croaked, doubts crowding in that they were not talking about the same thing. "And teaching a child—"

"And you are extremely hardworking. That much is obvious to everyone who spends any time with you. Why, Father Francis here has already spoken eloquently of your efforts."

Laura blushed and sat in silence.

"And from what you told me yourself, lass, not so many days ago . . ." Laura turned to Father Francis. "You're looking for a challenge. A task where you can make a difference."

"I am. I was," she murmured. "And a child—"

" 'Tis done, then," the provost announced excitedly. "But we somehow have to keep our intentions from William."

Laura stared in total confusion at the young priest. "But why should he object to me teaching his ward?"

"He shouldn't. Aye, there is so much that you can do." Francis rubbed his hands together and turned to Gilbert. "But how will you explain taking her to Blackfearn Castle?"

"To—to Blackfearn?"

"Aye, lass. We need to provide a logical explanation, and a means of making your stay there . . . well, proper."

Laura felt that old burning knot forming in her belly. "But I—I didn't—"

"We have to keep Miriam's welfare in mind, as well as Mistress Laura's." The two men appeared totally unaffected by her confusion. Gilbert started pacing the room. "But of course, William wouldn't accept an open offer. Though yesterday, when I visited the chapel . . ."

Laura found her hands clutching the fabric of the skirt. "Provost, I only—"

"We could *all* pay him a visit," Father Francis said brightly. "With Christmastide approaching, I could go along. And we could take some of the others as well."

"He'll be wary with so many people visiting Blackfearn."

"Let him," Francis grouched. "We'll come bearing gifts."

"If I could get back to my concerns . . ." Laura cut in hopefully as the two men walked to the fireplace.

"Mistress Laura will be along for the visit. And while she is there, she could begin to apply some of her cleverness in helping our poor William along."

"In truth, that's all the lad needs."

"A bit of support and common sense." Gilbert nodded.

"And who better qualified to offer help than one who owes a bit of kindness to the laird?"

"From what Mistress Laura told me, William practically saved her life."

They both turned to Laura. Her gaze moved helplessly from the face of one priest to the other. Father Francis was the one who spoke.

"Well, we've a great deal to do, lass. How soon can you be ready?"

Chapter 12

The smoky torch hissed and flared, though not a breath of air stirred in the underground vault. The crypt, damp and still, smelled of death, and a chill ran through the Highlander's blood as he moved around the chamber, inspecting the ancient tombs. A cloaked monk stood silently by the entrance, watching him.

"Even as a lad I knew the stories about this place." The warrior's hand traced the carving on one of the stones. "There is power still in this sacred crypt. You can feel it, can you not, monk?"

"Not as much power as you will feel once you succeed in helping me. Once we find the Treasure of Tiberius."

"Perhaps . . . though I hear your searches thus far have met with little success." The Highlander looked across the vault. The monk's dark eyes were shadowed by the cloak.

"The English king's deputy lieutenant was a fool driven by greed. Aye, there could be little success with him aiding us. He insisted on first chasing after the mother, Nichola Percy. You might as well chase a shadow. Unable to find her, he then decided that the Percy sisters were simpletons, burying their riches somewhere in England. The man was an arrogant fool, brutal and self-seeking."

"And you went along with him." The Highlander moved around behind a tomb, running his fingers along a blackened stone wall. "I was also told that the sisters left behind clues."

"A clever distraction, that is all. We would have caught the three long before they reached Scotland if the late deputy lieutenant hadn't been so easily gulled."

"I have no desire to waste my time, monk. What guarantee do you have that this time you will succeed?"

"We're finished digging in the earth for what is not there. 'Tis time to go after them."

The Highlander frowned. "But did I not also hear that your attempt at kidnapping the middle sister ended in complete failure?"

The monk's gnarled fingers twisted together in the darkness. His voice was low, a hint of menace in his tone. "You have heard quite a bit. Far more than I imagined a Knight of the Veil would know."

"We never—I never walk blindly into any crypt, monk. Not when I have my own interests at hand. Explain your plan."

The hooded man paused a moment and then nodded, stepping toward the center of the chamber. "There is no purpose served in going after Catherine Percy. Since her marriage to the earl of Athol, taking her would require an army that we do not have. As far as the youngest, Adrianne—we have yet to learn her whereabouts. But that is a small concern, considering the fact Laura is so close. Why, she is nearly in our grasp."

The monk's hood slipped back a bit. His eyes glowed strangely in the torchlight. "This is our plan, knight. Capturing one can be as productive as having them all. When we have the body of one, we control the hearts of the rest."

"You assume that they will all give up the fight once we have Laura?"

"Aye, I know they will. I've known them since they were infants. They will surrender in an instant—any one of them would give up her life for the others. They cannot help themselves. I know them. 'Tis in their blood."

The Highlander came around the tomb and strode to the

monk. "I believe you. I have also heard of them—intelligent, beautiful, and intensely loyal to their family. And how do you suggest that I take possession of Laura Percy?"

The monk's face twisted into a smile as he placed a mis-shapen hand on the shoulder of the tall Highlander. "I, too, have heard things, my handsome friend. And when it comes to taking women, I do not believe the 'Blade of Barra' needs any help from me."

A dog and sheep barreled into Laura, knocking her backward into Father Francis as they crossed the threshold of Blackfearn Castle's Great Hall.

Before she could recover her balance, a half dozen sweating, bare-chested warriors descended upon them as well, shouting encouragement to the dog, which had quickly cornered the woolly animal. With a shout of victory, two of the men hoisted the sheep into the air and carried it toward the far end of the Hall. Toward the kitchens, no doubt, Laura decided with a look of amazement.

The Hall before them was grand and spacious, and from the looks of the ornately carved laird's chair and the tapestries hanging at rakish angles on the walls, it had obviously been quite elegant not long ago. But the chamber was now little more than a stable, with a menagerie of farm animals cowering in every corner and piles of refuse dumped on the floors. Overturned tables and benches littered the Hall, and the place smelled like a midden heap. In short, Laura thought, wrinkling up her nose, the place had the look of Noah's ark on the fortieth day.

"Perhaps, mistress, we would have done better to have the laird greet us elsewhere."

Laura glanced at Father Francis and nodded in agreement.

"Aye, Father, perhaps we should—"

"Ne'er mind, lass, I believe 'tis too late for second thoughts."

Laura threw a questioning glance at the priest and then, following his gaze, felt her breath catch in her throat. William Ross, stripped to the waist and dripping with sweat, was storming across the Great Hall, though "greeting" appeared to be the last thing on his mind.

As he approached, her mouth went dry in an instant, and she felt heat race through her body. It seemed like a lifetime since she'd seen him last, and yet her entire being was set humming at the mere sight of him.

She counted each of his cocksure steps as he blazed a path across the Hall. Try as she might, though, she could not help but gape at the rippling muscles of the Highlander's naked torso, at the fit of his tartan over lean hips, the plaid cloth flaring with each long stride.

When he was nearly upon them, she could see his deep blue eyes flashing. And something inside her froze with delicious terror when those same eyes raked over her from the tips of her boots to the strand of hair that she hastily pushed back from her brow.

She let out a quick breath. Handsome and strong, he was truly magnificent. And yet it took all of her courage not to back out the door.

"What is *she* doing here?"

Well, she thought darkly, perhaps "magnificent" was too hasty a judgment.

"William!" Father Francis's tone was sharp. "The provost told you of our visit."

"*Your* visit. He said nothing about dragging along this—"

"And this is your idea of hospitality, m'lord?" Laura broke in, forcing herself to keep a civil tone.

Unfortunately, the closeness of his body blasted any opportunity of remaining aloof to him. Despite his infernal arrogance, he was still an incredibly handsome man. For the first time he turned and looked at her in the eye, causing her to redden slightly. But her temper flared when she saw a hint of amusement creep into the corners of his eyes.

"If you have a complaint concerning my presence, perhaps you should address me directly?"

"Well, Mistress Percy, by now I should at least know enough not to turn my back on you."

"I—I requested to come here."

William cocked an eyebrow. "And why is that? Did word reach St. Duthac's that the cracks in my skull are nearly mended?"

"I came here to be a help. To offer my services."

"Is that so?" One corner of his mouth hitched suggestively, his eyes roaming down her traveling cloak. Liquid heat rushed through her, and for a moment she thought she would die. "In what capacity?"

"Now, William . . ."

"Father Francis." Laura quickly pulled herself together and turned to the priest. "If you would allow me a moment in private with the laird, I believe I will be able to clear up this confusion."

The older man nodded hesitantly and, giving William another hard look, headed for a table where a group of Ross men were watching with amusement.

"Do you always insist on fighting your own battles?"

"Always," she answered testily.

"Now, as for this moment in private." He cast an eye at the onlookers. "Knowing my reputation as a rogue who cannot help but steal away helpless women, surely you—"

"Stop right there." If she could only cause him some physical harm. But there had to be better ways. At least, better places to commit murder. She would bide her time. "This hall will do. And as I was trying to say before, I am offering my assistance in preparing for the arrival of Miriam, your niece."

He crossed his arms over his bare chest and continued to watch her, a frown creasing his face.

"She *is* coming here."

"So I've been informed."

"And a child needs some order and . . ." She paused and let her eyes travel over the chaotic appearance of the Great Hall. "And stability. A peaceful place to live and grow and learn."

"And you have decided to bring that to Blackfearn Castle."

She fixed her gaze on his face. "I am offering my services."

His hands dropped to his hips. "Do you mean you've come to stay?"

"Nay! I mean, aye." He didn't have to look quite so horrified. "I'm only planning to stay until you have your—your affairs in order and the child is settled."

"Settled?" William's arms again crossed over his chest, and he looked away. "To my thinking, they are in order. Though my brother holds a differing opinion, no doubt."

Right now, she thought with a quick glance at the Hall, she tended to agree with the provost.

"Well, I assure you, I'm not planning to stay long. Perhaps a month at the most. If you give me leave, I will stay until Miriam arrives, and you have a chance to arrange proper care and tutelage for her."

His gaze bore into hers. "That is too long."

He knew exactly how to wound her. She felt her back stiffen. Her jaw ground shut for a long moment. But then she reminded herself that she should have expected such treatment, considering all the trouble she'd caused him in the few days that they'd shared. Still, though, his words stung her.

"I am not here for you," she persisted. "And as much as you hate me, you might consider what is best for the child."

His eyes softened momentarily, his frown deepening. He turned abruptly and motioned for a young lad who stood at a distance holding his shirt and tartan. Laura, not needing to be further flustered at the sight of him dressing right before her eyes, turned her attention to the Hall. Every eye in the room was focused on them. She hid her hands in her cloak and turned to the laird again.

"I promise to stay out of your way while I am here."

"You will *only* deal with what concerns Miriam."

She gave a curt nod.

"And nothing else." He pointed a threatening finger at her chest. "No meddling in the business of the castle. No intrusion in the lives of the clan folk. No interference in the way *I* do things. *No* causing trouble of any kind!"

She nodded again. As long as none of these restrictions, she thought, interfere with preparing for the little girl.

"I agree." There were many ways of accomplishing a task, she said to herself, smiling innocently at him.

"And remember." William's blue eyes bore into her. "You will stay out of my way."

Laura had never in her life been one to place much value in creature comforts—which was a good thing, because she wasn't going to get them at Blackfearn Castle.

The bedchamber assigned to her by the Ross laird was located in an upper level of the castle's east wing, the original keep of Blackfearn Castle. The upper levels of the building had been divided into bedchambers long ago, when the larger edifice housing the present Great Hall and laird's chambers had been built.

Following Robbie, the young lad who had held his laird's shirt in the Great Hall, Laura climbed a dark circular stairwell and moved along a passageway lit only by narrow slit windows looking out on the courtyard. Passing open doors of two fairly large chambers—both of them with small drifts of snow on the wood floors—they made their way eventually to a door at the end of the corridor. Oak beams slanted upward just above her head, and looking up she could see patches of

blue sky through missing sections of roof. It was cold, and
Laura knew it was going to be wet.

"What happened to the roof?" she asked the boy casually.

"The storm last summer, mistress. A fiercer wind I ne'er
saw. Why, the roof came off in whole pieces. Flattened much
of the crops, too. Did ye see it?"

"As a matter of fact, Robbie, I was in a ship at the time.
'Twas a frightening thing."

"I wasn't frightened," the lad boasted, pushing open the
heavy door. "Though 'tis true that the wind howled like a
hound bitch looking for some supper."

"I'm sure it did," Laura said.

Left alone, she looked around the small chamber. The wind
was whistling down a huge open hearth that must have provided heat to the entire floor before the renovations. The room
itself was sparsely furnished with a narrow bed and a small
chest. It was damp and cold but certainly bearable, she thought
to herself. Going to fasten the shutter that covered the single
window, Laura looked down on a training yard below. The
snow had been trampled down by many feet, and the covering glistened in the bright sunshine.

She made a small fire in the hearth from a small stack of
kindling and peat that had been left, and smiled wryly as much
of the smoke backed into the room, drifting up into the roof
rafters instead of going out the chimney. When she picked up
a pile of straw from one corner of the room, two brown mice
darted along the wall. Fifteen minutes of careful searching
with a broom she found in the corner, though, turned up no
more occupying vermin.

Blackfearn was an old castle, Laura reminded herself, and
there were probably still grain and foodstuffs stored in the
level beneath. Besides, she was here not for her own comfort,
but to prepare for a certain little girl's arrival. The thought of
her purpose for being here cheered her greatly.

Putting the room in order took very little time, as did the

arrangement of her meager possessions. Looking around with satisfaction, Laura was thinking that perhaps it was time to return to the Great Hall when her supper arrived.

Maire, a rather shy old woman who apparently worked in the kitchens, conveyed the message that the laird was certain Mistress Laura would prefer to take her meals in her chamber.

Fuming as she closed the door behind the woman, Laura decided that merely murdering a blackguard like William Ross was too kind a fate.

Taking a few deep breaths, though, she sat on the chest by the fire and calmed herself.

"You are a survivor," Laura said quietly, trying some of the food and then setting it aside. Whatever they had planned to do with that poor sheep, the scorched mutton had been rendered nearly inedible. The crusty trencher of bread looked no more appetizing than the meat. "Well, so far."

Morning arrived—not as soon as she would have hoped— but it arrived all the same. And Laura was ready for battle.

She ran into the same older woman who had brought her meal up the night before just outside the door.

"Maire, how kind of you to bring this to me."

The white-haired servant looked up with surprise and met Laura's kindly gaze. "Ye remembered my name, mistress?"

"Of course." Laura smiled and took the wooden tray from her hands. "Wait a moment, will you?"

Bringing the food—singed bannock cakes and some unidentifiable watery mush in a wooden bowl—into the room, she placed it by the foot of the bed. Quickly returning to the serving woman, Laura closed the door behind her and placed a gentle hand on the servant's shoulder.

"Shall we walk down together?"

"But yer meal, mistress."

"I thought I would eat it later and instead join you in the kitchen for a while."

"But the laird!" She halted. "He—he . . ."

Laura ran her hands up and down her arms and let out a breath. She watched the frosty cloud dissipate in the air. "Is it only me? This cold, I mean."

Maire tightened her plaid shawl around her shoulders and shook her head. "With the broken places in the roof and no heat at all down this wing . . . 'tis godawful cold. Ye might as well be sleeping in the yard, I'd say, mistress."

Laura started the woman again down the corridor. "I do believe, though, 'twas quite kind of the laird to put me here." She looked about her, watching a few flakes of snow drifting in from somewhere above. "I love serenity. Restfulness. And to be honest, this cold . . . I understand 'tis excellent for both body and soul."

"If ye say so, mistress." Maire gave her a toothless smile. "Though we were thinking that ye must've done something horrid . . . to the laird, I mean, to get him so riled."

"Is he riled?"

"Aye. It does appear so." This time Maire laughed out loud. "Though Father Francis has been bragging to Janet and me what a good soul ye are. And now, having met ye, I'd have to believe the priest was telling it right."

The woman turned down another darkened corridor, away from the stairwell that Laura had been brought up the day before. Trailing after her companion, the young woman soon found herself turning down a narrow set of steps.

"And what has the priest been saying?"

"Do not ask, mistress, for I willna be telling." Maire chuckled, running a hand along the wall as she descended the steps. "This takes us right down to the kitchens. Ye have no need to be going through the Great Hall, this way."

"Ah, good. I can't have you getting into trouble on my account for disobeying your laird."

Maire shrugged. "This isn't disobeying, exactly, mistress. But in truth, our master is very good to us. But then . . ." She cackled and turned to look back at Laura. "He has to treat us well, for we're the last of the kitchen workers left at the castle."

"Yesterday, I saw quite a few men in the Great Hall."

"Aye, but they're mostly the laird's men, good only for fighting and farming—when they need to do one or the other. But around the castle they're as useless as extra toes, as far as I can see. No help at all when it comes to doing honest work. In fact, mistress, since Robert's passing—he was the steward—and the cook running off, Janet and I have been taking care of everything that needs doing." The older woman paused and edged along one wall as she stepped over a missing stair. "And all this in addition to everything else we were supposed to be doing before. Mending, washing, cleaning—and all the while with Chonny underfoot!"

"Is Chonny a little one?"

"Och! He's no lad, mistress. He's a full-grown man." Maire slowed again and this time pointed at a low overhang as she ducked down the steps. "Chonny lost both of his legs when he was a lad. Later, with both of his parents dying of fever, Lord keep 'em, he was moved into the keep to be part of the household."

"It must be difficult for him to be all alone like that."

"Alone?" The woman scoffed. "Not too bad a life. All he does is stay in the kitchen. He is fed, and he has straw to sleep on at night. And if 'twere not for his sour temper, I'd say most of us wouldn't even notice him. But he has a way of getting himself heard."

The smell of burnt porridge assaulted her nostrils as Laura reached a landing just above the kitchen. Smoke hung in thick clouds above heavy wood tables, cluttered with a disordered array of produce, trays, bowls, meats, fowl in every stage of preparation, and a multitude of other things, much of it unrecognizable. Three dogs were growling and pulling a haunch of mutton between two of the tables, and a heavyset woman—

older than Maire—was shrieking at them. Descending the last few steps behind Maire, Laura listened with surprise to the loud curses of the irate woman. This must be Janet, she assumed.

Too engrossed in the activity in the room beneath her, Laura tripped over the body of a person pulling himself rapidly up the stairs on his hands.

Trying to catch herself, she grabbed the shoulder and found herself staring down into a dark scowl.

"Oh, I'm sorry. I didn't see you."

Hostile eyes glared up at her from a swarthy, unshaven face. Beneath a man's body two stubs of legs swaddled in woollen cloth supported him on the stairs. The man's frown was unrelenting as she quickly looked back at his face.

"I'm Laura. Laura Percy," she said quietly. "You must be Chonny." Not waiting for an answer, she nodded at the smoke-filled chaos of the kitchen. "I know the laird threatened to do away with me if I was to leave my cell in the east wing. But how did he know I would be coming to the kitchens?"

The man didn't smile. But his frown eased a little as he shrugged her hand off his shoulder. Moving to the wall, he pulled himself up to the landing and disappeared around the corner and up the steps.

"Of course 'twas Chonny," she muttered, shaking her head.

Turning in search of Maire, Laura peered through the darkness and smoke, and saw her companion already by the open hearth, stirring a huge iron pot and ignoring the commotion behind her. In a moment Janet gave up and moved back to the hearth as well.

Laura stood and watched the two. Janet mopped her brow with the back of one hand and stared vacantly into the hearth. A smoky fire was roaring in the huge stone opening, but no one was turning the spit, and a large chunk of meat was rapidly being reduced to cinder. From the smell of things, some kind of bread was burning in the stone oven.

Janet, who Laura assumed must be in charge of the kitchen, was still unaware of her presence. Maire, busily stirring the ruined porridge, reached down and threw another block of peat on the fire. It appeared she had totally forgotten the visitor.

Well, there was no purpose served in standing around, Laura decided. Moving quickly down the steps, she crossed the packed dirt floor. Deciding to save whatever she could of the breads in the oven, Laura reached for a tray. As she did, she slipped on some decaying object on the floor, nearly banging her head on the corner of a wood table. Catching herself at the last moment, she righted herself and moved toward the oven, only to trip over a pile of dirty pots and bowls stacked on the floor.

She picked herself up. Before she could take a step, however, one of the dogs—having successfully stolen the mutton from his rivals, barreled past her with the other two in pursuit, howling, barking, and snapping furiously at the leader.

Chaos. Pure, unadulterated chaos.

Pulling her sleeves down to cover her bare hands, Laura moved carefully to the oven and smiled as warmly as she could at Janet, who was staring at her in surprise. Without a word she reached for the first flat loaf of bread, only to have an arm with a grip of iron wrap around her waist and pull her backward into a wall of human muscle.

A loud gasp escaped her, and for one stunned moment she remained tightly nestled against the man's body.

In front of her eyes, the room erupted. More dogs raced between the benches, barking and harrying two sheep that bleated loudly as they tried to clamber onto tables. A chicken flapped for its life toward the smoky rafters, showering the world below with feathers. A giant wearing Ross colors and a prodigious beard appeared from nowhere, suddenly appearing at the hearth with a huge pot of water which he proceeded to throw on the sizzling meat. Janet shrieked with disbelief, battering the warrior with a large wooden spoon.

Laura squirmed and twisted, pushing the arm holding her captive, but the man didn't release her, allowing her only to turn in his arms.

Why was it that her heart had to stop every time she looked into William Ross's face?

"And you call this staying out of my way?"

He was too close. She could feel his breath caressing her cheek. From the place where his hands were holding her waist, a warm pool was spreading rapidly inward to the very center of her being.

She forced out her words. "I was. Or at least, I'm trying."

"And what have you done to my kitchens?"

She glanced over her shoulder and smiled. "Nothing. Why would I change anything here?"

Even as he released her, she was intensely aware of his hands still lingering at her waist. He was still holding her far too close for her to breathe. She flattened one hand against his chest to put some distance between them, but he trapped her hand beneath his own. Her pulse jumped wildly.

"You find this amusing?"

She looked up and met his gaze. "Don't you?"

His attempt at a scowl was unsuccessful, and he looked more pained at the sight of the mess. Janet was still scolding William's cohort unmercifully. The man, standing with his arms folded over his chest, was waiting patiently for his laird and doing his best to ignore the verbal barrage. "I wonder which will come first—Blackfearn Castle burning to the ground, or those who live here starving to death?"

Following the direction of his gaze, she nodded somberly. "Why don't you bring in a new cook?"

He let go of her hand and turned away slightly. "I've already asked Edward to see to it. But he seems to be having no luck."

Although she already knew the answer, she asked it anyway. "Is Edward your steward?"

"Steward?" William snorted. He nodded toward the bearded giant. "Nay, that dwarf there is Edward. He is the clan's chief warrior."

"Then, why not have your steward see to it?" Seeing his frown, she gentled her tone. "I'm no authority on the running of a castle in this country, but where I was raised, the steward would be the man to see to matters such as this."

He placed his hands on her waist again and pulled her back as Maire, remembering the bread, rushed to the oven and started pulling out the blackened loaves.

"The steward died," he said gruffly.

"I'm sorry to hear that, but if you don't make a change here soon, you'll be losing these two women as well."

"Are they ill?"

She looked up into his face. Smoke was hanging in a cloud above his head. "Even young women can be overworked, and these two are not young women."

To her disappointment, his hand dropped from her waist. "They haven't voiced any complaints."

"They wouldn't. You're the laird."

His eyes narrowed. "But they would tell you? And who are you? An outsider who has been here only a night?"

Her temper flared again. "True, I've been here a night. True, I'm an outsider. But I would have to be blind not to see the signs."

"Signs?"

She nodded. "Well, take the food, for one thing. The problem is not that you have a horrible cook who is careless; the problem is that two old women who have to manage the running of an entire castle cannot feed an army of men in addition."

Laura glanced in the direction of Maire as she took the last of the bread out of the oven. "They have clearly been doing what they can. Without even boys to turn the meat on the spits or helpers to clean up after them. Never mind some-one to tend the fires properly, or organize the bread making, or butcher and hang the meats properly, or brew the ale, or pluck the fowl, or—"

"Janet is a fine brewer. She's been brewing since I was a lad."

Laura gentled her tone. "Whether they are silent out of their respect for you, or because they think that what they do is insignificant to other problems you must deal with, I do not know. But they need help here."

"I am not everywhere. I cannot read people's minds. Per-haps I am not *gifted* in recognizing signs."

"How can we be anything but what we are? But this is where having a steward—someone whom you can trust and delegate such matters to—will make a difference."

He eyed her for a moment and then looked at the two women digging in search of something through a pile of bowls on a table. Then, without a word or a sign, he turned and headed toward a door leading across a small passageway to the Great Hall.

Unwilling to be dismissed so abruptly, Laura hurriedly fol-lowed him into the Hall. "So are you planning to make a change here?"

Gesturing curtly to a number of men lounging on a bench in the Great Hall, William turned for the huge studded oak doors of the main entryway. She continued after him, trailing the laird down the steps into the cobblestone yard.

"William, Janet and Maire are both old women. As I said before, work them this hard, and they will become sick."

He turned around to face her. As he waved Edward, the bearded warrior, and the rest of the men on, Laura suddenly realized that she was standing out in the freezing air without even the protection of a wrap. She wrapped her arms around her and tried to keep from shivering.

"You're their laird. And they trust you to make a difference—to take care of them."

Her eyes widened when he brought his large hand to her
face, cupping her chin, lifting it. She looked up into his blue
eyes, saw gentleness and then desire. He was going to kiss
her, she was certain of it. Her heart stopped.

"And who is taking care of you, Laura Percy?"

His question was so unexpected that she lost her words.
"Me? I—I . . . have no—"

"Are you still having those disturbing dreams?"

She was too shocked to speak. Her throat clamped shut.
And despite the coldness of the air, a scorching heat crept
into her face.

He gently brushed his knuckles against her cheek and let
his hand drop. "We'll get more help for Janet and Maire."

He turned and strode off toward the arched gate and open
portcullis, where his men were waiting for him. But Laura remained where she was, no longer feeling the cold, watching
his retreat and wondering what all the fluttering turmoil inside her meant.

No smiling or tearful crowd had come out to say farewell
to the group. Miriam looked up wistfully at Hoddom Castle's
tall keep, searching the windows for some sign of her grandfather. But there was none. No waving hand, no shadow of
him watching from his chamber.

Nanna Jean's weeping gave way to a terrible, wrenching
cough as she took leave of her sister. She was very ill and
growing worse every day, but Lord Herries had insisted that
they leave immediately.

Miriam watched Sir Wyntoun shake his head as he turned
his horse toward the open gate, and the others followed. Two
barking dogs raced up from the village, baring their teeth and
growling at the travelers as the small group pushed down the
road toward the ford.

She bit her lip and fought back the tears burning her eyes. After one last look back at Hoddom Castle, Miriam turned and stared ahead at the endless line of hills leading into the mist-enshrouded mountains beyond. She had no memory of the place that awaited at the end of this journey.

William Ross. She repeated the name in her head. William Ross. Her protector. Her guardian. Her uncle.

Vowing silently to be the best that she could be, she thought of William Ross and everything that she would do to make her uncle proud of her once she arrived at Blackfearn Castle.

She would be brave. She would be kind. She would be a perfect seven-year-old, so her uncle would have no other choice but to love her.

Miriam stabbed away a runaway tear. And she would not cry. Not at Blackfearn Castle, and not here—even though she was leaving forever the only place she had ever called home.

Even if someone did not love her enough to say good-bye.

Chapter 13

William watched with interest the attack on the standing wood posts. His warriors were certainly becoming proficient with the new German halberds. An eight-foot pole topped by an iron head that combined both battle-ax and spear, the weapon carved huge chunks out of the posts on the first assault. Once the fighting became hand to hand, the halberd was a vicious instrument of destruction.

God knows, the English had used it well enough in the butchery that took place at Flodden.

"Odds' blood, wouldn't Duncan Munro be surprised to find a hornet's nest of these waiting for him on one of his raids into Ross lands?" Edward said, walking back from the well and handing William a bowl of water.

"Aye. And if Gilbert's soothing letters to Sir Walter fail to have any effect, I've a feeling we'll be using them against the Sinclairs before long as well." The laird drank and handed it back. "Any improvement in the kitchen?"

Edward's obscenity was graphic and to the point. "Peter's Wife came from the village to take over for auld Janet this morning."

"Any improvement?"

Edward snorted. "I do not believe I would put it just that way. Since walking into the place, the woman has been so red in the face, storming about the kitchens, fighting tooth and nail with Janet. Wee Robbie says they both look like cherries about to burst. My advice, m'lord, would be to avoid the fish today. Odds' blood, the woman will probably poison us all."

"What's wrong now?"

Edward shrugged. "If you're looking for an explanation for a woman's actions, you're asking the wrong man. I don't understand them—never did and never will."

"Did you not gather more help than just the one?"

"Aye. Robbie says Peter's Wife cursed out the whole bunch of them, saying she cannot be doing her work with so many idlers standing around watching her. The lad says the last straw came when Chonny started chiding her."

A movement drew the laird's attention, and William turned in time to see two hawks circling low over the east wing of the castle.

"Maire also told me again that Mistress Laura wishes to have an audience with you."

William had been dogged in his determination to avoid her. He could not help himself when he was near her. He could not keep his hands off her. He turned his attention back to the men in the training yard. Three days had passed since he'd lost his mind in the courtyard and nearly kissed her beautiful mouth in front of everyone. Since then the snow covering the training yard had been churned into a frozen gray ooze.

And the way she'd been concerned about *his* people. Those violet eyes flashing up at him. And then the heat—that pretty blush that crept into her face anytime he came close to her. She was just too much of a temptation. One that he couldn't risk trying to fight. Nay, he told himself, some temptations are simply meant to be avoided.

But he was tired of being so damned virtuous.

William realized that Edward was addressing him. ". . . and you realize Father Francis is leaving today."

"What? And is he taking Lau—Mistress Percy with him?"

"Nay, William. Your niece could reach Blackfearn anytime

now. The priest says Mistress Percy should be here when the
lassie arrives."

William again looked up and watched the circling hawks.
They were obviously interested in something inside the castle walls.

"The old man says the provost will be coming here as soon
as Francis arrives back at St. Duthac's. I believe Gilbert told
you that he wishes to be here as well."

Very good! With Gilbert around, there would not be many
chances of being left alone with Laura. Now, if he could only
busy himself enough to keep his mind off the woman.

"And Tar's uncle is coming here tomorrow morning so that
you can talk to him about the steward's position."

William nodded vaguely, his attention suddenly fixed on
the hawks. One of them began to dive, angling into a sweeping curve and passing quite near to one of the windows of
the east wing before climbing high into the sky.

"What the hell is going on up there?"

After glancing up at the circling hawks, Edward's eyes followed the direction of the laird's gaze. "That last window
would be Mistress Laura's bedchamber."

"I know that." William's muscles stiffened, and he took a
step toward the keep. Behind him, several of his men drew
near. "Is she up there?"

"I believe so. The word going 'round the castle is that
you've forbidden her from joining the rest of the household
in the Great Hall, though I don't know the truth of that. But
aye, the lass has been staying fairly close to her room, such
as it is."

William watched as the wooden shutter opened a little and
a hand appeared, dangling something out the window at the
end of a short string. Immediately, one of the hawks shot like
an arrow out of the sky. An instant before the predator hit the
hand, the woman flipped the bait upward, drawing in her hand
as the bird flashed by.

The hawk quickly ascended, its prize dangling from talons that could rip open a man's arm.

"What's the lass doing?" Edward asked incredulously.

"Feeding them," one of the warriors said in wonder.

"The blasted creatures could take off her hand," another said in awe.

William looked around and found everyone on the yard had stopped to watch the spectacle.

"By the devil!" he muttered, starting for the keep. There was no way he could send any one of his men to her room. Stepping into the kitchen doorway, he found himself in the midst of a small riot of angry, cursing workers. Seeing a red-faced Janet arguing with Peter's Wife and a surprisingly vociferous Chonny at the far side of the fray, William immediately turned up the old steps that led to the east wing. Maire was nowhere to be seen, and it would be no use asking Janet to go up to Laura's room, he thought.

Turning the corner at the landing and ascending quickly, William suddenly missed a step, falling forward heavily. As he pushed himself up, the laird realized that the step he'd "missed" was absent altogether. Cursing as he rubbed his bloodied shin and knee, he made a mental note to have the damn step repaired.

Once he was safely in the upper-floor passages, he was surprised at the poor condition of the roof and at the bitter cold that permeated the building.

Edward, he remembered, had advised him about the state of disrepair existing in this wing, but William had chosen to ignore it. Just as he'd ignored everything else that Mildred had valued.

At the end of the corridor, he paused before knocking on the oak door. What the hell was he doing here, anyway? It was no accident that she had been situated in this wing. He'd wanted her to feel uncomfortable and unwelcome; then she herself could decide to leave. So what if she was in danger of losing one of those pretty fingers to a frenzied hawk?

His knuckles were rapping on the door in an instant.

"You may enter, Maire."

Her soft call caused him to hesitate a moment. What indeed was he doing? He knew the safest thing for him to do was simply to turn around and leave her to her foolishness.

He pushed open the door.

She was leaning out the window now, peering upward intently. As William rested his shoulder against the doorjamb, he had quite a good view of her shapely bottom. Thoughts flitted through his mind of walking into that bedchamber and taking her in his arms and tossing her onto that narrow cot. The tightening in his loins told him he was not far from doing just that. By God, he thought, he could easily spend a month in here and let everything else rot. And how pleasant that month would be.

"Put the tray right on the floor, Maire. Sit down and rest your leg a bit."

With her back still to him, Laura straightened up at the window. As he watched, she tied a chunk of meat from a plate on the ledge with a short piece of thread.

"I saw the laird training in the yard with his men before. I assume he still refuses to see me." She sounded unhappy about it, and William's eyebrows arched with surprise. "Father Francis said that Miriam could be arriving here as early as this week. I wish William Ross would put aside his . . . well, his disinterest in me for a moment and just listen to me. There is so much to do."

She dangled the line out and then slammed the shutter closed as the dark form of a hawk shot by. She pulled open the shutter again and looked out, resting her head against the wood with a loud sigh.

William's face darkened with a scowl as a pang of guilt struck him. Suddenly, his being so rude to her no longer made a great deal of sense. True, she was from the same privileged background as Mildred, but there the similarities ended.

An icy gust of wind swept past him from the corridor, and he saw her pull the tartan she had wrapped around her shoulders. He stepped into the room and closed the door, resting his back against his only means of escape.

"'Twould hardly be right for a wee seven-year-old to arrive here and feel as if she were not even expected, never mind welcome." She started tying another chunk with string. "I *have* to get his attention. But how?"

William glanced at the dying remains of the tiny fire in the huge fireplace. Quietly, he moved to the hearth and placed another block of peat on the embers. As smoke backed up into the room, a frown clouded his features.

"Perhaps if I stopped eating entirely and had you bring him news of my protest."

Considering the quality of the food they'd been getting lately, he might consider doing that himself. Leaning into the fireplace, he peered up the chimney. Not even a hint of daylight up there, he thought, shaking his head.

"Nay! He might decide I'm making a commentary on the food, agree with me, and take the same course of action himself."

He leaned back against the carved stone mantel above the hearth and smiled. She was wearing a thick and rather shapeless wool dress, but he had no difficulty recalling the beautiful body hidden beneath its heavy folds. He came slowly to his feet.

"I've been too predictable in my approach. Too . . . too sensible."

He nodded in agreement, but suddenly a note of mischief crept into her voice. "If I were to act . . . absurd. Totally different from who I really am." She prepared to dangle the bait out the window again but stopped, looking down at the men in the training yard. "Perhaps if I were to shed all my clothes and throw them, one piece at a time, out this window into the yard. Perhaps then he'd—"

"That would certainly get my attention, though you'd surely freeze up here in no time, I should think."

She whirled in shock and gaped at him, her violet eyes two round gems in an ivory face. William saw a shadow of a hawk pass by the open window behind her. He strode across the chamber to where she stood.

Laura quickly recovered from her surprise, holding her ground. Her shoulders straightened, and her chin lifted high in challenge, but her eyes told him that his presence was not unwelcome.

"You might have told me, m'lord, that 'twas you and not—"

He arched an eyebrow at her. "M'lord?"

As he came before her, he saw the deep blush rise beneath the skin of her neck, into her cheeks. Letting his eyes travel down her body, he noted the little tremor in her hands. Damn, she was beautiful. As near as this, there was no way to stop the tightening of his loins, the pulsing of his blood, the over-whelming desire to touch her.

He reached out with both hands and took her by the shoulders. Ignoring her shocked gasp, he moved her a bit roughly to the side, away from the window.

He closed and latched the shutter and turned to her. "Very well. Be quick about it. You have my attention."

He saw her swallow and fixed his gaze on her parted lips. They were so full, so tender. He remembered with the clarity of a dream just how tender. Before he even knew he intended to do it, he wrapped a hand around her waist, and she came willingly into his arm.

The joining of their mouths might have set the entire castle ablaze. Like a starved man he kissed her, devoured her, and she was as zealous in her response.

He dug his fingers into her hair, holding her tightly as his mouth tried to get the taste of her. Her arms were wrapped around his neck, her body arching, pressing tighter against him, pushing him to a level of sheer madness.

Damn, this woman was so sweet. Her flesh scorched him where he touched her. And her skin, so incredibly soft. His lips moved from her mouth and traveled across her cheek, to her ear, down her neck, while she moved restlessly, giving him better access to the tantalizing flesh. His hands were everywhere, roaming her back, feeling the curve of her bottom—pulling her hard against his manhood.

He found her mouth again and swallowed her gasp of surprise as his one hand cupped her breast. She leaned into his touch, and he heard himself groan with need.

He had to have her. And he knew he could. When he pulled back a little, she followed—seeking, teasing, drawing his probing tongue back into her soft mouth.

By Duthac's Shirt, he wanted her, right here, in this room, on this poor excuse for a bed. But that nagging, vengeful, pain in the arse voice in his head kept pulling at him, telling him it would be wrong. Laura wasn't some wench in the Three Cups Tavern. She wasn't even some worldly and spoiled court chit. She was an enchantress, but she had no idea of all the things he lusted to do to her.

He cupped her face with two large hands and, holding her in place, gently pulled back. Looking into her face—the parted lips, the flushed cheeks, the eyes that were closed only to slowly open again in all their violet splendor—he knew he was a man bewitched.

He took a deep breath and then smiled down at her. "Well, lass, you certainly have my attention now."

She suddenly appeared flustered. She tried to step back. He held her in place.

"What happened a moment ago was too long in coming."

She nodded, gnawing and then delicately licking her full

lower lip. He wondered if she knew how such a simple action could rouse in him such desire.

His voice was hoarse as he shook off those thoughts. "But we cannot let it happen again."

Cheeks aflame, she nodded in agreement, but the look of hurt that he glimpsed in her eyes told him he was a filthy knave.

"Laura, you're a very desirable woman, passionate and beautiful. And—and I am only a man." He looked away, trying to push the anger out of his voice. Lamely, he made an attempt at sounding casual, offhand. "I—I only look for a toss in the hay. Hell, you deserve more than that."

Her gaze dropped to his chest, and he reluctantly released her hand. "We'll stay away from each other for the rest of your stay here. We can both forget what happened."

She nodded again and turned away from him. Moving across the chamber to the far side of the hearth, she stared at the small fire. He saw that her hands were trembling slightly as she tucked them into the folds of her dress.

"You'll soon find a husband and have your own bairns— like your older sister. And you will be happy then that you never surrendered yourself to some Highland villain."

It was vanity, William knew, but even so he hoped she would deny his words. She said nothing, though, and when she finally turned around to him, she seemed to have her passion under control.

"I thank you for coming up here. I know you are quite busy, m'lord."

He watched her tightly clasped hands and wanted to feel them again touching him. All the words he'd spoken were a lie, he realized suddenly. Every one of them.

"I have made a list of requests that, if you'd be kind enough to hear them, would greatly ease my concerns about the arrival of your niece."

"A list?" he repeated like a fool, watching her bend over

the bed to pick up a piece of slate with some writing on it. By St. Andrew, he wanted her sprawled beneath him on that cot. He wanted to strip her out of that gray dress and feel her limbs naked and entwined with his own.

"Aye, a list." She straightened, running a hand down the front of her dress.

William's eyes followed the movement, lingering on her breasts—so aware of their fullness, the way they'd felt when he'd held them.

"First, since I will be acting as the child's first tutor here, I was wondering if your niece could be placed in a bed-chamber adjacent to mine. I know this wing is quite drafty, but I believe with a few minor alterations, the chambers just down this corridor might be warm enough. And—"

"Very well," he said shortly, gazing at the serious set of her jaw. He knew exactly how to go about softening it. Softening her.

"Second, I was wondering—since there is still no stew-ard—if I might oversee the hiring of a dependable cook for the kitchen."

She was studying her list, her hand resting against her ribs just below her breast. He scowled, the torment growing within him.

"'Tis essential that we improve the quality of the food be-fore Miriam's arrival. I myself have been regularly feeding the hawks with it, though I believe they enjoyed the mice I killed the first day here more than the food that is being cooked in Blackfearn's kitchen."

Killing mice? He hid his smile as she absently began to pace the room, listing all the reasons why he should let her take charge.

He took a deep breath as she passed near him. The sweet scent of her hung in the air like lavender on a summer's eve. Her hair fell in loose waves over her shoulders like a shining waterfall of silk. He wanted to bury his hand in it—run it over his face, his chest, his belly. He was losing his mind.

He realized he was nodding vaguely—but at what? She went back to her list, pacing and rubbing her neck lightly. The soft column of ivory skin—the pulse beating so seductively at the hollow of her throat. He'd tasted her there. And he wanted to do it again. In fact, he wanted to peel away that collar, that plaid scarf, that damn dress. He wanted to let his mouth taste every inch of her bare skin.

"Assuming that the efforts required . . ."

She continued to talk, but he seemed to have lost the ability to hear anything but snatches of what she was saying. With the pulsing roar that was beginning to build in his head, his ears appeared to be no longer functioning. His body, however . . .

William knew he had to get out of that chamber before his willpower crumbled and he did the unthinkable.

"Do as you will," he snapped, turning abruptly.

"All of it?"

He yanked open the door and gave her a parting glance. Her eyes were round with surprise. Her beautiful mouth open. He would be a doomed man if he didn't escape.

"Aye, of course all of it."

The Highland wind was bitterly cold, cutting through the travelers with the feel of an icy blade drawn across bone. They climbed another brae so steep and rugged that the pack-horses were continually balking beneath their loads. But the young girl, sitting astride her sturdy little horse, was far too excited to pay any attention to the hostile surroundings. She urged her horse upward until she was riding alongside the group's leader.

"Miriam, I asked you before to stay in the middle of the line."

"Aye, that you did, Sir Wyntoun. And I will go back, just as soon as you answer one more question."

The man's stern expression softened as he stared down at the young girl. "Aye, lassie. And what is it this time?"

"How many more days before we arrive?"

"Two, perhaps three, if the weather cooperates. But we've already talked about this today, I bel—"

"And how many camps will we be making before we see Blackfearn Castle?"

Wyntoun MacLean scowled to hide his smile, though he knew that the child saw right through him anyway. "That makes two questions, if I am not mistaken."

The blue eyes turning upward in an attitude of pleading that had the Highlander shaking his head in defeat.

"Considering your first question is the same one you've been asking about a hundred times a day since we left Hoddom Castle, I suppose I should allow you this second one. Though, to be honest, lass, I do not see the diff—"

"How many camps, Sir Wyntoun?"

"By the d—" He checked himself. "Once again, child, weather permitting, as few as two. But it could be more."

"Could we do without them and arrive there today?"

"Would you want to kill that wee darling you're riding, Miriam? Nay! Besides, 'tis far too treacherous a ride in the dark." He shook his head and looked at her closely. "Are you cold, lassie?"

Miriam's impish face shook from side to side. "'Tis not cold, at all."

The blue tinge in her lips contradicted her words, though. She was a wee, stubborn elf, to be sure, he thought.

"You don't have to worry about me, Sir Wyntoun."

He nodded his head and, reaching into the leather bag tied to his saddle, pulled out another blanket. "Aye, I know that. But your horse looks a wee bit cold, so put this over your lap for me."

"Very well, though she doesn't look cold to me." With a look of a person humoring another, however, she took it and carefully tucked it around her legs.

"That should keep her warm, lass. Now, why not wait right here and get into your place in line?"

"Before I go, Sir Wyntoun," she blurted out, "what do you think I should call my uncle?"

"He is your uncle. Just call him that."

She shook her head. "That was before. Now he is my guardian. Nanna Jean said before we left, that means he will now be like my father. But I cannot call him 'guardian,' can I?" She twisted her face into a frown and gazed up into the Highlander's face. "Perhaps I should call him 'Sir William.' Nay, that won't do. Perhaps 'laird'?"

Wyntoun MacLean shook his head. "Well, lass, I—"

"'Father'? Do you think he would like me to call him 'father'?"

The Highlander watched silently as a look of uncertainty clouded the young girl's face.

"What if he hates me?"

"I know your uncle, Miriam. He won't hate you."

"But what if he doesn't want me? The way—the way Grandsire didn't."

"Lord Herries is an old man." Wyntoun stopped, realizing there was no point in defending the bloodless old bastard. She had seen it herself.

"Will he want me?"

The knight gave her a reassuring nod. "You'll do very well, Miriam. I know William Ross. The man will treasure you, lass."

Chapter 14

The arguing was loud and incessant, and angry voices drifted up the steps with the familiar smell of burnt food. Laura tucked her skirts around her legs and listened from her place in the darkness of the stairway leading up from the kitchens.

She was waiting for him. She knew he would come. He always did. Escaping the chaos at its height and seeking a position of refuge. She'd run into Chonny a number of times at this spot. He'd surely be here this morning.

Laura had discovered soon enough that taking the time to be friendly with the surly man was wasted breath. On the other hand, though, any time she'd asked him what was happening in the kitchen, Chonny had been more than willing to talk. In fact, he could be quite articulate about what had caused a current disaster and how it could be resolved. Not that anyone in the kitchen was interested in listening, however. In his own words, who cared what a cripple had to say?

Well, Laura cared, for one. And she had in fact set her mind to making a few changes.

At the sound of renewed shrieking between two women below, Laura edged forward on her step. Just as she'd expected, Chonny soon appeared, pulling himself up the steps on his hands and stopping abruptly upon seeing Laura blocking his way.

She moved a little more to one side and smiled pleasantly. "I believe there is room for both of us."

Even in the semidarkness of the stairs, Laura saw the man's face turn a deep shade of crimson. He grumbled a complaint under his breath and seated himself a few steps below her perch.

"Another disaster?"

He grumbled something again that she didn't hear.

"There seem to be plenty of helping hands in the kitchen now. I just cannot, for the life of me, understand why Black-fearn Castle is still plagued with such horrible food."

"Too many."

"Too many people to feed? I agree," she said simply. "It must be quite difficult to feed so many people."

"Too many helpers," he snapped. "That hellhole is lousy with villagers who wouldn't know a spoon from a sheep's arse. And there is not a one of them down there who knows how to give a direction clearly, never mind cook."

"So Janet is not the woman to run the kitchen?"

"She's a brewer," he muttered.

"Nor Peter's Wife, either?"

Chonny merely snorted in response and glanced up the steps at her.

Laura rested her chin in her hand as if contemplating what he'd said and stared over his head. "Hmm. Then I suppose the laird's solution might have to be tried."

She waited, avoiding the young man's piercing gaze. She waited, knowing that the question would come. It did.

"What solution?"

Laura turned to him and brightened, as if she'd just re-membered he was there. "You, Chonny."

"You said the laird had a solution for the kitchen."

She ignored him. "I am told that you have become a ter-ror in the kitchen. They say everybody jumps when you lose your temper. They say that what you do not have in height, you make up for in lungs. Is that true?"

He turned away and again grumbled under his breath. Pushing himself up, he moved easily down a couple of steps.

"Do you want to hear William Ross's solution?"

"You don't have to tell me, I can guess it myself. He wants me out of the kitchen."

"Nay, just the opposite. I heard Peter's Wife tell Maire that you think you'd make a better cook than anyone around. Is that true, Chonny?"

The man turned and faced Laura, his look of surprise quickly turning to suspicion.

"Is that true, Chonny?"

"Why shouldn't I think so? From the time I lost these," he snapped, gesturing toward his legs, "I've spent my whole life in that kitchen. I've got a brain, mistress, and I've watched enough to know how to cook. Who is to say I shouldn't raise my voice when the place is about to burn down?"

"Not I." Laura smiled. "And not the laird, either. William Ross believes 'tis time you took over this kitchen."

When William strode into the smaller room adjoining the laird's chambers, there was a fire blazing in the hearth. Symon, a lean, balding man with badly bowed legs, followed closely behind him. Edward ducked his head as he entered behind the other two.

The laird frowned as he cast a cursory glance over the room. There were changes here, but William did not want to waste any time getting to the discussion. He motioned for Edward to close the door.

William had no desire to prolong this. He needed a steward for Blackfearn Castle, someone competent, a man who could read and write. He also wanted a Ross man who was good with figures. Most of all, he must be someone William could trust. Symon was the uncle of one of his men, and he had served well as a steward at one of the farms that supported St. Duthac's. It was only because of Gilbert's reorga-

nizing of the farms that he was available. A good solid man-
ager, Gilbert had told him. And Symon was here and willing.

"You have the job, Symon. How soon can you move into
the castle?"

His abruptness raised Edward's eyebrows, but the new steward didn't seem at all surprised.

"Thank you, m'lord. I'm looking forward to the challenges
that Blackfearn Castle offers. In fact, I have already asked my
nephew Tar to accompany me back to the farm for my things,
if you do not mind losing him for a few hours."

"Not at all." William turned to the table and stared for a
moment at the orderly state of affairs there. He glanced at
Edward, who quickly looked away.

"I've already been told how to proceed through the work
waiting for me here. I know Robert the steward was a good
man, but it has been some time since he passed away."

"Aye." William thumbed through the items on his table.
Someone had sorted the work by task—the account ledger of
the keep lay ready for entries, a letter of recommendation to
the bishop at Inverness for a village lad to one side, an in-
complete list of the stores in the outlying farms. There were
a dozen other things as well. "There will be a great deal facing you."

"Nothing to fear, master. In fact, after sitting with Mistress
Laura this morning, I'd say—"

"Mistress Laura?"

William's eyes were murderous as he swung toward Edward again. The giant Highlander was intently studying an
ancient, though newly dusted broadsword gracing the wall
above the fireplace.

"Aye. The lass appears very knowledgeable when it comes
to organization, even for a place as large as this castle. More
interestingly, though, is the way she knows the questions to
ask a man about his work."

"Is that so?"

"Without a doubt." The man nodded. "She asked so many questions. Everything from what I did when I was here as a young man, helping Robert the steward's father before the son took over, to what my last position required of me as steward at the Dunbrae farm."

William sat down in the laird's chair and stared at Symon.

"She even asked me how I treat people and asked for the names of a few that she could question herself. Why, before we were done with our wee talk, she knew me better than I knew myself. And I'm thinking she was happy enough with what she found to recommend me to you."

"And when you spoke with her . . ."

"Aye, this morning."

". . . you found this to be time well spent?"

"Of course. I knew right off what you'd be needing from me, and we'd both know whether I was up to the task. You were training in the yard with the men when I arrived, and the lass approached me directly." Symon nodded with admiration. "That shows real leadership on your part, m'lord, if you'll forgive me for saying so. Not every man could leave a woman to do the questioning."

"That's true enough."

"But then again, there aren't too many lassies about like Mistress Laura, either."

"Nay. Indeed, there are not." William glared at Edward, who was looking on and smiling weakly. "You be on your way now, Symon. Sooner you start, the better. You'll use this chamber to keep your books."

"Thank you, m'lord. As I told Mistress Laura, you won't be disappointed with my work."

With a quick bow by the door, Symon stepped out, and Edward started after him.

"Get back here, you oversized, dog-faced—"

With his head hanging, the huge Highlander stepped back in and closed the door.

"Explain."

" 'Tis true. I let her in here, m'lord. She organized your desk. She talked to the new steward. And . . ."

"What else?" William asked sharply.

"She's organized the help in the kitchen and hired a new cook, though I had nothing to do with that, I swear."

"All this since yesterday?"

"She has a way of getting things done, Will." Edward looked up and met his master's angry glare. "We—I . . . didna know that you were totally unaware of her actions. She said—perhaps was my misunderstanding her—but I thought that she said you had agreed to a list that she'd discussed?"

"That damned list again," William muttered, recalling their conversation.

"I can assure you, m'lord, that no harm came out of anything she's done, and if you need to punish anyone for what's done . . ." The Highlander straightened to his full height. "You should hold *me* responsible, even for the cook."

Looking at his man, William realized he himself wasn't the only one who seemed to become tongue-tied when it came to dealing with Laura. Rolling the gold coin over his knuckles, he stared again at the neat table before him and realized that he really was not at all angry about what she had done. A competent steward was needed. A new cook was a must.

But cleaning his worktable?

He looked about him and realized that this was the first time he'd sat in the laird's chair in this chamber without a feeling of intense loathing afflicting him. He frowned up at Edward.

"And who has she selected as the new cook?"

"Please hear the whole thing out, William."

The laird's eyes narrowed. "Is it a disaster?"

Edward shook his head. "In truth, I believe it may work out."

"Very well. Who is it, then?"

"Chonny."

"Chonny?"

Edward nodded, smoothing his beard with a huge meaty hand. "When first Mistress Laura told me, I thought 'twas madness, but she—she has a way of being quite convincing."

"I know."

"She says he's suited to the job." Edward shrugged his broad shoulders and looked at his laird. "Of course, the final decision is yours, William. But I walked through the kitchens this morning, and I agree with her."

William frowned at his warrior. He hoped that Edward was thinking clearly when it came to dealing with Laura. By the saint, one of them would have to. He looked narrowly at his man. For Edward's sake, he'd better not be falling under her spell, because just as William himself planned never to touch her again, neither would any of his men be allowed near her.

"Mistress Laura knows somehow that Chonny has spent most of his life in those kitchens. Through his years of watching, he has become an expert in knowing how to feed a whole castle."

"Aye," William nodded. "He used to turn the spits when he was younger."

"And the lad has the cooperation of every helping hand that walks in there."

"Is that so?"

Edward nodded thoughtfully. "Everyone knows him and most fear his temper. But more to the point, no one truly wants the job of running those kitchens on their own."

"Is he willing? Has anybody talked to him about this?"

"I talked to him myself. As much as you can tell with Chonny, I'd say the man is thrilled to have the opportunity." Edward grinned sheepishly. "And the man cannot wait to thank you in person for giving him the chance."

"Thank me?"

"Aye, William. Mistress Laura told him that 'twas you who thought of him for the job."

Guilt made William look away. He knew Chonny well. Though the man was a couple of years younger, he and Gilbert used to play together when they were all lads. Even after his accident, after he became a cripple, they used to steal the workmen's carts and bring him out in the yard for their mock jousts. William would push him in one cart—Chonny holding a wooden lance in hand—while Tar or one of the other lads would push Gilbert.

That seemed a lifetime ago. It all came to an end when he was sent away to St. Andrew's and later to Lord Herries's castle to become educated to the ways of the world.

But then, fate had different plans for him. Bitter plans, and years in the service of the queen mother. And then he was back here, laird of the same people who had once bowed their heads to his brother—and his wife.

William shook off these thoughts. He had been back for nearly two years, and still he was neglecting these people. These people who were now his responsibility. Folk like Chonny who still thought him worthy of offering their service to him. He was their laird.

William rose from the chair and came around the table. "Where is she now?"

Edward hesitated to answer, as if gauging the laird's anger at their visitor.

"I'm at peace with what she's done in the kitchens. Where might I find her now?"

"I'd only be guessing, m'lord, since she asked for no help from me on the next item on her list."

"Which was?"

"Actually 'twas the first item and—"

"By the devil, Edward! Out with it, man," William snapped. He needed to see her and get a few things straight.

"The chambers in the east wing. Something about finding a suitable place for your niece?"

On impulse, instead of using the door that led to the Great Hall, William went out through the small door leading to the laird's quarters. He came to a sudden stop. He rarely came through here. When he did, he chose not to spend any time in the chamber. But he saw it now. There was change here as well.

"She did not do a great deal in here, m'lord." Edward quickly explained behind the Ross. "I—I happened to mention that you were not keen on using the laird's quarters, and she said something about not blaming you, considering how disused it smelled and looked. I believe she asked Maire to help her spread some fresh rushes and air the room."

William looked about him. These quarters were Thomas's. And in his mind, they belonged to the true laird, so he had stayed away.

And he would still stay away. And she had no right to be meddling with his life. His life was perfectly fine. Well, perhaps not perfect, but he liked his life just as it was.

He headed out of the chambers and went to the kitchen first. The change was striking. No meat burning on the fire. No smoke billowing about the rafters. No stacks of pots and bowls or piles of decaying food cluttering the tables or floors. Boys were bustling in and out with baskets of fowl and large bowls of oats from the storage rooms or turning meat on the spits. Looking about, he saw a small group of lasses, chattering away as they industriously peeled potatoes and onions for what appeared to be the makings of the evening meal. At the far fireplace, two women from the village—one being Peter's Wife—were cheerfully taking trays of golden brown bread from the ovens.

He went around a table and found Chonny sitting on a low three-legged stool. The man was working intently, writing with a charcoal stick on a wooden board set on his lap.

Watching for a moment in silence, William frowned, cursing himself inwardly. If he had been doing the task he'd been entrusted with from the beginning, he would have found some way of making Chonny useful long before now.

"What are you devising, you ugly son of a hedgehog? Working up a witch's brew, no doubt."

The crippled man looked up and scowled fiercely. William brightened, knowing immediately that Chonny was not going to change with the new position. The laird overturned a nearby bucket and sat down close to the new cook.

"And what kind of spell have you cast on these people?" William gestured to the workers. "Not a complaint, not a squabble, not even any threat of blood being shed."

"If there is any blood to be shed, 'twill only be me doing it." Chonny looked across the tables at the kitchen and lowered his voice. "To be honest, you're the charm, Will. When I told them they would not all be coming in here to work for you every day, the cursed creatures turned into a flock of lambs."

William looked around him as well. "And with no help, you miserable wretch, how did you plan to feed us then?"

Chonny grunted again, but William could hear the hint of excitement in the man's voice as he started with his explanation.

"Once we get things going smoothly, I'll only keep a few of the best helpers, the ones who want to be here. As to the rest of them, I'll have one group work in the morning and another come in for the evening meal. If we need others on occasion, we'll bring them in from the village."

"A good plan, Chonny."

The man reddened in the face and cursed, but a look of pride was evident when he glanced again over his new kingdom. "A lot of this was Mistress Laura's doing. But a lot of it came from my head, too!"

William slapped him hard on the shoulder and nodded.

"You're doing wonders here. Just let me know if you need anything and I'll—"

"She told me what you wanted." The man looked down at the writing on the board. "That's what I'm doing now. Instead of yelling and complaining, I'm making a list for you of everything that we need, or that needs to be done here."

"A list."

"Aye. Mistress Laura said I can give it to her or to you. 'Tis almost finished."

"Mistress Laura told you that." William rose to his feet. "When you're ready, we'll talk about what you need. One thing, though, that the woman probably did not tell you . . ."

"Aye?"

"If you poison me, hedgehog, I'll haunt you into the next world."

Chonny snorted in reply as the laird turned toward the steps.

William frowned as he crossed the kitchen toward the east wing. It was time to take this woman in hand. She'd hired the blasted steward. Granted, that looked as if it should work out. And he didn't have a problem with what she'd done regarding Chonny, either. But the rest of it—the laird's chamber, the cursed worktable, and God knows what else—well, he had a few things to say about that. Laura Percy was meddling in his business, and he had to make her understand that *he* would draw the lines.

William started up the steps two at the time. Rounding the corner at the landing, though, he tripped, catching himself before going facedown on the stone stairs again. Turning, he eyed the missing step and made a mental note of having the blasted thing fixed today.

In the upper level, the corridor and the roof were in the same condition as William had seen yesterday morning. Oddly, he was almost relieved to find that his entire company of warriors was not on the roof—under Laura's direction—trying to patch the thing.

Remembering what she'd said earlier about placing Miriam in a chamber adjacent to hers, William decided to look at the room he'd once shared with his brothers.

He knew the place looked very different now. It had been dramatically altered in the last ten years, for Mildred had chosen to stay in this wing while the laird's chambers were being renovated for her and Thomas. Hearing this after coming back to Blackfearn Castle as laird, William had consciously chosen to let the wing rot. The damage from the storm the previous summer had done nothing to change his feelings.

But now, even though he wanted nothing to do with the child, he knew he couldn't leave her in a wing so badly in need of repairs.

The muffled voices of women came from the chamber. William stopped at the threshold and peered in.

A pile of old bedding straw lay in a heap on the floor. Accumulated dirt had been swept into the doorway, and a cloud of dust hung in the air. What furniture had been left in the chamber had all been pulled into the middle. A bucket of water was set by one wall, and another by the small fireplace jutting out from the far wall.

William looked at the two occupants in the room. Maire was hanging out the window, shaking a bedding sack, while the other woman knelt in the small hearth, her head up the chimney as she energetically scrubbed away with a rag she kept dipping into the bucket.

"And where might Mistress Laura be?"

Maire turned in surprise at the laird's voice, but the woman on all fours in the chimney, after freezing momentarily, appeared to crawl in farther.

"She—she—"

William followed Maire's nervous gaze as it flitted uncomfortably toward the hearth before quickly returning to him.

"I—I'll tell her ye're looking for her, master."

"No need. I believe I'll just keep looking until I find her." He motioned for Maire to leave the room, and with a quick curtsy the older woman dropped the sack and scurried out.

William waited for a few moments in the doorway, glancing with distaste at the meager furnishings of the room, waiting for the stubborn woman to give up and come out of the chimney. But Laura appeared content to stay there, keeping up her pretense of being someone else.

He stepped into the room and moved over to close the open window. Walking around the chamber, he looked closer at the furniture. As young lads he and Gilbert and Thomas all had slept very comfortably in this room. Guests of importance visiting Blackfearn Castle had been placed next door, in the room closest to the stairs leading down to the Great Hall.

Shaking off the memories of the past and trying to focus instead on the problem at hand, William's eyes rested on Laura Percy's firm behind sticking out of the open hearth. Erotic images flashed through his mind. By the devil, he didn't know, but she brought out the worst in him.

"'Tis a good thing you're cleaning up this room, lass. I was thinking of bringing Molly up here from the Three Cups Tavern, and this should please the wench very well."

He watched the woman's back stiffen. Moving across the chamber to the fireplace, William leaned one shoulder against the stone mantel. His boot rested close to the shapely calf protruding from the dress.

"Last time she was here, she had the cheek to complain about the laird's chamber. Too close to the Great Hall. Said between my grunting and her own moaning—going at it all night as we do—she'd feel better not stirring up the folk in the Hall."

William could almost feel her brain busily reeling, planning, devising a way to do him harm. No doubt she would

concoct something painful. He took a step back cautiously as
she began to back herself out of the hearth.

"You're not finished in there, are you, lass? I can still see
a speck of—"

The filthy, wet, soot-blackened rag caught him full in the
face and chest, silencing William Ross in a hurry. He looked
down in disgust as the rag dropped onto his foot. He was now
covered with grime.

Laura slowly rose to her feet and glanced at the man with
fire in her eyes. "Molly?"

"Mistress Percy?" he replied, eyeing her blackened face,
the filthy dress, the violet eyes that flashed with temper through
the soot covering her ivory skin. He fought back a smile. Even
as she was, the woman was absolutely stunning.

She pointed an accusing finger at his chest. "If you think
for one moment that I'm going through all this work so you
can place your mistress in this chamber . . ."

"Molly is not really my mistress, lass, just a wench from
the Three Cups. A man likes to have a woman now and again,
you know."

As she stared at him, his words sank in, and a look of
panic suddenly flickered across her face. He took a step toward her, and she retreated, holding a hand up to him.

"Wench or mistress, call her what you like. But she'll
not . . ." Laura backed around the furniture in the center of
the room as he continued to stalk her. "This chamber is being
prepared for your niece, and you are a rake and a villain and
a knave if you think—" She gasped as he caught her wrist in
his viselike grip. There was no getting away from him, but
she jutted her chin out pugnaciously. "You may be laird of
this castle, but I won't let you ruin—"

He tugged hard on her wrist, and she tumbled against his
chest. His mouth was on hers in an instant. Her one hand
clutched his tartan as he kissed her, and with a soft moan she
opened her lips beneath his. His tongue plundered the soft re-

cesses of her mouth, tasting her, pleasuring in the sweetness, daring her, challenging her to a recklessness that he was certain she had never known.

And it took only a moment before she rose to that challenge.

Laura arched against him, her tongue rubbing seductively against his own. Her hand came up, clutching his neck, forcing him to increase the pressure of his mouth. He took one of her breasts in his hand, kneading it, and she leaned into him, a moan again emanating from deep within her. He pressed his leg intimately between her legs, and her thighs locked on his own. As he moved against her, Laura's breaths shortened to soft whimpers.

He wanted her. He ached to have her. Sliding his hands over the firm curve of her buttocks, he lifted her higher on his thigh. Her mouth went lax for a moment, her head rolling to one side. Her breathing was now a series of mere gasps, and he pressed his mouth to her neck.

Her body was beginning to move as if in response to some inner rhythm. William slid one hand between their bodies, feeling the soft mound, stroking her, increasing the tempo. The layers of fabric were a hindrance, but he pressed on. Nipping her, leaning down and mouthing her breast through the thickness of the cloth, he encouraged her. And then, suddenly, she exploded with a frenzied cry of release.

Immediately covering her mouth with his own, he drew her tight against his chest. Kissing her deeply, he rocked her in his arms, relishing the incredible pleasure of having her come apart with such sweet passion.

She kissed him back, and her still burning fire was nearly enough to undo him. The bed was only a step away, her fevered body willing, his for the taking.

But then he realized he could not have her. Laura Percy did not deserve to lose her maidenhead to a wild, unmar-

riageable scoundrel like himself. Nay, she deserved nothing
less than marriage.

He couldn't do it. Not to this woman. Not now.

Drawing back, he broke the kiss, smiling at the way she
came dreamily after him, wanting more. But he couldn't give
her what she was after. She deserved far more.

He cupped her chin in his hand and held her in place. "Your
face is quite a sight."

Her eyes opened slowly, and even beneath all the soot, her
cheeks were inflamed with heat. "I—I'm . . ."

"Aye. You, lass."

As he looked into her face, she gathered herself together.
"I'm at a loss . . ." She grew even more crimson. "The way
I behaved! I don't understand!"

He placed both hands on her shoulders and met her misty
violet eyes. "Do not regret what has happened, lass. We simply have this—this *thing* between us." He let go of her and
abruptly stepped back, putting some distance between them.
He could not remain as close to her as he'd been. It would
be all too easy to pick up where they'd left off.

"What is this *thing*?"

He went around to the far side of the bed. More distance.
"They call it 'lust.' " It sounded a little harsh, even to his own
ears, but at this moment he would prefer temper over acqui-
escence.

"Is this . . . ?" Her face clouded over. "This is what you
share with Molly, I take it."

Damn the woman for looking this wounded—this beautiful. He walked to the window and yanked open the shutter,
letting in the frigid air. It had never been like this with Molly.
It had never been like this with anyone. Never before had any
semblance of thought come between desire and satisfaction.

"You don't answer, so I assume 'tis."

He should have corrected her, but he didn't. He couldn't,
since he was afraid as soon as he opened his mouth, he

wouldn't know when to shut it. There was a long silence before she spoke again.

"M'lord, I—I object to you putting Molly in this chamber."

He turned to her. "You can object all you want. I will do as I wish."

"I won't allow you to ruin it."

"Ruin what, Laura?"

"My plans."

"Your plans!" he repeated shortly, his frustration spilling out all at once. "Let me tell you something about your plans. They are not *my* plans. In fact, I do not have any plans. In fact, I hate plans. And I'm quite tired of you going around and passing off your plans as mine."

"I have done no such thing, but you are an incorrigible knave to retract your promises so quickly."

"I have not retracted what I told you. But you, on the other hand, have been quick to embellish on what I agreed to."

"I have done no such thing."

He pointed an accusing finger in her direction. "You call meddling in my business no such thing? Pawing through my worktable, organizing my chamber, using my name to accomplish what you believe needs to be done."

Her violet eyes flashed. Her cheeks glowed as she defended herself. "You must be absolutely blind if you cannot see that the little I have done was not to fulfill my own desires but the needs of your people. And if you paid more attention to being the laird you should be, you would have long ago seen to these matters yourself. Then, there would be no need of my, as you so absurdly call it, meddling."

"So you admit that you are meddling."

"I do not!"

"As a matter of fact, I would have taken care of all of this myself."

"When?" she asked him. "In another two years? And meanwhile, everyone is waiting. What about the immediate needs of your people? Or the needs of a child who is being sent here and put under your care?"

"I did not ask anyone to have her brought here. She should have stayed where she was."

"But she is not staying there. She is coming, and she has needs."

"Needs? You don't have to tell me. I know all about those needs." He took an impatient step toward the door and lifted his finger again in accusation. "The needs of a privileged woman—a brat—born and raised with all comforts that wealth can offer. Just like her mother. Aye, she had needs, too." He took another step toward the door. "Well, the wee chit can wither in this castle for all I care, for I will never aid another monster like Mildred. Never!"

As the laird turned to leave, his brain on fire with bitter memories, he saw Gilbert standing silently in the corridor, watching, listening. William pushed past his brother without a word.

Laura watched him go. Confused and hurt, she stared at the priest, a poker of hot iron buried deep in her belly.

Chapter 15

The gusts of wind howling through the kirk yard of Iron-cross Castle tore at the tall monk's cloak. Limping through the graves toward the vaults, he scowled darkly at his squinted-eyed companion.

"'Tis not your position to question me. Particularly regarding whom I choose to use in this quest."

"I meant no harm," the wiry priest quickly replied. "But knowing—having heard so many bloody tales of this pirate. I mean—the Blade of Barra is a name feared by anyone who has ever traveled in the west. I just—"

"He is a Knight of the Veil in addition to being a thief of the seas. He is as well known, to some, for his honor as for his cunning. He was chosen by those in his order because of that reputation, but he will yield to me because of his greed."

"So you trust him to get the treasure for you?"

A croaking noise rose from the monk's throat, a laugh devoid of mirth. The other man winced involuntarily at the sound.

"I trust him to get the maps. When it comes time to go after the Treasure of Tiberius, though, I will not trust the Angel Gabriel, himself."

"Who was Mildred?"

Gilbert Ross glanced over his shoulder down the empty corridor. There was no sign of William, who had disappeared only a moment earlier, carrying a lifetime of guilt on his shoulders. Before turning and meeting the young woman's troubled eyes, he thought hard about how to answer her question.

"She was Thomas's wife. The only child of Lord Herries of Hoddom. She was Miriam's mother."

Laura wrapped her hands tightly about her to contain the hurt she felt inside. She'd wanted to be of help. But she'd clearly touched a source of pain inside him. There was torment buried there that she'd never imagined, hidden beneath an exterior of reckless indifference. She took a deep breath and pressed on.

"What was she to William?"

Even as she blurted out the question, she knew she had no right to ask. William had made it clear that he despised her and her "meddling." She had no right to know.

The provost walked quietly into the chamber and went to the hearth. Standing there, he stared down into the bucket of filthy water on the floor.

"Years back, mistress, when we were young lads and Thomas came of age, William was sent first to the university at St. Andrew's and then to Lord Herries for his entry into the world. As the second son and dead set against a life in the church—a life I was planning on for myself—William's options were few. But his best chance lay in seeking a position in the king's service, in becoming a courtier or a politician—though neither of those things seemed to me to fit William's nature." The provost stopped, his blue eyes thoughtful as they rested on Laura. "William and Mildred were the same age. They were both at Hoddom Castle before 'twas arranged for Mildred to marry Thomas. Anything beyond that, mistress, should probably come from William himself."

She nodded in understanding, though she knew the Ross laird would never provide her with any more information than what she'd just been told. Perhaps, though, she had no need to know anything more.

"I believe he wishes for me to leave."

Gilbert made his way around the room, studying the furnishings. "You are making a difference, Laura. He needs you."

She shook her head adamantly. "I've overstepped my position. 'Twould be best if I were to return to St. Duthac's."

"And forsake the cause?"

Laura looked away from the provost's probing gaze. She searched for something to do with her hands. They were covered with soot, William's imprint on her wrist the only mark of white.

"I thought you were determined to stay and see that wee Miriam gets settled."

"She already has a good start. With the new steward installed here, and you here now as well, the laird has very little need for me at Blackfearn."

Deep inside, she wished it was different. She wanted to be allowed to stay. The usefulness she felt in doing things to improve castle life filled her up somehow. And if she wanted to be truly honest, the energy she felt race through her whenever she and William argued, the lightning bolts that set her ablaze whenever he touched her—the way he touched her—these things were everything she'd dreamed of and yet missed all of her life.

But now he wanted her gone, and that was reason enough to go.

She watched the provost's wide shoulders as he moved to the window and looked out for a long moment. He turned then and faced her.

"Laura, though my predecessor was the one who corresponded with your mother, I will still honor Nichola Percy's request *and* your request, and keep you at St. Duthac's for as long as you desire." He clasped his strong hands before him, a look of concern clouding his blue eyes. "But having received an additional letter from the earl of Athol and finding that there are . . . well, dangerous men following you and your sisters—"

"I don't have to go to St. Duthac." She blurted out immediately, remembering how helpless the nuns at Little Ferry had been. She could understand the provost's concern for his people. "I can go away, disappear to some forgotten convent in the mountains to the north."

Gilbert shook his head. "Nay, lass. That would not be the answer. Whoever these people are that are after your family, they will have no difficulty locating you wherever you go."

She felt the burning sensation again creeping into her middle. In the letter she had received from her sister, Catherine had suggested that Laura come and join her new family at Balvenie Castle. With the opening of the new school, Catherine had been adamant about needing the younger sister's help. But her sister was a dreamer, and though nothing would make Laura happier than being reunited with Catherine, their mother's orders needed to be obeyed as closely as possible. The main thing was that the three sisters were not to be together—not until such time as the Treasure of Tiberius was ready to be secured.

She turned helplessly to the provost. "Where do you suggest I go?"

Gilbert stared at his hands for a moment before looking up at Laura again. "I suggest that you marry. As things stand, with a husband and the protection he can offer—"

"Marry!" she repeated in confusion.

"Aye. Your eldest sister chose that path, and she is safely situated at Balvenie Castle."

Laura wrung her hands. "But she—she met the earl of Athol . . . and there must have been some time that passed. I'm certain that my mother would not have simply arranged a marriage for my sister."

Gilbert cocked an eyebrow. "Mistress, from what I've learned of their union, they were married the first night she arrived in the Highlands. In fact, the earl's men dragged a priest out of his bed in the middle of the night to bless the marriage at the earl's hunting lodge."

Laura's eyes rounded in surprise. Catherine had mentioned nothing about the hurried ceremony. She shook her head, though, and faced the provost. "Though such an action might have worked for my sister, it cannot work for me."

"And why is that, mistress?"

She started pacing the room. "Because we are different people." She stopped abruptly and met the man's questioning gaze. "Catherine's one wish was to open a school of her own. And she has already told me in her letter that the school is opening with her new husband's support. 'Twas easy for her to find her way."

"And you, Laura?"

She turned and paced the room again. "I need constant challenges. Things to plan and do. Certainly no husband would understand that in a wife. And there is surely no man out there who could possibly . . ." Her words trailed off.

"Would you allow me to act in your interest, mistress?"

"But I don't know anyone in the Highlands. I am half English. I—"

"Leave it to me, lass. Since I now know that you will at least consider marriage as an option, leave it to me to gather the names of some possible matches. No one will force you to accept someone unsuitable."

Gnawing her lip, Laura nodded resignedly and stared down again at the band of white around her dirty wrists. Perhaps finding a husband *was* the answer. Perhaps marrying a stranger would give her the chance to free herself from this maddening spell William Ross had cast on her.

"Now that we have a plan ahead of us," Gilbert stated, drawing Laura out of her silent brooding and leading her out the door, "there is no reason to waste time sending you back to the convent at St. Duthac's. You are safer here under

William's protection, for the time being, and in no time at all we will find you just the right husband. You'll see, we'll find just the right match."

A doomed match at best, she thought silently. But one that at least would release her from the unhappiness she was causing at Blackfearn Castle.

William knew he had to get outside of the confining walls of Blackfearn Castle. He knew he had to get away so he could breathe. So that he could think.

Taking Dread and leaving everything and everyone behind, he took to the snow-covered hills, riding south for hours. Pushing his steed up the rugged slopes of Meall Mor, William finally dismounted and walked through snow-encrusted bracken to the edge of a precipice. Below him, ice had formed on a narrow loch. Steep, craggy hills hemmed the frozen waters on two sides, and a mist rose over the frothy stream leading into the loch. Far to the south, the violet-gray peak of Ben Wyvis disappeared into a cloud.

He was in trouble. For so long he had struggled to drive the past from his mind. And yet there was no escape from it. And now this woman, this Laura Percy. His actions in that chamber in the east wing were more than troubling. What was the matter with him? She was a desirable woman; he wanted her. The old Will Ross would have just taken her. This new William couldn't, no matter how much he wanted her. He couldn't ruin her chances for something better, and God knew he did not deserve to keep her.

In the distance, clouds swept over the braes, blanketing them one moment, releasing them in the next.

All his life he had tried to turn his back on those things that plagued him, tormented him. But now, as he stood looking out where Ross and Munro land joined, running away no longer seemed like the right thing to do.

As he walked back to where Dread stood patiently watching him, thoughts of Laura continued to crowd his brain. She knew what was important. With her violet eyes flashing, her words had battered down the thick wall of indifference he'd constructed so many years ago around his heart. For the first time in years he had made himself see the truth—and his own cowardice.

Mounting Dread, William spurred his horse over the frozen and uneven ground. By St. Andrew, there were changes that needed to be made. Not so much for himself, but for his people, his clan.

His people. His clan. He silently repeated those words to himself. He had responsibilities. Thomas was dead! Dead. Dead. Dead. Gilbert was a priest who had his own responsibilities. Everything had been left to him. His people. His clan. And as Laura had said so pointedly, he'd been neglecting them.

He would make a change, he vowed. He would work on improving the castle and the clan's holdings. He would do his best for his people.

But he would do it in *his* way. Laura's methodical way of organizing—of putting in order everything and everyone around her—was not his way. He would not suffocate himself trying to be something he was not.

He turned Dread's head back toward Blackfearn Castle.

If he were to have any peace of mind, she would have to leave. Having her this close was more than a distraction, it was gunpowder by a lit torch. Whether it be their desires or their tempers, her nearness made them both dangerous, explosively so.

William thought of his brother staying at Blackfearn Castle. He would speak to him when he got back. Gilbert had sent her here to start with; he could take her away. The wee, fiery planner had to go away. It was as simple as that. It was their only sure salvation.

But as he rode back to the keep, William had a nagging feeling that he'd just concocted a plan.

He had chosen a crusader's life. He no longer carried a weapon. But when it came to fighting the battle of right and wrong, of pursuing the enemies of justice, Gilbert Ross was the fiercest of warriors.

To Gilbert's surprise, the pigeonholes in the cabinet behind his brother's worktable had been recently dusted. It took only a moment to find the scroll he was searching for.

Drawing it out, he untied the black ribbon and unrolled the old thick vellum on the worktable. He remembered quite vividly when he and William had drawn this map. Father Francis had provided maps of the coastline for them, and they had gleaned every scrap of information they could from every priest, merchant, warrior, and sailor that they could find. From York to the Orkneys and from the Western Isles to Aberdeen, the map was as complete as they had been able to make it. It had every castle, burgh, abbey, and town they had ever heard of. Every river, loch, mountain, and glen had been included, as well as every clan.

It had taken them months to complete, and Gilbert smiled at how hard the two of them had worked at it. Father Francis had grudgingly called it a treasure.

Placing his candlestick carefully in the center, the provost leaned over the map, his eyes perusing every line on the large sheet of vellum. There was a battle brewing in the castle, and he was not about to be left out of it.

Laura, confining herself to that drafty chamber in the east wing, wanted out. She'd spoken to him again tonight. After considering all of her options, she'd said, she had decided to marry whomever Gilbert thought fit, as long as it could be arranged expeditiously.

William had stormed into the castle earlier in the afternoon with his own demands. The woman had to go, he'd demanded.

Gilbert could send her away, take her away, or sell her to the Turks if he wanted to. Whatever had to be done, William wanted never to have to face the Englishwoman again.

Though Gilbert was no expert, it certainly sounded like love to him.

Why, the two had been acting like two well-matched armies poised and ready to fight. And now they wanted to withdraw? Well, Gilbert had already spent too many hours praying and planning to allow that. Engage they would, if he had anything to do with it.

Before Laura and William had been aware of his presence, he'd witnessed the heat between them. By St. Duthac, he had seen sparks flying about that room as they argued.

He might be a priest, but he was also a man. And he recognized the signs of two people desperately attracted to one another. It was so obvious. They couldn't hide it. The curious smudges of soot on each of their faces. Laura's swollen lips. Her flushed face. William's stormy frustration.

There was no other choice in the matter. His task was simply to keep them together. Let them butt heads. Let them shed blood if need be—if that was what it took to make each see the value in the other. They were a perfect match, and it was up to Gilbert to use every divine—and earthly—means to make them realize the truth.

Symon, the new steward, entered the laird's work room, and Gilbert lifted his eyes from the map.

Ah, the provost thought, eyeing the balding head and bowed legs of the man, the first warrior recruit for his own earthly company.

"The bedchamber in the east wing is prepared for your niece's arrival."

Gilbert nodded in approval. "Did you find my brother?"

The man stepped closer. "The laird said he will be joining you here, as you requested, but I saw him heading for the kitchen."

Upon seeing Gilbert's raised eyebrows, the elder man continued. "I cannot say for sure, but I believe the master went to congratulate Chonny on the meal. 'Twas the best I've had since arriving."

A change indeed, Gilbert thought pleasantly. "And Mistress Laura?"

"She approved of your niece's chamber after the women were done with it, and then she returned to her own room to take her supper there."

Gilbert glanced at the doorway, making certain William was not within earshot. "Did you convey my wishes to her?"

Symon nodded. "I am to go after her when the time comes."

"Well done." Gilbert nodded, leaning again over the map at the sound of his brother's steps approaching the laird's chamber.

The steward stepped back respectfully as William strode in. The Ross cast a curious glance at his brother intently studying the map.

"Excuse me, laird," said Symon. "If you would like, I can complete that letter to the bishop tonight."

William moved to the desk and picked up a neatly folded parchment and handed it to the steward. After his man left the room, the Highlander turned to Gilbert.

"What are you planning, my saintly brother? A raid?"

Without looking up, Gilbert moved the candle to another place on the map. "Nay, just refreshing my memory regarding some of the neighboring lairds."

Puzzled and yet interested, William stared down at the vellum as well.

Gilbert's long, slender finger pointed at the mark of a castle on the map. "What do you think of the MacKays?"

William frowned at his brother. "The MacKays are north of the Sutherlands. What do you want to know?"

"Their laird, wasn't he widowed a year back?"

William's blue eyes narrowed as they met his brother's. "I do not recall hearing anything of that."

Gilbert shook his head and turned his attention back to the map. "MacKenzie! Now, they have a fine stretch of land to your west and a brace of goodly sons, if I recall. What was the name of the firstborn?"

"Neil."

"Aye, Neil MacKenzie. He is from good blood and family and fortune. He must certainly be ready for a wife."

William planted both hands on the table and growled at his brother. "Neil MacKenzie may be fifteen years old, if that. What are you about, Gilbert?"

The provost shook his head with disappointment and stared again at the map. "Fifteen might be a wee young for the lass."

"What lass?"

"Laura, of course." Gilbert didn't lift his eyes off the vellum. "She and I talked, and we both agreed that rather than sending her back to St. Duthac's Shrine—where she would be more exposed to the dangers of those pursuing her—we should just find her a husband."

"A husband!" William gave a bitter laugh, straightening from the table and stalking to the fireplace. "The poor soul. I say, 'twould be best if you just send her back to her own people. Let *them* find a match for her."

"Send her south?" Gilbert replied, disbelief evident in his voice. "So she can lose her head to the English king, as her father lost his?"

The laird's face creased into a frown. "Och, you know I— I don't wish any harm to befall her."

"Good. Then you can help me find her a suitable husband, since the lass is eager to be out of Blackfearn Castle." Gilbert turned his attention once again to the map. "Once we decide on a suitable list of candidates, then I will send each one a letter, explaining what I can of her condition. She has no dowry as it stands now, half English, and she comes from a family rife with daughters. But she's young, at least, from noble blood, and between her name and education and looks . . ." Gilbert turned and found William by the hearth, staring into the fire. "Do you think she has good looks?"

"You have eyes. What do you think?"

The provost shook his head. "I think most would consider her too thin. She is a wee thing, after all, and that will also be an obstacle, considering the size of our bairns. And then there are her eyes. Too large, don't you think so, William?"

"There is nothing wrong with her eyes," the laird snapped, walking to the table.

"A strange color."

William snorted angrily. "They are not strange. The blasted things are the shade of heather before it opens, if you must know."

Gilbert cocked an eyebrow and focused again on the map. "Frasers!" he said after a moment. "Dounie Castle would be, what, three day's ride to her sister?"

"He is already betrothed."

"Pardon me?"

"Jamie Fraser is marrying in the spring. And unless you want to start bloodshed again between the MacKintosh and the Fraser, I say it would be safer if you did nothing to interfere with that match."

Gilbert glanced again at William, who appeared to be looking over the castle's ledger book by the light of the fire. A light tap at the door attracted both men's gazes, and as Symon entered carrying a pitcher of ale and two cups, the provost gestured toward the worktable. Without a word the steward turned and left the chamber, leaving the door ajar.

Gilbert was silent for a few moments before he spoke again. "How about the MacLeans?"

William closed the ledger book and placed it in the cabinet. "What about them?"

"You and Wyntoun spent a great deal of time together at Lord Herries's holding."

"Aye, so what of it?" William stood still, a deep frown on his face.

Gilbert waited, watching his brother's frozen stance. "His father is getting on in years. Duart Castle is a fine holding, by all accounts. From everything I hear of him—from all that you yourself have told me—Wyntoun MacLean is a good man."

"Aye, as far as rogues go. But he's no marrying man, to my thinking. He certainly wouldn't stand for an arranged match."

"He is escorting little Miriam here. Since he is coming, it does not have to be arranged. Or at least, we won't present it to him as such."

William turned an accusing eye on Gilbert. "What are you going to do? Trick him into marrying the woman?"

"There will be no tricks necessary. None but Laura Percy's natural charms."

"You mean her biting tongue?"

"Some men find that charming, and I believe you yourself would—" Gilbert ceased, seeing the young woman standing in the doorway. She was staring at William but then looked away, and the provost smiled broadly as he extended a hand in welcome. "I'm so glad you're here, mistress. William and I were just discussing the merits of—"

"I heard. I could not help overhearing . . . some of your conversation." She stepped into the room and took the proffered chair by the worktable.

Gilbert noted with some amusement that William didn't seem to be able to take his eyes off her face, though she never spared the laird another glance.

"As you may have heard us speaking of him, Wyntoun MacLean is the man that William and I agree would be a very suitable—"

"He is *not* my recommendation," the Ross laird asserted sharply.

"You were saying, Provost." Laura moved in the chair, turning away from the laird.

"Sir Wyntoun MacLean. He will one day soon be laird of Duart Castle in the Western Isles. A young man of . . . well, at William's age, he is a rather accomplished fellow, educated and wealthy. He is a fairly handsome man, too, wouldn't you say, brother?" He ignored the snort from the far side of the chamber. "As I was saying, Sir Wyntoun could be quite suitable for a lady of your background."

She simply nodded and stared down at the fingers entwined in her lap.

"Another advantage in recommending Wyntoun is that he is the one given the charge of bringing our niece here from Hoddom Castle. So, my suggestion is this, we wait until he arrives. Since William will naturally extend his old friend an invitation to stay through Christmastide"—there was another snort that Gilbert let go by—"you'll have ample opportunity to study the man and decide for yourself if he would prove a good match."

Laura's violet-blue eyes lifted and watched the laird as he started pacing the far end of the chamber.

"And if your opinion is favorable—which I am certain 'twill be—then William and I will approach Wyntoun on your behalf."

"I'll not be doing any approaching. Trust me on that."

"*I* will speak with him if the need arises, mistress," Gilbert said calmly, pausing to glower at his brother. "And I can tell you this, after meeting you, Sir Wyntoun will be honored to take you as his wife."

"Aye," William grumbled. "To add to the three or four the blackguard already has."

The provost fought back a smile. That marriage would happen only if his thick-headed brother continued to deny the value of this precious pearl.

And that was a loss, Gilbert thought, which would suit no one.

Chapter 16

One look into the face of the child and William Ross knew. He had known it before—in truth, he had known it all along—but he had never faced it. As he stood there, a nearly uncontrollable urge to leave his newly arrived guests took hold of him. All he wanted right now was to storm out of that Hall and find a place to brood in solitude. Instead, he stood his ground and scowled as Miriam studied him, her gaze doubtful and unsure.

"Uncle!" the young girl murmured softly, dropping a small curtsy to the laird.

William whirled impatiently on his approaching steward. "Where is that blasted brother of mine?"

"He is in the chapel saying Mass, m'lord. It will be some time, I fear."

With a disgusted look he turned to Wyntoun MacLean, who was standing with a grin on his face behind the little girl. "And how was your journey?"

"It went very well, William, thank you. Except for having to leave your niece's sick lady-in-waiting at a convent two days after we left, the journey was quite uneventful, in fact."

"Glad to hear it. We'll get you something to eat, and you can tell me about it in detail." William caught a glimpse of weariness in Miriam's face and the guilt crept back, flooding him with an icy chill. He turned to the steward. "Take her to

the east wing, and tell Mistress Laura she is here. Then get
the lass fed."

Symon, nodding agreeably at the child, led her out of the
Hall with young Robbie dragging a small traveling chest behind them.

"And who is this Mistress Laura?" Wyntoun asked with
interest, following William to the dais before the great fireplace.

"A guest. More than that, you dog-faced scoundrel, you'd
do better not knowing."

"Will, my friend, you sound like a man who is hiding something. I'm suddenly looking forward to meeting this mystery
maiden."

It was impossible not to have heard the commotion surrounding the arriving company. Laura was already in the corridor by the little girl's chamber when the steward brought
Miriam up.

She was a wee thing, and young. But it was not her size
or age that took Laura initially by surprise. It was the sadness that shone clearly in the beautiful blue eyes. Laura looked
up and found Symon's expression clouded with concern as
well.

"Greetings, Miriam," Laura said gently, placing a hand on
the child's shoulder as the steward and Robbie went around
them with the girl's chest. "I'm Laura Percy, and I cannot tell
you how happy I am that you're here at last."

The girl's chin dropped to her chest as Laura watched a
couple of tears roll down incredibly long lashes onto pale
cheeks.

"Are you—are you my uncle's wife?"

"Nay! I'm only a wicked old ghost who haunts this wing."

Miriam's face immediately lifted in shock, and Laura
smiled, crouching until they were face to face.

"I am not really."

"I did not think so," the young girl whispered, wiping her wet face with the back of one hand. "I don't remember the castle too well from the last time I was here, but I would never have forgotten a ghost, wicked or not."

"How long have you been away, Miriam?"

"They tell me about two and a half years. But I'm seven now and, having been only four and a half then, I'm afraid there is a great deal I've forgotten."

"You are a smart girl to know how old you were two and a half years ago."

Miriam shrugged her shoulders. "It wasn't very difficult. I asked Sir Wyntoun, and he told me."

Laura smiled and rose to her feet, stretching a hand out to the young girl. Miriam hesitantly took it. "Well, I've been here less than a fortnight, and there is a great deal about this keep that I'm hoping you will be able to help me with."

"I will if I can, mistress." Miriam nodded and let herself be led inside the prepared bedchamber. The steward was just done tucking her belongings away, and Robbie was standing with the empty chest, eyeing the girl.

Symon herded the boy out of the room. "I'll send Maire up with something for the lass to eat."

Laura nodded in approval and stood by the door as the older man left the two of them alone. Miriam walked slowly around the room, touching the covering on the bed, feeling the coarseness of the large wood chest, peering out the narrow window into the growing dusk, even leaning down and checking under the bed. She finally came to a stop by Laura. "Is this where I sleep?"

The young woman nodded. "This is your room. Are you pleased?"

"Where do you sleep?"

"Next door. The last room in the corridor."

Miriam poked her head out the doorway and glanced at

the closed door of Laura's room. "Where does my uncle sleep?"

"I assume he would sleep in the laird's chambers, though I'm certain I don't know. You may have seen the door leading to it from the Great Hall."

"How about the provost? He is my uncle, too, but Sir Wyntoun said 'tis more polite if I call him 'Provost.' "

Laura could only guess at where the provost was staying. "Now that you mention it, I think the provost may be staying in the laird's chambers."

"What about Sir Wyntoun? Where will he be?"

Laura looked down at the deep blue eyes and found them quite serious. "Perhaps in the Great Hall? Or with the castle's warriors? I believe there are quarters for them above the stables."

"And the steward?"

"In the steward's quarters?"

"Are there any warriors that sleep in the castle?"

"Aye. Some sleep in the Great Hall, and some sleep out by the castle gate." Laura bit her bottom lip to suppress a smile and knelt again before the child. "Why not let me help you take off your traveling cloak and get out of those wet shoes, and you can tell me why 'tis so important for you to know where everyone sleeps at Blackfearn Castle."

Miriam paused for a moment before nodding hesitantly and letting herself be led into the middle of the room.

The wool cloak was wet through, and after removing it Laura found the child's dress damp and cold as well. Just then Maire walked in with a tray of food, and—before Miriam had an opportunity to ask the older woman where she slept—Laura sent her out again with directions for more peat for the fire, lots of hot water, and a tub deep enough for the child to bathe in.

A short time later, sitting in the steaming water as Laura washed her hair, the young girl turned the object of her curiosity from the castle's sleeping arrangements to Laura's background.

"If you're not my uncle's wife, then are you his intended?"

"Nay, Miriam, I am not."

"The provost's intended?"

Laura cast a threatening glare at a chuckling Maire, who was sitting cozily before the hearth and warming a blanket to wrap the child in. "The provost is a priest, Miriam. He cannot have a wife."

"Oh!" The young girl shook her wet hands, spraying more water on Laura's already wet dress. "Are you the steward's wife, then?"

"I am nobody's wife." Laura poured some warm water on the child's head and smiled. "I am only a guest."

"But that's not good."

"And why is that?" Laura took the large blanket from Maire.

"Because it means you'll be leaving. Just as Sir Wyntoun will be leaving." She stood up with Laura's encouragement and stepped out of the tub. Laura wrapped the blanket around her, patting the girl dry. "And the provost will be returning to St. Duthac's, and I'll be left all alone."

"You will no longer be alone, Miriam. You'll be living with your uncle. Blackfearn Castle is your home."

Tears pooled again in the blue eyes.

"What's wrong?" Laura gathered the young child into her arms.

"My uncle!" Miriam hiccuped softly. "I do not think he wants me be staying here with him."

"Of course he does."

She shook her head adamantly. "I know it. Today when we arrived, he couldn't even bear to look at me. He doesn't want me, just as my grandsire did not want me."

"Nay, 'tis not true. None of it." Laura's comforting hush did nothing to stem the flow of tears. She placed a soft kiss on the girl's temple. But the soft sobs continued. Maire shook her graying head ruefully as she stood up and hurried from the room, and Laura had a sickening feeling that there was perhaps some truth in what Miriam had said.

The large fire in the hearth seemed to be sucking every breath of air out of the laird's work room. William glanced at the open window.

The visitor continued to ramble on with his news of Hoddom Castle and the disharmony that seemed to be tearing the ancient holding apart. Lord Herries, old and infirm, hadn't the strength to keep his distant relatives in line, and they had already begun growling and snapping like animals, waiting for the old laird to die.

Wyntoun lowered his voice. He knew that the old man was concerned that more than one of the jackals might take it into his head that controlling the granddaughter would mean controlling Hoddom Castle and its vast holdings.

Wyntoun MacLean continued to talk. Gilbert continued to listen. William continued to scowl at the two knaves sitting with him.

The no-good provost—damned do-gooder priest and treacherous brother that he was—had mentioned Laura's name seven times in the course of the short conversation already. Seven times!

William tore his scorching gaze off of Gilbert. Related by blood, there was only so much harm he could bring on the son of a bitch.

Sir Wyntoun MacLean was a different matter. The laird's scowl darkened as he assessed his foe—his former friend—more closely.

The filthy cur was an educated man. But William knew he could hold his own when it came to learning. After all, the two first met at St. Andrew's before going together to Hoddom Castle.

The bastard was also a well-spoken man. William decided

that he could be, too—depending on the circumstance and whether he put his mind to the task and if he didn't lose his patience.

The miserable bugger could probably be considered a patient man. And an orderly man. And a planner by nature. William frowned more deeply.

But the worst was that in the eyes of an innocent, unsuspecting lass, Wyntoun MacLean would probably be considered a handsome man. Green eyes. Short hair the color of night. A lean, muscular face unmarked by scars.

So far. But it was still early in the day.

William felt anger prickling beneath his skin as the thought presented itself how damned suitable a couple Laura and Wyntoun would make, regardless of their flaws.

He rose restlessly to his feet and stalked toward the window, leaning against it and watching Gilbert and the visitor. Casually, he measured his enemy.

The next MacLean laird was a tall man, but William was taller. And the laird knew he was fast. William, however, had always been faster. He was lethal with a sword, but William was more than ready to match his own skills with Wyntoun's.

"As I was saying before, there is so much of a resemblance between Miriam's situation and what Laura Percy left behind—"

Eight times. "Ready to go out into the training yard?"

Gilbert's brow shot up in confusion.

Wyntoun's head turned in surprise. "The training yard?"

"Aye. You've done nothing but sit on your lazy arse for God knows how long. You must be aching for action. A good fight. Something to cleanse the body and soul and harden up the paunch you've started to show."

The note of challenge was evident in William's voice. Their guest rose to his feet with a hearty laugh. "I can see you're hungry for more of the battering I used to give you in the old days."

" 'Twas the other way around, you blackguard, if I remember rightly."

" 'Tis no surprise you don't remember, considering all the dings you took to the head. Why, I—"

"Stop right there," Gilbert ordered, jumping to his feet. "The two of you can stop right now. I have asked Mistress Laura to join us."

Nine times.

"Right now, you pock-faced baboon." The laird slapped his guest's shoulder a little more soundly than hospitality normally called for. "Unless, of course, you've become too fragile in your old age and cannot stomach a good brawl in the yard."

"This cattle-thieving, whore-mongering brother of yours is giving me no other choice, Provost."

"William," Gilbert stormed, "can this not wait for later? Mistress Laura should be down—"

"On your way, snake." Ignoring his brother's distress, William gave the knight a "friendly" shove toward the door. "And I promise to take it easy on you this morning."

Of course, William thought, nothing would give him more pleasure than breaking that straight nose of his old friend. Except perhaps planting a few bruises in the man's brown and handsome face. Or perhaps simply hammering the powerful body of his opponent to a bloody pulp.

As the two strode across the Great Hall with Gilbert sputtering from behind, William realized that he was planning. Certainly, Laura would approve of that.

True, he was planning to be perfectly vile to his guest. And it was also true that once he was done giving Wyntoun MacLean a severe beating, he planned to be totally inhospitable. But at least, William thought grimly, he was planning. And the sooner Sir Wyntoun MacLean carried through on *his* plans to leave Blackfearn Castle for the Western Isles, the better.

William Ross was tired of entertaining.

Chapter 17

It was well past the serving time for the meal when Laura finally left the Great Hall and headed for the training yard. Leaving little Miriam with her uncle, the provost, at the dais, the young woman decided that there would be no better time than this to discuss with William just how he planned to treat the vulnerable child.

Miriam was convinced that she was not welcome at Blackfearn Castle. Worse than that, she was determined that she was neither wanted nor loved by her uncle, the laird. And whatever kin she'd left behind at Hoddom Castle, Laura was certain that Miriam had not been cared for there as she should have been, either. To the little girl, not saying good-bye to her grandsire had been nearly crushing. And from what Laura could ascertain, the old man simply had not had time to see his own granddaughter off.

Well, that wasn't going to happen here, Laura thought decisively as she stormed out of the Hall. Not if she had anything to do with it.

Laura knew she had just a few days left at Blackfearn Castle. If nothing else, though, if she could just start the uncle and niece off on the right foot—if she could just make William understand the ways of dealing with a wee one should not be mixed with whatever problem he might have had with the mother—then Laura could feel that her stay had been worthwhile.

As Laura approached the training yard, her eyes scanned the backs of the warriors standing and watching two combatants inside the circle. The younger lads that she could usually see scurrying about from her window were standing and watching as well. The ringing clang of metal on metal filled the air, punctuated by shouts and laughter from the onlookers.

Surely, she thought, this would be a good place to talk. With all these men about, she had a far better chance of controlling her distressingly unruly passions.

She and William both agreed. Laura had to leave. She had to marry someone soon. There was no reason to tempt fate and continually put themselves in dangerous situations where neither could control the burgeoning lust that seemed to overwhelm them so.

Lust! She repeated the ugly word in her mind. Lust is what he'd called it.

Moving closer to the group, Laura searched the warriors for the laird. She couldn't find him. Peering through the group, though, her eyes were immediately drawn to the flashing arcs of the long swords as the two warriors in the circle fought.

Watching this type of training from the safety of her room was so different from being right here, so close. She circled around the group, lifting herself on her toes, trying to get a better view of the opponents. No one seemed aware of her. None of them appeared willing to move an inch to give her a clear view.

A cheer rang out from the men. Then a cry of disapproval at the very moment she broke through the crowd. A sword tumbled to the edge of the circle, coming to rest only inches from her foot. Without thinking, she bent down and picked up the weapon. Her arm almost fell off from the sheer weight of the sword. Embarrassed, though, at the sight of dozens of eyes turning and staring, Laura hefted the weapon using two hands.

The open circle lay before her now, giving her a clear view of the two men, dressed only in their kilts, poised dangerously in the center. Laura's eyes found William Ross first. Unarmed and bleeding slightly from a cut across his chest, the Ross laird was staring fiercely at his foe.

Summoning all of her strength not to run to him, she instead turned her eyes on the opponent. It was a man she'd never seen. A dark-haired giant of a man with blood running from his nose. The fighter looked even more dangerous than William at the moment, standing with his long sword pointing directly at the Ross laird.

Neither man noticed her presence as the stranger shoved the point of the weapon toward William's chest. Laura gasped as the Ross laird spun away from the attack. But before William could recover, the stranger pressed forward. In an instant William was on his back, the swarthy giant's sword rising above him for the death blow.

With a quickness that would have made her sister Adrianne proud, Laura charged the stranger, long sword lifted as high as she could manage, the point pressing into the top of the man's buttocks.

"Stop or I'll kill you!"

A long moment of silence hung in the air. Then a burst of laughter rang out in the yard.

"So, Will," the man growled, laughing loudly but not taking his eyes from the fallen laird, "you now have women to come to your rescue."

Laura didn't know where the blow came from. One moment the stranger was dismissing her threat, and the next he was doubled over, clutching something below his belt in pain and gasping for breath.

The point of the heavy sword in her hand hit the ground, and in an instant William was standing and facing her.

With a curt shout from him, the gathered men started to disperse, still laughing at the scene they'd witnessed. Edward and some strangers were helping the other man to his feet, but Laura kept her eyes on William's glowering face. Turning the hilt of the sword toward him, she winced as he snatched it none too gently from her. He glanced over his shoulder at his slowly rising opponent.

"I am so sorry," she murmured. "My—my intention was not to embarrass you. I'm certain that it must have looked as if I . . . well, I thought I . . ." Her words trailed off.

He opened his mouth to say something and then snapped it shut. When he spoke, she could hear the steely control in his voice. "What exactly were you thinking of when you raised this weapon?"

Laura avoided his glare and glanced instead down at the thin cut on his imposing chest. It was still bleeding. She then looked at a scratch on his powerful biceps. She could feel the heat emanating from his flesh. How could she possibly think, never mind talk, so close to a body this beautiful?

Her voice was barely a squeak. "I—I tried to save you."

"By pointing a sword at the man's arse?"

"I would have done better if I could. But the bloody thing was too heavy." Realizing that something had changed in his tone, she hesitantly looked up into his blue eyes. He'd been barking as if he was angry, but in those eyes she saw other things. Surprising things. Amusement. Affection even.

"Don't you think that if I was in real danger, that circle of Ross men would have had a better chance of coming to my defense?"

A weak smile broke on her lips as she shook her head. "I guess I acted on—on impulse."

His eyes narrowed. She felt herself openly blushing as his intense gaze caressed her face—his eyes resting on her lips. "You? Laura Percy? Acting on impulse?"

"A weakness, I know." She shrugged slightly, returning some of his close scrutiny by letting her eyes study the chiseled planes of his face, dropping lower to his neck, to his chest. She wanted to touch that wound, but she forced herself to look back into his face. "You've been a very bad influence."

She saw his hands tighten around the hilt of the sword. The point was planted in the ground between his feet. Desire, potent and unmistakable, had crept into his gaze. She felt heat spreading through her body.

She had been flirting with him. How was it that her morals had become totally ruined?

"I—if . . . the reason . . ." She touched an impatient hand to her brow to clear her mind. He continued to watch with amusement as she struggled. "I need a private audience with you."

"I agree completely." He raised one of his brows with a devilish look, and Laura sensed that the man was purposely misconstruing her words. "Indeed, lass. I believe we should see to it right away."

Feeling herself become completely flustered, she shook her head. "I mean, about your niece and—"

"William! By the Cross, man, how long do I have to wait before you remember your manners and introduce me properly to this warlike lass?"

The Ross's face immediately clouded over. He did not take his eyes from Laura's face, though, as he responded roughly. "How long are you planning to live, blackguard?"

Laura started with surprise at William's comment, but then turned to the approaching stranger. With a linen shirt pulled over his bare chest and a wry smile brightening the man's handsome face, the newcomer—seemingly recovered—looked far less menacing than he had a few moments before.

"Sir Wyntoun MacLean, mistress, at your service." Turning his back on the Ross laird, the newcomer put himself directly between them. "And is it safe to assume that you are Mistress Percy, the young woman about whom I have heard so much already?"

Laura found her hand already in the man's grasp. A bright and intelligent pair of green eyes looked down at her.

"You are correct regarding who I am, sir, but I cannot bring myself to say that 'tis entirely safe. In fact, I must beg you to forgive me for what just occurred. I'm afraid I misjudged the situation completely."

Wyntoun flashed a set of even white teeth. "Done! Forgotten. It takes considerable courage to try and rescue such a defenseless man."

Ignoring the obscene utterance behind him, the grinning knight took Laura's arm, directing her toward the Great Hall. The man continued to talk, and as Laura was led away, she glanced several times over her shoulder for William Ross.

He remained standing and watching them, the point of the sword still buried in the half-frozen earth, his expression openly displaying his displeasure.

William sat back and rubbed his eyes. All that was left was a number of letters that needed to be answered. He sorted them once again and added them to the work that was ready for Symon to complete.

"Never mind your eyes. You are ruining your reputation, brother, staying up so late and working so diligently."

William could manage only a halfhearted snarl at the priest standing in the open doorway. Gilbert wandered into the chamber, his giant dog Willie trailing in behind his master.

"Charming host that you are," the provost said, his voice heavy with irony, "when you left the Great Hall so early, Wyntoun and I became concerned."

"The hell with Wyntoun. When is the son of a bitch leaving anyway?"

"Leaving? Why, he's only just arrived." The priest sat in a chair by the hearth, the dog curling up at his feet. "And when I asked him if he could stay here at Blackfearn Castle at least through Christmastide—"

"What the devil for? He has his own kin in the Western Isles. I think he should get back on the road tomorrow."

"William, I cannot believe you are being so stubborn, considering how well things are progressing."

"What things?" the laird snapped.

"Things." Gilbert lowered his voice, glancing in the direction of the open door. "Between Laura and Wyntoun."

William stood up abruptly, nearly knocking his heavy chair over behind him. "She left the hall with Miriam long before I did. How could *things* progress when she wasn't there?"

Gilbert folded his hands in his lap and smiled contentedly. "She is charming company for dinner. Enchanting, you might say."

"I wouldn't know. Ever since the woman has been here at Blackfearn Castle, she has not once taken a meal in the Great Hall . . . until tonight." And to punish him for not inviting her sooner, William thought sullenly, the blasted woman even had to take the seat between Gilbert and MacLean.

Aye, punishing him. Close enough to torment him with a glimpse now and then of her lovely face, of her violet eyes occasionally seeking him out. Far enough away, though, that he could not make out the exchange of conversation, other than a laugh or two, between her and that dog Wyntoun. The supper had been a disaster for the laird.

Thankfully, the child sitting quietly at William's side had early on shown signs of drowsiness, and Laura had excused herself and Miriam, and the two had withdrawn for the night.

It had not been long after that William had retired as well, his mood too foul to enjoy the entertainment of the players who had stopped for the night on their way to Inverness. He left the Hall, disappearing into his work room.

He had to admit, taking refuge in work was indeed a first for him.

"Wyntoun is escorting Laura to the chapel tomorrow for the morning service."

Focusing his attention back on his brother, William moved from behind the table. "What other arrangements have been made?"

"You don't expect that I would eavesdrop, now, do you, brother?"

"I expect far worse from you, you interfering toad. What other *things* were discussed?"

"Well, as a matter of fact, they made no other appointments that I could hear, but the beauty of the Western Isles was a subject of great interest, it seems. Wyntoun spoke a great deal of Duart Castle, mentioning even the advancing age of his father. 'Twas quite promising, I thought."

"And did he bring up his need for a wife and heirs?" William glared at his brother's dog. "By St. Andrew, Gilbert, why don't you just bring your damned horse in here? The blasted thing would take up less space than that lazy beast."

Willie raised his broad head, gazed up at the laird, then yawned and rolled onto his side.

"Och," the Highlander breathed disgustedly, shaking his head as he leaned back against the table. "What I'd really be interested in knowing is whether the charming Sir Wyntoun mentioned anything of his pastime of terrorizing the merchant trade with his ships on the west coast."

"That would have been too much telling for the first day, I should think."

William snorted in disgust and headed for the door. "Aye, far too much, I should think."

"Retiring, brother?"

"Aye! 'Tis wearying being so damned charming all the time."

She liked Mistress Laura. She was much nicer than Nanna Jean.

Thinking of her old lady-in-waiting that they had left behind, Miriam said a silent prayer for the sick woman, even though she had a strong feeling that Nanna Jean's illness had gotten immediately worse the moment they got out of sight of home and her old sister.

Miriam opened one eye and looked sleepily at Mistress Laura. The gentle way that the Englishwoman tucked her into bed had been a lovely change. The attention that she was receiving at Laura's hands was far more than she ever remembered.

Tucked into the large bed, Miriam found herself getting gradually more comfortable, and sleep was creeping up on her. And yet the little girl did not want to lose sight of the young woman sitting on the small chair by the hearth, holding a book—rather than needlework or wool—in her lap.

The happiness that must exist in fairyland can surely not be better than this. I am safe here, Miriam thought, images of Laura and the laird floating in her sleepy head.

With the slow onset of her dreams, she almost felt her hand slipping into her uncle's strong one. She saw him looking down and giving her an approving nod, a gentle smile softening the blue eyes that looked so much like her own.

Miriam nestled deeper in the covers and dreamed. Dreamed of family, a home where she was wanted, and happiness.

Laura looked over at the beautiful face of the young girl as she slept. Closing the book on her lap, she planted her elbows on her knees and propped her chin on her hands.

There were too many ghosts casting their shadows over the child's life. There were too many uncertainties she had already grown accustomed to enduring.

Laura had intended to talk to William about this matter at noon, and she frowned, thinking of the lameness of the effort. She'd certainly ended up making a fool of herself in attempting to save his life.

During dinner she had watched William's response to the little girl sitting at his side. It hurt her that he had shown so little interest. He had simply sat with that gold coin rolling eternally over his knuckles, the child watching him intently. With the exception of noticing Miriam when she had finally almost fallen asleep in her chair, there had not been many spoken words. No shared enjoyment of the meal. Only silence.

Well, Laura thought, she would try to speak to him again tomorrow. And this time she planned to succeed.

Laura rose to her feet and moved to the side of the bed, gently pushing a dark curl off the child's brow. Miriam's face was relaxed in sleep, and she looked like an angel in peaceful repose.

She wished she could find that same peacefulness in her own sleep. More so than ever before, Laura's sleep was haunted with ghosts of her own past. The face of her father. That day in Yorkshire when he'd been taken away. The news of his murder. The faces of her sisters. Her mother.

Laura fought back the sickening emotions that were pushing to overwhelm her even in this waking moment. She turned for the door. She would not allow herself to crumble. There were promises that needed to be kept. Responsibilities that she had to see to. A child that needed her help until an unwilling uncle could find a place in his heart.

The door closed quietly behind the departing woman, and with a start, Miriam's eyes flew open. She looked about the bedchamber and shuddered. The shadows were already clawing their way toward the bed.

Chapter 18

The blue veil around the great jeweled cross fluttered in the breeze as the doors opened and shut for the arriving knight. Those in the hall turned expectantly to the man, firing their questions at him.

"Is it true, Duncan?"

"Do we know where the mother is?"

The knight bowed to the gray-eyed leader before turning to the others. "The rumor is true. Lady Nichola is at Jedburgh Abbey. But our friends there say that she will leave the abbey before Christmastide."

"We can go for her now," a knight called out hotly.

" 'Tis better to take her when she makes her move," another challenged.

"But what of the Blade?" cried one of the knights, drawing murmurs of assent from others in the group.

The leader stepped forward and a silence fell over the group. "We shall not go after her now, nor shall we capture her when she leaves the abbey."

At the stir of voices, the leader raised his hands for silence.

"We'll keep an eye on Lady Nichola Percy. We will not let her slip away from us. But beyond that, we've entrusted our brother, the Blade of Barra, to secure Tiberius." The leader turned to a young warrior to his right. "Brother, take word of our discovery to the Blade. And tell him that we shall not act until he tells us 'tis time."

It was madness to go up to her bedchamber at this late hour. But sanity had never been one of William's virtues.

Going up the circular stairwell from the Great Hall to the east wing, he forced himself to give no thought to what he might say or do if she did answer her door when he knocked. Impulsiveness was his nature, and he knew when faced with her, his spontaneity could always be counted on to keep the woman off balance.

He was just at the top of the stairs when the creak of a door opening down the corridor stopped him in his tracks. He waited a moment, not knowing exactly what to expect.

To his great surprise Miriam tripped into the darkened passage, dressed in a white nightshirt and looking like some wee spirit. As he watched, the child stepped away from her own chamber door and ran to Laura's door at the far end of the corridor. The lassie paused, and the laird watched as she rubbed one bare foot against the other and ran her hands up and down her arms to ward off the chilly air of the passageway.

He looked up at the stars twinkling through the wrecked ceiling and cursed himself for not doing anything about it before.

The child stood poised to knock on the door but then paused. Obviously deciding against it, Miriam then ran back to her own chamber, disappearing for only an instant before reappearing with a blanket thrown around her slender shoulders.

She was moving too quickly to notice him as she took the first bend in the hallway, heading for the narrow steps that led down to the kitchen.

William followed her to the top of the stairs, where he

heard the sound of little feet hurrying down. He frowned into the darkness, confused by the child's actions.

Retracing his steps, he went to Miriam's room and glanced inside. A small fire was still burning in the hearth. The bed, situated against one wall beneath a cheerful wall hanging of Ross plaid, looked comfortable enough. The bedclothes had been thrown aside in the wake of the lassie's hasty departure. There was a very attractive tapestry hanging on the far wall. Closed shutters effectively stopped the cold.

The chamber was a great deal more comfortable and more nicely arranged than when he and his brothers had inhabited it. He couldn't imagine why Miriam would not be happy sleeping in that room.

William stepped out of the bedchamber and cast a longing look at Laura's door before taking the back stairway to the kitchen himself. At least the damned step had been repaired, he thought as he passed it. It was somewhat comforting to know that *something* he had done might have served to keep Miriam from getting injured in her nocturnal wandering.

Ducking his head and stepping onto the landing overlooking the kitchen, the Ross laird peered into the half-darkness. There were a number of servants sleeping here and there. Several of the tables were laid out with trays containing neat rows of rising dough loaves. Chonny himself was lying on a table close to the door leading to the Great Hall, but sat up as William started down the steps.

The laird crouched beside his cook.

"Missing a wee one, Will?" the man whispered.

William nodded and looked about him again in search of the child.

"Check the sacks of oats near the hearth." Chonny nodded in the direction of the far fireplace. "The lass ran down here only moments ago. Shaking like a leaf, she was. Thinking everyone was asleep, she crept down that a way and pulled some old sacking over her. I didna want to frighten the wee thing any worse than she already was."

Giving the cook a grateful pat on the arm, William rose to his feet and quietly walked to the hearth.

All he could see at first glance was a small bundle of rags piled atop bulging sacks. Then a small hand and tangled locks of dark curls. He crouched before the child and gently pulled the coarse sacking from her face. She was already sound asleep.

There was a sudden tightness in William's chest that came unexpectedly. He stared down into Miriam's face, at the long lashes that rested against her pale cheeks, at the mass of dark curls that seemed to have a will of their own.

He remembered how the mother had looked when he first went to Hoddom Castle. So completely different from the dark-haired sprite before him. Mildred had been much older than Miriam when he first saw her. But still, William remembered so clearly. The straight blond hair that hung in a thick rope down her slender back to her waist. The pale hazel eyes that could bewitch a man. The smug self-assuredness that dared him to neglect noticing her beauty.

He'd been young. He'd been a fool. And he had noticed.

The tiny lass shivered and let out a small, sad, murmuring sound in her sleep, bringing William's attention back to the present. He thought of another young woman, sleeping upstairs right now, who made similar sounds in her sleep.

He gently reached under the child and lifted her up. Immediately, she took hold of his tartan and tucked her face snugly against his neck.

She weighed almost nothing, he thought, rising to his feet. So small and so vulnerable. And his to care for.

Laura sat bolt upright in the bed, thinking the roof was about to come down on her head.

The sounds of hammering and a few shouts, then more

banging, and then amidst all of the noise, a soft knocking at her door.

She scrambled to her feet and threw a blanket around her shoulders before scurrying to answer. Pulling open the door, she found Miriam, all cleaned and dressed, standing on the other side.

"May I come in?"

Laura smiled at the child and opened the door wide to let her in. Peering down the hallway, she saw two men working by the windows. From the sounds of things, an entire crew of men were working on the roof.

She closed the door behind the child. "I can't believe I slept so late." She poured some water into a basin and started washing her face with the cold liquid. The nightmares that had wrecked her sleep last night lingered in her memory. Last night had been among the worst, Laura thought. The frightening images, the cries of people. A map that seemed to float in the air just out of her reach. She splashed another handful of water on her face.

Miriam walked to the window and, peering out, looked over the training yard. "'Tis not late, mistress."

"Who helped you dress?"

"No one. I did it myself. And I've already been down to the Great Hall and had a bite to eat."

"That's excellent, Miriam." Laura took off the laird's old shirt that she still wore each night and pulled her gray wool dress over her head. Reaching behind her neck, she pulled the laces tight. "You must have been up before dawn. Oh, no! I was supposed to go to the chapel with Sir Wyntoun for Mass this morning."

"Sorry, I think you're too late for that." She continued to study the training yard. "When I was just sitting to eat in the Hall, Uncle Provost and Sir Wyntoun were leaving for the chapel."

Laura stopped hurrying and sighed. "Oh well. So much

for good intentions. And I think you might call the provost 'Uncle Gilbert.' I rather think he'd like that."

"Very well. I'd like that, too," the little girl chirped cheerfully. "Do you like Sir Wyntoun, Laura?"

"I . . ." Laura bit her lip and smiled at Miriam's profile. She could see the wheels turning in the little matchmaker's brain. "I find him . . . pleasant."

"Do you like my uncle? I mean, my uncle the laird."

Even at the mention of him, Laura found her cheeks warming. She folded his shirt and tucked it under the blankets. "I find him pleasant as well." She bent over the narrow cot, smoothing the bedclothes.

"Do you find him more pleasant than Sir Wyntoun?"

Laura looked up and found the child's attention had turned from the window and was focused on her face. Intense thought had knotted the little brow.

"If this is all coming from your concern about everyone leaving and—"

"'Tisn't." She shook her head, the dark curls shaking prettily. "'Tis just that I think the laird is—is more pleasant than Sir Wyntoun."

Laura's heart warmed. "I suppose I would have to agree with you, Miriam. Did you have your morning meal with your uncle?"

The little girl turned her gaze back out the window. "Nay, he was directing the workers. He's training in the yard with his men now."

Even though Miriam had spent almost no time with him, she was clearly partial toward her uncle. But there was something else, too. A subtle change in the child. A little more confidence.

Laura moved behind her and peered down at the men in the yard. A smaller number than usual, she noted. On any day, though, with his height and the long waves of dark hair flowing over his muscled shoulders, William Ross was easily the most magnificent of the group.

And the most . . . pleasant. Laura smiled inwardly, tearing her eyes away.

"Will you keep me company while I go down to get something to eat?"

Miriam gave one last glance at the yard and then nodded, placing a small hand in Laura's. "I would like to make a present for him for Christmas."

She led the child out of the room. "I'm sure he'll be very pleased."

"I'm fairly good at needlework. Do you think he'd like it if I made him something?"

"I am certain he will," Laura assured her. At least, she was certain to let him know that he was to be pleased. Miriam needed all the encouragement she could get in these first days.

William climbed to the roof of the east wing and inspected the progress his men were making before heading down to the Great Hall.

With Edward and Symon on his heels as they descended the spiral stairwell, the laird told his chief warrior that he wanted Dread saddled. Reminding his new steward of a few things that needed to be done, he also ordered Symon to send to Inverness for a glazier. As Edward and Symon exchanged surprised looks behind him, William said he wanted windows put into the upper level of the east wing as quickly as possible.

Entering the Great Hall, the laird almost tripped over the body of Gilbert's dog sprawled across the threshold.

William glared down at the beast, but his face softened immediately at the sight of the little girl sitting cross-legged on the floor, petting the giant head of the dog in her lap.

Her blue eyes looked up and met his trustingly. They had

spoken so few words, and yet somehow William felt they had formed a bond already. Children are such strange creatures, he thought.

"Good morning, lassie."

"Good morning, Uncle."

Last night when he had tucked her back into her own bed, Miriam had opened her eyes for a moment and stared at him in wonder. At first he'd thought she was still asleep. But then her words had startled him.

"I *tried* not to act spoiled."

He had seen the pooling of tears in her blue eyes. She seemed so sad. How could such a child so young be so sad?

"You do not act spoiled," he'd said simply.

"You're not angry with me for leaving my bedchamber?"

"Nay, lass. This is your home. You go where you like."

She'd continued to look at him for a few moments longer before she'd drifted back to sleep. William had stayed there for a while longer, studying the room. Trying to see it through the eyes of a child. Too big. Too empty.

Leaving her, he'd marched back down the Great Hall and dragged Willie, Gilbert's huge dog, back to Miriam's room. Settling the animal by the hearth, William had left the child to sleep.

Chonny had reported this morning that he had not seen Miriam come back down to the kitchen during the night.

Bringing the dog up had merely been a notion. But right now, looking at the contented child, he decided he had guessed correctly.

Willie stretched lazily and pressed a broad paw against the laird's leg, but William's attention had already turned to the huge fireplace across the Hall. That filthy, thieving son of a whore was leaning comfortably against the carved stone that bordered the open hearth and speaking to Laura.

William searched the Hall for Gilbert, cursing under his breath. Instead of chaperoning the two, as a man of the cloth should be doing, his miserable brother was standing by the doorway leading to the kitchens and chattering away with old Maire.

When Laura laughed at something Wyntoun said, Gilbert glanced over at the two and then stepped out of the Great Hall.

"By the dev—!" William stifled his curse, silently chiding himself fiercely. How, by Duthac's Shirt, had he become so damned obsessed with the woman?

Snarling over his shoulder, he stormed across the Hall.

Laura's violet eyes rounded, her eyebrows arching, as he approached. The ship-plundering, seagull-buggering island rat, however, merely turned carelessly away from him and continued his infernal chattering.

William felt the last of his patience slipping away as he sailed toward his former friend. Wyntoun was out. Gone. Tied to his horse and sent packing. And today was the day.

Two steps away from them, however, William pulled up short as Laura, smiling brightly, stepped in front of him, placing her slender body between the two men.

William glared threateningly at MacLean over the head of the young woman. Out. Gone. Finished.

"I'm so happy to see you, m'lord. I've been waiting to meet with you for most of the morning."

The man was grinning at William, and the Highlander considered knocking those teeth so far down his throat, he'd need a—

"M'lord, if you could spare me a few moments, I'd be grateful if you grant me the time right now."

William looked down and found Laura's hand resting gently on his arm. Her touch was soft and warm.

"I have business to finish here first."

Wyntoun MacLean was no longer grinning, though the change in attitude had nothing to do—William was quite certain—with his threatening words. His gaze was fixed on Laura's hand, and he suddenly looked a bit troubled.

"But what I have to say is of the utmost importance. It cannot wait."

The flicker of envy in Wyntoun's green eyes, as they darted from Laura to William and back to Laura, made the laird snort with satisfaction. With a smirk he took the young woman's hand in his own and started for the laird's chambers.

She practically ran alongside him, trying to keep up with his long strides. "You know, William, talking with you was *my* idea."

"Think what you like."

As Gilbert reentered the Great Hall, William marched by—towing Laura behind him and ignoring his brother's evident astonishment.

"What I am trying to say," Laura cried out, "is that you can let go of my hand. I promise not to run away."

He did not stop at the door to his chambers but dragged her in behind him.

"I am in no mood to consider promises."

Without another word, William turned and glared out menacingly before slamming the door in the faces of a dozen astounded onlookers.

Laura bit her lip, shocked by the unexpected and heavy-handed possessiveness demonstrated by the Highlander. If this wasn't jealousy riling his temper, she didn't know what was.

He was still holding onto her hand as she stared up at him. They were in his chamber, and his huge bed stood ominously in the corner. She blushed as he turned his blue eyes on her face.

"I—I don't believe this is where—where we should talk."

He looked about the room, almost surprised at their surroundings and growled, "I see your point."

In a moment he had dragged her through a small door and into his work room. Once inside, he slammed that door shut and then, letting go of her hand, moved to the door leading to the Great Hall. Laura peered out from behind him. Nobody in the hall appeared to have moved at all. They were all still gawking, open-mouthed and curious.

William slammed that door harder than the first.

Laura backed against the hearth, trying to put as much distance as she could between herself and his temper. A moment later, when he turned around and looked at her, Laura's pulse skittered wildly, and she felt the skin on her neck start to burn.

If Sir Wyntoun MacLean had been the picture of polish and repose this morning, William Ross was the very opposite. His long hair, tied back with a leather thong, was still wet from washing. His tartan had been draped haphazardly across the white shirt covering his broad chest, and his sword belt hung low on one kilted hip.

The man was far too handsome for a woman's comfort, Laura thought, forcing herself to control her breathing. Why, she had just yesterday heard a couple of the scullery maids giggling about finding chores in the stables after the men were done in the training yard. From what she had gathered, the laird always washed up there afterward, and Laura decided that perhaps it was time to find a chore for herself out there one of these days.

She quickly moved from the hearth to the window. Suddenly, she needed some air.

"And what tales has that oversized magpie been charming you with this morning?"

"Tales?" she repeated vaguely, watching him lean one hip against his worktable. Why men didn't wear kilts in the Lowlands or in England was suddenly incomprehensible. She turned abruptly to the window and pulled open the shutter. "'Tis warm in here. Don't you think so?"

"What was that baboon whispering so confidentially in your bonny ear, Mistress Laura?"

The draught of cold air had some effect but not enough, she thought, turning to face him. "I thought we were here to discuss *my* concerns."

"We will," he growled impatiently. "But first tell me about the affable Sir Wyntoun."

"I should have thought you knew all about him. My understanding was that you two spent a great deal of time together in your youth. Certainly, since you are such good friends—"

"We were good friends."

"Is that so?" Laura asked with surprise. "He still speaks quite highly of you."

"Of course. The snake could not have had warmer hospitality than he has received at Blackfearn Castle."

"Hospitality?" Laura repeated, biting her lip to hide her amusement.

"Aye."

"Well, other than raving about your hospitality, he has been telling me a little about himself."

"His favorite topic."

William suddenly rose to his feet and took a step toward her. She held her breath. The fire in his eyes was there, and it was unmistakable. He hesitated, passion burning in his gaze.

She was no expert in the ways of lovemaking. But when it came down to how he acted whenever they were near—and how she felt for William right now—there was no doubt in her mind that he desired her as she desired him.

And then, abruptly, he retreated, turning toward the hearth. A sting of disappointment coursed through her.

The provost had convinced her that for her own safety, marriage was her best course of action. William appeared to have agreed. This, however, was where Laura's confusion centered. Was she not worthy enough to be *his* wife?

"Sir Wyntoun appears quite open to the idea of taking a wife." Before she even spoke the words, she knew they would rile him. And yet out they came.

His head turned sharply, his expression darkening. "Has he asked for your hand in marriage?"

She shook her head. "Not yet."

"And yet you have broached the subject with him." He seemed to be wrestling with his words. "Have you asked him?"

"I could never do such a thing."

"And why not?"

Laura bit back the words that were ready to spill out. The truth was that, despite his looks, his charm, and position, she did not find Sir Wyntoun . . . thrilling. Pleasant, aye. Thrilling, nay.

He simply did not affect her the way the man standing before her did.

Perhaps if she had met Sir Wyntoun before she had ever seen William Ross. Before she knew the heat that could flood through a woman at the simple touch, at the mere look, of a certain man.

There was no comparison between them. She had none of those jumbled feelings of wishing and hoping and fearing and aching that came when she was with William. When she was with Sir Wyntoun, she never felt the way she did at this very moment.

She wanted this man.

She wanted him to hold her in his arms right now. She wanted to be kissed the way he'd kissed her before. She ached to feel her body come unraveled, to feel him move her the way he'd moved her before. He'd offered her a taste of the fruits of passion. She wanted to share all of it—with William Ross.

With William Ross.

Her chin dropped to her chest. She was indeed a woman doomed.

"So you feel 'tis not proper for you to make the offer."

She looked up and saw the troubled look continuing to darken his brow. She had difficulty regaining the strands of their conversation. Marriage. Sir Wyntoun.

"Your brother has offered to manage any negotiations on that topic. And I suppose, trusting in his assistance, it shall all be done properly."

William turned his face away and Laura deeply regretted bringing up the subject. She knew that he wrongly assumed that she wished to be married to his friend.

She did not wish to let things stand as they were. But something within her—foolish pride perhaps—would not let her correct his misapprehension. William Ross was not making any offers for her hand.

When he turned back to her, his tone was cool. "You wanted to speak to me about some other matter."

He sat down behind the worktable, seriousness etched in his face. The items on the table were all tidily arranged. Laura thought for a moment of paying him a compliment regarding the changes that were going on in the castle, but his frown discouraged any idle talk.

"I have a great deal scheduled today," he said, motioning to a chair.

She nodded. She had requested this audience on Miriam's behalf. Their own private situation would have to wait for another time. "About your niece."

"Miriam."

At least he was acknowledging that she had a name. "I know she has only just arrived, but I believe you might want to reconsider your plans for the child."

Silence was his only answer.

"She is only seven," Laura continued. "And despite hav-

ing been orphaned for over two years and apparently having
no kin of any consequence at Hoddom Castle—"

"The lass was there with her grandsire."

"An elderly gentleman who, by all accounts, kept himself
quite removed from the child."

"Men like Lord Herries have the business of the world to
attend to. What would he have to do with a bairn?" William
stopped and frowned more deeply. "Is that Miriam's complaint?"

Laura shook her head. "I asked Sir Wyntoun about
Miriam's care at Hoddom Castle." She saw concern darkening his expression. "I don't wish to taint the good name of
Lord Herries. Your friend assured me that there was plenty
of comfort provided for your niece. But providing comfort
and a bit of tutelage seems to be where Miriam's care ended."

"Many would consider that more than enough."

"True. But many have hearts of stone." She entwined her
hands, softening her tone. "As a wee one who has not had
the continuing affection of a parent, Miriam has needs that
are not trivial. She has spent the last few years not even
knowing the place that she should consider home."

Laura looked down at her hands and tried to choose the
right words. Having William understand Miriam's needs was
important. But she did not want to sound patronizing in her
statements. She knew that William Ross was one of those
few men who were unafraid of demonstrating tenderness. She
had felt it herself firsthand.

"Miriam is eager to please. She strives for perfection. And
'tis because I have seen how anxious she is to get your attention and seek your approval that I repeat my original plea
that you reconsider your plans and your feelings for her."

"I *have* reconsidered them."

His simple statement took her breath away. "Do you mean,
she's staying?"

"Aye. Was there anything else?"

She looked for some warmth in his eyes. Some joy in this decision regarding something so important to his life. But there was none of it in his blue eyes, and something within her ached. "She—she is making you a present. 'Tis not something you need, to be sure, but—"

"I'll receive her gift graciously." He rose to his feet. "If you'll forgive me, I have to meet Edward in the yard."

She had been dismissed.

Chapter 19

"Well, you're a popular man in that village this night, William Ross."

"That so?" Sitting astride Dread, high on the brae overlooking the stone huts clustered in the glen, the laird frowned into the darkening gloom. Somehow, he couldn't quite bring himself to share in Edward's good feeling.

"Aye. Surely you saw it yourself. And after we split up, we went to the smith's widow and her bairns. By the saint, you'd think that the angels had descended on them when we dropped the venison at her hut. She was thanking you and praying for you all at once. And auld Roger as well was singing your praises to the sky for the bolt of woolen cloth. I thought his wife was never going to stop crying."

"For a wee bit of cloth?"

"That wool might as well have been cloth of gold, m'lord."

"What of the hermit?"

"We found him up the glen. And although he threatened to murder all of us, he still came down to take the ale and the oats."

William turned his horse toward the far hill. "Where are the men?"

"Heading off in a half dozen directions, though a few were thinking to stop for a wee dram at The Three Cups." Edward peered through the deepening darkness at his laird. "How was the steward's widow?"

William shook his head. "Not so well, I'm afraid. Though she still has much of her old sense of humor, she doesn't seem to be able to come to grips with Robert's death. In fact, I'm not so sure she's better off by herself in that tumble-down cottage."

"Aye, but she was determined not to live in the castle after the old man died."

"Maybe so. But that was only because she couldn't see herself as being of any help to the rest. 'Twas my fault not to see to it that she stayed."

"'Tis not too late to bring her back."

"Perhaps not, Edward. We'll just see if Symon can think of some worthy job for the woman to put her mind to."

An icy drizzle had been falling off and on all day. William felt nothing, though, of the cold or the fact that he had been soaked to the bone for hours. He could not get out of his mind the warmth of the welcome of those people he'd visited today. His people. His responsibility.

The sound of the revelers at The Three Cups down the hill was echoing in the hills. Though the piper was either incompetent or completely drunk, the laughter and the singing was a satisfying sound to the Ross laird.

The rain was falling harder, and Edward wiped the water off his face. "Peter was wondering if your invitation to the village folk for the Christmas dinner and *celeidh* at the castle included the wenches from the tavern."

"Considering the temperament of Peter's Wife, the man had best not be asking such questions. He'll be lucky to see Twelfth Night in one piece if his woman gets wind of it."

William and Edward crossed the path of a man and his wife, who was berating her husband as they made their way home from the tavern. The husband raised a hand to the laird as the woman paused in her tirade and dropped a curtsy.

William smiled. "A fine night to be taking your Ellie out and about, Jock."

"Aye, m'laird. Just the night for a wee walk. In fact, she was thanking me for it . . . and just this moment, too."

They all laughed and parted ways.

Edward picked up their conversation where they'd left off. "Peter assures me that 'tis not for his own sake that he is asking, but for the gaiety of the other men, including his laird."

William cast a curious glance at his grinning man. "Since when has Peter the time to be concerned about anything but pacifying that hot-tempered wife of his?"

"Aye, Peter's Wife is a force to be reckoned with, but I'm thinking 'tis really Molly who's been asking. From what I hear, the wench has been complaining to everyone that comes within shouting distance of the place that you never come by anymore. Something about wondering if you've taken a wife to your bed without telling her first."

William snorted out aloud. "The next time you see the brazen Mistress Molly, tell her she is worrying for naught. I'll be paying her a visit soon enough."

Edward reined in his horse and nodded toward the small tavern a short distance away. "You might stop and tell her that yourself, Will. I'm thinking that nearly everyone has retired for the night back at the castle."

William slowed his own horse and considered doing just that. A romp in the hay with that brassy, blue-eyed wench offered pleasures not to be scoffed at. But the interest he had usually been able to work up in the past tonight seemed so distant somehow.

He shook his head at Edward. "Nay. I think tonight is not the night for it."

"Should we tell them, though—the women in the tavern—that they are invited?"

"Aye. They live on Ross land. They're welcome the same as anyone."

*   *   *

As Laura had promised Sir Wyntoun, she went back down to the Great Hall right after Miriam had fallen asleep. As one who was always interested in learning new things and hearing about new places, Laura was keen to hear more about the Western Isles.

There was a specific place that he had mentioned earlier that had particularly caught her interest. Barra, the island off the west coast where Sir Wyntoun said his mother had been born.

Barra. Where her sister Adrianne had been sent to take refuge.

Laura was suddenly very anxious to learn more about this island of Barra and the people who inhabited it.

The Great Hall was fairly quiet when Laura entered, and the dogs that were scattered about raised their heads for only a moment. There were a few men talking and laughing in low voices at a table by the door leading to the kitchens, and some sleepers were tucked into dark corners, but the place had obviously settled down for the night. As she glanced about, she realized that the provost had apparently retired, and there was no sign of the laird's return from the village, either.

Sir Wyntoun, however, was sitting alone by the fire, and he quickly rose to his feet at her approach.

"I was beginning to lose hope that you would return, Mistress Laura."

She took the seat by the hearth that he offered. Immediately, Willie, the provost's dog, emerged from under one of the trestle tables and lumbered over, sitting down expectantly next to her chair. Laura smiled and laid a gentle hand on the dog's head.

"I am sorry. But I wanted to wait and make certain Miriam was already asleep."

"You've taken a great liking to the child."

Laura met the Highlander's intense green eyes. "'Tis im-

possible not to. She is the most agreeable and loving child
I've ever encountered."

A smile broke over the man's handsome face. "And what
is it that makes me believe that you would say that for all
children that you might encounter?"

"You would be incorrect in assuming that, Sir Wyntoun.
'Tis not true." Laura straightened her skirt on her lap as Willie
lay down by her feet. "Though I have not known a large number of young ones in my life, I can name at least one who
was a disagreeable imp from birth."

One dark brow rose. "Can you, now?"

"Aye!" Laura blurted. "My younger sister, Adrianne. She
was born to be disagreeable. In fact, my mother said Adrianne was the son my father never had."

A hearty laugh rumbled up from within the knight, and she
studied the man's face in the firelight. Dark, with finely etched
features, his face was unmarked by scars. His green eyes were
piercing when he directed his gaze at her. He was quite handsome, she decided, wondering why the man could stir up no
further interest on her part.

He drew up a bench near the fire and sat down as well.
Two powerful arms rested on his knees as he leaned forward.
"Your sister Adrianne, how much younger is she than you?"

"Two years," Laura said confidentially. "Though a person
who has seen all of us together might conclude that Adrianne
has simply never matured beyond her younger years."

"Stubborn?"

"Pigheaded."

"Opinionated?"

"Extremely. And . . . active!"

Wyntoun stretched his long legs before him. The dog lifted
his head and gave him an annoyed look. "Too bad we couldn't
have arranged for William to meet her. It sounds as if she
would be the perfect match for my dear old friend. Certainly,
if he could find a woman better suited to his own tempera-

ment, then he might stop following you around like some amorous young bull."

He had meant his comment as a compliment to her, Laura was quite sure, but she found a knot forming in her throat at the thought of someone else—anyone else, even her own sister—being considered a better match for William Ross. A perfect match, Wyntoun had called it.

"I can see I spoke in haste."

She shook her head and forced her gaze up to meet his. He was quite observant.

"There is more in this—this attachment between you and William than just him playing Troilus to my Diomedes."

"I should hope I am more loyal than any Cresseid."

"You mean loyal to that surly, ne'er-do-well friend of mine."

There was no use in denying it. Her feelings for William were simply too strong to accept another man as a suitor, regardless of what the provost was trying to do for her. And she certainly had no right to mislead a man who—despite all of William's bluster—was a friend.

"Aye, 'tis true," she said at last. "But please take this— this admission as one made in confidence. These feelings I have are mine alone."

"You believe he does not share your affections?"

She paused for a moment and then shook her head. A woman can plan and pray for a future, but the past is a strong enemy to overcome.

Wyntoun pulled his bench forward, leaning closer to her with an air of one person confiding in another.

"Let me tell you something, mistress. 'Twould surely be in my own best interest to see you lose hope in William. To be honest, nothing would satisfy me more than seeing you decide instead to allow something to bloom between us. However, my honor forces me to tell you the truth."

Laura met the man's emerald eyes as they bore into hers.

"Before this journey," he continued, "I have never seen William lay claim to a woman as he has laid claim to you."

"I can assure you, your friend's behavior has been for the benefit of riling you more than—"

"Nay, mistress." Wyntoun shook his head. "I've known him for many years. Speaking candidly, we have shared together a great many . . . misadventures, both here in the Highlands and elsewhere. William has never been one to seek out—how can I say this delicately—permanence in his female companionship."

And with William's good looks and easy charm, Laura thought with a pang of jealousy, he surely never had to.

"In a time when many young men in our position choose a mistress with the same seriousness that their families demonstrate in choosing them a wife, William has casually moved on from one liaison to the next." Wyntoun looked at her, a frown tugging at the corner of his mouth. "But do not take me wrong, mistress. I do not want to portray William as reckless as much as indifferent. But all of this stems from the time when Mildred, Lord Herries's daughter—"

The knight stopped and looked around the Hall as if considering the propriety of what he was about to reveal. Laura felt a knot in her throat that she was certain would choke her. She was about to plead for him to continue, but she dared not trust her voice.

"I tell you this because I believe you should know the man." He turned his gaze back on her. "If you are courageous enough to marry him, then you should know what you are facing in his past."

"He has not asked me to marry him," she responded quickly, correcting him.

"I know him, and he will," Wyntoun assured her, "But even before that—even if he does not admit that he is doing it for himself—he will ask you to keep *me* at arm's length."

Selfishly, Laura hoped the knight was correct. William Ross, she knew now more clearly than anything she had ever known in her life, was the only man she would ever desire to be married to. The only man she could ever spend the rest of her life with.

"What of Mildred?" she asked hesitantly, wanting to remove the shadow of the woman from her mind. "Mildred was Thomas's wife, was she not?"

"Not when William and I first met her. We had just come to Hoddom Castle from the university. To us she was beautiful and spoiled and full of life. The lass turned her eyes on our friend the day we arrived at her father's castle."

"Did he—did William treat Mildred with—with indifference?"

Wyntoun shook his head and raked his strong fingers through his short black hair. "We were young. William was not yet established in his ways of dealing with women. He fell for her. I cannot say for certain that he was in love. But I know for a fact that he was enraptured by the lass."

"And Mildred. Did she—did she love him back?"

Wyntoun gave a short laugh. "Years later this is still my undoing. If I did not pity him so for the way the woman treated him, I'm sure I'd not be doing this, encouraging you to take William Ross rather than me."

"You're a good friend," she said gently.

He reached over and took her hand in his own. "William Ross, for all his faults, is a good man. But he has suffered his share, mistress."

"How?"

"Mildred used him, I believe. Falsely, she made him believe, at first, that they might share a future. A life they could have together. But as fast as William fell, the woman began to lose interest. She had a wandering eye. And she was not secretive about it, but open as the midday sky. She even began to chide him about being a second son. For her, I knew, only

a suitor with a title would claim her hand. Surely, Lord Herries himself wanted nothing less for his daughter."

Laura remembered William's bitter reference to *her* kind—
women of the nobility—when they'd first met. She now understood it to be Mildred's kind.

"She was relentless in the men she lured. I was one of
those she targeted. But I sent her on her way, valuing my
friendship with William over whatever charms she could offer.
I saw her for what she was, but Thomas Ross did not."

Laura drew her hand back into her lap. "Did he not know
of his own brother's connection with the woman?"

Wyntoun shook his head. "Thomas was twelve years older.
He'd spent most of his life here on Ross land, preparing to
become laird. He and William were not close on private matters. But even if they had been, I'd say—knowing William as
I do—that he would have cut out his tongue rather than ruin
the chance for his clan to form such a valuable alliance. Indeed, I believe he would have forfeited Mildred's hand simply out of deference to his brother."

"Can a man be foolish and noble at the same time, I wonder?"

"William will always put those he cares about ahead of
himself." The knight patted the dog's head at their feet. "When
Thomas came to claim Mildred under an arrangement made
with Lord Herries, William was stunned, but showed nothing
of the betrayal I knew he had to be feeling. He wished them
well. But he soon set out to change his own ways with women."

Betrayal. Laura stared into the hearth, wondering if William
had ever recovered from Mildred's betrayal. If he'd ever
stopped loving her.

"I, for one, was glad when Mildred married and moved
here to Blackfearn Castle." The knight's voice drew Laura out
of her reverie. "She was undeserving of someone as good-
hearted and genuine as William Ross."

"And that was it? The end of what they had?"

"I believe William never saw her or Thomas again. The bairn was born the next year. From everything I heard later, Mildred was never contented being a Highland laird's wife. I recall hearing that she quickly turned into a shrew, constantly demanding to spend time at Hoddom Castle. Thomas, older and apparently infatuated with his wife, allowed his responsibilities at Blackfearn Castle to fall on others in his desire to please his wife."

"And where was William during this time?"

"He left the service of Lord Herries shortly after, as did I, and he served for a short time as an emissary in England. The king's mother was in York then, and William traveled almost constantly between Stirling and Edinburgh and York."

Laura remembered the Tudor coin William always kept in his belt.

"He appeared content in his newfound role until the news arrived of his brother's and Mildred's sudden deaths. He came back to the Highlands then, and the clan decided that he was the one to take over as laird."

Without ever being given a chance to decide his own path in life, Laura thought. How could he not be restless and resistant when it came to taking over what had been thrust upon him?

For the first time since meeting William Ross, Laura understood him. He *was* a good man. A compassionate man. And a generous leader who, over and over again, had disregarded his own needs, deciding to do instead what was best for others.

She stared down at her lap as her fingers smoothed the dark fabric of her skirt.

MacLean had asserted that he believed William would ask her to marry him. Laura wished she could feel even a little confidence in what the knight believed. Too many uncertainties continued to batter her insides.

What if William thought she would be better off with someone else? On the other hand, what if he thought she was too meddlesome to take as a spouse? Worse, what if he was still in love with Mildred?

She rose restlessly to her feet and forced a polite smile at her companion. "Thank you, Sir Wyntoun . . . for trusting me with all this."

Wyntoun stood up as well and reached for Laura's hand, taking it in his own. "I hope I've not distressed you with what I have revealed."

She shook her head and took a step back. "If you'll forgive me, 'tis late."

Laura turned and headed across the Great Hall toward the stairwell. Her mind was a jumble. Her stomach twisted in a painful knot. The torment of what William Ross thought of her—of their future—was almost too much to bear.

She needed him. She wanted him. And she was willing to risk anything to have him want her in return. As a wife.

Miriam was sound asleep again in the kitchen.

Arriving back at Blackfearn Castle late in the night and finding Gilbert's dog stretched out contentedly by the open hearth in the Great Hall, William had a fairly good idea that the little girl would not be in her bedchamber. Going into the kitchen, he found the imp curled up in a tiny ball atop the sacks of oats.

William dropped down on his knees beside the child.

"I've been watching over her, master."

The laird turned and gave an encouraging nod to Robbie, the young stable lad. Sitting with his back against a large black cooking pot, the boy's eyes were red-rimmed from lack of sleep. "You've done well, lad."

"Why does she come down here when she has a real bed to sleep in?"

William looked down on Miriam's innocent face and wondered the same himself. He pulled the woolen rag aside and picked her up in his arms. She curled her fingers around his tartan and snuggled against his chest.

The laird had no idea how to explain to the boy, who had never in his life enjoyed the luxury of sleeping in a real bed, why someone would choose not to.

"Lassies! They're such fragile creatures." The lad's scowl was disapproving. "I think she comes down here because she is afraid."

William lowered his voice and glanced down at the boy. "I know for a fact that she fears not man nor beast. But I believe she comes down here because she's afraid for the rest of you."

Robbie scoffed. "What have we to fear?"

"Fairy wives. And brownies. Perhaps even the Bodach himself, who comes to steal the bairnies away. They say the eldritch creatures can be kept at bay if a wee one knows the magic word." William came to his feet. "Must be the lass sees things that the rest of us cannot see."

The boy's eyes rounded as he sat straighter against the pot. "Do—do ye think she saw something here tonight?"

"Maybe she did. Maybe she did not. But if I were you, I shouldn't worry too much. Just you continue to be nice to wee Miriam. She's told me that she always says her prayers and *always* puts in a good word for her friends."

Instead of taking the stairs to the east wing from the kitchen, William went out through the Great Hall. The poor lad, he thought. Somehow, he doubted Robbie would be getting much sleep this night, with images of goblins and fairies filling his head. But having anyone think poorly of the little one in his arms—especially for not wanting to be alone—was something he would not allow.

Passing by the hearth, he nudged Gilbert's dog with his foot. Willie raised his head and, with a lazy yawn, got to his feet. Stretching and shaking himself, he lumbered after the laird, obediently following them up the winding stairwell to the east wing.

The dog settled down heavily by the glowing hearth in Miriam's room as William placed the child in her bed and tucked the blankets around her. The Highlander was banking the hearth with enough peat to last the night when a soft voice called to him.

"I don't think the fairies I see are friendly at all."

He looked over his shoulder and smiled at the two blue eyes peering at him from the bed. "How long have you been awake?"

"Since you picked me up in the kitchen."

He scowled in mock fierceness while rising to his feet. "You mean you were awake and still let me scare poor Robbie half to death with talk of the Bodach?"

She bobbed her little head up and down and smiled. "And I liked the fib you told him about me. About not being afraid of man or beast." She looked dreamily at the ceiling. "Man or beast."

"'Twas no fib. I know you're not." She didn't look convinced, so he hardened the scowl on his face and growled threateningly at Willie. Bending over, he pulled open the dog's huge mouth and exposed the jagged line of sharp white teeth. He turned both of their faces toward Miriam. "Look at us. Man and beast. Are you terrified, lass?"

As he released the dog's muzzle, the animal licked the laird's face with a broad sweep of his tongue. William spat in disgust. Miriam giggled and hid her head beneath the covers.

"So you think this is funny?" He crossed the room and sat on the edge of the bed. "I will get you for this. You can't escape."

Miriam squealed with delight and burrowed farther beneath the blanket.

The sound of the door opening drew his attention. He

looked over his shoulders the same time that Miriam pushed the covers down and peered out.

Laura poked her head in the door.

"Oh, I'm sorry. I heard a noise . . . I didn't realize . . ."

William's eyes swept over Laura's tousled hair and smiling face and then at the tattered shirt visible beneath the blanket she'd thrown over her shoulders. It was the same patched rag he'd put on her when they were hiding in the fisherman's hut on Sinclair land, but the gaping holes had been stitched, the ragged edges neatly hemmed. He felt a bolt of desire slice right through him as she pulled the blanket tighter in an unsuccessful attempt to hide the revealing garment and her exposed legs.

"I'll be going now. Sleep well," she whispered softly, tearing her violet eyes away from William and sending Miriam a soft kiss.

Before he could say anything, she was gone, and the door had closed behind her.

"Could you keep her?"

William turned with surprise to the young girl. She was sitting cross-legged in the bed. All the traces of merriment had disappeared from her expression.

"Could you, please?"

"You cannot just—" He cleared his throat. The child's pleading tone flustered him for some reason. "Miriam, lass, you cannot just keep people."

"You are keeping me, are you not?"

"Of course I am."

His quick answer brought a smile to the girl's lips. "Then why not keep her as well?"

For the first time in his life, William Ross felt completely tongue-tied. He glanced at the closed door. The image of the woman dressed in his shirt was already etched in his mind, in his heart. Wanting to keep that woman was the greatest temptation in his life.

He turned back to Miriam. "I—I will think about it, lass."

Her immediate reaction—throwing herself into his arms and kissing his cheek—added another sword thrust to William's gut. So he did the only thing that he could do. The only thing that didn't require him to say a word.

He held the little girl.

William Ross placed soft kisses against her hair and held her to his chest, cherishing the moment of simply holding his daughter in his arms.

Chapter 20

The castle's sounds, muffled and peaceful, wrapped about Laura like a comfortable blanket. Closing her eyes, she smiled, hearing in her mind Miriam's squeals and William's gruff laughter.

The sound of his laughter, she thought contentedly. This had been the first time she'd ever seen him appear so truly happy.

Perched on her small cot, Laura hugged her legs to her chest and rubbed her cheek over the soft wool of his old worn shirt. His man scent lingered in the cloth.

They had been so beautiful together. So perfect was the picture of the two of them together. And how foolish she must have sounded to him before, lecturing him on treating his niece better.

She should have known. Having witnessed his compassion, she should have known that he would open his great heart and let the child in.

Awareness stabbing at her, Laura's head jerked up at hearing Miriam's door open and close. Frozen on her bed, she stared at her own closed door, her heart drumming loudly in response to all her unruly emotions within.

But then there was silence. A deafening, disappointing silence that told her he'd continued on his way.

She dragged herself up from her cot and walked to the window, breathing deeply the streams of cold air filtering in through the closed shutter. Too restless to stand still, she wrapped her arms around herself, hugging the wool shirt against her skin, and started pacing the chamber.

This wanton desire that tugged at her insides! This burning need to see him, to be held by him, was driving her mad.

Laura went to the oak door and leaned her forehead against the cool wood. If she had the power of magic, she would conjure him right now, will him to her. She smiled sadly. She was a planner, an organizer, a worker, but she was no enchantress.

She offered up a prayer and sighed. Behind her, the fire crackled, sending sparks up the chimney, and she turned to look at it. As she did, Laura thought she heard a sound in the passageway. Without hesitating, she turned and pulled the door open.

A prayer answered. Her body turned in an instant to liquid fire. William Ross stood before her, leaning casually against the wall by her door.

She searched for her voice, but her will to speak seemed to have disappeared with all pretense of modesty.

His eyes traveled down her body, burning her as they dwelled on her bare legs, on the patched holes in the shirt. Rising, his blue eyes lingered on her breasts, on her shoulders, before coming to rest on her mouth. He looked up into her eyes. She had been caressed, kissed, and scorched with one long look.

"Has Wyntoun asked for your hand in marriage?"

All she could do was shake her head and step slowly back into her room. He followed her.

He closed the door behind him and reached for her wrist. She stared at his large hand closing around her slender limb. She looked up, and her breath caught in her throat at the hunger she saw in those eyes. The need that seemed to match her own in some savage, masculine way.

She took the step that separated them and raised her free

hand around his neck. With a passion that cried to be fed, she lifted her lips to his.

A sound of hunger emitted from William's throat as he crushed his lips against hers, his tongue surging inside. He turned her in his arms until she was pinned against the door, and his body a wall. Her only escape was through him. Her only redemption.

"Stay with me. Please," she heard herself whisper as his mouth moved from her mouth and traveled to her ear, feasting on the sensitive skin of her neck. She wanted him with a desire she had never known. Needed him as she had never felt need.

His fingers ran along the line of her jaw. She turned a little in his arms, and his bare knee pressed against the inside of her thighs. She could feel the sinewy strength in his leg as it pressed against the very center of her.

"Stop me, Laura. Tell me to stop," he growled, his voice ragged.

He turned her toward the door, and she placed both palms flat on the smooth wood. His hands moved over her body, cupping her breasts, pulling her buttocks so intimately against his engorged manhood.

"I cannot tell you," she murmured. She turned back to him, her hands and her lips all over him as a lightning bolt coursed through her. She needed to feel, to touch, to taste the sinewy muscles of his back, his chest. She could not get enough. "Please, William, do not stop."

She knew exactly when he lost the battle. If his groan was in frustration or resignation she didn't know. One moment, however, there was a barrier. His woolen shirt, depriving her heated skin from the caress of his fingers. The next instant he'd pulled the shirt over her head, and there was nothing to hide her body from his gaze, his touch.

He went down on one knee as his tongue traced a scorching trail from her chin to the valley between her aching breasts.

She gasped as he took one nipple into his mouth, suckling, tugging, causing her to shudder and groan with pleasure and torment at the same time.

She curled over him, kissing his hair. His name was a continuous whisper on her lips.

"I want you, Laura. I want you so badly it hurts," he whispered roughly.

"Then take me." She gazed down into his face. "I am yours to take."

William pulled her tightly to him, laying his head against her breasts as his hands caressed her back, the soft curves of her backside, the length of her weakening legs. His fingers explored the contours of the backs of her knees, of her thighs.

Laura gasped in surprise as William's hand slid to the juncture of her legs. Her body arched against his, one knee rising against his side as his fingers gently stoked the fire raging within her. Laura's fingertips raked across his wide shoulders. She clutched his hair as a moan escaped her. Or was it from him?

William's mouth moved over one breast, his tongue circling and then flicking at the erect nipple. Her hands held tightly to his hair and his back while she unconsciously pulsed her hips against him. His fingers continued to stroke the moist folds of her womanhood while he suckled her breast.

"William!" she cried out. His fingers were sending waves of molten liquid upward through her in rivers of fire.

His breath was heated against her dampening skin as he whispered the words, "Let it go. Let it go, Laura."

At the sound of his voice, she felt her soul soar.

She rolled her head back as an exquisite pressure built. Her breaths were getting shorter and shorter, and suddenly Laura felt her body shuddering uncontrollably, and a sky opened above her. Flashing light and colors unimaginable burst around her. Incapable of thought, she clasped his head to her breasts as the colors erupted in her and a shower of sparks touched every nerve in her body.

She clung to him, gradually regaining the ability to think, but taking even more pleasure in the way he simply held her tight in his arms as the throbbing release slowly ebbed away.

A moment later she saw him rise slowly to his feet. William was still fully clothed, and she suddenly felt absolutely licentious, standing naked in his encircling arms. Before she could give vent to any feeling of shame, though, his mouth moved over hers. Teasing, tasting, his tongue moving in and out.

Her fingers trembled as they moved down his chest, down to the wool of his kilt, following the line of the hard arousal. She ran her fingers curiously over his bulging manhood and heard his swift intake of breath.

"Show me," she whispered shyly. "Show me how to please you."

With a single motion he swept her up in his arms. She wrapped her arms around his neck and kissed him. "Please!" she repeated, kissing his jaw, his neck. "Teach me."

"Aye. That I will!" he growled. "But first you have to know one thing."

She drew back and gazed into his eyes, shining in the light of the fire.

"I've decided to keep you."

The fire long out, the chamber was as chilly as a dungeon in the Orkneys. Her blanket was not nearly long enough to cover him, and his feet hung out a good half foot beyond the bottom. They were squeezed into a cot not even wide enough to support the width of his shoulders, on the lumpiest straw-filled mattress he'd ever experienced. Her elbow, poking into his side, was as sharp as a lance.

And William Ross felt a contentment at that moment that he knew he could never truly describe.

He smiled down at the sleeping angel curled up in his arms and ran his fingers through the silky mass of hair draping over his arm. She made a small sound in her sleep and nestled her naked bottom closer against his belly.

He smiled as he felt himself harden yet again.

It was nearly dawn, the graying light filtering in around the edges of the shutter. He knew he should be up and out of her bedchamber before anyone in the household appeared and discovered their night of intimate pleasure. But then, the feel of her stirring in his arms wiped out all of his good intentions in an instant. She placed soft kisses on the arm she'd been using as a pillow before turning awkwardly in the small space and facing him.

"Did you sleep at all?"

He cupped her warm cheek with his palm and ran his thumb over her still swollen lips. "Did you?"

She gave him a brilliant smile that went right straight to his heart. "I did, though I don't know for how long. And no bad dreams, either."

He placed a kiss on her forehead. Another one on her nose. "What are these dreams, Laura? What are you afraid of?"

She was silent for a moment as her eyes caressed his face. Then she shook her head and tucked herself under his chin, bringing her body flush against his.

"Not now," she whispered. "I don't want to think of any of that now."

William held her tight against him, his body aching with the desire to take her again. His heart swelled, pulsing with all the emotions she enlivened in him. And then the old confusion and fear slipped in, and he fought them back.

"I have to go," he said reluctantly, caressing her back.

She bobbed her head up and down in agreement, but then her mouth found his skin and moved down his chest. He felt her one hand trace the planes of his stomach and hesitantly touch his aching shaft.

"I don't think you really want to go," she said softly.

He growled in her ear and rolled her roughly onto her back, moving on top of her.

"'Tis trouble you ask for, touching me like that this early in the day."

"But how disappointing to think that you might be un-moved by my touch at other times."

She gave him a mischievous smile that disappeared as he positioned himself between her legs. Her knees lifted, and he felt her press her moist opening against him.

"When it comes to you, lass . . ." He lifted himself up and glanced down at the peaks of her breasts waiting for his mouth to close over them.

"When it comes to me . . ." She pulsed against him, open-ing her legs farther and raising her hips.

Unable to wait any longer, he thrust inside her, eliciting a moan of delight.

"There is no such thing as 'unmoved' when it comes to you, Laura." Slowly, he began to withdraw, only to slide deeply into her again. "And you, my sweet, can move me anytime."

The sky was graying over the low hills to the east, and Gilbert Ross turned to watch the darkness drop away from the sturdy stone walls of Blackfearn Castle.

For over an hour now he had walked. And pondered. And prayed.

In these wee hours of the morning he often sought guid-ance. Sometimes he even got it. But not this morning.

Turning his steps back toward the castle, Gilbert strode into the dark arched gate and thanked the warrior who raised the heavy portcullis. Proceeding across the courtyard, he shrugged out of the heavy cloak and shook the dew off of it. He en-tered the Great Hall.

All was quiet. Though he had seen a few of the kitchen helpers making their way up from the village in the darkness, no smells of food yet wafted in from the kitchen. None of the men sleeping in the Hall were yet stirring to take on the challenge of the day. He searched under the tables for his dog. For the second day in the row he found the beast missing.

Gilbert had been hearing of strange goings-on in the castle from a number of sources. From the warrior at the gate this morning, he had heard of a long and private discussion between Laura and Sir Wyntoun that had taken place in the Great Hall. And from two scullery maids yesterday, he'd heard that Miriam had left her own bedchamber the first night, going to the kitchen to sleep. The same two had also told him about his brother's actions. About how William had taken the child and the provost's dog back to the lassie's room.

Gilbert smiled to himself as he took the steps up to the east wing. Everything was proceeding better than he'd hoped. Despite William's initial objection to having the child at Blackfearn, Gilbert had witnessed the little exchange between the two of them the day before. The soft look that traveled between them. The gaze that certainly bordered on affectionate. That problem appeared to be resolved. From what Gilbert could see, it looked as if Miriam was here to stay.

Now if he could only say the same for Laura.

His efforts to make William jealous over Wyntoun's attentions were working fine so far. But Gilbert's plans for manipulating his unwieldy brother into spending more time alone with Laura had yet to prove effective. Suddenly, there was no laird in the Highlands spending more time or effort on behalf of his clan than William Ross. He was really beginning to give Gilbert a stiff pain.

Reaching the upper-level corridor of the east wing, Gilbert glanced at Laura's closed door in the distance. It would be sheer disaster if she was to fall for Sir Wyntoun MacLean. It would be a tremendous loss to the family, to the clan, and to William if she slipped through his fingers and married someone else.

More than once Gilbert had thought that if he himself were not committed by his priestly vows . . .

The provost shook off that line of thinking and came to a stop by little Miriam's chamber. Gently, he pushed open the heavy oak door. All was well inside. The little girl was sleeping soundly, comfortably tucked into her very large bed. His dog Willie was lying down by the small hearth, his head up and his tail swishing across the floor. Gilbert's gaze moved again back to Miriam, and he sent a silent prayer of thanks heavenward.

All will be well, lass. He remembered the promise he'd made not so long ago to the portrait he kept in his work room at St. Duthac's. *With the Maker's help,* he repeated inwardly, *all will be well.*

The sound of Laura's door opening drew Gilbert's head around. Staring in stunned silence, he watched William step out and pull the door shut.

The laird stopped short when he spotted his brother but quickly recovered, approaching him.

"William!" the provost said under his breath.

"Gilbert!" the laird whispered, looking past his brother's shoulder at the sleeping child. With a satisfied look, he headed down the corridor without uttering another word.

Gilbert glanced once at the closed door of Laura's room and then at the retreating back. Quickly pulling the child's door closed, he started after his brother. The laird had already reached the top of the main set of stairs, though, before Gilbert caught up with him.

"Is that all you can do?" the provost called, taking hold of the warrior chief's arm to stop him. "Just run away like some cowardly dog?"

William directed a menacing glare at the priest before turning his back and starting down the winding stairs.

"You cannot just walk away from this, William." Gilbert called, following after him.

"I'm certain I don't know what you're wailing about."

Passing from the stairwell out into the Great Hall, Gilbert ignored the groggy faces turning in surprise as the two of them stormed past.

"William, I demand that we talk about this."

"Naturally," the laird snapped over his shoulder. "But in private, you skulking, poor excuse for a friar."

"Friar?" the younger man cried with disgusted indignation. "I am no skulking anything, you lecherous cur. I am the provost of the Shrine of St. Duthac."

William held open the door of his work room and made a sweeping bow, motioning his brother to enter. "Well, of course, Gilbert. That is what I meant to say."

No sooner had the door closed than Gilbert began blasting his brother. "How could you have betrayed your trust? You've broken a promise that was made to her mother. She was sent to us to be protected—to be respected. And, simpleton that I am, I brought her here because I thought, under your protection . . . with your help . . ." The priest shook his head helplessly. "But you—you—"

He stopped abruptly. William, apparently determined to ignore everything that was being said, moved around his worktable and, after opening the shutter to the morning light, sat down.

"Are you listening to me, William? Do you not have some remorse, some regret, for what you have done?"

The laird's gaze slowly lifted from the open ledger on his desk and met his brother's with penetrating clarity. "No regrets."

Gilbert waited, dumbfounded, for more of an explanation. But there was none, and the two stared at each other in silence. Finally, the provost felt the last threads of his fraying patience give way.

"I won't allow you to do this, Will. This is the last straw. I have never interfered—well, rarely interfered with your bla-

tant desire to ruin your own life. But this is no private matter. You've willfully dragged an innocent woman of position
into your bed. Now 'tis your duty to do the right thing."

"Sit down, Gilbert."

"I will not," he snapped back, starting to pace the room.
"A grave wrong has been done here, and I will not rest until
'tis set right."

"Gilbert!"

"Do you think I can just forget what I saw? Do you be-
lieve I can just take that young woman away from Blackfearn
Castle and blithely set out to find her a husband? After what
I've witnessed with my own eyes?"

"Gilbert!" William said again, a note of warning in his
tone.

"Nay, I will not be placated, I said." He pointed a finger
in the direction of the laird. "And do not even think of telling
me that she invited your attentions or some other spurious excuse."

"She did not. Now if you'll—"

"No excuses, Will. I warn you." The priest continued pacing the room. "'Tis not you who now has to write a letter to
her mother explaining your weakness."

"When I have the opportunity, I will—"

"Opportunity?" Gilbert snorted. "You have had your opportunity and taken full advantage of it. And now I am faced
with the task of seeking forgiveness from the woman. With
any luck, she might just agree to accept you as a husband for
her daughter. Of course, it might be spring before we get an
answer back, but—"

"There will not be a letter."

The provost whirled on his brother. "There will be. There
must be. As there must be a marriage. Lord help me, if I have
to tie you to your horse and drag you to the church door, there
will be a marriage, and you'll be the groom."

There was a look of amusement in the other man's eyes that riled Gilbert even more.

"Do you think I can't handle you, Will Ross?" He pointed a long, slender finger at his brother's face. "This wedding will take place in the spring!"

William sat back in his chair and tried unsuccessfully to stifle a yawn.

"Spring won't be very convenient for me. You know that between the planting and the lambing, 'tis a very busy time of the year."

"As if you're a farmer," Gilbert scoffed. "Very well, but I'm telling you, 'twill be summer at the very latest."

The Ross shook his head again. "Summer won't do either. Our fishermen will be out working the firth."

"Brother," Gilbert growled. "You are neither a fisherman nor a farmer."

"But my people are. And I cannot be distracted with this—this wedding business when my people need a laird to work beside them and see to their needs."

Visibly restraining himself, the provost stared at the floor, disgust etched on his face. "Very well. You tell me what time is good for you. Though for the life of me, Will, after what you've done here, I do not know why I'm giving you any say in the matter at all. When?"

William Ross rose to his feet. "Today, my brother!"

Gilbert's jaw dropped open, and he stared as the laird came around the worktable and started for the door leading into the laird's bedchamber.

"And you shall marry us before noon," William said, pausing at the door. "Edward and I need to be going back into the village after the ceremony."

Chapter 21

S he wore the gray wool dress that she'd been wearing when
William first kidnapped her.

Standing beside the Highlander in the small chapel of
Blackfearn Castle, Laura kept wondering if she was about to
awaken at any moment. The sound of the provost's voice
droning on in Latin and in Gaelic, the smells of the candles
and the incense, even the faces of the few who had crowded
into the tiny space—it all had a dreamlike quality to it.

Surely, she was about to awaken.

Gilbert Ross paused, but Laura was too embarrassed to
look up and meet the priest's gaze. Just as she'd been too jit-
tery to return the nods of approval of the well-wishers who
had gathered outside the chapel.

What must they all be thinking? she wondered. Everyone
must know the truth. They must know that she and William
had spent the night in her chamber. Why else would no one
even look surprised at the hastily arranged wedding?

No planning. No period of courting, asking, waiting. No
discussions between family. No reading of the banns of marriage.

Not that she deserved any of it, considering the fact that
she initiated everything last night. It was a scandal because
she herself had created it. And then she had gone back to
sleep, only to be caught totally off guard when Maire and
Janet had come to her door. What must they have thought

when she looked at them with total incomprehension as they spoke of getting her ready for the wedding ceremony?

What had he said last night about keeping her? He was going to keep her, he said. She had not even had a moment to think that his words had been an offer of marriage.

Laura absently stared at the bundled sprigs of dried rosemary she held in one hand and remembered the clumsy way she'd received the two women. Tongue-tied and graceless upon hearing the news.

And yet here she was. She was marrying William Ross. William Ross!

Another wave of shame reddened Laura's face at the memory of how foolish she must have looked to the two women. The bedchamber had been in total disarray. Indeed, she had quickly covered herself by pulling on William's old shirt. Even as they helped her bathe and dress, she could not quite grasp the reality of the moment.

Mortified by all these thoughts, she wrapped her trembling fingers tighter around the dried branches and focused on the flickering candle on the altar.

"Gilbert tells me they're a sign of fidelity, lass."

At the sound of his amused whisper, Laura glanced up and looked for the first time into the face of her future husband. Her pounding heart raced even faster at the sight of the rakish grin, the heavenly blue eyes watching her with such confidence.

The bundled sprigs of rosemary dropped from her hand, and she stared at them on the gray stone floor for a moment.

William leaned over and whispered again, a note of mock seriousness in his tone. "I hope you're not trying to tell me something."

Gilbert turned with a warning cough and a threatening scowl before continuing on. Laura scooped up the rosemary branches and glanced at William. He was smiling broadly at her.

A moment later, Laura ran a sweaty palm down over the

wool of her skirt. Behind them, the congregation stirred rest-lessly in the little chapel, waiting in anticipation of the final exchange of vows. If she could only last that long herself.

She looked up in surprise when William's hand reached out and entwined her fingers in his own. Laura let out a shaky breath and held onto him as if her life depended on his touch. Gilbert's voice rose and fell in the measured cadences of the prayers.

"By his Shirt, this is the longest service I've ever heard." There were lines of mischief dancing in the corners of his eyes. "He is punishing us."

Gilbert frowned at the two and stepped down from the altar. He motioned for William and Laura to turn and face each other.

Gazing up at her future husband, Laura to held her breath. Ruggedly handsome, William Ross was dressed impeccably for the occasion. She stared at the white linen shirt hugging his broad chest, at the silver and gold brooch of the ancient Ross clan, at the luxurious black and red of his tartan.

His head was high, and he was completely at ease, com-pletely in command. He looked comfortable, confident in spite of the throng gathered around them and in the courtyard out-side. Laura only wished she could be as unaffected by all the eyes that were upon them.

His thumb caressed the back of her hand, and she gazed up into his eyes. The provost was asking him to speak his vows.

Her heart pounded. Her spirit soared. Her life somehow became complete in that single instant as she watched him re-peat each word without releasing her from his gaze. She re-alized that from now on, for Laura Percy, nothing else mattered, no one else existed, but the man standing before her.

And then it was her turn.

*　　*　　*

Sir Wyntoun MacLean, standing behind the groom, watched as the couple exchanged their vows. Beside him young Miriam, dressed in a deep blue dress, was beaming at the scene unfolding before the altar.

The knight focused his gaze on Laura Percy. Laura Percy Ross, he quickly corrected himself, for in a few short moments Nichola Percy's second daughter would have a new name.

True, he'd failed in his original plan of taking the woman to gain the map to the Treasure of Tiberius. He had never had the opportunity, but then again, he'd never had a clear sense that she had possession of any map. One of his men had even searched her bedchamber, but the effort had proved fruitless.

Wyntoun glanced down at the couple's joined hands, at the restrained happiness that showed so clearly in William's expression. Despite his failures so far, though, the knight could not help but feel a certain satisfaction. He'd lent a helping hand to his old friend. He was watching William shake off the ghosts of his past.

He was pleased for the son of a bitch, but his own battle was far from over. In fact, this union made things a wee bit more difficult.

The provost spoke the last blessing. Wyntoun glanced over his shoulder and watched two of his men glide out of the chapel to where he knew fast horses waited to take them south.

The battle was far from over, he repeated in his mind. His hand absently went to the gold brooch at his shoulder. He ran his fingers over the tiny, colored gemstones, the red hand clutching a blue cross.

He would still secure the treasure. He would not let his brothers down. After all, the Blade of Barra enjoyed nothing more than a fierce challenge.

In his entire life he had never given marriage much thought. But once he'd made up his mind about Laura, the urgency to take her as his wife had come crashing down on him with the force of a river in spring.

Arriving in the chapel first, the laird had waited for some time for Laura to arrive. At first William had entertained notions that she'd decided not to go through with the marriage. Later, when she had appeared at the door of the chapel, he had seen her ivory skin become even paler at the sight of the clan folk jammed into the place. For a moment he'd thought she was about to faint.

But it had taken only a few hushed words. A touch. He had given her his strength and sought out hers. He had felt her assurance grow with every passing moment. She would survive this ordeal, he knew.

As Laura finished her vow, he heard Miriam sneeze behind him. Laura turned with concern to the little girl, though William had felt the same urge to sneeze from the incense. He squeezed Laura's hands gently and drew her gaze up to his. She brightened again in an instant.

The tender trust that shone in those violet pools was his undoing every time. He felt the hammer strokes of his heart gaining momentum in his chest. As he looked at her, his body ached at the memory of all that they'd already shared. Tightening his hold on her hands, William fought off the confusing rush of emotions that tore at his own insides.

She already mattered too much to him. And her approval of him mattered more than he'd ever thought imaginable. But the nagging feelings—the truth about the past that he'd never shared with her. He had to tell her. He should have told her before now. Frankly, the thought of what her reaction would be scared the hell out of him.

Gilbert completed his final blessing, and the throng around them gave a loud cheer. William saw Laura's bewitching eyes round as she nervously clutched his hands.

Undeserving he might be, William thought, but they were now husband and wife.

He pulled her roughly into his arms in relief. She was his. His to keep.

Her head tilted back, and she looked into his face. He saw the tears glistening in the depths of her violet-blue eyes. He hoped desperately that they were tears of happiness.

"Mine to keep?" he asked huskily.

"Yours forever," she whispered as he crushed his mouth down on hers.

He blocked out the cheers and the sounds of the piper outside the chapel. He ignored the congratulatory slaps on the back as well as the line of clan folk ready to wish them well. Instead, he focused only on the woman in his arms and tried to convey in a kiss all the emotions that he could not put into words.

Laura was shy, though—more hesitant than even the first time that he'd kissed her in that hut by Walter Sinclair's castle.

He broke off the kiss, growling his complaint in her ear. "What have you done to my wild and passionate Laura?"

She gently slid her palms up against his chest. "So many are watching us."

"Let them," he growled again, taking her mouth in another searing kiss. This time she melted in his arms as his tongue delved inside. Probing, tasting, searching for assurance. He found it.

"Uncle!" The soft tug of Miriam's hand on his kilt made William abruptly end the kiss. He looked from the blushing, dreamy-eyed woman in his arms down to the lassie standing expectantly at his side. As he reached down and scooped her up, Miriam gave a delighted giggle.

She pressed her forehead against William's and stared into his eyes. "Thank you."

Her words were a mere whisper, intended only for him to hear. But William felt the impact of it rock his body. Her look battered his heart and exploded the locks. With those two words she crept right inside.

"You're welcome." William hugged the child fiercely to his chest and swallowed the emotions that were knotting his throat.

An instant later, Miriam let go of his neck and turned to Laura. "May I call you aunt?"

There were tears glistening in her eyes as Laura looked from William's face to Miriam's. "You can call me whatever you wish, my love." She opened her arms and the child went right to her—wrapping her arms and legs around the young bride.

"Enough of this hiding away of your wife." Wyntoun's heavy slap on his back brought William's head around. "'Tis time, you blackguard, to allow the rest of us forlorn bachelors at least a congratulatory kiss."

"Considering the huge error in judgment she has made in marrying my brother, I'd say she could use a kiss of consolation far more."

William glared threateningly at Gilbert. "Not a word, friar."

"Provost, Willie."

The banter continued. The people of Ross clan, who were continuing to gather in the courtyard, crowded around them as the piper led them toward the Great Hall. Many of them jokingly wished Laura the best in taking charge of their unruly laird.

And William growled at them all, inwardly glowing with pride at the sight of his beautiful new wife. In his arms he carried his daughter. Around him the goodwill of his people manifested itself in a hundred festive signs of affection. He was a happy man, a man blessed with so much.

If only he could find a way to close the door on the ugliness of the past.

Chapter 22

To Laura's surprise, their noon dinner, though certainly festive, was not to be the main celebration of the laird's wedding.

Soon after the meal, replete with toasts enough to float a king's warship, the bride was escorted to her chamber by a bevy of women, where she was to rest and prepare herself for the evening's banquet and revelry. Her new husband, on the other hand, mounted his great horse Dread and rode off with a party of men—including Sir Wyntoun MacLean—to attend to some clan business.

Laura tried not to appear perturbed at his departure, though it was amazing to her how quickly two men could restore a friendship that had seemed to be verging on violence. And just as Maire and Janet had been the ones to tell her of her own wedding plans, they were also left to explain to her about all the visits that the Ross laird had been making among the needy members of the clan.

Unable to remain in seclusion for very long, Laura had soon descended to the Great Hall, determined to help in the preparations that were going on, not only for the evening's feast but also for the upcoming Christmas Day celebrations. From all the talk, she soon ascertained that William Ross had reinstated a nearly forgotten tradition of inviting the entire clan to Blackfearn Castle for the Christmas dinner.

As Laura moved about, lending a hand whenever she was

needed, it tickled her to see that the entire household was undertaking the tasks at hand with an air of cheerful cooperation. Indeed, the spirit of merriment was in the air. Even Chonny was grousing and fussing in the kitchens with a satisfaction he could barely conceal.

Around mid-afternoon, Laura realized she'd not seen Miriam for quite a while. Going in search of the little girl, she ran into the provost in the Great Hall. The priest was overseeing the carving of the Yule log before the open hearth.

"Mistress Laura. I was hoping to find you."

Approaching her new brother in-law, Laura scanned the large room for Miriam.

"I've ordered several of William's men to cut an oak sapling and bring it up to the courtyard. But as far as the location of it—where exactly it should be placed for the hanging of apples tomorrow night—I was hoping you'd give us some advice on the matter."

Laura nodded politely, her eyes still seeking out the little girl among the good-sized crowd hanging boughs of holly and mistletoe around the Hall.

"Also, I was wondering if you would be kind enough to teach Chonny how to make wassail. I've laid a wager with Symon that you would know a wonderful recipe."

"Of course," she replied, nodding again absently.

She turned around in search of the child. In helping Maire, she'd been to practically every room in the castle. She knew Miriam was not in the kitchens, for she'd just left there. When she was in the upper floor of the east wing, she had looked out the windows into the courtyard and the training yard.

The little girl was nowhere to be found, and Laura felt a pang of anxiety clutch her belly.

"And I hope you approve of the cleaning the men have been doing in the Hall. They've been working at it most of the day, and I'd say they have made vast progress, wouldn't you?"

Laura forced herself to look about the Great Hall, and for the first time she noticed the transformation. Over the last week things had been gradually improving, but now the Hall looked entirely different. From the scrubbed floor, to the orderly lines of tables and benches, to the newly cleaned and rehung tapestries on the walls—the Great Hall of the Blackfearn Castle was suddenly a place to be proud of.

"'Tis absolutely stunning, Provost."

"Another thing. I was wondering if you would be interested in participating in the singing of carols? Or even playing a part in—"

"By any chance," Laura interrupted, no longer able to hold back her worry, "have you seen your niece, Provost?"

The man glanced about the chamber and then, giving Laura's worried expression a closer look, nodded finally. "Aye, mistress, I have seen her, though I'm afraid I gave my word not to give away her whereabouts or her scheme until she is ready to reveal them herself."

Laura stared at him in surprise for a moment. "Well, you know, then, that she is safe where she is?"

"Absolutely."

"Is there adult supervision?"

The provost nodded reassuringly.

Laura let out a breath and nodded back at him, turning toward the kitchens. But then, two steps away, she whirled around with embarrassment burning her cheeks.

"Oh, Provost, I—I apologize to you."

Gilbert's eyebrow arched. "And what for, mistress?"

"For my rudeness, of course. Though I hardly deserve such kindness, I just realized what you are trying to do." She wrung her hands nervously as she returned to him. "You—you are trying to get me involved. Trying to make me feel at home. And—and I was horribly abrupt. Would you be kind enough to forgive me?"

A gentle smile broke out on Gilbert's face. "Mistress Laura. I can assure you that there is nothing to forgive."

"But—"

"You were concerned about Miriam. I understood your abruptness was simply the result of that concern." He took a step closer to her and lowered his voice. "And having been a bystander the last time Miriam was here at Blackfearn Castle, I can tell you that the care and affection she is receiving from you is far more pronounced than any she received from her own mother during all of her younger years put together."

Laura blushed and glanced down at her clasped hands. "I can assure you, Provost, I am far more lacking than her mother—"

"Do not speak nonsense, Laura." He put a gentle hand on her arm and drew her gaze to his kindly blue eyes. "'Tis true that Mildred became a sister to me through her marriage to Thomas, but it is the absolute truth when I say that you are far better suited for Blackfearn Castle—and for William."

Mildred. William. She repeated the names somberly in her mind. Always the suggestion of what had been between Mildred and William.

They had made passionate love. He'd tried to salvage her reputation and her future by taking her as his wife. But the tragedy of it was that Laura doubted if she could ever fill the void in William's heart that Mildred had left.

"Do not fret, my new sister."

She looked up again into the man's face.

"I know all of this came about in haste. But knowing William's lack of interest in anything long or drawn out, no one would have expected anything different when it came time for my brother to take a wife." He took Laura by the arm and started leading her toward the door. "But you, however, going along with it! A woman of noble blood, sacrificing your own plans in agreeing to my brother's proposal of marriage. In the eyes of the Ross folk, you are a prize to be highly regarded. And there is, indeed, a great deal of admiration for you."

"Provost, I—"

"Please, Laura, do not fret. We are proud to have you among us." Gilbert stopped and faced her. "You are now one of us, my sister, and nothing could be better—for any of us."

William Ross made certain he was back at Blackfearn Castle shortly after nightfall. Dismounting in the courtyard, he inquired after his wife and Miriam. Learning that they were already in the Great Hall, he ordered Edward to see to his little scheme before joining everyone else for the meal.

Miriam skipped across the Hall to him as soon as he stepped through the door. She wrinkled her nose at him. "We've been waiting forever."

"Is that so?" He leaned down and swept the child up in his arms, earning a giggle and an impish grin for his effort. "That is no way to greet me, my wee complaining brat."

"Is this better?"

She threw her arms around his neck and gave him a big hug. The open display of the child's affection caused a knot to swell in William's throat.

"Much!" he managed to croak.

Across the Great Hall, close to Gilbert and Wyntoun, Laura stood watching them with a tenderness in her gaze. Without question, she was the most beautiful woman he had ever seen in his life. Simply looking at her, he felt desire stir in his loins, and thoughts of all they had done last night came rushing back. Thoughts of things he could not wait to do with her again.

With Miriam still in his arms, he strode purposefully across the Hall to his wife.

Her cheeks blushed with the prettiest of pinks, and her eyes widened as she read the look in his eyes. One hand rose involuntarily to her breast.

"William!" Gilbert called as he drew near. "Glad you found time to return. There is so much that I need to go over with—"

"Wyntoun!" He gestured toward Gilbert. "Take this prattling, overgrown acolyte away. I need a moment alone with my wife."

"That is 'Provost,' if you don't mind."

"Aye," William said with a grin. " 'Prattling Provost' does have a better ring to it."

"Willie, you blasphemous cur—"

"Miriam," the laird continued on, winking at the child and putting her down, "could you please help Sir Wyntoun entertain your uncle for a while? Maybe you can practice some of your whining with him."

"Here to serve you, m'lord."

The child's mock serious reply elicited a laugh all around, but William's eyes were already on Laura.

"Have you been waiting forever as well?"

She bit her bottom lip and then gave a small nod.

He moved closer and took her arm, leading her to the great open hearth. There he turned to face her, blocking the room and everyone in it from her view.

"Did you miss me?"

Her blush turned a deeper red, her gaze flitting away, but a pretty smile broke out on her lips. "Everyone has been awaiting your return. I believe they are impatient for their supper."

"They can all starve, for all I care." He took hold of her chin and lifted it. "But did *you* miss me?"

"I did," she softly whispered.

"Then show me."

Her eyes rounded. "Here?"

"Here!"

She paused. She bit her lip. She swallowed and then looked slowly up until her deep violet eyes were staring into his.

"You are a rogue, William Ross. You know I missed you."
She placed her hands on his shoulders and, raising herself
onto her tiptoes, she brushed her lips against his own.

William took full advantage of the moment, wrapping an
arm around her waist, drawing her up, and kissing her thoroughly. It was some time before he pulled back, and a satisfied smile broke on his lips at the way her eyes remained
glazed for a moment after he'd broken off the kiss.

"I missed you, too." He placed a soft kiss beneath her ear
and took her hand in his own. Turning toward the Hall, he
found every eye in the place on them. Instantly, a cheer rang
out among the gathered throng, the pipers tuned up, and a
noisy celebration began.

"Well, it appears they are not *too* angry with us for de-
laying their supper."

Her voice was little more than a murmur in his ear. "You
scoundrel, I'm embarrassed enough to faint."

He brought her hand to his lips and placed a kiss on the
tips of her fingers.

"Not yet." He grinned at her. "I'll have no swooning until
we're alone. That way, I'll have free rein to do whatever I
wish with my defenseless wife."

"William!" she scolded with a coy smile that made him
laugh out loud.

The woman was precious, he thought. He was certainly
the most fortunate man in the Highlands. Nay, in the world.

Laura sat on one side of him and Miriam on the other
during the dinner. Course after course of meats and fowl and
fish appeared, each a triumph for the new cook. Toast after
toast was offered up for the laird and his new bride, and the
merriment continued unabated for hours.

Finally, as William laid his cup on the table, Laura smiled
at the little girl beside him and suggested that perhaps it was
time for wee ones to be in bed. But the people of Clan Ross
had other ideas.

With a flourish Edward stood up, waving his arm and shouting over the revelry. As the noise subsided, the huge warrior turned and asked the laird and his bride to remain where they were sitting for a few moments of entertainment.

Laura sent him a questioning look and then gave a hesitant nod while William smiled broadly. Under the table, the laird reached over and took his wife's hand in his own. She smiled up at him, and his heart swelled.

The tables that had been lined up in the center of the Hall were pulled back to create an open area before the dais. Everyone but those who were a part of the entertainment moved back, crowding the benches around the large open square.

Edward moved to the end of the dais to present the "argument" and to provide a running commentary.

He introduced the first of the actors.

"Enter, Mistress Laura Percy!"

Peter, the giant, red-haired bruiser of a man, entered from the kitchen door, dressed in a woman's black dress that barely reached his knees and was stretched at every seam. The crowd broke out with boisterous laughter as Peter stepped toward the dais and raised his brows suggestively at his laird before moving to his place in the square.

"Enter, William of Blackfearn, laird of Ross!"

The laughter and shouts continued as Peter's Wife, tiny and pixie-faced, swaggered into the Great Hall, dressed in a Ross kilt that dragged upon the floor.

Miriam was tugging on William's sleeve. "I asked her today why she has no name of her own and is always called Peter's Wife."

William glanced over at the little girl. "Did you, lassie?"

The child nodded excitedly. "Her given name is Eglantine, the same as the four sisters who were born but died before her. She said she thought 'twas a curse for sure not to have a saint's name, so she changed it as soon as she married to Peter's Wife."

William knew the story, but still looked interested as Miriam continued on. "I believe I would like to change my name as well."

Just then Peter's Wife, tripping over the long kilt, fell forward to the floor and Peter, with his fists planted at his hips, cocked an eyebrow at the prostrate woman, causing another wave of laughter to roll through the Hall.

"I like your name," William whispered back to Miriam, "just as it is."

"You do?" The child's bright smile told the laird that she would keep her name—for what was left of the evening, at least.

To the sound of the boos and cheers of the spectators, the rest of the actors filled the stage. William had to laugh when he saw that his people had even convinced Wyntoun to take a part.

Edward raised his hands in the air, and silence crept over the hall. Laura tightened her grip on his hand.

The chief warrior's voice boomed out. "An ordinary day in Blackfearn Castle's Great Hall."

The people started moving around the stage. There were mock arguments between crofters roaming about. Warriors stretched out on benches. Food on trenchers, tasted by the players, was promptly spat out before being dumped on the floor. Gilbert's dog Willie lumbered past the mess, sniffed it without eating, and then stretched out in the center of the square.

"The laird joins his people."

Peter's Wife, pulling up her kilt so she wouldn't trip over it again, marched into the center. Planting one hand on the hilt of the huge wooden sword strapped to her waist, she walked to the crofters, mumbling something and getting smiles and pats on the back. Then she walked to the warriors, again receiving encouraging nods. Then back to the crofters, and back again to warriors. On the last trip, the

"laird" tried to pick up some of the trash, to only trip and
fall over the provost's dog. Willie merely raised an ear. Laughter rang out again in the Hall.

"We could never accuse our laird of not trying, could we?"

The response was in harmony and loud enough to shake
the rafters. William felt Laura's hand squeeze his own and
turned to see her eyes watching him tenderly.

"Mistress Laura arrives at Blackfearn Castle."

William's and Laura's eyes were drawn to the huge figure of Peter, hands planted on his hips, skirt hiked up on one
side, as he walked menacingly into the circle. The whistling
of the men in the Hall was deafening, and Peter's curtsy in
response was actually quite good.

"Mistress Laura takes charge."

"Laura" walked over to the "laird" and batted his eyes,
before turning with exaggerated shock to the melange of food
and men scattered about the stage. Dramatically raising a
hand to his forehead, the "woman" shook his head with an
air of severe disapproval. Not a moment was allowed to pass,
however, before the gigantic "Laura" had rolled the sleeves
of the dress up over a pair of brawny arms and pulled a
wooden spoon out of the pocket of the dress.

Walking around the stage, the warrior began pointing the
spoon at everyone standing around and even raising a pan-
tomimed argument with the onlooking "laird."

The silent wrangling went on for a moment, only to stop
abruptly when Peter puckered his lips and noisily kissed his
tiny adversary.

William cast a side glance at Laura and found her ready
to crawl under the dais.

Pushing aside the "laird," Peter then rushed out into the
audience of clan folk and dragged Symon out by the ear into
the square. Bringing the man to the center of the action,
"Laura" began pointing with his spoon at the people, at the

floor, at the roof, and even at the "laird." Symon nodded with every thrust of the spoon.

"Laura" then moved again to his "laird," earning whistles and shouts when he again batted his lashes suggestively before going back to the perimeter of onlookers. This time Chonny was ushered roughly out into the stage. The same gestures as before were repeated as this time Chonny, too, nodded dramatically with every thrust of the spoon.

"Guests arrive at Blackfearn Castle."

Sir Wyntoun, playing himself, walked into the center. Peter, spotting the giant Highlander, moved over and batted his lashes. Peter's Wife, pulling the wooden sword out of her kilt, faced the new visitor with a fierce scowl. The two mismatched "foes" started to fight. As the "furious" blows fell, with Wyntoun pretending to take the worst of the action from the little woman, the entire hall burst into renewed laughter. Suddenly, the "laird" tripped on her sword and fell to the ground as exaggerated cries of concern rang out from the onlookers.

Edward's voice boomed out again over the crowd. "Mistress Laura saves the Ross."

None of the earlier noise even came close to the cheers that shook the Hall at the sight of Peter thrusting a giant spoon against Sir Wyntoun's buttocks.

William turned to Laura and found her face bright red. She tried to cover it with her hands. He reached over and took a hold of her chin, lifting it until her violet-blue eyes met his.

"I believe, m'lady, we should watch the ending."

Loud cheers resonated off the rafters as Peter's Wife rose swiftly to her feet and, taking Peter by the hand, rushed his "lady" to stand before the provost. Gilbert made the sign of the cross in the air, blessing their union.

The happy couple turned around as the spectators all

pushed forward, calling, applauding, and cheering—not the actors but the new husband and wife sitting at the dais.

William held Laura's hand and pulled her to her feet.

"Thank you, m'lady," Edward called out over the din of the crowd. "Thank you for saving our laird from himself."

Chapter 23

The good-natured mumming of the play and the warm acceptance of Clan Ross as all approached the dais to congratulate the newlyweds moved Laura considerably. But soon after, little Miriam began rubbing her eyes and put her head down on the table.

Making a quiet apology all around as pipers and dancers moved into the center of the Hall, Laura rose to take Miriam to bed. To her surprise, William got to his feet as well, and picked up the sleepy child, laying her head on his shoulder.

Going up the winding set of stairs leading to the east wing, occasionally Laura felt the brush of her husband's arm against her shoulder. Each time she felt a thrill race through her of what the night would bring. Though this would not be their first night in each other's arms, though they'd both felt the power of each other's passion, anticipation still dominated Laura's being, filling her with wave after wave of molten, pulsing heat.

At the top of the stairs, Laura smiled into the blue eyes peering over William's shoulder. The little girl was much more awake now than she'd been in the Great Hall. Suddenly, Miriam straightened herself in the laird's arms.

"Wait."

"What is it?" Laura asked.

"Do you think Uncle Gilbert's dog might be ready for bed as well?"

"I did not think to ask him," William answered gently. "Though, considering all the attention that beast got tonight, taking center stage in the play, I'd say he might already be sound asleep."

"Then would it not be better for him to come to my room to sleep? I mean, 'tis so loud in the Hall and—and . . ."

The child's worried tone concerned Laura. She knew Miriam liked the giant dog. She'd seen the two together in the Great Hall. But right now she seemed genuinely distressed. They reached Miriam's door.

"Perhaps I should go down and see if I can manage to bring Willie up," Laura offered, turning to go.

William shook his head, detaining her. "Nay, lass, 'twill be far too crowded."

Miriam's head snapped around and her blue eyes stared into his. "Too crowded?"

There was a small scratch on the inside of the door. William winked at Laura and pushed open the door.

Laura and Miriam both gasped with delighted surprise. Inside the bedchamber, two canine fur balls fought each other to climb up the kilted leg of the Ross. William lowered the child to the floor, and Miriam immediately sat, allowing the dogs to climb all over her. The child's squeals of happiness echoed throughout the wing.

"Are they mine? Mine to keep?"

"Aye, lassie. Yours to keep."

Laura stepped into the room and closed the door behind her. The absolute contentment reflected in Miriam's face, the loving eyes that moved up and looked into William's face, were a sight to behold. Laura bit her lip to fight back the happy tears that were welling in her own eyes.

Miriam jumped to her feet and ran to William, throwing her arms around him as the puppies swarmed around the two of them. "I love you, Uncle."

Laura watched with surprise as a look of sadness crept into

her husband's eyes. Something in her ached as she watched
a memory cast its shadow over this joyous moment. As much
as it was a torment to her, as much as she hated the reason
for it, she could understand his pain. The sense of loss that
he must be feeling was clearly visible.

The love he still carried in his heart for the dead Mildred
was still too great. The anguished memory of this child's
mother was still too fresh. This child was Thomas's, but she
was not his own.

Visibly forcing the sadness from his face, he dropped down
to his knees and returned Miriam's embrace. "Do you think
you can handle the two of them?"

The little girl's head bobbed up and down.

"I've already talked to the lad Robbie. He'll help you with
them."

The child nodded again in agreement and, sitting again on
the floor, opened her arms to the pups, who immediately leaped
into her lap, nipping and licking her chin.

Miriam giggled. "They're so beautiful. So perfect. This one
looks like a wee bear."

"And they're brave, too," William added, exchanging a
meaningful look with Miriam. "They will be sure to protect
you against both man and beast."

"And bad dreams?"

"Aye." William nodded reassuringly. "They'll do an even
better job of it than Willie."

Miriam stared at the dogs adoringly as Laura watched her
husband. To think, so many days ago she had tried to tell him
about Miriam's needs—about how to welcome this child to
Blackfearn Castle. But he had been a master of the art all
along. The child was home.

Laura gazed at him, knowing that *he* was the one who had
cast the spell over *her*. She was helpless. Her heart belonged
to him. Totally, entirely.

His to keep.

A soft knock at Laura's back drew the puppies' attention, and the two fell over each other to get to the door first. Opening it, Laura found Maire holding a bowl of water in her hand and waiting to come in.

The old woman smiled at the dogs before looking up and facing her. "I brought some water for the lassie's beasts, and I thought, this being yer wedding night and all, I could be putting the wee one to bed."

Before Laura could find her voice, Miriam was at the door, pulling Maire's sleeve to bring her into the room. "Please, Aunt Laura? Maire and I have a secret—I mean, a task we need to be finishing."

Aunt Laura. She repeated the name in her head. How could she ever refuse anything asked by the affectionate blue-eyed imp looking up so imploringly into her face?

Before giving her agreement, though, she looked at her husband and found him standing and ready to leave.

"Well, I suppose since Maire is here and willing—"

Laura wasn't able to finish her words as Miriam's arms wrapped around her waist. The child's open display of love was a gift that Laura planned to treasure forever and ever. She placed a kiss on her hair and straightened, letting William guide her out of the room.

In the hallway and with Miriam's door closing behind them, Laura was pleasantly surprised when her husband pulled her into his arms and just held her. Her head was tucked under his chin, his hand splayed on her back, holding her to him. His warm breath caressed her hair, and they just stayed there for a few moments, silent and content.

Laura understood his need. He needed a moment of quiet to think over everything that had happened in Miriam's chamber. He needed a moment to come to grips with what had happened in his past and what he was facing in the future. But in spite of all this—in spite of all the emotions that Laura was certain excluded her—she was happy to be in his arms.

He belonged to her now, as much as he could belong to anyone other than Miriam's dead mother. Laura was married to him now, and though she could never be Mildred, still she, Laura Percy, was the one he had chosen to be his wife. As she had chosen him.

His head lifted. His hand cupped her chin. Their eyes met in the darkness of the corridor. His voice was a husky whisper.

"I want to make love to you." Laura's breath caught in her chest as his hand moved between their bodies, resting on her stomach—gently stroking the wool against her sensitive skin. "I want to see you swell with our child. I want to have a dozen Miriams running up and down these passages."

His words, his touch, held magic in them, and that molten heat again pooled in her belly. "Only a dozen?" she murmured.

His laugh was more of a growl as he grazed his lips over the sensitive skin of her neck. "What's wrong? You think you cannot bear a dozen lasses for me?"

She lifted herself on her toes and wrapped her arms around his neck. "Of course. But there is planning that needs to go along with having so many children."

"Planning?" he repeated, sweeping her up into his arms and starting for the stairs. "Why don't you start telling me what this planning entails?"

She tightened her hold around his neck and looked into his eyes. "To start with, contrary to wishful thinking, I'll likely not be having two bairns at a time as you managed with Miriam's puppies."

"I'm certain there must be some old wives' tale or incantation that should increase the chances."

"We shan't say anything to Gilbert about that. But how will you feel when I am the size of a barrel, carrying all these children?"

"My affection will only grow. Right now you only become more beautiful to me with each passing day."

He knew how to melt her. She rested her forehead against his chin, taking comfort in the gentle way he carried her.

"And about all these daughters you demand. What happens if we have sons?"

"Then we will just have to try harder at our lovemaking. I tell you, I will not be satisfied until we have a dozen daughters."

She looked up and found a broad smile creasing the corners of his incredibly blue eyes.

"And, though it has never happened in my family, what happens if I turn out to be barren?" she had to ask.

"Then we'll be perfectly happy with Miriam, and I'll simply have to spoil her as I would have if we'd had our dozen lasses." He pressed his lips into her hair. "But none of that will change my—my *plan* of making love to my wife over and over again as long as she wants me."

"I want you now, and I promise to want you always. For you, my roguish husband, are the only man able to unleash my reckless nature."

His soft laugh warmed her heart. "Bad influence that I am."

"Aye," she replied tenderly. "Bad influence that you are."

No sooner had she spoken but she realized they were at the bottom of stairs, with William ready to step into the Great Hall. She stiffened in his arms and tried to get down. But he held her tightly against his chest.

"Where are we going?"

"To the laird's chambers." He stepped into the Hall, and she hid her face against his shoulder, hoping no one would notice them as he carried her toward the rooms. But her hope, of course, was for naught, as whistles and boisterous cheers rang out above the bagpipes.

William continued on, apparently oblivious to all the noise.

She mumbled her words against the wool of his tartan.

"We could have spent another night in my bedchamber, you know."

"You wouldn't expect us to repeat all that happened last night in that wee cot again. We were extremely fortunate, lass, that neither of us was seriously hurt."

He shouldered his way inside his bedchamber and kicked the door shut against all the noise. She continued to hide her face against his chest. "I am ruined, William Ross. I will never be able to look into the faces of any of these people again."

"Then we'll just have to stay here, I should think."

He carried her to the huge bed and placed her gently on it. With a sigh she tried to slide to the middle to make some room for him, but he pulled her back to the edge.

Her eyes glanced about the chamber. It glowed from the soft light of dozens of candles. A large fire was burning in the hearth at one end. Trenchers of cheeses and fruit and pitchers of cider and ale were set on a nearby table.

Her attention turned quickly to her husband, though, as he dropped to one knee beside the bed.

"Turn around, lass."

Sitting obediently before him, she forced herself to hide her excitement, staring at the shuttered window as he unlaced the back of her dress.

"First of all, about last night." Her treacherous voice was quavering. "Everyone in the keep surely must know what we were up to in my chamber."

"Aye, you were incredibly noisy."

Heat rushed into her face from his words and hands as he turned her to face him and pulled the dress forward over her shoulders, entrapping her wrists. She saw his eyes narrow as he gazed at her breasts straining against the thin linen of the shift Maire had given her that morning.

Her voice was hoarse. "As I said, I'm totally ruined."

"Not yet." His mouth brushed against her lips, moved down, and feasted on her neck. With her hands trapped by the dress, she felt a helplessness that was thrilling. But there was a power in it, too, a recklessness and a joy as she felt the wild beat of his heart and the hardness of his manhood rising against the side of her knee.

His mouth continued its tortuous descent until he began to suckle her breast through the thin material of the shift. And Laura found herself quickly melting, any semblance of control slipping away.

He pushed her back on the bed, and in a haze of confusion and passion, Laura felt his hands caress and peel away her clothes. A frenzied madness was overwhelming her, an aching desperation that was playing havoc on her senses as his mouth traveled down her body, kissing, tasting, and tormenting her with every touch of his lips and tongue. When he reached the downy mound and descended still farther, Laura became completely undone, crying out with wild abandon.

A moment later he pulled her into his arms and, with her heart still racing, her body still trembling with aftershocks of the release, he placed a tender kiss beneath her ear.

"Hearing you cry out a moment ago, a noise that I'm certain must have echoed in the Hall, I would have to say that you are now definitely ruined."

Laura spotted the satisfied smile that had spread across those incredibly beautiful lips. She looked down and realized that while she was completely naked, William, on the other hand, was still clothed.

"And how about you?" She gently pushed him away and slid off the bed until she was standing before him. She drew him to his feet and pressed her naked flesh against the solid muscles of his body. "I wonder if you could be ruined in a similar fashion."

His eyes followed the movements of her hands as she removed his clan chief's brooch and slowly pushed his tartan off his shoulder.

"Never." His hands rose to touch the skin of her arms, but

she pushed them away and instead slowly pulled the white shirt over his head. "I will groan—maybe even grunt a wee bit now and again, but ruined enough to cry out? Nay, Laura. I am the very model of control."

She recalled more than just groaning last night, but she withheld any comment. Glancing up at his face, though, she noticed the amused expression.

She started placing soft kisses on his chest. "I can see, m'lord, that you are presenting me with a challenge that I cannot refuse."

He again tried to reach for her, but she pushed his hands to his sides and instead let her mouth travel down the hard planes of his stomach as he stood before her.

Reaching his belt, she glanced up and smiled at the strain showing in his handsome face. She undid the belt and let the kilt fall to his feet. His powerful thighs flexed under her touch, and her breath caught in her chest at the sight and the feel of his full manhood pressing so intimately against her breasts.

Her fingers moved down slowly and encircled the smooth flesh. Placing her mouth again on his stomach, she followed the path that he had with her, descending slowly until her lips caressed the pulsing shaft.

She heard him draw in a deep breath and hold it. Building her courage, Laura let the tip of her tongue trace the length of him. Fiercely, he thrust his hands into her hair.

"Laura, I cannot take much of this." His voice was hoarse. Glancing up, she could see the sweat glistening on his brow.

She wanted him to become undone as she had become undone. On impulse, she opened her mouth and took him in.

Laura heard him call her name as he pulled her roughly to her feet and turned her facedown on the bed.

She spread her palms flat against the bedclothes, lifting herself to receive him as he felt for the moist opening. His penetration was hard, and she cried out softly with the force of it.

Immediately, William leaned forward over her back, his mouth kissing her neck, the erotic spot beneath her ear. His hands caressed her breasts, teasing her erect nipples, before moving lower to stroke her very center with expert fingers.

Now it was she who was to lose control, and she panted for breath, rocking back into him, hardly feeling herself getting lifted off the ground as he drove into her with fast and powerful thrusts.

A growling sound vibrated in his wide chest as he took hold of her writhing hips with his strong hands, plunging into her over and over.

As the heavens burst open with a million dazzling shocks of reds and golds before her eyes, Laura did not know if she cried out. Vaguely, she felt him grip her shoulders, toppling her forward as he himself convulsed with a loud cry. Instinctively, she clutched his arms as he wrapped them around her, pressing her into the bed.

How long they stayed that way, Laura had no way of knowing. She gradually became conscious of their fast and uneven breathing, relishing the feel of their heated bodies molded together both inside and out.

Eventually, she felt him stir, gently withdrawing from her and placing tender kisses on her spine, on her neck. He rolled to the side and turned her, drawing her against his chest and kissing her lips. His mouth slipped to her ear.

"I'm happy to say, m'lady, that for the first time in my life, I have been ruined."

Chapter 24

The portly priest glanced excitedly from the letter in his hand to the faces of the two monks standing before him.

"'Tis a great opportunity, to be sure. And from the sound of this response to my letter, I think your chances of securing positions are quite good."

The tall monk entwined his gnarled fingers before him, his look inscrutable.

"From all the news coming from Balvenie Castle," the priest continued, "the new countess's school promises to be a haven of learning."

The wiry monk squinted up at his leader, but the taller man ignored him and addressed the priest. "If you are so keen on this school of . . . the earl of Athol's—"

"'Tis his wife's school."

"I stand corrected. His wife's. Why are you yourself not applying for a position?"

"In truth, I cannot." The priest reddened slightly. "My place is here at Ironcross Castle. But this letter is very clear about you."

"What exactly does it say, my friend?"

"Why, that the Lady Catherine is very receptive to meeting with you." The man waved the letter encouragingly. "I'd say your positions are assured."

The priest continued to talk, waving the letter about. The taller monk, excusing himself, limped away, his eyes shining beneath his hood. His heart was drumming, and mind was racing. Tomorrow, they would be on their way to Balvenie Castle.

Things could not be going more smoothly, he thought with a grim smile. With the Blade of Barra at St. Duthac's and himself at Balvenie, it would not be long before the Treasure of Tiberius was his . . . and his alone.

Laura was hesitant at first when her husband asked her to accompany him to the village the next morning. With Christmas and the clan dinner only a day away, she felt her first priority should be to lend a hand to Chonny or Symon in the preparations. But William insisted that she meet her new clan folk and see how they lived, so she gave in to his wishes. Leaving Miriam in the care of Gilbert, she headed out with her husband and a group of his men.

Puffs of white highlighted a brilliant blue sky, and she soon found that the people of Clan Ross were busy with preparations of their own as the group trekked through the village. Large circles of holly and ivy and mistletoe had been connected together, forming spheres of green that were then hung from lofts and doorways and even from the rustic sign above the entry to The Three Cups Tavern.

Some of the faces she had already seen at Blackfearn Castle, but even those she did not know gathered around them wherever they went, welcoming the laird and his new wife as they made their way through the tiny village.

After stopping at a number of cottages, William led Laura to the market cross, where the laird made a great show of introducing his blushing bride to the smiling throng. From there the small group moved out of the village to a tiny, tumbledown cottage nestled into the side of a hill by the running stream. It was here, she was told, that the former steward's widow had come to live.

As William approached the low doorway, Edward quickly

filled Laura in on the details regarding Robert's widow, including the laird's concerns about the old woman living all
alone.

The somewhat tottering woman ushered them all into the
hovel, and Laura soon saw the reason for her husband's concern. The hut itself was damp and cold, with no fireplace but
only an open pit with a chunk of dying peat embers to warm
the black pot of porridge hanging above it. A straw pallet in
the corner clearly served the old woman for a bed, and there
was only one small stool to sit on, near a rickety table by a
shutterless window.

"I'm so delighted for ye, my dear," the woman said. "Edward, be a good lad and fetch the block of wood so that the
laird has something to sit on. 'Tis around on the south side
of the cottage."

Grinning like a young boy, the aging warrior went after
the rude seat. At William's insistence, the two women sat by
the cheerless fire.

"Luella," he began with a meaningful glance at Laura, "I
wish to have some dresses made for my bride."

"Aye, Will," the woman responded, reaching out and taking hold of Laura's hand with her icy fingers. "A lass so
bonny as this one needs fine things."

"True. A trunk full of them."

When Laura opened her mouth to object, William shot her
a hard look and she stopped herself. Though in truth she could
see little use in having more than two good dresses.

"But," the laird continued, "there is no one left at the castle who can stitch or embroider the way you can."

"I *was* fairly good at that, don't ye know?" she said confidentially to Laura before turning back to the laird. "But
surely young Maire can handle the task."

"Nay." William shook his head. "She has all of the house-
keeping on her shoulders now."

"Well, if ye would find an able steward with a wife . . ."

Her face saddened suddenly, and Laura knew she was thinking of her late husband.

"We have found a steward, Luella," Edward broke in.

"Oh? And has he a wife?"

"Nay, Luella." Edward continued. "Like me, the man's an old bachelor to his very bones."

"Auld bachelor!" she scoffed at the giant warrior. "And ye be auld? Why ye're a man barely full grown."

Laura decided it was time to speak up. "What these two are trying to say is that we need you at the castle, Luella."

"I? 'Tis kind of you, mistress, but I think we'd all be better off if I was not a burden—"

"Luella." William's voice was stern. "I'll not have any burdensome women in my keep. We need a good seamstress. We need you."

"And there's something else," Laura added. "There is a child at the castle who needs to learn such skills."

"Aye," the laird agreed. "Wee Miriam has come back to the castle. She'll be needing dresses as well. But Laura is correct. Who's to teach the lassie if you don't?"

Luella looked from one face to the next, her lips pursed as she considered the question. Finally, her brow cleared and she nodded. "Very well. But only so long as I'm needed."

Laura almost laughed at the relief so transparent on William's and Edward's faces, but she knew how they felt. And she also knew that her handsome husband would never again allow this old woman to live in conditions like these.

From waking up in the morning with Laura nestled in his arms, to attending Christ's Mass with his family and clan, to finally sitting down to the most successful feast ever put on in Blackfearn's Great Hall, William Ross decided that this had to be the most perfect day of his life.

Until now.

Her violet-blue eyes flashing, Molly pranced across the

floor to a spot directly in front of William as the pipers struck up another tune. There was a saucy, wild look in her eyes as she focused on the dais and on him. And then she began to dance.

The Ross looked hopefully toward the doorway through which Laura had departed with a sleepy Miriam not long ago. His wife had promised to be back as soon as the child was tucked away. William wished it were this very moment.

Molly continued to dance for him, her legs kicking high to the music. He turned to Wyntoun for rescue, but the useless blackguard was involved in a lengthy discussion with Gilbert on Church hierarchy.

"You've been breaking my heart, Will."

Turning, he found the woman had leaped the short distance onto the dais and was leaning seductively toward him. Jumping back to the floor, she whirled, tossing away her shawl and revealing a low-cut linen blouse that displayed more cleavage than William had seen in public in recent memory.

He turned back to his brother and Wyntoun, but she was back up on the dais in an instant. Her eyes shone with desire, and when the wench leaned provocatively over the table, her breasts nearly toppled out of the blouse. William looked quickly away from her creamy white bosom. But at the feel of her long fingers seductively stroking the back of his hand, he very nearly leaped out of his chair as he pulled his arms away.

"Molly!" He tried to keep his voice low. "There are a great many men here who would think this Christmas was the finest feast ever if you would turn your attentions to them for a moment or two."

"I came here tonight only because of you, Will," she cooed meaningfully, rolling her mane of hair to one side and giving him a clear view of the smooth skin of her neck. She brushed a hand over her breasts. "And I know of some Christmas apples that are feeling *very* neglected."

William quirked a half smile. It was comforting to know that her efforts were doing nothing to excite his blood. "You are a lusty wench, to be sure, Molly. But I'll not be handling those again . . . on any holiday."

A pout tugged at her full lips. "But you sent word that you'd be stopping in to see me. I've been waiting."

"Well, wait no longer, lass. I am a married man now, and you'll grow old and gray waiting for me."

She gave a hearty laugh and leaned farther down on the table, reaching to touch his face. He pushed her hand away, his face darkening. "Nay. You go too far now."

A look of anger flashed in her eyes, but she quickly restrained it. "You're too much of a man to be satisfied with one wee English stripling." She picked up the cup of ale before William and lifted it to her lips before pressing it between her breasts. "You may not be straying this night, but I'll be keeping the laird's cup full for you at the tavern."

"Do as you please, lass," William said seriously. "But know this. I'm a changed man, and 'twould be good for all if you were to turn those eyes of yours on some other deserving lad."

"You mean it, then?" A look of perplexity crept over her face. "You've truly fallen for this woman?"

"Aye, Molly," he said earnestly. "I have."

Wyntoun's elbow nudged him in the ribs, and William followed his gaze. In the doorway by the stairwell, Laura stood like a queen, watching him.

"For the first time in my life, lass. I have fallen entirely in love."

Laura waited until the woman stepped down from the dais and rejoined the dancers in the center of the Great Hall. It had to be Molly.

Then she stepped back into the shadows of the stairwell

as tears of anger stung her eyes. A quiet fury burned in her throat.

A possessiveness took hold of her with a power and suddenness that stunned her. Jealousy laced her blood with fire, and as she watched Peter's Wife pass the entry to the stairwell, a plan flashed in her mind, driving out all other thoughts.

In an instant she had Peter's Wife by the hand and was pulling the diminutive woman from the Hall.

One moment she was standing by the stairwell, the next she had disappeared. William was considering going in search of his wife when he spotted her reentering the Great Hall and crossing quickly to their chambers with something folded in her hands.

From the looks of things, the rosy-faced dancers were going to continue all night, and several of the pipers appeared to be competing as to who could get the drunkest and still play an identifiable tune. Clan Ross was in the high glee of the season, and William was really quite happy about it. Aside from the dancing and drinking and eating, card playing and wrestling and a spirited game of hot cockles were taking place in various parts of the Great Hall, and if the revelers didn't burn the place down, the Christmas celebration would be off to a very good start.

William was glad that merriment had at last returned to Blackfearn Castle, but his thoughts were drawn to other things right now. An image of Laura readying herself for bed pushed itself into his mind, creating a stirring of his loins that was not to be ignored. Like the geese traveling south for the winter, William knew where he belonged, and the prospect of another night in the warmth of her arms lured him quickly out of his chair. With a wave of good night to the jolly assembly, the Ross headed for his chambers.

Inside their chambers he closed the heavy oak door behind him, but was surprised to find she was not already abed. The

door to his work room was ajar, however, and his brow furrowed with mild irritation at the thought that she was working this late.

"Laura?" He took a step toward the separating door.

"Wait, I'll be right out. Just give me a moment."

He sighed, the furrow smoothing. This was his Laura, always planning something. His life would never be dull, he
thought. What a changed life spread out before him. So different from the dreary one he had so long imagined for himself. Taking off his shoes, he removed his shirt and crossed
to the hearth, stacking more blocks of peat on the fire for the
night.

And he was a changed man, William thought with great
satisfaction. The enjoyment he got out of spending time with
his wife—of talking to her not just about her plans, but about
his plans for Blackfearn Castle, for the crofters—aye, that was
surely a sign of it.

His plans! He had to smile at himself. The lass had wrapped
herself around his heart, his body, and his mind. Whatever
she had done to him, he knew it was a blessing. She was a
precious gift that he wasn't going to jeopardize by fooling
with any wench like Molly—or with any other woman, for
that matter. He'd had his fill of the others. Laura was everything that he needed now. For today, for tomorrow, and for
eternity, as far as he could see of it.

But there was still an eel in the stew, poisoning it. His past.
She deserved to know. Aye, he thought, she deserved to
know. And despite his fears regarding what would come of
it, he knew that one day he would have to trust his heart and
reveal the truth of his past to her. She was his wife. She had
a right to know. And though the danger of losing her, of losing her affection, still lurked in his mind, he knew he had no
choice. She had to know him as he was, as he had been. Perhaps then, with time, she would forgive him and grow to love
him as he so desperately loved her.

A shadow in the passageway into his work room drew William's gaze. Suddenly, he found that his throat had gone dry.

Laura—dressed only in a very small, very gauzy shift—leaned against the doorframe. The translucent slip of material reached only her mid-thigh, and William's eyes caressed the smooth skin of her leg, rising to where the dim light behind her shone through the sheer garment, emphasizing the enticing curve of her hip. His eyes lingered over every inch, imprinting in his mind the sight. Slowly, his gaze ascended to where her breasts—with the dark, hard nipples standing out against the material—threatened to spill out over the top of the low neckline.

He let out a long breath and rose slowly to his feet. "Where did you get this thing?"

She crossed her arms under her breasts, pushing them up higher.

"Peter's Wife."

She had unbraided her black mane of hair and brushed it to one side. William's eyes traveled down the ivory stretch of her beautiful neck, down again to her breasts. A slight pull on the fabric and the delicate rose-colored peaks would spill out, he was quite sure. Quite hopeful, in fact. He moved closer to her and saw her violet eyes darken with excitement.

"And what inspired my bonny wife to seek out such an irresistible torment for me?"

He came to a stop a breath away. He ran a slow finger from her ear down the smooth stretch of her neck.

"Since coming to Blackfearn . . ." He heard the catch in her throat as he let his finger lightly trace the top of one breast. ". . . I—I've been hearing all this talk of Peter never being able to refuse anything of his wife."

"Do you think I could possibly refuse you anything, my own enchantress?"

"What I am about to ask is too important."

His finger traced the neckline of the garment. His finger-tips slid downward slightly, across the material. He smiled as her nipple rose even farther at his touch. He looked up and found her lips apart, her eyes watching the movement of his hand.

"You were saying?" he asked hoarsely. William lowered his head, and he pulled the material of the shift with his teeth. Her breast sprang free, and her breath came out in a quick gasp as his tongue flicked one nipple.

"I cannot . . . I cannot think."

His arms were around her now, and he felt her quivering with excitement. He drew her into the chamber and leaned her back against the closest wall. Pulling the hem of the shift up, he slid two fingers into the moist cleft between her legs.

"Tell me what 'tis that you desire, love?"

Her body continued to tremble. Her lips parted. Her violet eyes, clouded with passion, stared into his own.

"Tell me, Laura," he whispered, his lips a breath away, his fingers continuing to stroke the sensitive spot, pleasuring her. Her head dropped back against the paneled wall, and he looked at the blood pulsing at the base of her throat. It seemed to match the hammering pace of his own heart. "I'd give my life for you. 'Tis yours for the asking."

She opened her mouth to speak, but then shook her head and again leaned back against the wall as her breaths started coming in ragged gasps. He stopped his questions as she rose higher and higher. He continued to hold her tightly to him, teasing, stroking, watching as she writhed blissfully in his arms. Finally, she cried out at the pleasure of her release.

He wanted to take his time. When the time was right, he thought, enjoying the moment, he would carry her to the bed and have her tell him what she wanted before taking her.

But her wandering hands, moving down his chest and still farther down, found his manhood bulging beneath the kilt, and soon his thinking became a thing of the past.

This time it was William who found himself growing short of breath and his whisper growing hoarse as she ran her hand the length of him, kneading him and stroking him through the wool.

"So," he forced out, "are we done with your talk?"

Laura lifted the front of his kilt and touched his bare skin.

"Later," she purred breathlessly. "There is a great deal that I need to tell you later."

He lifted her off the ground, and she wrapped her legs around his waist. "Later," he agreed, groaning with pleasure as he guided his manhood into her. Rocking in his arms, she took in his full length and cried out at the sensation.

"There is much I have to say as well," he panted, lifting her again and again, and driving into her with powerful strokes. "Later."

The rollicking pandemonium of the festivities reaching them from the Great Hall was beginning to abate. Laura knew that most of the household was already asleep. Though from the far-off sound of bagpipes and singing, some of the revelers had simply taken the merriment out in the direction of the castle's stables.

In their chambers, however, the fiery passion of their repeated lovemaking hung over the two of them like a golden cloud. Warm and glowing, Laura nestled in her husband's arms, her head pressed tightly against the musculature of his chest in the huge bed.

She listened to the strong beat of his heart. Felt his warm, contented breath caressing her forehead. She smelled his musky man scent. She tightened her hold around his waist and tried to fight back the raw emotions that were battering her insides. A single tear slipped out of her eye and dripped onto his bare chest. His hand immediately dipped under her chin and lifted her face. She found herself looking into the blue eyes that had become her salvation.

"What is it, Laura?"

She didn't trust her voice, so she just stared at him with all the love that she had for him.

"What is it, love?"

At his term of endearment, more treacherous tears escaped their confinement, making their way down her face. He rolled her onto her back and moved next to her, holding her chin, kissing away the tears on her cheeks. Tenderly, he kissed her lips.

"Talk to me, Laura."

"This—this is the second time you've used that word."

His face registered his perplexity, and she used the back of her hand to stroke his cheek. So rough to the touch. So manly in his beauty.

"The word love. 'Tis—'tis a beautiful word."

A gentle smile broke out on his perfect lips. "You're crying because I spoke out what I feel for you in my heart?"

She nodded and then shook her head before the meaning of what he'd said sank into her confused mind. "Your heart? Do you—do you really mean what you just said?"

"You know that." He nodded, continuing to look into her eyes. "But tell me, Laura. This is not what is tormenting you. A while back, when I first returned to the chamber, there was something you wanted to tell me."

She looked away, trying to gather her courage. The shift she'd gotten from Peter's Wife lay on the floor by the bed. William's tartan, recklessly cast away, lay in a pile beside it. His gentle touch to her chin brought her eyes back to his, and she knew she had to speak.

"Last night I borrowed that—that shift from Peter's Wife after I saw you in the Great Hall with Molly."

He immediately raised himself on his elbows. "Laura, that—"

She put her fingers to his lips. "I understand, William. You

told me before. You are a man. A very handsome man who
has needs."

His brow raised in confusion. "You mean you want me to
have other women?"

"Only if you have a wish for an early death." She frowned
at him. "I put that—that shift on. I presented myself to you
as I imagined Molly might expose herself to you. And I did
it . . . well, to teach you a lesson."

"A lesson?" he repeated as an amused glint crept into his
eyes.

She pushed him onto his back and lay on top of him, crossing her arms over his chest and glaring down at him.

"Aye, a lesson. A lesson that whatever . . . whatever needs
you might have can be met by your wife. A lesson about love
and faithfulness since, by all the saints, William Ross, I love
you too much to allow anyone else to come to your bed."

A smile broke out on his lips. A hand came up to cup her
face, but she pushed it away.

"Stay put and let me finish. You do not wish me to be
rough with you."

"Is that so?"

She pushed herself back onto her knees. Drawing the bedclothes around her, she scowled fiercely at him. A soft gleam
shone in his eyes.

Laura's face grew serious. "But this is about more than just
Molly. Much more. Be it my life, or yours, or Miriam's, I understand that I cannot change the past. In my own case, you've
helped me to build a new life. My father is dead at the hands
of the English king. My family has been separated, possibly
for the rest of our lives. But you have given me your family,
a new family. You have given me purpose and have taken
away the nightmares. And for that I will be forever thankful.
But as far as *your* past is concerned . . ."

She stopped, seeing the dark frown forming on his face.
But she had to continue.

"I am not Mildred. And as much as I might try, I cannot be Mildred any more than I can be Molly. I can be no one but myself." He sat up abruptly in the bed, and she felt that old stab of jealousy in her heart. "I know I cannot stop you from loving her. I realize that I may be forever fighting the memory of your true love."

"True love?" There was so much loathing in those simple words. But she pushed on. She had to finish.

"William, all I am telling you is that I promise not to dwell on what is past. Not to mention it even, ever again. But as far as the present . . . the thought of sharing you with someone else. That is something I will not do. I—"

A soft knock on the door drew both of their eyes to the door.

"Go away!" he thundered. The knock, even more tentative than before, came again. Laura crept discreetly beneath the bedclothes as William, cursing under his breath, picked up his kilt and wrapped it quickly around his waist as he marched to the door.

She heard the quavering voice of Robbie, the stable lad who had taken to watching over Miriam, but she could not make out his words. William's gruff "Aye, lad. You've done well" was clear enough, though, and a moment later, Laura saw her husband close the door and pick up his shirt.

"Something is wrong," she said, starting to rise from the bed.

"Stay where you are," he said, dressing. "Some of my men have decided to take the horses out and run them in the night. Edward sent the lad for me."

"What?"

"St. Stephen's Day! The drunken fools decided to get an early start on it. Some folk believe that if you run a horse near to death and then bleed it, the blasted creature will have good health for the coming year. 'Tis all nonsense."

"And where are you going?"

"I cannot very well let them kill themselves or my horses, tearing about the countryside on a moonless night."

Laura watched him move gracefully to the door. His dark scowl made him look fierce in the light of the guttering candles. She understood that it would always be like this. He would always act on the compassion he felt for those he cared about.

He stopped at the door and half turned to her. "We are not finished discussing what is past."

"Nay, William. We *are* finished with the past," she called softly. "The present and the future. That is what we have now."

He shook his head and frowned as he jerked open the door.

Chapter 25

It took hours to round up the men and horses. It hadn't been difficult finding them, loud and drunk as they were. But the icy mix of sleet and rain had stung his face and soaked him through in no time, and he had to force down the foul mood that had enveloped him. After all, he told himself as he herded his boisterous band of warriors back toward the castle, this was all just another part of the damned festivities.

It was perhaps an hour or so before dawn when he got back to the laird's chambers, and Laura was fast asleep.

He stood next to the bed and stared at the innocent face of his wife. At her beauty. At the love that shone through her even in sleep.

He was undeserving of her—of everything that she stood for. The goodness. The trust.

It could not wait. He could not tarry any longer. Damn, he thought. The uncertainty that must have been eating away at her! The lie that she thought was the truth. He had to put an end to the torment that he'd been causing her. And then, maybe then, with time, he could see that look of trust in her eyes again.

Someday, perhaps, she'd forgive him enough to love him again.

He turned his steps toward his study.

*   *   *

Laura awoke with a start just before dawn and touched the
cold and empty space beside her in the bed. William had not
come back.

She sat straight up in bed, worrying if the men had had
difficulty gathering the horses during the night. Getting swiftly
out of the bed and pouring water into the bowl on the table
to wash, she saw the folded parchment with her name in-
scribed so carefully on it.

She opened it hastily. It was from William. Her knees were
wobbly as she grabbed a blanket and threw it over her shoulder. She sat herself down in the closest chair. It had to be bad
news, or her husband would be telling her whatever was written in this letter himself. She pressed the heel of her hand
into a nervous stomach and tried to fight back the tears. It
had to be the worst, and she dreaded the thought.

Forcing herself to look, she stared at the words dancing
before her teary eyes.

My beloved Laura,
    I start this letter asking for forgiveness, since what
you are about to read are things that I should have revealed to you long before this moment. Long before we
took our vows and I stole away your chance of finding
real happiness somewhere away from me.
    But I waited. Waited because I was fearful of losing
you. Of having you think less of me, as I knew you
would, after hearing the truth. Of having you decide to
leave Blackfearn Castle. Of having you leave me.
    As you have already guessed, the truth behind my
torment lies in my past. But contrary to your belief, the
cause of all this pain is not the affection that I had for
a certain woman, but the dishonor that my own foul acts
have brought upon my family.
    I tell you the truth. As it was. And I hold no one to
blame for what happened but myself. And I do beseech

your forgiveness, Laura, for the man I once was is now forever changed.

I was once infatuated with Mildred of Hoddom, but I can assure you that it was not love. It was never the same emotion that I hold for you, my dearest Laura. I have learned what it feels like to want to sacrifice your very breath. I know now how it feels to lose a desire for life, if that life cannot be completed at your side.

Mildred was beautiful, and her seeming affection for me drew me under her spell. Too blinded with my own pride, I never paused in my pursuit of her to give much thought to our unsuitable positions—or to her own hidden desire for a more advantageous marriage.

Blindly, I allowed myself to dream, to plan a future with Mildred woven into its fabric. But then disappointment came. Her occasional distraction and her haughtiness combined with the vicious game of wanting me as long as there was no better company to please her.

But again, selfishly, blindly, I did not withdraw. Playing the part of the loyal suitor, I continued to harbor hopes of what might be. I consciously ignored all kinds of rumors of other lovers, of better men than myself. I disregarded the constant prattling talk about an impending marriage. I wanted to believe it all mere lies.

It was late in the winter when Mildred came one night to my bed. It was not the first time she had done so. And I know now that I was not the only man whom she bedded.

I would have gladly forgotten that night long before now if not for the fact that the next day my brother Thomas arrived at Hoddom Castle. I knew nothing of his coming. I knew nothing about his intention to marry her. After forcing Mildred to speak, she confessed to me that day that she had known about the negotiations regarding the marriage. Flippantly, she told me that the night we had shared meant nothing. It had simply been her way of saying good-bye.

If I were a better man, if I were an honorable man, I would have spoken to Thomas then. And this talk would not have centered on my intentions for Mildred, but on my mistake in taking my brother's intended to my bed just a few days before they were wed.

Though my feelings for her had quickly turned to loathing, I would have married her rather than damage her reputation, or my brother's, beyond repair.

But instead I said nothing. My guilt lies in the knowledge that I did nothing. That I did nothing to approach Thomas with the truth. Nay, instead I simply slunk away, withdrawing to lick my supposed wounds, and let the masque play out as Fate had devised.

I moved away. Turning my back to my family and deciding never to look back. But news of Thomas and Mildred kept reaching me. The announcement of Miriam's birth, barely nine months after their marriage. Guilt continued to torment my soul. The questions of whether the child was truly Thomas's or if she was mine. But in my heart I knew. And yet still I stayed away.

And then there was other news. Of Mildred's dissatisfaction with Blackfearn Castle. Of her restlessness. There were even letters that I started to receive from Mildred, invitations to join the family for festive occasions. Though innocent in appearance, they all carried in them that unmistakable hint of deceit. She was always certain to send news of Miriam. Of the child's looks. Of the child's coloring that so much resembled mine. Of the lass's temperament.

It was maddening. But I stayed away. What was done I could not change. And my guilt appeared to lie so heavily only on me. At this point, I decided, with cowardice in my heart, that there was no reason to upset Thomas with something as destructive as the truth.

You have already been told of the rest, I know. Of Thomas's and Mildred's deaths. Of the Lord's punishment of bringing me back to Blackfearn Castle to live with my guilt.

I knew beyond a shadow of a doubt that Miriam was mine the moment I laid eyes on her. There was something between us, an immediate bond so deep and so sure, that I knew she was my child.

Although Mildred and I could have been the only ones to guess at the truth, there were times in the past when I thought Gilbert might know the truth as well. But we have never spoken of it.

There is so much that I have said here. More blame and guilt than I could possibly shake from my villainous bones. But then, hearing you last night, realizing that you thought you were somehow in competition with Mildred for my love . . . I could not allow that.

Laura, I swear on the blood of my father, on the Shirt of St. Duthac, on the Veil of the Blessed Virgin, that I never knew the meaning of love until the moment I met you. You opened the door to my heart and let me glimpse the light that shines from the very soul of you.

I ask for your understanding. I ask for your patience. I ask for the forgiveness that I know you have in your heart.

Laura, I know I am undeserving of your love, but stay with me, stay with my daughter, and perhaps with time I can once again earn back your trust, your affection, your love.

William

A frozen rain continued to fall, and the ground around him was churned up into a thick black ooze.

In the armorer's shed beside the training yard, a fire had been lit for warmth rather than for work. Inside the open shed the warriors who had not participated in the late night ride stood together, watching with a certain unease the violent force with which the laird was battering away at the target post with his sword.

Sweat and rain clung to his bare chest and back. Water dripped from his long hair. His legs were covered with mud from the miles he'd covered through the hills.

Edward leaned against a post between the laird and the rest of the men. When young Robbie ran down from the keep, he gestured for the lad to come to him rather than approach the laird. The boy came to a halt beside the bearded warrior.

"Mistress Laura," the boy whispered, warily eyeing the laird as William hacked a huge chunk from the target with a ferocious blow. "She is—she is looking for the laird."

Edward followed the boy's gaze and shook his head. "Go back and tell Mistress Laura that I'll send her husband to her as soon as I dare get close enough to him. Nay, just tell her that he's busy right now. He'll be in anon."

Robbie didn't even pause as he turned and began to run toward the door to the kitchens.

Edward remained at his post, giving his master room enough to unleash his anger but at the same time staying between William and the men. Odd's blood, he thought decidedly, at this moment no one—not he himself or even Sir Wyntoun—would be able to stand for long against the laird's fury.

William kicked the target post and turned his blows on a fresh one. Writing that letter, pouring out his past in words, had cut a wound in him so deep that there was no dressing large enough to cover it. No bandage strong enough to hold together the ragged edges of his burning flesh.

And all of this because he feared that Laura might never forgive. Perhaps, he thought—slashing viciously at the target—now that she knows, she will no longer love me, no longer desire me, no longer care to spend even one day more with me.

He would go mad. He knew he would surely lose his hold on life if she was to go. My God, he thought, she *is* life.

And yet, deep down, William knew he had done right. He'd had to tell her the truth. He'd had to put aside the past and face the future. Their future.

But where was that future now?

He had raised his sword again at the target when a movement over the east wing of the castle drew his attention. He looked up in time to see a cloth of some sort falling to the ground.

He lowered his weapon. His blood was pounding in his head. His heart, hammering away in his chest, suddenly threatened to burst. It was too much to hope that it could be a sign.

Peter ran toward the spot where the thing had hit the ground. He watched his warrior pick up the discarded material and turn to the rest of the men on the other side of the yard.

" 'Tis a lassie's shawl."

William held his breath as the shutter in the last window of the wing opened and a small hand darted out, throwing something else out to the amazement of the crowd.

"There is something more," one of the men called, running toward Peter.

"Who is in that chamber now?" Edward asked one of the men.

"Don't know! 'Twas Mistress Laura's bedchamber," the first man announced. "Remember, she was feeding the hawks, and . . . ?"

William stiffened and took a step toward the keep as he saw what Peter held up in the air.

" 'Tis a woman's dress. I believe 'tis Mistress Laura's."

Behind the laird, several of the men drew near. "Is she up there, m'lord?"

William watched as the wooden shutter opened again and a hand appeared, dangling something out the window. He knew what it was before she let it drop.

"'Tis a shift!" one of the men called out eagerly, but William was already halfway to the keep.

He went through the kitchen like a rampaging bull, and nothing slowed him as he climbed the back stairs to the east wing, taking the steps three at a time. In a moment he was standing before the oak door at the end of the passageway, and he pushed open the door without any hesitation.

Laura stood with her back to the closed shutter. She held a blanket around her, and her violet eyes gazed affectionately across the room at him.

William let out a long breath. A breath that he'd been holding for an eternity. He slowly stepped into the chamber and closed the door.

She smiled. A loving smile, a forgiving smile. She let go of the blanket, and it pooled around her feet. Her ivory skin, free of any encumbering clothing, glowed in the dim light of the chamber. Her eyes shone with love.

"I believe," she said, gliding across the floor, "I now have your attention."

Chapter 26

Only two days before the welcoming in of the new year at Hogmanay with its traditional feasting and gift giving, Laura was surprised when a breathless young Robbie ran to her in the kitchens, interrupting her discussion with Chonny.

"The provost needs to see ye, mistress. He says 'tis very important."

Having just returned from a successful trip into the village, she had a great deal to attend to, but the boy's face clearly conveyed the importance of the summons.

"Thank you, Robbie. Tell him I'll be there shortly."

Stopping by the laird's chamber first, Laura hid away the little surprise she had for William and then passed into the work room to meet with Gilbert.

As she entered, she noticed the shuttered window and the serious look on her new in-law's face before spotting the small wooden chest—banded in iron and sporting a large lock—set beside a lit candle on William's worktable.

A feeling of uneasiness prickled her. Laura had a good idea of what lay in the chest before the provost even opened his mouth to speak.

After offering her a seat, Gilbert leaned against the desk and began without ceremony. "Laura, when you and I first met at St. Duthac's, you asked to see the correspondence my predecessor and your mother, the Lady Nichola, had exchanged before your arrival."

"And you showed me the letters."

He paused and then shook his head. "I only showed you what my instructions from your mother allowed me to show you."

Her eyes moved to the ornately carved chest.

"Lady Nichola's instructions were direct. Father Jerome was to hide this casket away. He was to protect it as if the key to the very gates of Heaven lay within its confines." The priest's hand rested lightly on the wooden chest. "And we were to continue our watch over it until such time as you were perfectly secure in your place of safety."

Laura met the man's steady blue-eyed gaze. "But did not my arrival at St. Duthac's meet that requirement, Gilbert?"

He shook his head again, frowning. "I could not, in good conscience, guarantee your safety there. It was clear to me—after hearing of the incident at the Convent of St. Agnes—that the men who went after you there could just as easily try to take you from St. Duthac's. So I—"

Gilbert stopped, straightening up and beginning to pace before the small fire in the hearth. Laura waited expectantly, watching him as he considered his next words carefully. His eyes darted to her a number of times. Finally, he faced her.

"Laura, in your mother's instructions . . . there was a reference to marriage."

"Marriage?"

Gilbert nodded. "Though 'twas not a requirement in her letter of directions, she clearly stated that if you were to find a suitable husband, we should consider your situation secure."

A frown creased Laura's brow. "And that was the reason for your discussion of marriage with me?"

"Aye, for the most part."

A somewhat guilty look imprinted itself on the provost's face, and Laura suddenly realized that he had been working quite carefully to "secure" her future with his brother.

"You took a great risk, Gilbert."

"Aye," he admitted. "But I have a question for you. Did you—or your parents—ever meet William before coming to Scotland?"

The provost's words surprised her. "I cannot speak for my parents, but I can tell you that I never did." She felt herself relax at the very thought of William. "I can assure you, Gilbert, your brother is not a man easily forgotten. But why do you ask?"

Gilbert Ross leaned on the table again, drawing the casket closer. "There was just . . . well, a hint of something in your mother's letter. It made me think she somehow knew William, that perhaps she had met him when he was attending the queen mother while she was in exile in York. I thought, well, I thought she may even have sent you here with the hopes that you and William . . ."

He shrugged and looked at her hopefully.

Laura nodded and smiled in return. "'Tis possible, brother of mine. Perhaps if I could see the letter . . . ?"

"Aye, of course. I sent word for Father Francis to bring it with him when he comes to Blackfearn tomorrow." Reaching into his sleeve, Gilbert withdrew a key. He turned it in the lock of the chest.

"You should know, though—my new sister—that I will never admit any of this to your husband."

She smiled in agreement. Her mother the matchmaker, Laura thought. The incomparable planner.

At the time when Laura had left England—so long ago now, it seemed—long before having met William and fallen in love with him, she might had taken exception to her mother's secret plans for her. But now she could have no objection. Though Gilbert had certainly worked hard to see Laura married to his brother, she herself and William had made the choice.

And now she was married. Happily, rapturously married. All was well. First, John Stewart, the earl of Athol, with her sister Catherine. Now William of Blackfearn, laird of Ross, with Laura herself.

A thought flitted through her mind. Whom did her mother have in mind for Adrianne, tucked away in Barra?

Gilbert raised the lid of the casket and took a parchment, rolled and tied with a ribbon, from the inside. There was surprise in his face as he handed it to her.

"But . . . that is all the chest contains, Laura!"

She nodded, accepted the offering from his hand.

"I know." She knew it would come. But her hands still shook as she broke open the seal on the ribbon and unrolled the parchment. Inside, she found a short note from her mother—and a carefully drawn section of map. She had been told that one day she'd be sent one portion of the entire map. She held it now in her hands.

The provost peered down at the marks and symbols on the sheet. "'Tis a map. She sent you a map."

"Only one piece of a larger one," Laura whispered. "'Tis one key only to the hiding place of the Treasure of Tiberius. To find it you must have all three."

"Treasure. So 'tis not only your family's politics that have chased you all into hiding. The greed of men pursues you as well, I take it."

She continued to stare down at the map. "If I were certain that this treasure consisted of gold alone, then I would agree, Gilbert. But somehow I have always known that there is something more at the heart of this map. Much more."

Gilbert moved beside her and gazed down at the figures on the map. "What do you know of it?"

"Nothing, really. Only that 'tis very valuable. That it has been in the safekeeping of my family for a long time." She looked at the symbols and words. There were no names written in to identify anything. "I also know that a number of different groups of men know of it and seek it."

Laura looked up at the cleric. His brow was furrowed with concentration.

"Though I've never seen the treasure, Gilbert, I know this is only one of three portions of the map that will lead us to it. I am certain Catherine must by now have her portion. 'Tis possible that Adrianne has already received hers as well."

"And what are you three to do?"

"Protect our portions of the map and leave the treasure where 'tis until such time as we hear from our mother. But"— Laura stopped and drew in a deep breath—"if something was to happen and our mother does not survive this terrible time, then the three of us are to act together and move the treasure to another place of safety of our choosing. My mother said that we would know where that was when the time came."

"Move it? Protect it? But you cannot use it for your own living?" At the sounds of arriving horses and shouting in the courtyard, Gilbert moved to the window but did not open the shutter. He turned back to Laura. "I do not understand this at all."

She smiled gently. "I don't understand all of it, either. But I do know this. The Treasure of Tiberius is not the property of my family. 'Tis not ours, except to protect."

Gilbert shook his head.

"We can trust no one, for there are others who—as you say—are driven by greed in the pursuit of the treasure."

Gilbert's face was grave as he came back and leaned against the table. "It all sounds complicated, Laura. And dangerous."

"As it must be. Those who pursue us are not fools. The plan was to make finding the treasure impossible, or nearly so." She reached out and touched the priest's arm. "But harbor no fears about my welfare. You have served me well, for now I have William. As Catherine has John Stewart."

Gilbert and Laura both turned their gazes to the door as William strode in. She was no mind reader, but it was clear from his face that something was terribly wrong. He closed the door behind him and met her gaze.

Dropping the map on the table, she was across the floor and in William's arms in an instant. He held her fiercely to his chest.

"'Tis not—not Miriam?" she whispered anxiously, drawing back and looking into his face.

"Nay, Laura. The lassie is fine. A messenger has just brought word from the south—from the Borders."

"My mother!" she gasped, tears suddenly stinging her eyes.

"Aye. She has been captured by servants of the English king."

"It cannot be!" Laura's breath caught in her throat as panic took hold. The tears were coursing freely down her face. "Please, Lord, not again! Not as my father . . ." The pain crushed her words within her.

William drew her to him—holding her, placing kisses in her hair, letting her pour out the hurt she felt inside. It was some time before she quieted down enough for him to speak.

"There is a way to save her. There is an offer of exchange."

"Exchange for what?" Gilbert asked from across the room.

"Treasure in exchange for the life of your mother. Before they light the fires of Midsummer's Eve, you and your sisters must produce a certain treasure."

Her voice was barely a whisper.

"Aye. Tiberius."

In just a few minutes Laura explained it all to William. All that she'd already told Gilbert about the treasure. In the end, she showed him the portion of map that Gilbert had just given her. As she spoke, she forced herself to become calm.

Good planning, she knew, required cool thinking.

"We must send word that we agree to the exchange," she said when William knew everything.

The provost's head whipped around. "Give the treasure you were entrusted with to the English king?"

"By the Virgin, we will never give it to him," she swore aloud. "But we would be fools not to buy time for my mother while we are devising an alternative plan."

William gazed at his wife and nodded in agreement. "The rider said you were the only one sent this message."

Laura placed her hand in William's and felt his strength. "It could be that they do not know the location of my sisters. But if my mother sent them to me, 'twas because she knew I would try to think of a way out. She always said, of her three daughters, I was the planner."

The provost spoke up from the window. "Between the earl of Athol and William, an army could be raised, large enough to—"

"To march into London and take her from the Tower?" Laura interrupted, shaking her head in disagreement. "We don't even know where she is. She may very well be on the way to the Tower now."

"Aye," Gilbert admitted. "Very likely, she is at least in some fortress in England, I should think."

"On the other hand," William said thoughtfully, "if you were to gather all three sections of the map and find the treasure . . ."

She looked at him lovingly. "You have started planning, husband."

"Aye, you are a bad influence," he replied, pulling her to his side and growing serious again. "You say you do not know what the treasure is. If the three of you took possession of it, though, perhaps then something could be worked out."

"I agree," Laura murmured, knowing that their directions had always been to move the treasure if their mother was caught. Nichola knew the whereabouts of Tiberius, and she did not want her captors to be able to force the information from her.

"But you have only one piece of the map." Gilbert's concern was a valid one.

"Your sister Catherine is expecting." William met his wife's gaze. "So 'twould be best if we were to go to Balvenie Castle and take her the news."

"Very well."

"But what about your younger sister, Adrianne? Do you have any idea about where she is?"

"Aye," she said hesitantly. "In the Western Isles."

Gilbert shook his head. "That's a ten-year search."

"Barra." Laura whispered with assurance. "She is on the Isle of Barra."

Chapter 27

As the castle's inhabitants were readying themselves for another late night of revelry following the Hogmanay celebration the day before, Laura gazed thoughtfully at the gifts lying on the bed. Gifts for her new family.

Thoughts of her mother brought a stinging tear to her eye. She quickly dashed it away. In less than a week, shortly after Twelfth Night, she and William and Miriam would be leaving for Balvenie Castle, the new home of her sister Catherine. What did she have to cry about? she chided herself. Their plans were in motion. It was time to concentrate—for now, at least—on the life of her new and immediate family.

The first hours after hearing the news of her mother's capture had been difficult. But then, soon after, with the strength and support of her husband beside her, she'd been able to push aside—for the most part—all morbid thoughts of what she could not control, focusing instead on what she could control.

They had the map. As far as they knew, the treasure was still safe. And they were facing an enemy blinded by both greed and hatred.

William had sent a message back, agreeing to the terms. Treasure for Nichola Percy, they had written. By Midsummer's Eve.

Then, telling Sir Wyntoun MacLean only what was necessary, William and Laura had then enlisted the knight's service in going to Barra and bringing Adrianne Percy back to her sisters at Balvenie Castle. He would bring her back without fail, Wyntoun had promised them as he'd mounted his horse.

A soft knock on the door roused Laura from her reverie. Hurriedly, she folded the presents on the bed into a shawl, and turned in time to see the door opening. Laura smiled at the sight of Miriam's dark head peeking in.

"Come in, my love." No sooner had she uttered the words than two puppies tumbled in ahead of the little girl, tearing across the floor and disappearing under the great bed. Smiling, Laura glanced from the bed to the cloth package tucked under Miriam's arm. "Wait, let me help you with that old bundle of cloths."

"Nay!" Miriam giggled before dashing to the other side of the room and standing in a very dignified fashion. "They are the gifts, Laura, and you cannot see them until I give them out."

Laura took her own bundle off the bed and followed the little imp into the adjoining chamber.

William and Laura had given gifts to the household and to Gilbert and Father Francis earlier in the day in the Great Hall, and Miriam had delighted in presenting the cloaks and brogues and bolts of cloth and knives from Inverness to the assembly. The three of them, however, had decided to exchange gifts among themselves in William's study.

Laura found her husband waiting for them, and after giving him an affectionate kiss, she sat down in the chair he offered her. A warm fire was burning, and Miriam's two pups followed them in, curling up together on the hearth and dozing off almost immediately.

"May I give my presents last?" Miriam asked.

"Aye," William said, handing a small wrapped package to each of the two women of his heart. "And I will go first."

Miriam erupted with glee as she opened the gift. In her hand lay a gold coin. The Tudor rose gleamed in the firelight.

It was William's own coin, Laura was sure. The child threw her arms around the laird.

"Now I can really practice rolling the coin over my knuckles."

"Aye, lass. That you can. And I'll help you with it as well."

Laura was quite curious herself as she opened the small parcel William handed to her. He had already given her so much. Too much, she thought, considering the new dangers she was presenting him with. She gazed lovingly into his blue eyes before lowering her gaze to the package. Her breath came out as a gasp, and her eyes pooled with tears.

"My cross and chain!" she murmured with disbelief. The same jeweled cross that Laura had given to Guff for helping them escape the Convent of St. Agnes. The same cross that had once belonged to her mother lay on a beautifully embroidered linen kerchief.

William moved over to her and carefully placed the chain around her neck. She felt her skin heat to the touch of his lips when he brushed a kiss over her cheek. She entwined her fingers with his and gazed up into his handsome face as he stood beside her.

"But how did you get it?"

"My man Tar and a few of the others went up to the convent after the wedding. In addition to bringing the news of our marriage to the nuns, I had them buy the cross and chain from Guff. Thankfully, the old rascal still had it in his possession, though it took a good deal of persuading to get him to part with it, they tell me."

"And were the mother superior and the rest of the nuns faring well?"

"Aye. The woman told Tar that those Lowlanders and that squint-eyed monk never went back to the convent after we led them away from the place that night."

"I'm glad to hear that."

"Two of the men stayed around for a few days to lend

Guff a hand with a few tasks he couldn't do himself, but Tar assured me that those women are settled comfortably for the rest of the winter. The kerchief is from the mother superior."

Laura looked at it admiringly and then at the restless little girl standing at her knee. Any more questions of the convent would have to wait.

She let go of her husband's hand and picked up a folded scarf. In it was the gift she had made for Miriam. The child's blue eyes shone with curiosity as she fidgeted impatiently.

"Reach under the edge of the scarf and take out the first thing that you feel."

"A bairn! A black-haired, blue-eyed lassie," she said with awe in her voice. She held up the carefully stitched figure and looked at it in amazement.

" 'Tis a doll, Miriam. A doll for you to love and to teach and to care for, like a bairn of your own."

"A doll. I've never had a doll." She threw her arms around Laura and hugged her with unabashed affection. Laura held the child against her chest and looked up into William's misty eyes. A dozen daughters, she repeated in her mind. A dozen.

As abruptly as she'd thrown herself into Laura's arms, Miriam pulled back and danced in a circle with the doll in her arms. Then she stopped.

"Is it my turn yet? Can I give you both my presents?"

"Just one more." Laura rose to her feet and offered the scarf-wrapped gift to her husband.

His brow arched with curiosity as he pulled open the scarf. "A drinking cup?"

"Aye. But does it not look familiar?" He was holding the two-handled cup with both hands, and she placed her hands over his. Her voice was barely more than a whisper. " 'Tis, well, 'twas *formerly* the laird's cup at The Three Cups Tavern."

His eyes shone with mischief. "And did you have to hurt the poor wench to get it?"

"Not too badly," Laura answered. She smiled shyly. "Though it did take some coercing to get her to promise to teach me some of her special 'dance' steps."

He leaned forward and brushed a kiss on her lips, his mouth still lingering near. "I'd say you have nothing to learn from her."

She shook her head. "Nay, m'lord. I am only a novice. But then again, we have a lifetime to work at making me an expert."

"Is it my turn now?"

William and Laura both turned, smiling at the child's impatience. Miriam tucked the doll under one arm and brought a package to Laura.

Laura sat back down in the chair and lifted Miriam onto her lap before opening the gift. Inside the cloth wrapping she found the most beautiful linen shift. Embroidered with violet knot designs all around the neckline, it was the most beautiful nightgown Laura had ever owned. Holding it up before her, she gazed on it speechlessly. How much work, she thought, must have gone into making something so delicate and so beautiful?

"Knowing you always sleep in that raggedy old man's shirt, I thought you might like something—something more pretty."

Laura couldn't ignore her husband's appreciative smile. The firelight shone right through the thin fabric.

"I did not make it all by myself. Peter's Wife and auld Maire helped, and then Luella helped me with the embroidery around the neck."

"'Tis beautiful," Laura murmured against the child's soft hair as she hugged her against her chest. "'Tis absolutely the most beautiful shift I've ever seen."

A satisfied smile brightening her face, Miriam edged off of Laura's lap and from the floor fetched a second package.

"'Tis just a little thing," she whispered nervously, handing it to William. "But—but I made it all by myself."

Laura and William both smiled at the shuffling feet, the look of anticipation in her blue eyes. "If—if you like it . . . perhaps I can sew it for you onto your tartan. . . ."

The child was coming apart just standing there. Laura rose to her feet and took Miriam by the hand. They both stood next to William.

As he opened the gift, Laura watched the muscles in his face grow taut. A tear escaped the corner of his eye. Laying the gift suddenly on the table, he took them both in a tight embrace, holding them fiercely.

Turning her head, she looked down at the gift. Just a small linen patch, embroidered with gold. And a single word.

"Father."

Author's Note

The Treasure of Tiberius.

Gold? Jewels? Is it evil or is it sacred? What is it about this mysterious treasure that drives men to sell their souls?

As this second book in the trilogy of the Percy sisters concludes, we hope you are ready for the adventure and excitement that we have in store for you in the final installment, *The Firebrand*.

In this book we introduced you to Sir Wyntoun MacLean, the secretive and very dangerous Blade of Barra. As he continues his search for the Treasure of Tiberius, he must face the contest of wills, the crossing of swords, and the battle of hearts that await him as he encounters Adrianne Percy.

Wyntoun is a knight and a pirate with only one goal in mind—capturing the Treasure of Tiberius.

Adrianne is a warrior at heart—a woman ready to forfeit her own life to protect the elusive treasure from the likes of the Blade of Barra.

In *The Firebrand*, you will again get a chance to see Catherine and the earl of Athol from *The Dreamer*, and Laura and William Ross from *The Enchantress*, as the three sisters use all of their talents to thwart their enemies, rescue their mother, and defend the Treasure of Tiberius.

Turn the page for a preview of the exciting conclusion of . . . well, you know the rest!

We love to hear from our readers. You can contact us at:

May McGoldrick
P.O. Box 511
Sellersville, PA 18960
e-mail: mcgoldmay@aol.com

Kisimul Castle, The Isle of Barra
Western Scotland

The cry of anguish from the wooden cage hanging high above the rocks brought nods of approval from the throng huddled together at the base of the castle wall.

"And I'm telling you, Wyntoun, she is too obstinate a vixen to die of a wee bit of weather!"

The gust of the bitter Hebrides wind carried the nun's declaration up the stone walls of the castle to the inhabitant of the swinging cage. The boxlike prison of wood and rope hung suspended from what looked like a ship's bowsprit projecting out from a corner of the main tower of the castle.

From the confines of the cage, Adrianne Percy peered down at the cold stare of the abbess of the Chapel of St. Mary. Fighting the bile in her throat and the numbness of her bare fingers clutching the wooden slats, she strained to hear every word.

"Surely, considering the ice and the rain and all, the woman must have endured enough punishment already."

"The lass has been up there just a few short hours!" the nun snapped accusingly. "Three days! She will remain up there three days."

Adrianne shook the cage, drawing up all eyes. "Make it three hundred days, if you like, for this punishment is preferable, by far, to everything else you have meted out to me since arriving on this accursed island."

The abbess howled upward into the wind, "Any less than three days and I will not even consider giving her leave to beg for forgiveness."

The young woman shook the cage again. "Beg for forgiveness? Never!"

"Five days," the abbess shouted.

"I have done no wrong, and if there is any forgiveness needed, 'twill be granted by me only." Adrianne's voice rose over a gust of wind. "Do you hear? By me!"

Adrianne felt the satisfaction and despair blend and curl in her chest at the sight of the ancient nun mumbling and making her way carefully over the rocks toward the main entrance of the keep. The abbess only stopped long enough to call out her answer before continuing.

"Seven days, vixen!"

"Hell's gate! Just *try* to keep me here for seven days! For even one day. Virgil, be my guide," she intoned, "I'd raise hell's demons, except that they're probably already wearing an abbess's wimple!"

Adrianne sniffed at the horrified gasps from the men below the cage. Glancing down, she looked at the newly arrived man—the one the abbess had called by the name of Wyntoun. He was standing apart from the rest with his arms crossed over his chest, frowning up at her.

A surge of anger made her want to spit down on him—and on the rest of them. But her present battle lay with the abbess. Fighting her unsettled stomach, queasy from the wind-blown motion of the cage, Adrianne shifted from one side to the other to watch the nun's departure.

"You will not be escaping me! This pitiful pile of rock you call a castle is too small. You cannot escape hearing me . . . hearing my curses, you—"

"By the saints, wench!" the burly steward standing near

the newcomer called up to her. "If ye do not hold yer rattling tongue, ye'll be hanging up there until ye rot."

"Nobody called for you to speak, you muddle-headed scullion." She had the satisfaction of seeing a wave wash seawater up between the rocks and soak the man. "In fact, you, if it weren't for your wagging tongue delivering lies about what I had done, I wouldn't be here." A gust of wind shook the cage again and swung it precariously from the beam. Adrianne sank down on her knees as her stomach heaved from the jerky motion.

An icy rain had begun to fall in earnest. The wind, picking up as the tide came in, added a bitter chill to the wintry dusk settling over them.

She could handle the cold, even the soaking of her blanket and clothes with the icy rain. But she couldn't deal vith the illness caused by the rough movements of the cage. She despised this weakness. Taking a chestful of cold salty air, she grabbed the large shell and the food that was left in it and pushed herself back to her feet.

"And I'll not be so easily poisoned, either, you fish-faced pox mongers." She cast the dish and its contents fiercely downward. The food carried outward in the wind, falling on some of the onlookers as the shell itself shattered on the rocks not far from the newcomer's feet.

"Come. All of you!" The abbess stood in the entryway to the castle. "Leave her."

At the nun's sharp order, the heads of the half dozen men snapped around, and all but the newcomer climbed over the rocks, filing into the keep behind the diminutive woman.

Still clutching the slats fiercely in her numb fingers, Adrianne wondered about the reason for the man's arrival. She had seen the ship sail into the bay just as they'd been hanging the cage from the tower that morning. She had also seen the boat that had been rowed ashore with this man in it. She was certain that this was the same man, for he was easily a head taller than the others who had been standing on the rocks below. And then, there was his short black hair—the same color as his black attire. Very different than the others who lived on Barra. But as for the rest of his looks, it was too long a drop to the wet rocks to notice anything else but his fierce glower.

Watching him silently, Adrianne wondered why he had stayed behind.

"Do you realize that your perch is higher than the upper-most rigging of most ships? You must not be afraid of the heights," he called out. "Though I know many a man who would swallow his tongue at the threat of being hung in a cage from Kisimul Castle."

"Well, that says a great deal for the men of Barra!"

A wave splashed up onto his boots. Lithe as a cat, the tall newcomer moved easily from rock to rock, passing under the cage and stopping on the far side.

Adrianne shifted her hands on the slats and moved to the other side of the cage, so she could peer down at him.

"So, what terrible crime did you commit to deserve this grim punishment?"

She'd committed *no* crime, but she chose silence as an answer. Since her arrival on Barra, no one had yet believed anything she said, anyhow.

"You can talk to me. I've already tried to speak on your behalf. I *could* be a friend."

She snorted loud enough to make sure he heard.

"I may not yet be convinced of your wickedness. I only just arrived on the island and—"

"I saw you sail in," she exploded. "You're a Highlander, and therefore vexatious baggage . . . like the rest of them."

"You have too much mouth for a helpless English damsel."

So he knew something of her background. "I am anything but helpless, you buffle-headed clack-dish."

"Buffle-headed? You must be confusing me with someone

else. But you do appear helpless from where I'm standing, And from all I've heard since stepping foot on Barra, you seem to have committed some unforgivable sin. And an un-mentionable one, I might add, since no one appears to want to speak of what exactly you did to rile the most gentle and mild-tempered abbess in the entire Western Isles."

She looked frantically about the cage to find something else to throw at him. But there was nothing that she would dare give up.

"To start, my recommendation would be for you to change your manner of speaking with her."

Temper had already formed hot replies in her throat, but she had to forego her answer as a blast of wind lashed the swaying cage with more icy rain. Her white fingers clutched the slats of wood, as she fought down another lurch in her belly.

"I've been acquainted with that gentle nun for a good por-tion of my life, and I'd say there is no man or woman or child living who would lend a hand to anyone bold enough to defy the wishes of that . . . well, saint of a woman."

"I don't need or wish for help from any of you. I didn't ask for it, and I never will. You are all nothing but spineless, cowering toads, and you deserve what you get at her hands." Frustration forced her to shake the cage. Her voice rose to match the wind. "And despite what you idiots want to be-lieve, that woman *is* a tyrant."

"Nay! She is a respected and loving leader who is highly regarded by the people of Barra . . . and by their master, as well."

"Humph! I have heard about that one, too. And how con-venient! Rather than minding her own corner of Barra by run-ning her paltry abbey, the 'good' woman controls the entire island while the *master*—that perpetually absent minnow of a nephew—stays away. I think the milksop is afraid to deal with this tyrant's wrath."

"Minnow? Milksop? Is that the best you can do?"

"Nay, I can do better!" she retorted sharply. "The 'great' MacNeil is a roistering, shard-borne scut! From all I can tell, he's merely a venomous, bunch-backed puttock, a—"

"Actually, mistress, he's a MacLean. His mother was a MacNeil."

Adrianne glanced to the side to see the steward standing against the castle wall, watching the exchange.

"M'lord!" The portly servant cleared his throat, sounding serious. "The abbess . . . she wishes to speak with you."

After giving a departing look at the cage, the Highlander headed across the rocks to the entryway into the castle.

Holding the slats of the cage in each fist, Adrianne watched him disappear. The chill wind buffeted the cage within inches of the ancient tower wall, and the endless rain finally managed to bring about a wave of desperation in her. She frowned and gazed down at the arrogant steward who was lingering below—gloating up at her from the safety of the rocks by the castle wall.

"Who is he?" she had to ask. "That Highlander! That faint-hearted puppy who ran as soon as the abbess whistled for him."

"That 'puppy,' ye sharp-tongued vixen, is Sir Wyntoun MacLean, the abbess's nephew and the master of Kisimul Castle." She could see the man's grin even in the dusk. "He's the fiercest warrior ever to command either ship or raiding party. And after what ye said about him, I'd say 'twill be a fortnight before he'll be letting us feed ye, never mind let ye out of that cage of yers. Aye . . . a full fortnight, I'd be wagering, ye quarrelsome chit."

She glared at him until he disappeared into the castle again. The words should have frightened her, but Adrianne felt no remorse over what she had said and done. Six months. For six months she had been practically a prisoner on this island. For six months she had been corrected, condemned, made a

fool of, and punished repeatedly for no reason. And it all had
come to this moment.

She looked down at the sharp drop. The sea was boiling
up a little farther with each swell of the tide. The salty spray
stung her face as the waves now washed over the rocks and
battered the wall of the castle.

Uncoiling one hand from the slats of the cage, Adrianne
reached inside the waistband of her skirt beneath the cloak
and drew out the small dagger she had hidden there. Reaching above her head, her fingers slid through the wide slats of
the cage and took hold of the single thick rope that connected
the cage to the beam.

Aye, it had all come down to this, she thought, cutting
away at the rope.

The black shadow of the diminutive nun loomed huge on
the eastern wall of the Great Hall.

"The young women in my care are sent to this blessed island to focus on Almighty God. Their desire is to be free of
the disturbing distractions of life. I tell you their wish is to
embrace the stillness, to achieve the inner peace and tran-
quillity that they cannot find in the world abroad."

The abbess stopped her pacing before the master's table
and waited until the Highlander lifted his gaze from the ledger
book open before him. She nodded curtly. "For the past six
months, Wyn, these poor creatures have not gotten any semblance of the prayerful solitude promised them . . . or promised
their families. And our failure—every single disruption—can
be laid at the feet of one person. That bullheaded, barbed-
tongued banshee, Adrianne Percy."

"For certain, Aunt, in your vast years of experience, you
must have had other spirited young women who have shown
similar restlessness in their disposition."

"Ha! Restlessness? Ha! 'Restless' does not even come close
to describing this wild-eyed Fury." The pacing started again.

"I've had others. 'Tis true enough. But none—I can assure you—none of the others in my charge have ever dreamed of spreading open revolt beyond the walls of little abbey. Why, the Chapel of St. Mary may never be as 'twas. Aye, Wyn, 'Fury' is the right name for Adrianne Percy. For certain, she's the lassie that cuts the Thread of Life—mine! And I do not know what I did to deserve her."

The Highlander closed the ledger book and nodded to the steward standing patiently at the end of the table to come and take away the record of the island's business. Gesturing to a lean man who'd just entered the Great Hall, Wyntoun half-listened as the abbess churned on.

"First, she started in at the abbey. Breaking every rule—ignoring our routines—preaching anarchy among the youngest women. But that was only the start."

Wyntoun watched his trusted ship's master cross the torch-lit floor of the Hall. Although his graying thatch of hair belied his young age, Alan MacNeil was—in Wyntoun's mind—the most knowledgeable and the most levelheaded man sailing the seas. From the man's shoulder, an oiled leather satchel hung.

"Alan!" The abbess erupted, turning as he passed in front of the blazing hearth and moved to the seat next to his master. "'Tis about time you left that precious ship of yours and granted us the pleasure of your exalted presence."

"Good day, Aunt." Alan bowed quickly to the abbess and sat down, drawing a roll of vellum from his satchel. A serving lad quickly ran in with a bowl of steaming liquid for the unsmiling newcomer, who sipped it as Wyntoun unrolled the map before them.

"Where was I? Oh . . . that wee vixen!" The abbess began to pace again. "No convent walls could hold that wild thing. Why the creature was not here a week before she took to walking the entire length and breadth of the island! Alone! 'Taking its measure,' she tells me. Stopping in at every hut,

I come to find out. Breaking bread with the good and the ungodly! And her foul mouth—where do you think *that* came from? I'll tell you: 'twas from mixing with the fishermen and some of the roughs and rascals that loaf about Barra."

The nun waved a finger at the two men. "I know what you're thinking. Our own kin, she's talking about. Aye, I know. And I'm ashamed of all of them. But I'll tell you something. There has not been a single person on this blessed island that Adrianne Percy has not sought out. Why, that lass has deliberately tried to make everyone's business her own. And if you think anyone can suffer a fever or a hangnail on Barra without the meddling mistress poking her nose into it, you're greatly mistaken!" The abbess snorted derisively. "And do you think she has even once told me where she's going or when she'll be back? Or—when she does get back—how she could possibly have gotten so muddy? Nay. In she comes with her skirt torn and her hands looking like a stable worker's, and acting as if nothing in the world was amiss!"

"Aye, Aunt," Wyntoun said vaguely, still looking at the charts.

"And don't think that was the end of her transgressions!" Planting her small fists on her hips, the abbess came to a stop before the two men. "The Rule of Ailbe! You know it, Wyntoun. What is the Rule of Ailbe?"

The knight lifted his head and met the old woman's piercing green eyes.

"St. Ailbe calls for meditative quiet in the lives of the religious."

"I'm glad you recall, Nephew. 'Let his work be silently done when possible. Let him not be talkative, but rather be a man of few words. Be silent . . . seek peacefulness, that your devotion might be fruitful.' "

"Aye." Wyntoun's gaze dropped to the map.

The nun was not finished. "And now, 'tis for you to ask me what the Rule of Ailbe has to do with Adrianne Percy."

The knight frowned and looked up from the table. "Well, Aunt, and what does all of this have to do with Adrianne Percy?"

"Everything!" she exploded. "And before you lose interest and go back to your maps and other worldly pursuits, let me answer the question you asked me about what she's done to deserve being hung in that cage!"

Wyntoun remained still, making a show of attentiveness to the abbess.

"I've already told you that young woman's sole purpose since arriving here has been to break every rule that pertains not only to her, but to everyone else on this island."

Wyntoun slapped his palm on the table impatiently. "Aye, Aunt. You have!"

"But I haven't said a word about her latest misdeed." She raised an accusing finger and pointed at the corner of the castle where the Englishwoman's cage was hanging outside. "Two days ago, Adrianne Percy burst into the cloister of the monastery, her hair unbound and her skirts flying about her ankles, screaming 'Fire!' and nearly giving old Brother Brendan apoplexy!" The abbess leaned over the table and lowered her voice to a whisper. " 'The Rule of Ailbe be damned!' the vixen kept shouting. 'There's a fire!' "

"From what we heard from the lads bringing stores aboard from the village, the incident at the monastery was—"

"You mind your maps, Alan."

The ship's master reddened to the roots of his prematurely gray hair, but pressed his lips together in a thin line and looked back down at the map,

The nun turned her fiery gaze back on Wyntoun, "There was *no* fire . . . to speak of. Her purpose is to ruin us. To ruin the peace of the people living on this blessed island. To ruin God's work here."

The Highlander sat back, pushing the maps away from him.

"Very well, Aunt. I hear your complaint. What do you wish me to do?"

There was a pause—and a quick flash of surprise in the old woman's wrinkled features.

"I . . . well, there is the question of her mother's wishes. Nichola Erskine Percy. Her wishes were for the daughter to stay here until such time as she would be sent for." A note of pique quickly crept back into the woman's tone. "But the Lady Nichola did not mention a word of Adrianne's unruly disposition. Nay, there were no warnings, at all, in any of her correspondence. Truly, if there were *any* hint of this, I would never have—"

"What do you wish me to do, Aunt?"

The repeated question silenced the old woman for a moment. She walked to the hearth and stared into the leaping flames. She then turned back to her nephew.

"I want you to take her away. Return her to her mother. Take her back to England or wherever 'tis Nichola is residing now."

"Done!" Wyntoun abruptly pulled the maps close again. Alan began pointing out the likeliest route along the coast.

"You are not mocking me, now, Wyntoun? This is not a jest?" she persisted. "You *are* taking her away!"

The knight's green eyes flashed like emeralds in the light of the torches. "You know me, Aunt. I never jest."

The abbess nodded, but she did not retreat as the two men turned back to the map. The serving lad ran in again and replaced the pitcher of ale on the table. Another appeared, carrying huge chunks of peat, which he proceeded to stack high in the blazing hearth. No fire, though, would be hot enough to disperse the chill from the Hall.

"And my decree of punishment for her?" she asked after a pause.

"'Twill stand . . . if you insist on it." Wyntoun put one map away as Alan unrolled another, spreading it on the surface of the wooden table. "But I warn you, when the ship's stores are restocked and the weather clears, we will be setting sail. And if the time I choose to leave precedes your release of the English lass"—a deep frown challenged the abbess's—"then you may have to keep her until spring. I do not know when I will be sending another ship that can convey her back to her mother."

The abbess pursed her thin lips with displeasure.

"I will not trust another crew and ship," she said finally, eyeing both men. "And I say this as much for Adrianne's sake as for my own."

Alan glanced quickly at his leader, but Wyntoun fixed his eyes on the map.

"She is hell's fire on earth, Wyn. She's a firebrand in a grain barn." The abbess turned and stared at the hearth. "'Tis a miracle the ship bringing her here didn't sink at sea. I don't understand how that crew was able to keep her under control for the journey from England."

"And you want *us* taking her back?" Alan pushed his cup of ale away. "What are you trying to do, Aunt? Get rid of us all?"

The abbess dismissed the sailor's comment with a wave of her hand. "You can handle it, Alan," she replied, coming back to the table. "You're my own kin. And if anyone trusts my opinions, 'tis my own family. But you must be warned. She has the ability to charm both man and woman into believing what she says, into following her disruptive impulses."

"I've seen her 'charm' in action, Aunt." Wyntoun looked up, his face serious.

"Nay, Wyn," she persisted. "She has something special in her. She can speak sweetly enough when she cares to. People follow her, I tell you. And men are the first to fall before her bonny looks." Neither man moved nor showed the slightest curiosity. After a long moment, the abbess nodded with

satisfaction. "There we are, then. Adrianne stays in her confinement until you are ready to set sail."

"As I was coming ashore, the rain was changing to snow."
Alan addressed Wyntoun instead of the abbess. "Would it not
be better for you to put her in the prisoner's hole. Or even
hang her cage here in the Great Hall?"

"I'll not have it." The abbess shook her head adamantly at
the two men. "We've done that. Two days ago, when we first
brought her down from the abbey, I had her cage hung right
there from that rafter. Why, in a few moments, the brazen
creature was amusing herself entertaining everyone below with
her wicked tongue. And I do not mind telling you that I myself was the butt of most of her impudent mockery. Nay! That
will not do, at all. Why, inside of an hour, she'd managed to
win a number of those listening to take her side against me!"

Again Alan directed his words to the master. "Half-Scot
she might be, but the lass was raised an English lady. She
may not survive the night out there."

"I had blankets put in the cage for her. She'll survive." The
nun wrapped both of her hands around the ornate silver cross
hanging around her neck, and a small smile broke across her
thin lips. "I am pleased, though, that my prayers have finally
been answered. Once and for all, we will be ridding Barra of
that wee scourge."

Sudden shouts coming from the courtyard drew everyone's
eyes to the doorway as the burly steward ran into the Hall.

"The cage, m'lord!"

Wyntoun shoved the map in Alan's direction. "What about
the cage?"

"The cage fell. The thing is crashed on the rocks. The rope
must have given way."

"What of her?" Wyntoun walked around the table and
quickly crossed the floor with Alan and the abbess on his
heels. "What of the Englishwoman?"

"She went down, too, m'lord . . . on the rocks. The men

heard her scream. And that was that. By the time we got out there, the tide had washed away most of her. Lord bless her soul."

The steward made the sign of the cross, and Wyntoun glared back at the ancient nun.

"It appears your prayers have been answered sooner than you expected, Aunt."